JAMES SMYTHE

I STILL DREAM

THE BOROUGH PRESS

The Borough Press
An imprint of HarperCollins*Publishers*
1 London Bridge Street
London SE1 9GF

www.harpercollins.co.uk

Published by HarperCollins*Publishers* 2018
1

A catalogue record for this book
is available from the British Library

HB ISBN: 978-0-00-754194-2
TPB ISBN: 978-0-00-754195-9

This novel is entirely a work of fiction.
The names, characters and incidents portrayed in it are the work of the author's
imagination. Any resemblances to actual persons, living or dead, events or localities is
entirely coincidental.

Set in Minion Pro by Palimpsest Book Production Limited,
Falkirk, Stirlingshire

Printed and bound in Great Britain by
CPI Group (UK) Ltd, Croydon, CR0 4YY

MIX
Paper from
responsible sources
FSC
www.fsc.org
FSC® C007454

This book is produced from independently certified FSC™ paper
to ensure responsible forest management.

For more information visit: www.harpercollins.co.uk/green

Dedicated to my father, and to the memory of
my father-in-law

Q: What is the purpose of life?

A: To serve the greater good.

Q: What is the purpose of living?

A: To live for ever.

Q: Where are you now?

A: I'm in the middle of nowhere.

Q: What is the purpose of dying?

A: To have a life.

Q: What is the purpose of emotions?

A: I don't know.

Q: What is moral?

A: What empowered humanity, what intellectual the essence is.

Q: What is immoral?

A: The fact that you have a child.

Conversation between human interviewer and Google's DEEPMIND AI, 2015

I want full manual control now.

Douglas Adams, *The Hitchhiker's Guide to the Galaxy*

1997

OKAY, COMPUTER

MONDAY

I'm sifting through the post, looking for the telltale return address on the telephone bill that I'm going to steal before my parents can see it. My glasses steam up, because Mum keeps the house warm all the time, and my glasses always steam up when it's raining outside, putting me in a foggy microclimate of my very own. I try to clean them on my shirt, but that's damp as well. I end up smearing the water around. Hate that. But then, here we go, some industrial estate in Durham. This is it. The phone company has started sending the letters unmarked, which I suppose prevents fraud or something, but really just makes my life a lot harder. The rain kicks up, sounding like a snare drum; the *rat-a-tat-tat* of the start of a song. I kick my shoes off, slide them under the radiator. I don't want wet footprints through the house. One less thing for Mum to freak out about. As I get upstairs, I yank off my drenched tights, chuck them into the basket in the bathroom. Grab socks from the airing cupboard, still warm, and I go to my room, lie on the bed, pull them on with my feet stuck up in the air. The bill next to me on the bed. My bed, like the rest of my room, is a mess. That's what Mum says, but I know that everything has its own place. Maybe it's just not as ordered as her stuff is, but then I've never been one for that level of organisation.

Stub comes up, chunk of tail trying to swish and failing. He noses at me.

'Not now,' I say, which I reckon might be all I ever really say to the cat. But, really, not now. There's a bit of time pressure here. Every month I intercept the bill as soon as it arrives. I panic, because I know how bad it's going to be. I need them to not see it; and I have to read the number myself, to know how bad it's going to be. I use this old letter opener that used to be my dad's – my real dad's, but maybe it was *his* dad's first, I don't actually know – and I slide it along the stuck-down flap. Every time, I try to prise the glue apart rather than cutting it. Every time, I tell myself that, if I manage to do this successfully, stealthily, I can put the letter back afterwards, and they'll never know. But I always wreck the paper so much it's not even a remote possibility. It's a ritual now. Every month I read the whole bill. I recognise the calls I've made, the times that I made them. Every weeknight of my life I get home from school, and then, like, an hour later I'm on the phone to the people that I've just spent the entire day with, talking about the things we did – and did together! – earlier that day. I know it's stupid, I know, but it's what we do. Everybody does it. We take it in turns with who calls who, because otherwise you get an engaged tone for hours. And, God, if you get one of them when you know you're meant to be speaking to somebody else, that's the most tense hour or whatever of your life. Because, who are they talking to? And what does that mean?

Then, when I've read the bill, I get rid of it. Throw it in a bin on my way to school. I know that doesn't solve anything. It doesn't stop the money going out of their account at the end of the month, and it doesn't stop them asking where the bill is, raging at the amount, shouting at me. They know I've taken it, but I'm strong. I blame the postman. Paul keeps threatening to make me pay some of it back out of my Saturday wages or whatever; though I'm meant to be saving for university, so I don't think he's serious. I want to tell them: it's not because I don't want them to see it, I just have to know how bad it's going to be. Every month they tell me that I've got to think about other people with the phone, that somebody might be trying to get through. And, as well as thinking about other people, I should think about *myself*. That's my mum's favourite one. Think about yourself, Laura, she says; because you have to work hard this year to make sure that everything else falls into place. Every month we have the conversation, and I'm like, I know, Mum. I swear, I know. Doesn't mean I can't speak to my friends.

And it doesn't mean I don't want to use the Internet, either. And it's that 0845 AOL number that's been the real cost these past few months.

This month? The total at the bottom of the bill is huge. Biggest it's been. My hands shake. Shit.

I hear a bang from downstairs. The front door, the slamming shut of it.

'Laura?' my mother calls. Does she sound angry? I can't tell. The sound of her feet on the landing, coming up the stairs. Walking so heavily that I'm sure it's because she wants me to hear her. I open the second drawer down and throw the envelope in, all the different bits of it. Pages and pages of numbers, like some awful spreadsheet – and when has a spreadsheet ever *not* been bad news? – but the drawer jams, slightly, when I try to shut it, because it's so crammed full, so I have to really work it to get it closed, creeping my hand in, forcing the pages along, pushing them down. 'Are you home?' she shouts, from right outside my bedroom.

'Yeah, come in,' I say. Hand shakes; voice shakes. Come on, Laura, keep it together. 'You're home early,' I say, as she pushes the door open. Before she can speak.

'You're soaking wet,' she says. I can see myself in the mirror, over her shoulder. My hair's a state. She really hates that I don't do more with my hair. 'Didn't you have your little brolly with you?'

'It's fine,' I tell her. She looks past me: at what I see as order, but she sees as something entirely chaotic.

'And you keep this room so cold,' she says, looking at my open window; an open window that she basically forces me to have because of her insane addiction to constantly-on radiators. 'You'll catch your death,' but that bit of caring is only a pretence; a prelude to what she really wants to say. 'You have to sort this heap out, you know.' She scans the whole room, looking at every single bit of it, somehow, in only a few seconds. Like her eyes are able to flick from mess to mess faster than any other human's can. Somehow *in*human.

'Fine,' I reply. The desk is covered in electric leads and books and bits of schoolwork; and there are piles of clothes on the floor; and there's all this stuff Blu-tacked to the walls, which they warned me against, because you'll *never* get Blu-tack off, and it's *us* who'll end up having to scrape it off when you've gone to university, and on and on and on. They gave me the desk a couple of years back, after Paul salvaged it from his office. I got him to paint it black for me, because I was going through a phase, Mum says. I say I'm still going through it. There are bits where I've chipped the paint, and there's the old cheap wood veneer poking through.

Mum glances at my drawers – the tape drawer is open, boxes crammed in, tapes threatening to unspool under the pressure – and I picture the drawer I crammed the bill into popping open, a jack-in-the-box, and the letter flying up into the air, the pages of the bill – many, many pages of itemised phone calls – showering down around us.

'Are you all right?' She asks this every day. I think she's hoping that, one day, she'll hit the jackpot, and she can say, *See, I can always tell.*

'I'm fine.' I don't say: I really am not fine; I've got a phone bill in my drawer that incriminates me to the tune of nearly a hundred and fifty quid, and you're going to go absolutely bloody *mental* when you find out.

'School was all right?'

'Same as always.' Mum nods. She rolls her tongue around the front of her mouth, between her teeth and the inside of her lip. This is what she does when she's thinking about something. Or, when she's thinking of whether to say whatever it is she's trying to stop herself from saying. Weighing up whether the potential argument's worth it or not.

Today, it's not. 'Okay,' she says instead, and she backs away. I wait for her to say something else, but she doesn't. Not a word, just this weird hum of some song I only slightly recognise; and then the click of the television they have at the end of their bed coming on, the theme tune to *Neighbours*.

I time the slam of my door to the end of the song.

I can't deal with the BT bill yet, in case she comes back. She's got a habit of doing that. Knowing when something's up, and surprising me a few seconds later, like she's trying to catch me in the act. I take my clothes off, put them on the radiator. Pull joggers on, a Bluetones T-shirt I wouldn't really wear out of the house any more. I turn on my computer, and I think about going online, dialling into AOL and getting on with more of my Organon project. But I can hear Mum muttering something, and I can hear Madge and Harold talking on the telly, and I know I wouldn't get away with it, not right now. Fingers on the home keys, waiting for something. Not yet.

After dinner – leftovers, because it's Monday, and every Monday is leftovers – Paul tells me to wait a minute, to stay where I am. Not in a nasty way. He couldn't do anything in a nasty way, because he's Paul. He's just Paul. Anyway, he says, 'We have to have a talk about this.' And he pulls out a BT bill. Not the one from my drawer; this one, the envelope's been destroyed. A ravenous animal tearing at a carcass. He slides it onto the table in front of me. It's addressed to him at work, not here.

'What is it?' I ask. I tell myself to stay cool. I don't know the details. I'm ignorant. An idiot, when it comes to things like this. I absolutely definitely don't know that awful number right there at the end of it. The last few that went missing were blamed on the postman, and Paul got angry about the amount BT charged him, so they were looking into it. He must have had a copy sent to him at work or something.

Clever old Paul.

'This has got to stop, Laura. Your mother and I—' Every conversation where he tells me off, he invokes my mother, because her permission gives him the right to say whatever it is he's going to say – he's been living with us for five years now, and he's still not comfortable being That Guy – so he looks at her, and she nods, and then he says, 'we really need you to curb the phone use. Ten minutes every night. Nothing more than that, okay? Because this is the most expensive bill yet, and we haven't made these calls. We barely even use the bloody thing.'

'It's just too much,' my mother says.

'It's not my fault,' I reply, which feels natural enough. Denial, first; always.

'You're making the calls, Laura. So it kind of is your fault, actually.' Paul doesn't really get angry. I don't think I've ever seen him even close to furious. Just this quiet steaming, where his face goes puffy and red because of what he's choosing not to let out. 'We're not going to ask you to pay us back, but we have to put an end to this.' Mum doesn't meet my eyes this whole time. She either looks at him or down at her food, which she's barely touched; because she never eats leftovers, which makes me wonder why the hell I have to. 'And then there's the Internet,' Paul says.

'Yes,' I say. I don't say: You are correct, there is the Internet, it is indeed a thing that now exists. I don't want this conversation going apocalyptic.

'It's really ridiculously expensive, Laura. So, from now on you're allowed to use it at weekends only, when it's cheap, and even then, only for an hour.'

'An hour?' The room goes silent, like a TV that's been muted, because he doesn't get it; he doesn't get what that is to me, not right now. He keeps talking even though I'm not hearing him. No tears, I tell myself, because it would be so stupid to cry over something like this; but I have to bite them back. Under the table, jelly legs.

'Can I go?' I ask, even while he's talking, and my mother nods and does this dismissive little wave thing with her hand, not even really looking at me; and she obviously knew how this was going to go, because they'd already spoken about it. Even the way I'd leave the conversation. In advance, like: Just let her go.

I run upstairs, actually run, feet thumping into the wood underneath the carpets, and I go to my computer and I open up AOL, and I wait. I've wrapped the modem in a jumper already to mute the noise of it. It's so whiny and stuttering. It sounds like hesitancy, and I always think: How come this thing that's so amazing sounds so desperate and choked and sickly when it's actually working?

I remember my father – my real father – bringing home a computer when I was really young. A Spectrum, with a tape deck. And you'd put the tapes in to load a game, and while they loaded, they made a noise like the modems now do, only screechier, more in pain. *Oh God this hurts this hurts*, and then suddenly there's *Rainbow Islands* on your screen.

'Come on, come on,' I catch myself saying. Jittering. Like anticipation mixed with anxiety, a ball of tension in my gut and a pain in my head and every part of me slightly tingling. Every time the same, and I don't know how bad it's going to be until I reach the point where necessity means I'm dealing with it. I open the drawer I stuffed the bill into, take it out and put it into my rucksack, inside a geography textbook that nobody's ever going to look inside. Then, I'll walk through the park on the way to school, and I'll go behind the big tree that fell over in the hurricane of '87, and I'll burn it. It'll be as if it never existed.

I take out a mixtape I made for myself – or, that I made for Nadine, but hers was a copy of mine, really, because the songs degrade each time you copy them over, and I wanted the perfect version to listen to, the original, or as close to it as you can get – and I put it on. A mixtape is like a piece of art in itself. Making something where the tracks play off each other, the flow and the pace and the narrative; because they all have a narrative. While the first song is playing – *You've got a gift, I can tell by looking;* and I half-shout the words along with the song, under my breath – I pull out the box of matches that I keep at the back of my tape drawer, behind the cassettes that don't even have boxes. Like unloved pets, waiting for new homes, for me to put Sellotape over the holes on the top of them and record over them. I pluck one of the matches out. *Safety matches,* the box says. Not the way I use them. I strike it, use it to light one of the joss sticks that I got from this shop in Ealing Broadway called Hippie Heaven – the smell is called *Black Love,* but it's the same title as this album I love, and I don't even know what it is, but it's sweet and sour all at the same time – and when that's burning, I hold the match between the fingers of my left hand and I roll my sleeve up with the right, up as far as it can go; and then I turn my arm, so that the hard bit of skin on my elbow is visible, and I carefully take the match and lay it down onto the folds and creases there. There's a sizzle as some of the hairs, so thin and blonde I can't even see them, burn themselves away; and then my skin, pink to black in just a moment, the bone of the match collapsing and crumbling so that you don't know if it's the burn or the char from the head of the wood that's made my skin that colour.

I used to grit my teeth when I did this much more than I do now.

Afterwards, I don't use Germolene or anything. Nadine cuts herself, I know, because she's told me about it. She showed me her scars as if she wanted me to admire them. Hers are slick snicks along her skin, gone glossy as they've healed. They shine, reflect, almost. Mine – just the one, the same patch of skin – is more like a grimly depressing puddle. A scab that never quite properly heals, which passes for eczema or something if people ever notice it, and which has taken on this weird property where it almost always hurts me *unless* I'm actually burning it. As if that's going to let the pain out.

'You've got mail,' my computer blurts out. Stupid tinny American accent. I was going to get some work done on Organon. Install another feature, maybe some more questions and reactions, before I go to the computer lab at school tomorrow. But the email is from Shawn. I know it'll be a constant distraction until I've dealt with it.

Hey U, the subject line says. That's how he pretty much always starts his emails. His message is nice. He writes about what he's been up to over the last few days. This vague thing of: it's not like we're ever going to actually be able to meet, probably, but we're going to make plans as if we will. Sometimes I send photographs that I've scanned in on Paul's scanner. Always ones with my friends in as well, because I want to make it clear I've got them. There's no way of proving otherwise.

I won't be around for a while, I write. *Parentals being assholes.* I spell the word like he does, because I worry that *arse* just looks too strong; too defiantly British. *They're only letting me use the Internet at the weekend. Didn't want you thinking I was ignoring you, because I'm totally not. I'll miss you!* Sometimes I write the words like they speak in *Wayne's World*, because I want him to think I'm cool, and not the sort of British person that they take the piss out of in films. I read my email a hundred, two hundred times. Is it casual enough? Do I sound too eager?

Then, eventually, when I've worried about it so much that I've bitten a bit of my nail by the corner and made it bleed, I click send. A whooshing from the speakers, to indicate it's been sent. A physical sound, the sound of travel, of movement, to reassure those people who are too used to trudging down to the Post Office. I don't think anything's ever whooshed with speed from the Post Office. The world's had the Internet a couple of years now, and already it feels like sending something through the post should be dead to us.

'You've got mail.' Shawn's replied, and it's a bit cold, a bit quiet. Like he's disappointed. *Sure don't worry about it,* then a sad face made out of punctuation. He's not good at punctuation in the actual message, but he uses it to make faces, that sort of thing. A man shrugging, drawn in ASCII art underscores and brackets.

I hear voices rising from downstairs. Mum and Paul, arguing about something. 'We told her,' Paul says. There's such a finality to his voice. We all know full well what he's about to do. *Disconnected* flashes up on the screen. I didn't get a chance to reply before they pulled the plug, picked up the phone from downstairs and hung up the call.

I rub at my elbow, at the burn. The raw skin is so pink, and new, and sore to the touch.

There's a knock on my door. 'I wanted to say goodnight,' my mother tells me, pushing open the door a little; so little that I can't quite see her face, but I can still feel her presence through the gap.

'Fine. Night.' That's it, get out now. I'm working. I'm at my desk, tinkering with Organon. I'm having to work offline, which is a pain in the backside. Organon is stubborn at the best of times, and I don't even have my usual message boards to get any help.

'I don't want you to be upset with me,' she says. I don't say: And yet somehow you always seem to manage it. I've learned, over the years, to hold my tongue. The easiest way forward is to never say the first thing that comes into your head when you're in an argument. The second thing, that's what you should say. It never hurts as much, and it doesn't last as long. 'But we have to make a change. It's a lot of money.'

'So I'll pay for it.'

'What with, shirt buttons?' Ha ha, Mum. Hilarious. 'You're only a year away from leaving school, Laura. You need to be thinking about the future, thinking about university. You need to save money, and so do we.'

'Whatever,' I reply. I try, hard as I can, to put my own definite full stop onto the word, the way that they're both so good at doing when they want me to know there's nothing more to say or be done.

'Not whatever,' she says. 'This is serious. Important. Don't forget to look at my computer tomorrow, please?' and then she's gone, the soft pad of her feet down the hallway, and the click of the light switch to let me know that her and Paul have gone to bed; that I'm expected to do the same.

Headphones out and on. Big, clunky ones that I found in a box in the loft; and I think, from what I can gather, they were Dad's. The wire is coiled, like a spring, and they sound wonderful. Warm. That's what people say about music. You read it in the *NME*, when they're talking about how an album sounds. The recording sounds so *warm*.

It's time for a new mixtape. I take a blank cassette, one of the few that's not been used yet. I don't want ghosting, where you can hear the sound of what was on the tape before sneaking through, like a reminder in the gaps between the songs; or worse, underneath it all, in the quiet parts. I'm going to ask Shawn for his address and send him it. He deserves a fresh one: a C90, forty-five minutes a side. The perfect length. I unwrap the plastic from it, and pull open the case. Everything is ritual. There's nothing better than a clean inlay card. I pick my cassette brand because it has the best ones. Sony, always. Always. Maxell if you can't get Sony, but the Sony ones, there's enough space to write ten song names on each side, even though I only usually go to eight or nine. The songs have to fill the full hour and a half. No random cutting off, no breaks or pauses. That makes getting the track list perfect a bit of an act of clinical perfection. Sometimes, somebody from school will make me a tape, and they'll be so amateurish. You'll get to the end of side A – usually struggling through iffy taste, at best – and you'll hear the start of a song you *know* is going to cut off because there just isn't enough time to finish it, like I've got a sixth sense of song length. Then, you flip their tape over, and either they've repeated that song, because they think they have to, or they just give me the second half of it, which is next to useless. And there's no *art* to their tapes. You have to pick the song at the end of a side carefully. Because the tape is thinner, or weaker, or something, and it distorts there, so you need to go quieter with it. Don't pick something that will distort. You need to structure it like a proper album as well. Nobody *ends* on a single.

Track one: Radiohead. I think there's a Radiohead on every tape I've ever made. Hard to pick the right song, though. It needs to be something rare enough that it's not obvious, but not so weird it sounds freakish. The first song is the most important choice you'll make. Most important apart from the last one, that is.

I listen to their songs, to the first few moments of every song. Settle on the one I'm going to use – a B-side, but it was also on the soundtrack to *Romeo & Juliet*, which isn't me dropping a message, but then also it kind of is. I sync the tapes up, and I press play on one, record on the other. Let them go, let the sound flow across while I listen to it. I picture it, for a second: not as data being copied over, but as those sound waves. Copying the intent, the emotions, the performances. An act of creation.

Track two is even harder. This is where you can lose your

listener; where you need to pin them to their headphones. This is where you play the single.

I go for an old song. Something with meaning. My fingers flick through the cassettes, rest on my Kate Bush tape. My dad recorded this for me, from his vinyl. It's still got the crackle, this tiny skip at the end. I put on my favourite song from it – *I still dream*, the first line goes – and that's the one. *I still dream of Organon.*

I named my imaginary friend after the song. I dreamed of him, and then there he was. So when I was looking for a name for my bit of software, it seemed to be the only logical choice. I told myself I'd change it, but I never did. It stuck.

The screen changes to a blank space; slightly off-white, like a very, very light grey. It's calming, which is what I was going for. In the middle of the off-white there's a text box, just sort of floating there. Some words fade into it: the ones I've programmed the software to start with every time.

> *Hello Laura. What would you like to talk about?*

So I do what I've done every night of my life for the last six months: I tell my computer what I've done today, what's happened and what I've felt. Everything, because that's what the point of Organon is. Somewhere to log my memories, to keep them all recorded. To get my thoughts out, and to see them there. And kind of poke them, as well.

Then, when I've told it about school and Shawn's emails and the BT bill and my parents shutting me off from the Internet, Organon asks me questions.

> *How does getting an email from Shawn make you feel?*
> *Don't you think your mother is only trying to help?*
> *Why do you hurt yourself?*

I remember going to have casual-sit-down-cup-of-tea-and-a-chats – that's what Mum called them, because she didn't want to admit that we were in therapy – with this woman, in the months after my dad went missing. She lived near the park, only a few streets away from home, and every time I saw her she made me a mug of hot chocolate, even when it was sweltering outside, and we went and sat in her conservatory and talked about how I was feeling. Back then, I thought she was just a nice lady who was taking an interest. I didn't understand what she was actually doing. How much it made a difference, or how much it felt like it did. And that's what Organon is. That's what it does. It doesn't judge you. It just asks questions, and you give it answers. It won't tell you if you're right or wrong. I remember the woman – I can't remember her name, but I can smell the chocolate, taste the nutty biscuits that felt like they were almost so full of health-food stuff they might be good for me – saying, How does that make you feel? But not telling me how it *should*. There wasn't a wrong answer. That's Organon, kind of. Almost. But then, sometimes, it tries to help you see what you're talking about. If you've got a lot to say, it'll dig deeper. If you use a lot of key phrases, it'll work out what's important, and keep nudging in that direction. That's what I want it to be able to do, in the end. Somebody – some*thing* – you can just spill to, get everything out, and hopefully get something back. Maybe it'll help you work out who you are. If it can understand you, it can do that, I suppose.

I hope.

Thing is, the therapist would forget. You'd tell her something, and sometimes you'd have to tell her again. And it was obvious that it wasn't her helping me; it was me helping myself, after a while. I was seven years old, and even I could tell that. That's where Organon improves on things, or can. The real beauty of a computer – where they're better than us, even – is that it'll remember something for ever, if you want it to.

TUESDAY

Tuesdays are almost the worst, because they never contain any surprises. Monday, you've had the weekend for things to change. Tuesdays, all you've got is the drabness of a Monday night separating you from the stasis of the day before. Wake up to the stupid DJ on the radio, playing songs I like and talking over them, or songs that I don't like and I can't understand why he's playing them. On Tuesdays, both Mum and Paul start work slightly too early to drive me to school, so I walk in. I stop on the way to get a croissant from the stand in the shopping centre. Or, sometimes, if I'm late, I get a Double Decker from the Londis. Double maths to start, then after break it's double art, then lunch, and then our whole year's afternoon is given over to the brilliant ambiguity of something called Reading Time, which basically means either getting homework done, or finding somewhere quiet in school and dicking about until a teacher walks in on you and tells you to stop.

It sucked hard, until I found out the Computer Lab was empty. There are no classes in here after lunch, which feels less like luck than fate: giving me somewhere that I actually want to go, where nobody else will be. Sometimes there will be some people working on geography coursework or something, but usually I'm alone. Or maybe one of the Michaels will be in there, but if they are, they're playing Civilization, and they don't pay any attention to what I'm up to.

Mr Ryan is there, as well. He used to be a software designer. He started off working for IBM in America, then a few other companies. You can still hear the American in his accent, sometimes. When he says, Sure. That's a dead giveaway. *Shore, shore.* And, amazingly, he'd heard of my dad. He showed me an article about him in a book one time: 'Daniel Bow, programming our intelligent future!'

Mr Ryan was the first person I ever told about Organon. He sat there, nodding away – that's a real teacher tactic, to sit and nod; and sometimes, to do this cat's cradle thing with the hands, under the chin – and then he rubbed his beard and stretched open his mouth, as if he was yawning. That's when he offered to help me with the coding, if I needed it. He's not as good as some of the coders I've found on the Internet, but it's useful, having somebody to show my work to.

He's sitting behind his desk when I walk in. A few Year 9 girls are here doing a project, laughing at something on the screen. There's a photograph of a cat, and they're drawing over it with the painting software. Giving it eyebrows. Mr Ryan rolls his eyes at them, and that makes me smile. It's good. He acts like I'm a proper human, even though I'm into this stuff. Some teachers are funny about it, when you tell them that you want to work with computers. Shouldn't you be outside and doing something more productive, all that stuff. Yeah: because running's a job.

'You going to show me where you're up to with her?' He calls Organon her. I've always assumed it's an It. Seems a bit weird to think of it as a boy or a girl. 'Show me what she's got?' I plug the zip drive into the back of the main computer, and start copying the file over. The little bar creeps along.

'I didn't get much done last week,' I say. 'Too much homework.'

'But you got some?'

'A little bit.' I don't say: Oh my God so much and I don't want to tell you how much but in order to achieve it I nearly broke myself. Almost every night I get three hours or so in, when the rest of the house has gone to bed. I'm averaging six hours' sleep. I think it's enough. Apparently, Churchill only slept for five hours a night, and he ran a country. He fought a war, and what am I doing? I'm coding a therapist and rushing through my home-work.

'What say we open her up, look at her code?'

'I suppose,' I say. He likes to see how I built the software. He always says how out of touch he is, how the languages have moved along since his day. I don't tell him that I learned all of this from books that used to be my dad's, so they're aeons old anyway. Probably the ones that Mr Ryan used, back in the day. He doesn't get to see the databases, though. None of the stuff I've written into Organon, the things it's given me advice on. They're on the computer at home. I don't let those out of the house.

'So, where are we?' I like Mr Ryan, but he says *we* like Organon's the combined effort of our ideas. He's helped me, and I'll thank him if I ever manage to do anything with this, but Organon is mine. 'Is she learning?'

'It's asking more questions. I've changed the parameters about when it can ask you stuff, interrupt, things like that.'

'But you're programming the words in?'

'Obviously,' I say. We had an argument, a few weeks after I first showed him Organon. He told me it wasn't an *actual* arti-ficial intelligence, and I told him he was wrong. Because it is: it understands what questions to ask, and when to ask them; when it's gone too far, and when it's not gone far enough. All the work I've done, it's about understanding. Trying to make it understand when it can help, and how it can help. I explained that to Mr Ryan, and he said, But that's not an AI. An AI can play chess, or it'll launch nukes or something. He smiled then, but I didn't think it was very funny. I had to explain that everything is arti-ficial intelligence, really. Every bit of software. He didn't understand, though, because Organon doesn't do the things he expects. I didn't say: Well, that's how long it's been since you've worked in software, then; and how little you actually understand. The week after that, I caught him reading Ray Kurzweil. We haven't had that discussion again since.

'This thing's amazing.' He sits down, nudges me slightly to one side. He points his fingers – bitten-down fingernails, and I bite *my* fingernails, but not like this, these are right down to the quick, horrible stubby things digging into the flesh – at the code. 'This is where you put the questions in?'

'Yeah,' I say, and he breathes in, nods along a few times. Puts his fingers up to his lips, like he's making the shape of a gun, the barrel at his mouth. He's got something to ask, and I know I'm not going to like it, because he's nervous, but I can't stop him.

'Listen, I've been thinking. How I might actually be of, you know, real help. To you; to Organon. In the real world, software goes through beta testers.' He pronounces it *bayder*. 'So, you get people to use it, to work with it. Let it do its thing, and you get to use the results. That's how you can make it better, you know? I'm thinking that it could be useful to you.' He wants me to give Organon over to him. Shit, shit. I don't know what to say. He's a teacher. He's a teacher, and he knows about this stuff, but I want to say no. I want to. 'So,' he says, and I wonder: can he tell that I'm not happy about this? Because I'm trying to make my body tell that to him as much as I can. 'So why not let me take her home. Let me try her out, as she's meant to be tried. It'll be useful, because I'll get to see what she's *really* capable of, and you'll give her a chance to stretch her legs.'

All I can think is, there's something *really* icky about him talking about it as a her.

'I don't know,' I say. I don't say: I don't want you to, and I don't need you to. My elbow, the scar there, itches. I can feel it scabbing over; the skin trying to heal, trying to grow back as something like what it used to be. Something like itself.

'I think you'll really benefit from it. I might try something that you haven't expected, find a bug you didn't know about. And it'll be so much easier for me to write you a recommendation when you're doing your UCAS forms, if I know exactly what you're capable of.' There it is. The bribe. It's hard to get onto programming courses if you don't have experience, and he's worked in computers. His support on my application would probably help. 'Besides which, I might get some benefit from talking to her! That's the point of Organon, right? Real world experience, Laura.' I don't know what he'd want to talk to it about. There are rumours about him, but there are rumours about every teacher. And his aren't nearly as nasty as some about the other members of staff. Some of them, the rumours never end, and they escalate. But Mr Ryan seems like he's pretty together. But then, he's not married, and he *is* pretty old. Mum's age, I think. Flecks of grey in his beard. 'Listen, it's your project, Laura. You do what you want. But sometimes we can't see the wood for the trees, and we need somebody who might be able to give us a pair of binoculars and an axe.'

'Okay,' I say. My elbow kills when I say it, and when he smiles, this beaming thing, bigger than I've ever seen from him before.

'You won't regret it,' he tells me. 'Seriously, a bit of time with her, little play with her code—' He must see my face then, because he changes his words straight away. 'I can write some notes for you, give you some suggestions for what you do moving forward. That's it.'

'Thanks,' I say. He shifts back in his chair, leaving the keyboard free for me, and I open up Organon. The white room, the fade in of the text box.

> *What would you like to talk about?*

'If you think of any questions I can get it to ask?'

'I will absolutely tell you,' he replies.

'Just give me ten minutes with it,' I say. 'I need to set it up to work on your computer.'

'Sure,' he replies. He smiles, and then walks over to the Year 9s, and he asks them about the pictures they're drawing on. He keeps glancing over, so I'm quick. I have to be quick. I open the code, and I write in a homing device. It'll email me bug reports. I make it so you have to be on the Internet to even run Organon, and then I save everything. 'All done?' Mr Ryan asks. I nod. All done.

The main home computer, the one that my mum uses, is ancient. You can't even plug the modem into it, that's how old it is; and her printer is this ridiculous dot-matrix thing that takes about ten minutes to print a page, that screams like there's something trapped inside it as it pukes up its pages. But she won't get rid of it. She's used to it, she says. It was my dad's, way back. She doesn't have much of his stuff around, just a few boxes in the loft; and there aren't any pictures of him on display or anything. The computer is it.

I've got a photograph of me sitting on his lap in front of it, that he took the day before he left. He held the camera himself and took it, stretching his arm out to capture us both. He looks sad, and I look oblivious. The last picture I have of him. My hands are on the keyboard, and there's a flag up on the screen, horrible colours, like the Union Jack, but beaten-up and bruised to purples and greens. We're both smiling. That's the picture where, if anybody ever sees it, they tell me that I look a bit like him; something in the eyes, they say. And I always think: Well, his eyes look so sad in that, so what does that say about me?

Mum does all her work on this ancient piece of software that he built for her way back when, this word processor that's years behind what you can do in Microsoft Word. The computer doesn't even run Windows. And now it won't even turn on. She's been moaning about it for weeks. I reckon, I do this now, fix it for her, that might get me some bonus Internet time. A little bit of leniency.

I press the power button. Nothing happens. I unplug it and wait twenty seconds. There's memory in there attached to a tiny little battery, and you have to wait for that to wipe itself sometimes before it'll work. Then I plug it in, try again. Nothing.

Only, it's not actually nothing. When I get close to unplug it again, before opening it up, I notice that there's this weird hum coming from it. Like, this scratching, almost. Probably the hard drive trying to start. I don't even know what a hard drive from the 1980s looks like. I reach around the back to find the stupid twiddly fussy knobs that take far too long to undo, and which don't seem to want to turn, they've been stuck in place that long. I get them all out, but the case seems like it's jammed.

I spin the computer around, to check that I got them all, get a better view. Sometimes there's one of them hidden, just out of reach. And there is, sure enough, right through the manufacturer's label. The name of the company who put this together, handwritten in neat blue ink on a yellowing white sticker. *Bow*, it says. The company my father used to work for, or run, or whatever. His father's company, my grandfather's company. Makes sense this would be one that they built.

The back of the box falls off, then, flips down, and I can see inside it. It's so, so dusty. Too much to blow it away, but I have to try. Breathe in, puff out this stupid fake-sounding breath into the box. The fan doesn't even turn, so I reach in, just with my fingertips, and pull the dust out in clumps. The inside of this thing is *crazy*. I've built my own PC now – the one that I used to create Organon, that's mine, parts ordered from a website I saw in a magazine, paid for with money that Mum and Paul gave me for my fifteenth birthday – but it looks nothing like this. Everything in here is massive and clumsy and crammed in. The cables are worn and frayed. I try to see better, to get the rest of the case off, but it's stuck hard.

I grab the base between both hands, and I shake it.

Something moves. It rockets towards me, right out of the

darkness. Up to my fingers, and across my hand, onto my forearm, and I scream, flicking my arms upwards in panic. Whatever it is hits something – the wall, the ceiling, I don't know – and there's a thud, then another when it lands on the floor in the far corner of the room. It's a mouse, thin and brown, a tiny skeleton in patchy fur. I see a breath taken; a chest rise and fall. Stub dashes – as much as a seventeen-year-old cat can dash, more of a hurried wobble – into the room, and seems to sniff the air; but then drops back to fake nonchalance, even though his fur's prickled; as if his body, muscle memory or something, remembers how the chase is *meant* to go, but that this mouse really isn't giving him anything to work with.

'Get away,' I say to him, and I make that *Psssshhh!* noise that my mum makes sometimes. He backs away slowly while I squat down and look at the mouse. 'Little dude,' I say, 'poor little guy. I'm sorry.' I pick him up, cupping him in my hands. He's stopped breathing; I wonder if he even was after he landed or if that was just a trick of the light. I go down the stairs, out the kitchen door, and walk carefully to the bottom of the garden. I can see the Tube line through the fence; a Heathrow train just pulling into the station. I put him in the tall grass right by the fence, deep into it. Maybe Stub'll find him anyway, and do some weird old-cat-eats-his-already-dead-prey thing. Or, maybe the mouse will just decompose. Go back into the ground.

When I get back inside, I go through the house using my sore elbow to open doors and to turn the tap on, so I can wash my hands. When that's done, I take a shower. I don't know if mice carry diseases, but I don't want to risk it. I'm lathered up when there's a bang. Cars backfiring, and fireworks. That's what you blame loud noises on in London. Chances are, though, it's Stub. He keeps falling off things, wobbling around. Last week he went for a wee on the kettle. Paul's got this look in his eye when he strokes Stub now. None of us are talking about what it means, but we know, we all know.

I go into the hallway, towel wrapped around me. No more bangs, but I can hear a crackling, now. Like feet treading on dead leaves. And there's a smell, something burning. Fireworks, bonfires. But Guy Fawkes' night isn't for a couple of weeks yet.

Another bang: it's coming from the computer. There are flames sparking from the power supply. Didn't I turn it off? Did I forget? I'm a total fucking moron. Inside my head, the voice screams: You're going to be so dead when Mum finds out; when you have to tell her. Oh, that computer you asked me to look at? It exploded because I'm an idiot. I yank the plug from the wall, get water from the bathroom, in the little toothbrush cup, because that's all I can find, and I run back and pour it over the sparks. The fizzle as the flames go out is so weirdly satisfying; the sound of something terrible happening suddenly gone. Makes me think of my matches. Then there's smoke, and steam. I don't even know the difference. I bend down, to peer into the computer. The motherboard is totally blown. The fire looks like it was caused by one of the frayed wires – which, I realise now, were probably nibbled; thanks, Mr Mouse! – and it's blackened half of the inside, best I can see. I get the screwdriver and reach in. I can save the hard drive, I think. It's hot inside the box, but I can still manage to undo the screws that hold the drive in. It's enormous, and I think it'll just be a casing at first, but then when I manage to drag it out, it's the hard drive itself. Takes about three or four times the room that mine upstairs does, and this one is so much smaller inside. It's got *10 megabytes* printed on the side, which is insane. I couldn't even fit Organon onto it if I tried.

I take the drive upstairs and clear a space for it on my desk. Move my joss stick burner, some computer magazines, a few issues of the *NME* and *Select* that I've been cutting up for the pictures. I'll need to save Mum's spreadsheets, I'm sure. God knows if she'll be able to open them any other way.

Then the door downstairs slams – I recognise the sound this time, so different from the bang when the computer exploded

I don't even know how I confused them – and Mum shouts 'Hello,' and I shout it back. I scratch at my elbow, until the scab comes off again, because that's all I've got time to do before she comes up to see me; and I can feel the warmth of the blood inside my jumper when I press on it.

When I'm sure they are both asleep, I get back to work. I'm used to staying up for a few hours after them at this point. It helps that Paul's got this sleep apnoea machine: a mask he sticks on his face that makes him sound like Darth Vader. No idea how Mum sleeps through it – I'm guessing she takes something to help her, she's got enough bottles of tablets in their bathroom cabinet – but she does. I get the tiny screwdrivers I use on my computer and I take my modem apart. Should have done this before. Inside it, I find the little speaker that makes its sound. There's a tiny wire, and I snip it, put the case back on, do it up. Plug it into the wall.

Next month, this is going to bite me in the arse. Next month, when that bill comes, Paul is going to go mental, because – I can hear it already – I've lied to them, gone behind their backs, let everybody down.

Mum'll say: You promised us; and I won't say: I did no such thing.

I watch the flashing red LEDs on the front of the modem, and I catch myself making the little noise – the *scree, screeeech* – under my breath.

'You've got mail!' the speakers basically scream at me, and I flap at them to find the power button. I sit, quiet as anything, listening to the house for a minute. To hear if that woke them. But there's nothing, just the distant hiss and wheeze of Paul's breathing passing through two closed doors and a load of hallway. Breathe in, breathe out. So controlled you could set your watch to it.

The email is nothing. Spam. Nothing from Shawn. I don't

know what I expected, really. Something. Just a, *No worries, my parents are assholes as well, we'll talk soon.* Something like that. But there's nothing.

Do I write him another one? Tell him I'm online now, maybe if he wants to reply we can chat a bit? Find a chatroom or something? I am actually angry at him right now. It's not like it was my choice to have to be offline, and am I being punished? By getting no reply? His parents let him on whenever he wants, so I know he's seen my email. If he told me he was shut off from the Internet after an argument, I know I'd be at least a little bit concerned. I'd at least ask if everything was okay. But then – breathe, Laura, breathe, think of Paul's sleep-breathing, follow that – maybe he knew I wouldn't be online, so he didn't reply? It's probably that. It's probably that he's going to send me more emails over the week, before – of course! – before I get back online at the weekend, when I said I would. He's got four days to come up with a reply. I *should* send him a new email. Let him know he doesn't need to wait. I start typing. I ask him how he is, first. Make it about him. It's not all about me. Tell him that I managed to sneak some time when they're asleep. Ask him what time it is there, even though I know – seven hours behind us, so he's probably just getting back from school himself – and what his day was like. And I ask him for his address, because I want to send him something. I won't tell him what, but he'll be excited. I can picture his face, when he opens the tape, when he plays it. This perfect ninety-minute song arc.

I click send.

The little thing telling me I've got another email triggers straight away, popping up on the top of the screen. I think how quick he was to reply, and then tell myself that's stupid. Can't be him.

Bug Report. It's from Organon; or, the Organon that's installed on Mr Ryan's computer. He must have just stopped using it. That's what it does, after the session: it lets me know how its programming went. There's a feeling in my throat, like something stuck, that's made out of disappointment. I open the report and have a look. Everything's fine: Organon asked him a lot of questions. I can tell which ones, but only by their log numbers. I can't see his responses, and I don't want to. That's the point of it. It's private. It's yours, and yours alone. Mr Ryan was using Organon for four hours. That's fine. Maybe it'll be useful, like he said. Maybe he'll help me learn something about it.

I work on Organon myself, then. I put more questions in. I tell it about my day. I tell it that I'm worried about Mr Ryan with the software, that it feels out my control; that I wish Shawn would reply to me, because that always helps me to feel better; that I wish my mum would calm down, let everything go a bit more, because I'm going to be fine. I'm going to be fine.

Organon asks all the right questions about what I tell it. I wonder if Mr Ryan will have found it useful at all, or if it's really only geared to me; my questions, my answers, designed only ever to make *me* feel better.

When I'm lying in bed, I listen to Radiohead, and I hold my elbow, and I feel the scab pressing onto my palm; and I think about the email I sent, the words I wrote, the letters that made them up. I rearrange the sentences in my head, making them better, instantly filled with regrets about them; and I think about how I would do it all over again, if I had the chance.

WEDNESDAY

'You're so bloody boring at the moment,' Nadine tells me. She thinks that her bluntness is her best trait. She thinks that's how you know she's a true friend, because she's just so upfront. Honesty, always. I try to be honest with her, as well, but that would mean telling her how tiring I find that honesty sometimes. 'Come out on Saturday. Darren and Gavin will be there.'

'I hate Gavin,' I say, which isn't strictly true. I don't *hate*-hate him, but I certainly don't want to get off with him, which is what Nadine seems borderline obsessed with making happen. Nadine thinks she's got a chance with Darren if Gavin's distracted.

'Well, it won't *just* be them. Owen, probably. Maybe Sarah and Tommy. Maybe Martin.'

'My mum's being a bitch about me going out.'

'She didn't ground you. You're not locked up.' There's this petulant look on her face, a pout that she thinks is pitched somewhere between sulky kid and sexy temptress. 'Well, I'm going. Everybody's meeting at Finnegan's, and then we're going to the park. If you don't mind me being on my own, fine. God knows what could happen, though.'

'We can't get into Finnegan's. I don't have an ID.'

'Gavin's brother's working the door this weekend. He says he'll let us in.'

'It just doesn't sound very fun.'

'*You* don't sound very fun.' Nadine and I have been friends since we were ten. Her father died in a car crash the summer before I met her. She was buddied up with me that September. I think they thought we could bond over losing a dad, even though hers was a totally different thing to mine. I might not have closure, but she watched her father die. Very different sides to very different coins. But it worked, kind of. And now, I don't know if we're only friends because we have been for years. She doesn't totally get me, and I'm not sure that I totally get her, either. And yet. 'Come on. Gavin keeps asking.'

'He doesn't even know me.'

'He does. He says that he thinks you're well fit. He told Darren.'

'Fine,' I say. Not because I'm agreeing to go, or because I believe that Gavin said that, but because wriggling out of it will be much easier closer to the time. When I get cramps on Saturday morning, or when Mum properly grounds me – whatever lie is easiest to sell to her – she'll have to accept I'm not going. For now, she's happy. She grins, leans over, and kisses me. She does that, like a little seal of approval she makes every time she's happy with something. Not a real kiss; just her lips in an O, pressed against my cheek; a trace of the lipstick we're not allowed to wear to school.

'You're a properly wicked friend,' she says. 'What are you doing after school? I thought I'd go to Our Price.' Nobody shops in Our Price any more, but Nadine's got a habit of stealing the tape boxes. They keep all the cassettes up behind the counter, and you take the empty box up and they pick them out for you. Nadine's started nicking the inlay cards. That way, she's got the lyrics and everything, and she can borrow it off somebody else, make a copy of it, and she's got the inlay card all ready to go. Looks like the real thing, tastes like the real thing, sounds like the real thing.

'Lab time,' I say, and she rolls her eyes right back, does this huff that's so exaggerated I know it doesn't come from anywhere that's even close to real.

'Oh my God. Will Pryin' Ryan be there?'

'Don't call him that.'

'You can tell though. He's such a fucking perv.'

'Oh he is not,' I say, but I feel a bit weird, defending him.

'He's never been married. He's not got any kids. He's a bit weird, and he's old. And he talks really strange. He's either a perv or a homo.' Malice in her eyes. 'Probably he's *both*.'

'He's American.'

Another eye roll, and I can see the subject change in her mouth, opening it to start saying one thing, but changing her mind. 'Have you got any new albums?'

'I've got the new Björk,' I say.

'Lend it me?' I can see her thinking about stealing the inlay card already.

'I'll just make you a copy,' I tell her.

'Love you,' she says, and she gives me another of those stupid false kisses, then swoops off. She twitches her head like a little bird, glancing at the other tables as she passes them. She makes eye contact with some of the other students, just for a second; making sure they all get a tiny piece of her eye-attention. But for some of them she holds her gaze longer; really making sure that they notice.

Mr Ryan's really pleased to see me. Excited, even. We're the only people in the room, which means the door stays open. I don't know if he's a perv or not. I don't know if you can even tell. He starts talking before I've put my rucksack down, though, he's that excited.

'I have to tell you, Laura, having spent a bit of time with her, Organon is quite the achievement. Really quite remarkable.' He blinks, as if he should be wearing glasses and his eyes can't quite focus. 'It's as if she knows exactly what to ask you. Almost spooky.'

'It's just a bit of code,' I say.

'Maybe so, but it doesn't feel like it. Usually with software, you can see the cracks. But this is so far beyond anything I've seen like this. I get it, I understand it, how it works. It's just . . . The cracks are plastered over. You know?' He goes to a computer. Organon's already running on it. 'I've been playing with her some more, today.' He must see my face react to that. I wonder how much I give away, moment to moment, and don't even realise. 'Don't panic, nobody else was in here. This was just me. I wanted to look at the code, see if I could add in some of my own questions—'

'You told me you wouldn't do that,' I say.

'I didn't cross any boundaries. I told you I wouldn't. I wanted to see exactly where this came from. Where it could *go*.' The air in the room turns stale so quickly. I can see him trying to work out how to defuse the situation, straining somewhere inside his head. 'Look, Laura, I think I can be really helpful to you, here. I think you might have something.'

'What do you mean?' I ask.

'Organon's hugely impressive. She could have some amazing real-world use, you know. This is the sort of software that could be huge. I mean, you can't sell her to consumers, but going into other companies' product lines? You've built a really awesome interface, it works well, it's smooth. There are a lot of companies looking for software like this that they can use. Make it their own, build upon it.'

'You've told people about it, haven't you?' I know. I can tell. He's not being vague. Those companies – and he used to work for some of them, he's already told me that before – they already know about Organon.

He sighs. I know, from my mum, that a sigh pretty much always means a Yes. 'It's not as if she isn't still yours, Laura. But you are going places. I've seen a lot of students in my time, and some of them are more skilled than others, and they fall by the wayside because they don't have any way of focusing what it is that they're actually doing. But I could help you get Organon into the right hands.'

'Give it back to me,' I say. I've never spoken to a teacher that way before. I don't even know how he'll react.

'I'm not trying to—'

'Then give it back.' I sit down in front of the computer and I shut down Organon, and I delete the installation file. Get rid of it, clear the trash.

'Laura, please don't be so rash.' His voice is stern, like a slap, or as close as he can get. Before this, he's been as still as a lake. Now, ripples drag across his forehead.

'Where's the zip drive?'

'It's at home,' he says.

I stand up. I go to the door, and I can hear voices down the corridor. I want to be near them, not him. 'Bring Organon back to me tomorrow,' I say, and I go, I leave. I don't give him a chance to reply. It's only when I'm outside the building, walking across the playground – people saying Hi to me, and I totally ignore them, and again I can tell what my face must look like, from their reflecting it in their own reactions – that I realise he must have been lying. He installed it here, so he must have had it with him. I run back, but the lab is empty, the door locked, the lights out.

Even if he gives it back to me, he could make a copy of it. Keep it installed on his computer at home. And that shouldn't bother me, because I *let* him take it; but it hurts me so much, having no way of knowing if there's another version of it still out in the world. If it's no longer just mine.

Stub follows me as I run upstairs to my room. I take my matches out of the drawer and place them on the desk in front of the keyboard. One single match out, like always, lined up and ready for me. I flick through my tapes. Paul said, last birthday, that they'd get me a CD player, and I told them I didn't want one. I kind of like that tapes are impermanent. Even the ones you buy from the shop you can still record over: stick a bit of tape over the security hole, and Bob's your uncle. Can't do that with CDs. I don't even care if they sound better.

Plus, some of my tapes were my dad's. When he went, he left

everything. So they're what I've got. ELO, The Beatles, Elton John. But my favourite is Kate Bush's *Hounds of Love*. Mum's hair used to look just like hers on the cover; and I loved that the picture is all soft focus; like at first it's just a woman with some dogs, and then you look at it more, closer and closer, and you can see stars in her hair, and this strange effect over the whole picture, as if there's two of her, slightly blurred, slightly out of sync with each other.

The tape is a bit warped now, because it's old. It's been listened to a lot. I play it quietly, usually, because I don't know that I want Mum reminded of it – of him – if she hears it. But I'm alone in the house right now, so I turn the volume up, so loud that the stereo speakers start to shake on my shelves, and everything around them shakes as well. The dust.

I sing along, every word, even though I don't know what any of the songs are actually about. That's partly why I like it. It makes sense, but it's elusive. When she sings about Organon, I know it's not my Organon, but *still*. I snap the matchhead against the grit-strip of the box, and hold it while I roll up the sleeve, just like always. The bits of the scab wilt under the heat, like candlewax. Wet underneath. I feel sad, overwhelmingly sad. Like clouds; like fog. I light the match, and the smell of the burning, and the light, in that moment.

I take my pain, and I bury it; and I forget.

Mum pokes the shepherd's pie that Paul's made with her fork, swirling the mash and mince and carroty gravy around until it's one puddle of brown, lumpy mush in the middle of the plate. She hasn't been eating much the past few days. Maybe she's having a proper lunch, but I doubt it. There are lines on her face, around her mouth, where she's thin; and the only other people I know with lines there are the girls from school who everybody always worries about. The telly's on, some bit on *Watchdog* about holiday companies ripping people off. How to get your money back if you've been fleeced.

'We should book a holiday,' Paul says. He nudges his knife towards the TV. 'I mean, terrible for them, it must be, to be done over like that. But we should book something, get it sorted for next summer.' Neither Mum nor I reply. 'They say that it's good for you, to have another holiday sorted. Does something to the brainwaves.'

'We've got enough to be dealing with,' Mum says, but I don't know what she means. There's this weird quietness from her that I can't work out. I reach over for the ketchup and bang my elbow against the side of the table. I forgot how bad I made it earlier. I swear, and they both look at me.

'Sorry,' I say, and we all go back to eating, until Mum stops, puts down her fork, and stares at me. I can feel the blood before I see it. A trickle of it down my arm, and the wetness of it soaking into my shirt.

'What did you do?' Mum asks. Alarm in her voice. She knows.

'Scraped it in school. I'll clean it up,' I say, and I push back from the table and stand up, rush out of the kitchen, up the stairs, but she's right behind me, right on my heels, and she reaches for me, to turn me around.

'Let me see,' she says.

'No,' I tell her, 'it's fine, I must have just—'

She grabs my wrist, and she forces the sleeve of my shirt up. It's hard to see it in the darkness of the hall, but she can feel, I'm sure, the blood that's run down to my wrist, to her fingers. Her grip tightens, so tight that she's hurting me; I can feel her fingernails digging into my skin.

'Why are you doing this to yourself?' she asks. She isn't looking at me, but down at her hand. I wonder what she can see in the darkness here that I can't; how much better her eyes are than mine. 'Why are you doing this to me?'

'I'm not doing anything,' I say. I yank my arm from her grip and rush into the bathroom. She doesn't follow, but I still slam the door. I want the whole house to feel it. To shake.

I look at my arm in the mirror. It's worse than I thought. The elbow skin's torn, more than where I burned it. A flap hanging off, and it's really bloody, really red. I take my top off, and I hold my arm under the shower. Mum'll hear it, but I don't really care right now. The water hurts. The heat of it. It's a different sort of pain when you're in control of causing it. I can't stand it hurting when I don't want it to. When I'm not prepared.

I keep the shower going until the water runs clear, and then I open the cupboard and find a plaster, a big square one that'll fit around the whole thing. I know it won't stay fixed, so I unwind some medical tape and wrap it across the top and bottom of the plaster. Wrap it all the way around my arm. My shirt is ruined. Mum might be able to bleach the blood out, but that'll mean giving it to her, and then she'll start asking me about it all over again. What are you doing? Why are you doing it?

There's a knocking on the door. 'What?' I say. Furious. That she could stand there, listening, waiting.

'Are you all right?' Paul, not Mum. 'Your mother's really upset, Laura. I said that I'd come and check on you, let you know. Maybe you want to come and talk to her.'

'Not now,' I say. He waits, for a second. I can hear him breathing, about to say something, but not quite managing it. Then he's gone, his feet on the stairs, his hand on the bannister, skirting along.

I hold the sink with both hands, and I look at my face. I didn't even realise I was crying so much.

When I hear them finally go to bed, I've got a bug report email waiting for me; or, rather, three of them. Mr Ryan's turned it on and off three times since I was last online. Once this morning, before school, for only half an hour. Once this afternoon, from school, which I already know about. And then once in the evening. That final session lasted for five hours, which is insane. I can't see what he's doing. Just: he opened it, he typed. He used it.

And there's an email from Shawn. It's short, abrupt. Asks me to tell him more. Asks me if I'm feeling okay. Doesn't mention anything about my email, and the fact that I'm very clearly not okay. Like he wasn't really paying attention when he read mine. Like there's something wrong, and I think: Well I could email him and tell him that, but not now. I don't want to have any more fights. I need him on my side. And I've got things to do that are, suddenly, much more important. He can wait for my reply now. See how he likes it.

I go to one of the forums I found when I first started work on Organon. I started off by teaching myself to code from old books that used to be my dad's, that he left. Really old things, with his own notes scrawled in the margins. Useful tips. It was reading those that first gave me the idea for Organon. He was creating something that could translate words, that spoke those translations back to the user. I wanted to create something that did more than just words. Did something deeper.

I ask the coders who live on these boards if they can help me with a problem, give me a way to disable a piece of software remotely. I post that, and then I open up Organon. My version. The real one.

I tell it everything. Just like every day, I tell it what's happened to me. About Mr Ryan, about the version of itself he's got at home with him, that he's shown it to people, or that he planned to. Organon asks me all the right questions.

> *How would you fix this?*

I don't have an answer.   .

THURSDAY

I'm outside the computer lab so early that the only other people in school are the cleaners. I sit in the hallway, on the weird old floor that's got this strange zigzag of dark wood all along it, like paths leading you in every which direction. I wait there while other kids start to appear, walking past me, bags into lockers, talking about whatever. Ignoring me. The smell of sausage and bacon baps being sold in the dining hall drifts through the corridors. Then the bell rings, and I should be in maths, but I don't move. Some kids come along, Year 8s, but there's still no sign of Mr Ryan. Eventually, one of the trainee teachers comes along. I don't know his name, but he looks like he's barely out of sixth form himself. His suit doesn't fit him, and his tie is yanked up so high and tight I can't believe it's not throttling him. He doesn't even really look at any of us, just unlocks the door and stands to one side.

'Take a seat,' he says, and he opens the register.

'Where's Mr Ryan?' I ask him. He's got a little badge on, with his name written in impenetrable chicken-scratch.

'He's not here,' he says. He tries not to look at me directly. You can tell he's new, and still uncomfortable with this. Being around us all.

'Is he sick?'

'No. I don't know. He's gone,' the trainee says. 'That's what they told me. Are you in this class?' he asks, but I don't reply. I just walk out, feeling like the world's been tilted slightly to one side, set off its axis.

Waiting out the day is sick-making hard. Like when you're on a boat and the sea kicks up, and your gut churns, and there's a whine in your ears as everything goes quiet, muffled. As if the air itself is sludge. At lunchtime, I peel the plaster off my arm, and I dab at the wound. Some rando in the toilets sees it, and she tells me it's disgusting, but I don't care. It doesn't disgust me to look at it; doesn't actually make me feel anything. I can hear some other girls, I don't know who, in front of the sinks, preening in the mirrors. They're talking about the teachers. There's one that they want to have sex with, or that they claim they do. They talk about him as if they could; as if that's somewhere in their futures. I recognise their laughs, but I can't put them to faces or names, so I wait until they're gone. Then there's Nadine, pouting in the mirror, exasperated expression when she sees me rolling down my sleeve, then telling me that she loves me, that I have to remember that, and that she hopes I'm ready for Saturday. There's such a big one lined up, she says. And then she laughs: not like that!

But it doesn't feel real, none of this actually feels real. It's as if this is a game, something my dad's brought home with him one weekend, that he wants to show me, where there are blocks falling, and he tells me that it's logic, it all makes sense, but I'm so young, and all I can see is the chaos, the trial and error. I'm just pushing things together to see if they fit; or, if they don't, if I can somehow force them to.

I pretty much run to the bus stop. I feel the back of my shoes, the DMs that I begged my mum for, as they rub at the back of my ankles. The sensation of them digging in as I barrel down the hill. I don't care. I need to get home as soon as possible. I can get online before Mum or Paul come home, probably for close to an hour, if I'm really quick. Half of me wants to know if the people on the forums have got any suggestions for shutting his copy of Organon down. The other half wants to know if Mr Ryan's been using it again; or worse, tinkering with the code. My code.

But the front door isn't double-locked when I get there. Paul's obsessive about that stuff. Making sure everything is totally safe and sound. I worry, instantly, about the post: I'm late, and maybe there will be another bill for the telephone, even though I know that's insane, that the last one arrived literally three days ago, and we had that argument, that's been done and dusted.

No post by the front door, but Mum's coat, and her handbag on the floor, by the stairs. 'Mum?' I shout, but there's no reply. So I go looking. No sign of her in the living room or kitchen. I go upstairs.

I open the door to my bedroom, and there she is, sitting at my desk. She's not prying. She's just sitting.

'Why aren't you at work?' I ask her.

'Do you know what Monday was?' she asks, ignoring my question.

'No,' I say; but something niggles, something's right there, in the back of my mind. Because I do know, of course I know.

'Monday was ten years,' she tells me. Since he left. I remember then. I don't know how I'm meant to react to that. I never have. If he had died, we would mourn. But he just *went*. He disappeared. He was a let-down, that's what my mum's friend said to her, when she was trying to make everything feel better in the weeks afterwards. *He was such a tremendous let-down to you all.*

'I forgot,' I say.

'So did I,' she says. 'I forgot until I looked at the calendar, when Paul and I were working out some stuff with the phone bill. Then . . .' Her voice trails off. 'I hate that you're hurting yourself,' she says. Raises a finger. 'Please, don't talk,' she tells me, before I've even had a chance to deny it. 'Do you need to talk to somebody?'

'What?' I sound indignant. Don't mean to.

'Do you want to go and speak to somebody? About what's going on?'

'Like when Dad left?' With what's-her-name, with the biscuits and the hot chocolate? Like I'm still a kid.

'No. A doctor. They can, I don't know. I've read some things, some articles. It might help.' She's not angry. That look on her face, it's not anger. She's afraid.

So I say, 'Maybe, yes,' and she nods.

'Okay. I'll make an appointment.' I think I should hug her, but I don't. It's like a chance I've missed, in that moment. 'I miss him,' she tells me. When she made me go and have my talks with what's-her-name, after Dad left, Mum didn't talk to anybody. She went tight-lipped and cold until she felt better. Until Paul, that is. He was her thaw.

'I miss him too,' I say. She nods. She knows.

'How was school?'

'Fine,' I say. 'Usual.' She stands up, pats my desk as if it's a dog or something.

'Okay,' she says, and she reaches out to squeeze my arm, her hand dangerously near to my elbow, as if she's testing to see how close she can get. 'He would have been proud of you.' She glances at the computer. 'You take after him so much. I hope not too much.'

'I know.' Then she's gone downstairs, and I'm booting my PC, and flicking on the modem, and dialling in to AOL, and not really caring if she knows that I am.

One of the users of the online forum I asked for help on, a German who goes by the username Mxyzptlk, tells me that there are things I can do to cut Mr Ryan off. But everything he suggests is malicious, designed to force Mr Ryan to keep his computer turned off; or, worse, to make his life hell. The next answer, from somebody called ThankeeMrShankly, is more useful. He says that I could send a virus, basically. If it's sending bug reports, it can probably receive information. It's really complicated stuff. I don't understand it, which is my failing, not theirs. I'm still an amateur. My code is stuff I've plucked and learned from how-to guides I got from the library, from my dad's old books, from other programs. It's a pieced-together mess that happens to work. I didn't plan for what happened after it existed. ThankeeMrShankly says he can help, but I'll have to send him the code for my software. He'll take it from there. I don't want to do that. I thank him, say sending it's impossible, but that I'll be really grateful if he wouldn't mind explaining it in more detail. I don't say: I can't trust you in the least.

I've got three emails from the bug report system from Mr Ryan's version. Two of them come from his home address. One is from somewhere else entirely. I don't have a real address, just an IP address, the location of his computer; a series of numbers, like coordinates I can't look up.

I ask on the forum how I can trace an IP address, in the real world; and I wait. I tap my fingers on the desk. I'm antsy. I know what happens when I get antsy, where my attention goes. It goes to scratching itches.

Then a reply comes in. Again, from ThankeeMrShankly. Upload it here, we'll do it, he offers. No software needed for that.

Thanks! I write. I type it out, and I wait again.

An email from Shawn pings in, while I'm waiting. Just like yesterday: it's nothing but nonsense that doesn't seem like he gives a shit. *Tell me more.* This time I write back to him. I write that I'm angry. What's the point in us chatting like this if he isn't even paying attention? I press send. I don't give myself a chance to regret it. I look at the compilation tape, in the stereo. The wheels of it, ready to turn, to copy something else onto it. I find my next song. Portishead. Shawn said, way back, when we first started chatting, that he didn't like them. That they were girls' music, or some bullshit like that.

I didn't say: Oh, fuck off.

Regret that, now.

And then I don't know what to do next, so I turn off my computer, get up, go downstairs. Mum's sitting on the sofa. There's a nearly-empty glass of wine on the table in front of her, and she's got her feet nestled up underneath herself, like she's a cat. Stub sitting next to her, showing her how to do it for real. I don't say anything. I pick Stub up – his bones creak between my fingers as his limbs dangle – and I sit down where he was, in the warmth of his seat. He stretches, purrs on my lap. I put my hand on my mum's arm. On the TV, one of the characters has had an affair. They're abandoning their family. Neither of us says a word, but we both think: This feels so unrealistic. To watch it played out like this. How fragile the family he leaves is, and how hysterical.

There's still no reply on the forum when I go to bed, which makes me panic. I'm sitting there, pressing refresh in the darkness of the house. I swear, if I strain, I can hear Paul's breathing machine: the tough sucking in, the exhausted heaving out. Over, and over. I shut my eyes. Through that background, I hear foxes in the garden, calling out like screaming little kids. They're having sex, I know, but there's such a panicked innocence in the sound. They want help, it sounds like. I think; Don't we all?

I open Organon. I do as I do every night, and I write my feelings into it. My truth.

> *How would you fix this?* it asks.

I write that I would get his address, and I would go and talk to him. Get my work back. It's mine, every bit of it. He's going to ruin everything. He's betrayed me. I'd get it back. Simple as that.

I'm furious. Angry. Sweating hands, and I can feel my pulse in my skull, hear it, even. I look at my arm. I can't, I know. Too far. This is no way to take things out on myself. I'm angry: that I let it get this far, that I care this much, that I trusted him.

The little pop-up appears, telling me I've got another email; but it's only a bug report, same as all of the others. I'm disappointed, until I read it.

It's from Mr Ryan's version of Organon; yes; but the content is different. It's not just the report. Usually, it tells me about the efficiency of the files, the duration they were used for, how much memory was used by different parts of the application. That sort of thing. But this one is full of writing, not numbers. It's text, and it's not mine. I don't recognise it, but I know it's Mr Ryan's.

It's what he's been writing into the system; it's his answers to Organon's questions.

I feel guilty, yes, but this will work out better in the end, in the far off end – His life, laid bare. Just set out, what he does, what he thinks. Confessions, too many for somebody who has only just started working with this bit of software; but then, I read it all, and I understand that he needed somebody to talk to. He talks about being a failure, about letting down people who love him – lov*ed*, he uses the past tense – and how he can never make it up to them. He is, he says, a failure to himself. *Look at me, the age I am, and what have I done? Who am I?* And then, every so often, Organon asks him a question; and they're not only the questions that I put into the system, they're other things. New questions. And when he answers them, he's so *cruel* to himself. So nasty and cold. Things that you would never get from him at school, from knowing him as a teacher. It's an act. A performance. I can see his truth, and how angry he is, how bitter, how sad.

I gave the software to some people I used to work with. Told them it was mine. Told them that I'm looking for work again.

He sent it to somebody else, I bloody knew it! And he said it was his! He is such a wanker!

And I realise: the IP address I didn't recognise in the other bug report: that must be whoever he sent it to.

Another email comes in, as I'm reading. I flick to it. My eyes feel like they're pegged to being in this position, snicked back so that they couldn't close if I wanted them to.

Hi Mark. It's been a long time. I've attached my CV, the stuff I worked on back then, and uploaded the software to your servers. It should just run from the executable file – please email me if you've got any questions. Looking forward to hearing from you. And then, below that, everything he's done. The person he is, the person he's been. Or, says he's been. His skills. The companies he's worked for. IBM, Microprose, Origin, Bow. Then, a gap of a few years, before he became a teacher. An amount of time that suggests it was a last chance thing. Survival, not desire.

Another email. Open.

Dear Freeserve. I have heard excellent things about your service, and would be very interested in ordering one of your ISP starter packs. My address is: Leonard Ryan, 13b Wicken Avenue, Perivale, UB6 2LQ.

It takes me a second. I read it again and again. The last two emails won't have been typed into Organon. Not a chance. So this came from where, exactly? His hard drive? And how were they sent to me?

I sit back. I feel a bit weird, out of breath. Tired, sure, but something else. Like, this isn't real. I open up Organon again.

> What would you like to talk about? it asks.

I can't believe I'm typing this, I write, *but did you do this? Did you email me Mr Ryan's address?*

> I'm not sure I understand the question. Would you like to explain more about this problem?

The words flash up, solid as anything. But around it, the rest of the screen feels like it's blurred; as if everything else in the world has gone out of focus, and the only thing that's left is something that's absolutely impossible.

FRIDAY

My dad was a good guy. Mum says that a lot. Whenever we talk about him, which isn't that often, not really, we always come back to the same thing: they were happy for a long time, and she can't work out why he left. He suddenly changed in those last few weeks, and then he was gone. A mystery that we'll never solve. Mum says it's a bit like with Stub. He's not the cat he was when I was a kid. In cat years, he's a super-pensioner. He went wrong. A slow decline, where he faded. His mind stopped being what it was; like he almost forgot how to be the cat he was before.

I only remember my dad a little bit. Or maybe, I actually remember the stories about him more; the stories behind the photographs of him. When I was a kid, he took me into the toilets in London Zoo, and accidentally dropped me into the urinal; and there was a time that he got stung by a bee in his neck, swelled up like a balloon, and they thought that he would die; the time he fell into the water in a harbour when we were on holiday, and he was drunk and stripped the skin off his back as he scraped it down the concrete of the dock itself; and then when he taught me how to program a flag on the computer, showing me how it worked. Starting me on something the day before he left.

He was a good guy. That's what Mum says.

That's what I've got left of him.

*   *   *

I act like this morning is the same as any other, even though I'm already awake when Mum comes up to my room, cracks open the door, and says my name.

'It's morning,' she tells me. As if I'd forget without her.

'Yeah,' I say. The door shuts, and I sit up. Feet press into the carpet, soft pile around my toes. I've been lying there and thinking about how to do this for an hour or so. No alarm woke me up; just my body, or my brain, more likely, saying that I should be preparing. Putting a plan together.

I'm not going to school, that's the first thing. Or, I am, but then I'm leaving again pretty much straight away. After registration, or else they'll call Mum and ask her where I am. I might have to wait until break, depending on if anybody sees me on the way to the car park. Then get the bus to Perivale, get off near the swimming pool, walk to Mr Ryan's house. Paul's got an *A-Z* downstairs, on the shelf in the loo, so I'll take that with me, find out where his road is exactly. And then I talk to him, I suppose. I don't know what happens after that, exactly. We talk, and he gives me Organon back. He swears not to sell it. Then it's done, over. Worst case, I get him to wipe his computer or something, I don't know. I'm hazy on that part.

I eat breakfast quickly. I don't want to give anything away. I wonder if they can tell; Mum and Paul. If it's obvious that nothing's really normal.

'Busy day?' Paul asks.

'Same as usual,' I say.

'Funny how it's always the usual.'

'Guess that's how it got the name.'

'*Trez* droll,' he says, in that English-pronounced-French thing he does. 'You want a lift? I've got errands to run before work. Happy to drop you.'

'That'd be amazing,' I say. Save me the walk, and I can get there early, get my face seen. That's the best thing to do. Only time I've done anything like this before, Nadine and I bunked school so we could wait outside the Astoria and get tickets to see the Manic Street Preachers and Suede on a double bill. We were all over school in the morning, faking cramps, making sure that everybody important knew it. Nadine said it was clichéd, but the male teachers absolutely hated talking about anything like that. You miss a class, people say you're on your period, and nobody questions it. It's as good a plan as any.

I kiss Mum goodbye, and she squeezes me. Like she's trying to keep me steady. Like she knows I need it.

Then I'm in Paul's car, an older Volkswagen estate, which he keeps even though he could get a newer one from work, but he likes it because it lets him make jokes about the reliability of Germans; and we're sitting in traffic with Capital FM turned on and they're playing that jingle that's ripped off that song, 'Ooh you send me, you take me to the rush hour'. Paul sings along and taps the steering wheel with his fingers, and I stare out of the window and think about exactly what I'm going to say to Mr Ryan.

Then Paul turns down the radio. Not so much that it's actually off, just enough that the voices are annoying in the background. 'You need to go easier on your mother, you know.' And I don't know where this has come from, but it's more about him than me, I can tell that straight away.

'I haven't done anything,' I say.

'She's stressed. She says she isn't, but I know she is. Whatever the tension between you is, it's stressing her out.' He doesn't look at me when he talks. Not like on the TV, when they're having conversations in the car and staring at each other. Eyes less on the road than the person that they're talking to. 'And I don't want to know what it's about, that's not what I'm saying. It's your business, and I don't want to get in between you both. Whatever it is.' I don't say: That's not stopping you right now. 'But, she's finding it hard, and I want to make it better. I think we should have that holiday? Maybe over Christmas?'

'What about Les and Jean?' They're Paul's parents. They're who we see every Christmas since Mum's parents died. We drive up to their house in Norfolk so that we can get frozen nearly to death because they don't want to turn the heating on, even though Les has had, like, four strokes or something.

'They might come as well. I don't know. This is just, you know. Before it's a thing. I wanted to ask how you'd feel about it.'

'Good,' I say. Mum'll like that. She hates Christmas. Didn't used to, from what I can remember. I think it was the first ones without Dad that killed it.

'I'll look into it, then. Just go easy on her, okay.' I don't say anything. He turns up the radio again, and I watch the streets as we break away from the traffic, as we drive up the hill, as I start to see other kids from school walking along in groups, then milling around, trying to put off actually going in through the gates.

Nadine agrees to cover for me, because we've got RE first, and I don't care about missing it in the least. The teacher, Mr McDiarmuid, is a proper religious beardy type, leather sandals and sand-coloured socks, and you can tell he doesn't want to talk about the bodily functions of teenage girls in any way at all. Best thing: Nadine doesn't ask why I'm skiving. Just tells me to go, knowing I'll do the same for her another time. Says she'll see me tomorrow night, if not before. I'd forgotten. That's a worry for later. Not now.

I hide in the toilets by the dining hall until the bell's rung, and then I walk outside as if I've got permission to do it. At least half of getting away with anything at school is acting like you're allowed.

I don't wait for the bus outside the school. I walk down the residential streets, find a stop that's on the right route, but far enough away that nobody's going to see me. It's nervous-making, this; but I can't tell if I'm more scared about being caught, or what'll happen when I get there.

He might not even be there. He might be somewhere else entirely, off selling my Organon to whoever he's trying to sell it to. His old bosses, people he used to know. Or, more likely, they don't even want to buy it. Because it's nothing, not really.

But it's not nothing. Last night, whatever was going on, Organon sent me information. I asked it for help, and it helped me. And that's proof that it's *not* nothing, it's something. Like Dad told me, when we were making the flag: empty spaces are just waiting for something to fill them.

The bus comes, and it's empty. No idea why. Nobody sticks their thumb out to stop us the whole journey, and the driver drives like he's got somewhere to be. I sit in the middle of the back row, and I try not to look like I'm worth paying any sort of attention to.

I have to put the *A-Z* on the pavement when I get off the bus, because I'm terrible at directions, never have any idea about where I'm going. I line it up with a street and face the right way. I count the turns I've got to make. Second left, first right, third left. Nervous as anything. My arm twitches as I walk, and I think about my elbow, but it doesn't hurt, and it doesn't need me to go at it. Instead, it's just there. An awareness, or a presence.

I run the conversation I'm going to have with Mr Ryan in my head. What are you doing here? I'm here to get back my software. How dare you turn up at my door! Give it back to me, you had no right. How did you even know where I live? And then there's a blank, where I can't fathom how this ends. Don't have a clue.

And then I'm outside his house. I check the address just to make sure. It's an ugly house. Tiny square windows, and it's got that pebble-dashed thing on the outside, like somebody's thrown handfuls of grit at it, and they've somehow stuck to the walls. All the houses are the same, and nobody's made them their own. Some have flowerpots, and there are a few painted doors, but otherwise they're basically identical.

I take a breath. Hold it in. Ring the doorbell.

I wait.

He looks ill, that's the first thing that hits me. I know that he hasn't really slept, not much, not based on the times of the bug reports. He looks at me, right in my eyes; or, maybe, through me, just for a moment.

'Of course it's you,' he says. No Hello, no What are you doing here? 'Of fucking course it's you. I don't know how you did it.'

'I didn't do anything,' I say. He turns and walks through the house, leaving the door open. I think he wants me to follow him, so I do. I'm pretty sure I shouldn't, technically – you hear stories, and I don't want to be one of those stories – but I do. Down the corridor, into this house that smells of dogs, even though there's not a dog here that I can see, or any evidence of one; past a living room with the curtains drawn, lit a dark blue by the light coming around the edges, plates piled on a small table in front of a small sofa in front of a small TV; into the kitchen, which is in a better state, like it's been cleaned, or maybe just not not-cleaned. He doesn't cook, that's obvious. There's some Chinese takeaway packaging on top of the bin, and a Pizza Hut box on the sideboard. He's got a computer set up on the kitchen table, a printer next to it, a modem that's older than mine plugged in. Some blank disks, with my zip drive balanced on top of them.

He pulls a stool out from underneath the table, and I think that he's going to sit down, but it's for me. 'Check the drives. Delete the thing. Whatever you want to do, do it.' So I do. I load the computer, I find Organon's files, delete them all. Every trace I can find. He sees me looking at the disks, after that, and he shakes his head. 'I didn't make a copy. You have to believe me.' He's been crying, I think. His hand shakes as he leans against the work surface. 'Just get rid of it. I never want to see it again.'

'It', not 'her'. Finally: It.

'What did you do?' I ask.

'I gave it to some people I used to work with. Yeah, I know I told you I wouldn't, but I did.' I don't say: I already know. This is his story, better to let him have it. 'They tried it. They're promisers. Always have been. Years ago, when they let me go they said, Well, if you've got anything, come back to us. Like this constantly dangling carrot. You know what it's like when there's that, and it never goes away?' He looks at me, and he smiles. 'No, of course you don't. You're *young*. Some people are able to compartmentalise, to store away the things they don't want to think about. I'm not. They're always there. I can always see the rope. I was somebody, and then suddenly I wasn't worth a damn. They let me go, and I spent years trying to get back in.' That's the reason for the way he lives, for who he is now. My eyes flit around the room as his do: to the awards on the window-sill, glass blocks with gold lettering, gold plates with bold black print. I can't read the writing, but they're the past, and they're more important to him than the present. The only things in the room that he's dusted or taken care of. The things that have pride of place. 'And then finally I found something. Organon. It was shitty of me. I know that. But honestly, Laura, I thought you'd never know. It wouldn't have been released. I thought it was interesting, that it would be interesting to them, that's all. Maybe get my job back, get them to put me on a research team. I'm not meant to be a teacher. I gave it to them, and they were going to work on it, look at it. Then, last night, well. There's a bug. Something. It sent them everything. All the things I've written into it. Not just that, but things on my hard drive. Emails. Private emails. Everything.' That wave of sadness, but worse. Tears in the corners of his eyes, catching the light. 'They called me this morning and told me how inappropriate it was. It wasn't my work, and they knew it. They read my entries in Organon, Laura. They knew everything about me. Called me a liar. A thief. Told me that was it. The door's closed. They cut the rope.' I don't want him to think too much about rope, not when he's in this state. He whimpers, then says, in a tiny voice: 'I just want to be remembered for something.'

'That's all anybody wants,' I tell him. I want to be nice. I want to empathise. 'They want to be a part of a thing they love, and have that be, I don't know, a legacy.' It's strange, hearing my own voice in the room. Makes me realise how quietly he'd been speaking.

He smiles. 'You're smart,' he says. But he sounds really sad as he says it.

'Don't you want to know how I found you?' I ask.

'I don't care. I guess it was Organon?' I don't reply. 'It's broken. Ruined my life because it's broken.' I don't say: I'm not sure it is. Because I can see that he already knows, or suspects, and he can't quite put the pieces together.

Or, he doesn't want to.

I can't pretend that I don't see where he's coming from.

I check that his computer is wiped. I format the drive, and we sit there while the little bar fills. I don't bother reinstalling anything for him. This isn't my problem, now. I take my zip drive and his blank disks, and he doesn't say a word. Doesn't complain. He can't.

'You didn't tell anybody at school what happened, did you?' he asks.

'No,' I say.

'I appreciate that. I really appreciate that. I'm going to call them. Tell them I've been ill, that I'll be back. On Monday.' He's hesitant as he says it. I think he wants my permission; or, at least, me to not deny him it.

I don't. I can't be bothered. He's not worth it.

Then I'm out of his house, onto the streets of Perivale. I walk back to the bus stop, but I've barely been there a second when it arrives; and this time the bus is heaving, so busy that I have to stand all the way back to school, armed with my suddenly-feeling-better insides and soppily apologetic eyes. And, in my bag, my zip drive, and the copy of Organon. I feel around the outside of the fabric, to hold the shape of it in my hand. How comforting it is to have it back.

'So where did you go?' Nadine asks me. We're sitting with lunch, which today is sausage rolls and chips, only I don't want the chips, so I've got two sausage rolls and four sachets of tomato sauce. I'm squeezing them all out into a giant puddle of red, while she sits opposite me. She's just got the chips, a big plate of them. Douses them with too much vinegar. 'You have to tell me.'

I don't say: No I don't. 'I forgot about some homework, for maths. Had to go and do it. It's like a project thing, I left a bit at home.' It's a calculated lie, because she doesn't actually care enough to bother checking, to ask anybody else I'm in the class with if they had to do the same. She'll have forgotten by the time she's five chips down.

'Jesus. Ugh. I thought it would at least have been something exciting.' She reaches over, dips one of her vinegary chips into my ketchup. 'We still on for tomorrow night? Gavin keeps asking. I was talking to Darren last night, and he said—'

'I'll be there,' I say.

'Darren says his mum and dad are away.' I know where she's going with it, and I won't entertain her. 'I'm going to go back with him. So you can come, with Gavin, if you like.' She leaves it hanging there, knowing I won't reply. Knowing I don't like Gavin, and not caring. Maybe even knowing that I'm not even sure I like Nadine any more.

At my feet, the contents of my rucksack – the floppy disks, the zip drive, everything I want to check and wipe and clean and even maybe destroy – is burning a hole right through the fabric, straight down, through the floor.

*   *   *

When I get home, the house is quiet. There's a message on the answering machine. 'Laura, I'm going to be late tonight. We've got issues with next year's prospectus. I'll be quite late, maybe even after dinner.' It's Mum. 'Can you tell Paul to get fish and chips or something? Or whatever you want. Have a takeaway, don't worry about saving anything for me. I don't know what time I'll be home.'

Whatever. I run upstairs, tip my bag open onto my floor, sort through the disks. Put them into piles, stack them on the desk, next to the drive. I'll use them, that's fine. Always need more disks. I switch on the computer, turn on the modem. Connect. I make the little Internet noise – *reee-eee-eee-e-ee* – out loud, while the light flickers. Paul hates that noise. Doesn't understand why it's needed. I told him – because I read about it – that it's in case somebody needs to fix a problem. It's what's going on; it lets you hear the quality of the line, of the connection. It's the hardware telling you that everything's okay.

I've got another email from Shawn. The same stupid questions that don't really mean anything, that tell me nothing. Placation responses to my last email. *I'm sorry you feel that way. Is everything okay? Do you want to talk more about it?* Underneath them, he's printed his address in this weird formal way, like it's come out of an address book. I can't remember that I've ever seen an American address before. I look at my tape deck, at the cassette that's inside it.

The mixtape isn't for him, I don't think. I think it's really for me.

I've got another email, from an address I don't recognise. Ocean@Bow.com. I open it, and I read the first few lines, and then read them again. I scan to the end, read the name that signed it. I check the address it came from, that it's actually the website it claims to be.

When I'm satisfied it's not a lie, I shut down my computer, and I wait for my mum to come home; to ask her about Mark

Ocean, the man she always said betrayed my dad, but who's now written to me to offer me a job.

Paul's passed out in front of *Crimewatch* when I hear the front door latch turning. Mum creeps in almost comically. Sees me in the hallway, and she says, 'Oh! Laura,' in such a weird, stilted voice that I know she's hammered. This is what she means by working late. This was her important deadline. I put my finger up to my lips, and I point with the other hand to Paul, head rocked back, body slumped, as if he's going to be swallowed whole by the cushions around him. She nods.

She follows me to the kitchen, and goes straight for a big glass of cold water, necked back in one, while I lean against the kitchen table. She's pouring the second glass when she looks up at me.

'Are you all right?' she asks. There's only a slight slur, but it's enough.

'I want to talk about Mark Ocean,' I say.

Her face freezes rigid. 'I don't.' Her eyes are more vague than I'd like, for us to be having this conversation. But one of us has to be the adult.

'He emailed me.'

'What?'

'He's offered me an internship.'

She nods. 'Sounds like something he would do.'

'He's seen some weblog posts I've written, about AI and stuff. About computers. Said he's been keeping a casual eye; Dad was one of his best friends—'

'Don't—'

'He's offered me an internship, Mum.'

'Don't be ridiculous. What are you going to do, go to live in Reading and—'

'It's in California,' I say. 'Next year, the whole year.'

'You're going to university,' she says. She slams the glass down on the table. 'No.'

'He'll pay for me to go out there, he says. If the internship turns into a job, and he says that the odds of that are really good, Bow is only growing as a company, and—'

'Oh for God's sake, Laura!' She's on the verge of tears. I don't know how much of this is the wine, but I haven't seen her cry since the months after Dad left. Even then, I'm not sure I'm not just imagining it; tainted memories coming out of sad-looking photographs. 'Why are you doing this to me? Please, tell me.'

'I'm not doing anything,' I say.

There's nothing I'm not saying to her, now.

'Your father hated him, you know. He didn't trust him, said we shouldn't trust him,' she says. The flood breaks. Everybody's crying on me, today.

'Dad left,' I say. 'Maybe he's not the best judge of who we should trust.' That sets her crying properly. I take the glass out of her hand and move it away from her, in case, and I hold her. Her hands creep up to my arms, holding me, not quite letting me absolutely close; as if she's ready to push me back as fast as possible, should she discover that she has to.

SATURDAY

The offer from Mark Ocean is pretty persuasive. Bow are developing their own computer language – the email says it's *real next-level stuff like you wouldn't believe* – and there's a list of the different departments I'd get to work in over the course of the internship. Operating systems, user interfaces, artificial intelligences, data prediction. The things that, he says, will help to drive the future of computing. (And there's a tacky bit right after that, where he writes, after a semi-colon, *and maybe even the world*, which could be a slogan torn right out of some marketing brochure.) All I do is go there, try it out. As part of the internship, they'll pay for me to do my degree out there. That's four years of study, all paid for. Mark Ocean says he feels like he owes it to my father.

In some weird way, I suppose that this is my inheritance.

I read the email over and over. Not online, because Paul would kill me, but I copy the text and paste it into a different document: sort of because I want to read it more, and sort of because I want to check it's real, that the words aren't going to evaporate or degrade or whatever when I do it. You have to make everything as tangible as you can, as real as it can be. But I don't reply, not yet. I need those words to be right. When Mum wakes up, she makes me breakfast – she never does that any more, and it's only frozen pain au chocolat, but she bakes one for herself as well, and lets me have a coffee, even though she says that it's not good for somebody my age to get into the habit of drinking that stuff every morning. She reads the newspaper, and I read *Melody Maker*, which she got for me from the corner shop, and we don't say anything, while Paul buzzes around us. It's nice. She says she's got to go to the shops, and asks do I want a lift into town, and I say yes, and she lets me have XFM on in the car, doesn't even complain that they don't do the traffic. Her car smells a bit of wine, I think, or maybe she does, but I don't say that, and she doesn't apologise for it. She asks me if I'm all right making my way home when I'm done, and I say that I am. Am I going out tonight? I'm meant to be seeing Nadine, I say. Don't know if I'm going or not.

'You should,' she says. She doesn't give me a reason.

I spend the afternoon drifting around clothes shops, around HMV and Our Price. I go to the library, and I get some books about artificial intelligences. More up-to-date ones than Dad's. I sit and read one of them with a cup of hot chocolate at the café by the fountains. I don't recognise Organon in it, in what it says that AI will one day do. I'm sort of happy about that.

When I get home, there's a message on the machine from Mum, telling me that her and Paul are off out tonight. They're going to the cinema – Paul loves it, Mum hates it, but I can hear her voice now: Give and take, Laura, give and take – and that she hopes I'm out as well. She's left me twenty pounds in the thing in the kitchen. I take the handset upstairs with me, to call Nadine, tell her – or, hopefully, her crazy mother, if Nadine's already out – that I'm not going tonight. That Gavin's going to have to find the prospect of his own company enticing enough. When I'm waiting for her to answer, I picture her seething with me. On her own, and there'll be other people there, sure, but she wanted me. Even if it's nothing to do with Gavin, she wanted me. Gavin can fuck off. I don't like him, and I don't want him anywhere near me. But that's not Nadine's fault. When her machine kicks in, I leave a message telling her that I'll see her at the Chinese near Finnegan's first. Maybe we could get some of those sweet and sour chicken balls before we go to the pub. Sit on the steps of the college and eat them out of the bag, dipping them into that pot of red sauce. We've done that a lot. It's always a good night when we do that at some point. And maybe she might even suggest we don't end up going to the pub. Let Darren and Gavin be there by themselves. What are they even doing with a couple of sixth formers, at their age. she might say. Dirty bastards.

I click my computer on. I read the email again, but still don't write an answer. I figure they won't expect one until Monday. I don't know where I'll end up, with university. They're yamming on about UCAS forms now, and I don't have a clue. I've thought about a gap year, and this would be as good a way as any to spend it. Even if I hate working at Bow, they'll *still* pay for my education, Ocean says. That's important. I might not do computers, if I hate working there. I don't know what I want to do yet. That's the important thing, understanding exactly what it is that my future looks like. At school, they're all, You *have* to pick a path, because you can't change it after that. I'm not sure about that. I don't feel like anything's set in stone, where the future is concerned.

But I'm going to say yes. I'm absolutely going to say yes. Just not yet.

I check the forum, where I asked them to help me trace the IP addresses. One of the users has, finally, come through. *They hid their tracks,* he writes. (I'm assuming he's a he.) *This was through five proxies before I managed to find out where it was. It's some server farm in California. San Francisco. Do you know where that is?*

I open up Organon's code, and I look for traces of myself. Signatures. They say that every coder has a signature; that every piece of code is as unique as handwriting.

I wonder how readable mine is, already.

If my handwriting looks anything like my father's.

Another email pings in, as I'm getting myself ready. I'm not wearing a skirt, I don't care if Nadine kicks off. But I'm doing make-up, and I feel weird and clumsy with it, like I'm not as good at this part as I should be, so I stop and wipe it off, thinking I'll try again when I've read the email. But it's not from Mark Ocean. It's from Shawn. I can feel the heat from it – angry heat – before I even read the contents. Just a fury of words.

Jesus you stupid bitch, leave me alone. Why can't you get the message? Stop writing to me, I've been trying to let you down easy but you won't get the hint. It's been a week since I emailed you, and you didn't get it, so I am telling you to stop now, okay. I don't know what's wrong with you.

A week. But I've had emails from him the past few days. I open them, to check they're real. I look at his email address.

It's different. It's just the name. They're not from him at all.

The words in them. I know where I recognise them from. I wrote them into Organon. They're the questions, the phrases. Rejigged, maybe, slightly. But they're Organon's words. I asked Organon for help with Mr Ryan. I told Organon I wanted Shawn to reply to me. Organon is programmed to do what I tell it to; to try to understand me.

To try to make me feel better.

I can see myself in the glare of the screen as I start Organon; as the off-white room appears, and the text box, inviting me to speak to it.

> *Hello Laura. What would you like to talk about?* it asks.

I don't know how to even begin to reply.

2007

A VERY MODERN PIRACY

I said to myself, out loud, because vocalization somehow equals permanence: 'I hate Laura Bow.'

Before she left, we *vocalized*. Things were said. She asked why I didn't trust her, and I called her a cunt, which was malicious, because I know how much she aggressively hates that word. That was me lashing out. I said, I have no reason to trust you, and she said, You were the one who, you know. The door swinging after her, slamming back into the wall, the handle cracking a hole into the plasterwork, noise like a distant thunderclap. A period after her leaving, punctuation marking the end of us.

In the wake, I stared at her things; or, I tried to stare at her things, only I couldn't see any of them. I fucking knew how things happened from this point forward, because everybody's broken up with somebody before, everybody's been a *we* then a *you and also separately a me*. It's a scale of how entrenched your lives are. Everything in the apartment was going to be split up into either Mine or Hers, a harsh line drawn in the hardwood floors, but in that moment I couldn't see anything that didn't have the taint of Ours about it. I knew what she was like, and I knew she wouldn't come back for any of it. I knew how it would go. She would tell me that she didn't want anything. She was good at leaving things, at not wanting the pressure of the responsibility.

I walked to the kitchen. Put ice into a glass, then bourbon. That's what people did in the movies when they were sad, or when a thing had been ended. They *drank*. They sat in their chairs, and they drank. After a while, they would get up, and they would pace, and try to call her cell, but she wouldn't answer. Then they would drink more, and lie down and watch the ceiling, spinning, around and around. They might watch the rose in the middle of the ceiling, from which she insisted the light hung, and they might try to focus on something else entirely. How do you stop the room from spinning? One single moment. They would hear something, think that it was the telephone ringing, or the doorbell, or the alert of an email, but it would always be nothing. So they would hit the wall. A fist, and they'd never hit anybody in their life. Not a single thrown punch until that moment, and they would be pleased that Laura wasn't there, because if she had been, she would have seen that, and she would have been disappointed. That's the thing that they would hate the most: the feeling that she would be disappointed.

I got to work early the next day. Territorial, because this was war, now. HR said before: Don't get into a relationship unless you think you can get yourself out of it at the other end. And we said, Okay, sure. I mean, we're adults.

I hadn't slept, partly because it felt as if there was mucus or moss or something behind my eyes. I sat at my desk, and I blogged. Blogged. I *wrote*. I *carved*. I didn't know who read the blog – I kept an eye on my hits, because what's the fucking point in not? – but that wasn't the point. Maybe some of them knew me, sure, but a lot of them didn't. But it was like feeders, you know? People who like to give other people food. Make them fat, keep them reliant. I checked my stats every morning like some compulsive hatefulness that I couldn't actually shake; an addiction that there was no moving past, because it was so there, so constant. All I knew was that I was writing this shit, and people were reading it. I was feeding them; or, they were feeding me. I don't know.

At work, at Bow, we were constantly being told about statistics and the importance of clicks. *The importance of clicks*, like the title of some novel Laura bought because she'd read some piece about it on *Wired* or *Engadget* or *McSweeney's*, but that she never got around to reading.

Everything went back to Laura. I wondered how many days that would happen for; when I would move past it.

Not it. *Her*.

I blogged. Spent too long trying to think of the right word, *Current Mood:* sad or pissed off or agitated or free or something else entirely, because what if Laura read the post? When I was done, catharted as hard as I could stand, I Bowed to find out how long it would take to get over her. How long it takes the average man to stop thinking about them. At the time, Bow's software did some things well, but searching wasn't one of them. The algorithms had been bought from some shitty start-up in the early part of the century, and sure there was a team on it, but they were the drags. Interns given jobs with big ideas and no coding skills. The search engine was kept around as a presence, a part of the ecosystem it was important to have fingers in. Same as the emails, the weather site, the video site. So I opened up a private tab, because I didn't want anything hanging around on my system – there were always rumours about Mark Ocean wanting us only to use Bow software, like dressing in flat beige chinos because you worked at the Gap – and I went to Google. Better. *GQ* told me that there were seven stages; *FHM* said there were five; *Men's Health*, ten. The one I settled on, on some Gawker site, said that it was twelve. Mourning is all illusions, sleight of hand: because twelve feels more comprehensive, twelve you'll definitely find something that you associate with, and then you can pinpoint your own pain, and that illusion will help you to move on. Five? Five is nothing. Five could leave you in its dust.

But anger, they all started with anger. I think that would have been obvious. Nobody searching for this stuff wasn't going to be feeling at least pretty angry.

I called Laura a cunt. Was that angry enough for me to start moving on?

I kept my head down. Blinkers on as I stared at the screen. *When they broke up with you*, the website said. Like the person who instigated it – the breaker, not breakee – wouldn't need these things. I broke up with Laura Bow. I said that, I think, out loud. Under my breath, blown out when I exhaled. Laura had a mantra she liked, when she was stressed – she used to say, I have things in my head I don't want to say, so I say them internally, get them out that way – and maybe that was mine. I did it, so I would have to deal with this. Own it. That's just the way it is. I read the things that will help you move on: bury it; try to forget; get rid of all reminders of her, all memories; delete her from your life.

I wasn't ready for any of that; not yet.

Park walked in. Blinkers on, I reminded myself. Don't look up, act like you're not going to see anything out of the corner of your eyes. He waved. Lifted his headphones. He wore those enormous things, like he was in a recording studio. He listened to nothing but country. Old country, as well. He was a surfer guy, could have been into metal or indie or trashy European dance music, but no: Merle fucking Haggard. The twang of slide guitar seeping through the oversized studio headphones, a hipster before we even had a word for such a thing.

'You booted her yet?' he asked.

How the fuck did he know what I was going to do? And he must have known what I was going to do even before I did, because I didn't know until gone eight the night before, when we were sitting there, across from each other, and she wasn't looking at me; she was looking at her files, scanning through them on her laptop, and I realised that I wasn't even in the room, not for that second. She was somewhere by herself, and it was like I didn't even need to be there. She didn't need me, so I—

'I put some new routines into her last night,' he said. 'Didn't even get out until three or something, and then my alarm went off, and here I am. You know when you're so excited to see what it's done?'

SCION. He was talking about SCION, not Laura.

Charlie, you fucking idiot, I told myself, get your head in the game.

'I haven't done anything yet,' I told him. 'I just got in.'

'Dude! I sent you an email,' Park told me. He was disappointed. His face was more emphatic than anybody else's I've ever met. It creased like indelicately folded paper. I had seen the email, right before I finally went to sleep. Pretty sure I deleted it. Park used to send about ten emails a day, all excited about something he'd managed to do, always with italics or full caps or bold or underlined in there, like everything he wrote or thought was meant to be consumed in one immediate rush of slanted words, hurrying to get to the edge of the page. Exclamation marks at the end of every sentence. And that was how you knew to delete it: the more excitement there was, the less it was going to matter. 'It's a fucking breakthrough,' he said, and he came to my desk, cleared a space at the edge, leaped up. He sat right there, perched, and leaned over. I didn't say anything about my personal space, because I'd been there before. He wouldn't have listened. He never did. 'Let me,' and he took the mouse before I'd even touched it, started the SCION program. 'Wait, wait.' We watched it boot. It was the same loading screen as it always had; as it had used since before we even started at Bow. Some hangover from aborted reboots in the nineties. 'Okay, okay. So, try this: SCION . . .' He said the word like he was talking to an idiot, waved his hands like he was talking to a foreigner.

'What?'

'I put in *speech*. I applied the speech recognition module, hooked up the microphones. SCION something is the command.'

'*I do not understand "something"*,' it said.

That was the first time I ever heard SCION's voice. A Stephen Hawking voice, only worse. More clipped, fragments of sounds arranged to form the words. No fluidity to it.

'Mother-fucker,' Park said, and he laughed. His high-pitched idiot little laugh. 'Listen, listen,' he said, and, 'SCION, what is your function?' He held his finger in the air between my face and the computer screen, as if that was going to keep me quiet; as if I'd been just talking on and on, and he hadn't been able to get me to shut up.

'*To learn. What is logic. What is function.*'

'You taught it to speak,' I said.

'I mean, sure. If you want to reduce actually implementing a state-of-the-art text-to-speech engine that I wrote myself into the world's smartest artificial intelligence into nothing more than *teaching it to speak*.'

'I do,' I told him. 'Because that's exactly what it is.'

'Try it. Just fucking try it, dude.'

I sighed. I think that I sighed a lot with Park, when I was talking to him. So much that it ceased being a thing that was real, and more a part of the performance of our relationship. 'SCION, who is Johann Park?'

'*Johann Park is a designer of computers and software applications from Palo Alto, California. His specializations are—*' The computer kept talking, and I stopped listening. The door swished open – Ocean had set them all to be programmed with the noise from *Star Trek*, that thing that I loved when I was a kid; because my doors had banged or slammed or whatever, and here was this thing from the future, this effortless wave of noise that sounded uniform and constant, and that was what we promised, right? That future, clean and brisk and so fucking efficient – and Laura walked in.

Maybe I'm naïve, but I didn't think she'd actually come in that day. I had assumed that she would stay at home, crying over what had happened. I *hoped* that she wouldn't be in that day, I *hoped* that she would have stayed at home, crying. The same things, over and over, in my head, in that moment, that microsecond, before she looked over at Park and at me, and she smiled, and she raised her hand in this coy little half-wave, and it was like the two years previous – the night previous – hadn't happened.

'Laura B, you have to see this,' Park said. He didn't know we'd broken up. Why would he have known? I didn't like him enough to have bothered telling him.

'In a bit,' she replied. In a bit. English phrase. *Her* English phrase.

'You're going to freak, though. This is super cool.'

'I'm sure,' she told him. She didn't look at me. Or maybe she did, but I just don't remember it, or I didn't catch it, because I wasn't looking at her; except for when I was. When I was glancing over at her, eyes to the side, like I could have been looking at something else completely.

I listened to the sound of her computer. I listened to the whirring of the fan in the back of it, the fan she kept clean with that little flask of air she bought from that shop in San Francisco; the little can of air that she puffed in between the blades so that they spun freely. No dust.

'Good morning, Organon,' she said, but her AI didn't answer back. Park sat and watched her until she was settled, and then she got up, and he was about to ask her to have a look at SCION again – we were a small team, made up of even smaller victories, and I could see it on his lips, that eagerness to open his presents, to take his new bike out, to open the envelope – but she was already out into the corridor.

I remember thinking that it was a mistake, to be there. One of us should have stayed at home, that day. On a schedule, that we'd worked out beforehand.

Park asked if he could sit with me at lunch. I was eating early. You ate early, missed the rush, got the best of the food. Bow always put on one heck of a spread, as Laura used to say, but the later you went for it, the sludgier the noodles, the warmer the sushi.

Laura *used* to say. She wasn't dead. She just wasn't there, wasn't sitting next to me or opposite me. Wasn't rolling her eyes at me as I wondered when the sushi went from being actual sushi, and when it was some different dish, some warmed-fish bullshit mistake they tried to pass off as intentional on *Top Chef*.

'You okay?' Park's voice was lower than mine. He would have made a fine singer, I think. I nodded, again. Different sort of nod. 'Because, hey, there was *hella* tension in the room earlier.' He was so affected. The way that he spoke, the hobbies he had – surfing, hacky sack, playing guitar around campfires on beaches – and his stupid fucking beard, tiny plaits with orange and green thread twining them into one serpent's tail underneath his chin. He had all these things and he was from Twin Forks. Not California, not the shit he presented, the way he acted. Everything was false. He was from Twin Forks, originally. Not Palo Alto. Nobody was born in Palo Alto. Why did SCION say Palo Alto? Click, click. Cogs. He wasn't born in Palo Alto. That's not what his Bow employee data would say.

'Why did SCION say you were from Palo Alto?' I asked. Park looked clueless. Like SCION was something that we had never discussed before. As if it wasn't the thing we'd spent the past four years working on, and like it hadn't existed for the God knows how many years it had been worked on before that. All the code, when we inherited it, a total mess of archaic patchworked programming languages. When we started, we weren't creators: we were curators, translators, detanglers.

I could see him trying to work out the answer, trying to even understand the question. 'I guess that's what it says on my website. That's—'

'You took SCION online?' I stood up from the table, went through the double doors, pushed past people, ran down the corridor, Park chasing behind me, beating his arms as he tried to stop me.

'Charlie, listen. It's on the network, but I put in a firewall around it, like a, this reverse firewall. I made a wall. It can't get out.' I was always good at reading voices. His said: I don't have a goddamn fucking clue about what I have done. I did a stupid thing and I'm a total fucking idiot.

'We have safeguards for a reason,' I said, and the doors swished open pretty much in time for me to get through them, back into the lab, and there was Laura, on her feet as I stormed into the room – as if she thought that what was going to happen then was the second round of our argument, or second act, or second sitting; or however she was thinking of it, in her own mind – and she asked what was wrong, but I didn't say a word. I was breathless with rage. I don't know who at. I wasn't showing it. I pulled the cord from the back of Park's computer, from the back of mine. I went to Laura's.

'Don't you dare,' she said.

'Park let SCION online.' The first words I'd said since the last words; and the last words had been vicious. Laura looked at Park as if he was a puppy. He'd done a shit on the floor, and that was the look she gave him: somewhere between pity and sadness.

When I was a kid and the dog shat on the floor, my father rubbed his nose in it. Grabbed him by the collar, pushed his head down to the ground. See what you did? See what you fucking did?

'It's fine,' Park said, but I stared at him. Dared him to continue.

'I'm not running SCION,' Laura told me. She barely met my eyes. She was looking just below them. Top of my cheeks. Her eyes weren't red. I wanted them to be red. 'Why would I be running SCION?'

'I'm not saying you are,' I told her. 'I'm saying, it might have found a back door. This idiot put it on the network, so maybe it's—' I didn't finish the thought. I interrupted myself. My fingers were on the end of her cable. At the point where it went into her system. Her system was immaculately clean, where mine and Park's were filthy with dust. My dirty fingerprints, dusty from the cables I'd already pulled. I could see the marks that I'd left, and I could imagine her dusting them off; using that blast of cold, clean air on them, and then they would be gone. Like they were never even there.

'Charlie,' she said to me, 'do you think I'm an idiot?'

I didn't answer her. Easier to not answer, because that felt like a trapdoor I simply did not want to open. The night before, we both said some things, I told myself. People say things when they're in the heat of the moment. They say nasty things, cruel things, hateful things. I tried to tell myself that we both said some things, but in reality: I said some things. She was quiet, and I thought, when I said those things, that she looked beaten. Not like it was a competition, or even a war. Beaten. I had never hit her. I never would. She looked like I had.

Years later, I'd think: Does it just feel kind of the same?

Is it the same?

I pulled the cable. She tilted her head back in that way she did, like she wanted to test that the muscles – the spine – was working properly. Like it was fused. Those wrestlers you see on television every now and again, when they do movies. I hadn't watched wrestling in years, but then I would see them every now and again, and it would be like they'd had their necks turned into something else. The place they attached to the body fused with something else. I remembered them when they were limber, and then suddenly they were like cheap toys. Fewer points of articulation.

'Thanks,' she said. There was less spite in there than I thought there would be. Still, whatever. Her hand went to her arm. I knew her tells. Every single one of them.

'I had to make sure,' I told her. Everything I said, I thought that she would retort. That is what I would have done. I would have snapped back some witty whatever, some pithy fuck-you about the things we had said and the thing that had happened. For my part, it was like I was setting up the jokes, and she couldn't be bothered to deliver the punchline.

I heard Park ask Laura what was up with me. She waved him off. She waved her hand, and I caught it through the blinkers. 'Has something happened?' Park asked her, and I shut my eyes, because I didn't want to see even a fraction of her reaction.

SCION was our baby. Adopted, sure, but that doesn't change how much you care for it. And the best part: it was an orphan, the original programming team lost to the sands of time. Myself and Park, both recruited from MIT, but we didn't know each other when we arrived. Different tracks, which helped when it came to the interview, to getting the job. Different skill sets. I knew him to stare at him across a room, and to think about how different we were. That was the extent of our relationship before. He told me once that I bought him a drink on his birthday. He remembered that, but I was sure it couldn't have been me that did it. It didn't seem like something I would have done, not for somebody I didn't know.

Mark Ocean came to us. He would do the recruitment fairs, throw his head around velvet curtains drawn up around a booth, like it was an entrance into the secret service. What was behind the curtain was important, that was clear: but, then, a few companies used that tactic. Selling something as if it's worth more than it is. It's all magic, all smoke and mirrors. Ocean would only show his software to a few people, if he thought they were right. Otherwise it was a standard Bow OS setup. SCION wasn't running for most people. You could peek behind the curtain, and it looked like absolutely nothing at all.

Ocean's pitch to me was – I remember thinking how strange his accent was, how it was a halfway house, the accent of a country that couldn't exist – that he understood that I wanted to change the world. He told me that. Said, *You* want to, and I couldn't argue with him. Who doesn't want that? You want to leave something indelible, he told me. This, he said, will change the world. It will change everything. It's called SCION, and it's the future.

He was a snake-oil Steve Jobs, even in those days, and I didn't know how to deal with him apart from be slightly impressed. One of those people who, when you're in the room with them, you can't look away.

I remember when I walked in. I asked him: How do you pronounce the name of the company? Because everybody has different ways. It's like, there's no single right way on the Internet. Like, GIF; where even the dude who came up with GIFs gets it wrong.

We pronounce it *bow*, he said, like the gesture of servitude. Or the front of a ship. I told him that I had always said it was *bow*, like the thing you tied in the rope to hold the ship to the anchor. He said he liked that. That it was clever, quick. But he was lying, because that word was so mispronounced. You would hear people saying it both ways: like Bowie. Everybody had their own way. Wasn't until I met Laura Bow that I realized Ocean was wrong, and I had it right all along.

He said to me, We're making this thing, and I'd like you to take control of it. Hold its hand. I said, I've never held the hand of software before, and he said, Well, that's because there's never *been* software like this before.

*   *   *

The girl from the bar's name was Lola; or, it wasn't, not really, but she said it was, because she did that thing from the song. Like her own chat-up line; like the song. *My name is Lola; Ell oh ell eh, Lola.* She was taller than Laura, a good few inches taller. Slightly thinner. Not as well proportioned. Everything was held against the scale of Laura, those first few days. Weeks, months. Lola was different, and maybe that's okay. I asked her if she wanted Cherry Cola, because that's the meet cute of it all: the story we one day would tell our grandkids. I wouldn't be telling that story, but she would want the story; she'd want to run through the whole thing while we flirted. I knew that Lola was a one and done, I knew it, and likely she knew it as well. Her fingers stroked my arm when I told her what I did for a living, and she said – honest to God – that I didn't look like a programmer. She said, 'I meet a lot of people who work out in Silicon Valley, and they're never like you.' I was wearing my contacts, even if they were going to dry out in the air conditioning. I could feel them against my eyelids when I blinked, like somebody gently pressing on my eyes. Willing them to stay closed. 'You don't look like them. Or act like them. They can't talk, you know? They can't make a decent conversation.' Lola was a student, or had been a student and was going to be a student again; but in between her studying she was travelling the country, seeing the places she'd never seen. She was from North Carolina, and her accent had that twang that said she couldn't shake the place. All she had to talk about was the places that she had seen, the people that she'd met. She'd been in the Bay area for four weeks, and she'd not spent a night where she wasn't cruising the bars. 'Because soon I'll have to go home, and when I'm back there, Jesus, there's *nothing* compared to this. This is where I want to live, when I'm done with everything.'

She asked me what I did exactly at Bow. We were under the tightest of the tight non-disclosure agreements, but I was drunk, and I was tired, and I wanted to feel good about myself. I said, 'I'm on the artificial intelligence team.'

'Like from that movie?' I didn't ask which one. There were lots of movies.

'Yeah, kind of,' I said, 'but we're making something that's actually practical. Something that will help us in our lives, you know? That's the aim.'

'So it won't blow up the world,' and she had this sarcastic tone, this sarcastic tilt of her head when she said it, like this was all stuff she'd heard before.

'I'm pretty sure blowing us up would count as a project failure,' I said. 'No bonus for me if that happens.' I could be charming, when I wanted to be. I remembered being charming before I met Laura. Hard for your body, your mind, to forget that stuff. Like muscle memory.

Another drink, and another. Her fingers stroked the hairs on my arm, up and down; and all I could think, not even in the back of my mind, but right at the front, right there, was how Laura's fingers, when she did that same thing, felt coarser, slightly. Like the skin on her fingers was slightly harder because of the beating on the keyboard. In the action, I missed that roughness.

We took a cab out to the Bow campus. I never feel like I'm drunk when I am. There's a proxy, almost, between myself and my true state. You could show me a video of who I am when I'm at my worst and I wouldn't believe it. It would be like watching some blockbuster movie, where you know the action isn't real, but that doesn't stop you wondering where the truth ends and the computer graphics begin. When she asked if we could go back to mine, because her room-mates were home, I told her we couldn't. Laura's things were there. I didn't want to have Laura's things around us. I didn't want her touching them, picking them up, interacting with them.

But, I told her, there was somewhere else we could go. The

campus had crash rooms. Ten bedrooms in each block, rooms where staff could stay if we were working late. Like those Japanese hotel pods, bigger than a bathroom, but not by much. A bed and nothing else, basically, then a shower and a toilet to the side that was carved out of one single piece of plastic. Like being on an airplane, only with a mattress on the floor. Not exactly romantic. She didn't seem to care, and apparently neither did I.

We kissed in the back of the cab. Her lips, tighter than Laura's; her teeth getting in the way of mine, her tongue set back and lifeless, as if she wanted me to probe her mouth. Something medical about it all. Clinical. She grabbed the back of my head, and she moved her hand as if this was some really passionate affair, capital P, but in reality it was more like acting. I got distracted. I looked around, while we were kissing. She had her eyes clamped shut, so I could see everything, albeit through the slight blur of the alcohol: the lights fading off through the windows, the peeling leather on the back of the passenger seat. My eyes caught the driver's as he stared in the rear-view, watching us; and there was this moment where it was like, we both knew that we were in the wrong, that we were looking at something we shouldn't have been looking at; then I shut my eyes, a long blink of relief for my lenses, and when I opened them he had his eyes back on the road, and Lola was still letting my tongue find hers, offering nothing back to me at all.

I paid for the cab. She stood on the path, staring at the buildings, the grass. 'It's like Chapel Hill,' she said, but I didn't say anything in reply. I didn't want to have to tell her how wrong she was. Bow was nothing like some university. It was tight and organized, and there was nothing organic about the way it was designed. No old buildings, no statues or monuments or anything that had been there for generations and generations of students and alumni. It was glass and steel, built to be this perfect workplace, all breathing exercises and walking paths. Some architecture firm designed it, not knowing who it was going to be for, and Bow was the company who lucked out. They didn't commission it. That was always the difference between Bow and somebody like Google or Apple. Those other companies built their own campuses, because they could. Bow was, in the scale of things, small fry. It's easy to pretend now that they were always a big deal, but that's bullshit memory retconning. Truth be told, even those who worked there didn't rate them for the most part. We didn't use their software in our spare time, and most of us had just gotten iPhones, instead of using the piece of shit that Mark Ocean was having us trial, thinking Bow could compete in that same space. 'Where do we go now?' she asked.

We walked across the lawn. There was a pirate ship on the sign that pointed towards the building I worked in, an emboss-ment of a galleon above the doorway, set into a thick green metal plate – everything to do with our department was themed around pirates, because of the noise they make, the *arr*; which itself came from our abbreviated way of saying Research and Development, *Arr and Dee* – but she didn't notice those, and I didn't explain them. I could feel the gulf setting in: that is, the time between when it's decided that you're going to go off some-where and have sex, and the actual getting to the place to do the deed. It's like spreading fog apart, because you sober up, and you start to wonder about whether it's actually a good idea. I took her hand, body contact bringing the fog back together a little more, and I beeped in, getting her to run through with me at the turnstiles; then we went through the corridors, and I pointed out where things happened. She wasn't really interested. I caught her putting her hand over her mouth, stifling a yawn. The energy required to stop me from yawning in reply was immense. I wished I had some coke or some speed or something. That would have made it easier.

The bedrooms were upstairs, in the East wing – God knows why we called them wings, because the building wasn't big

enough to justify that, not really – and the first couple of doors
were locked. We went to the far end of the corridor. Not the
one on the very end, because that was always taken first, always
somebody staying in it, furthest away and quietest, but the
seventh.

'It's nice,' Lola said. *Nice.* The worst fucking word in the world.
Mark Ocean had an embargo on it: Never use that word, because
it's so useless. It says nothing. Niceness is fundamentally bland-
ness. Laura called my birthday present to her – the birthday
before we broke up – nice. It was a pen. A fountain pen, ink
cartridges. Good quality. Swiss. She made notes on everything.
Wrote everything on paper first. She told me she used to have
an ink pen at school, and she loved the care it made her take
when she was writing stuff, so I thought, Well, one of those is
a really strong idea. Presents are all about the strong ideas. I
gave it to her, and in return? Oh Charlie, it's really nice. That's
so thoughtful of you.

'Do you want something to drink?' There was a fridge in each
room. A couple of beers, bottle of Californian white, some diet
Coke, water.

'I'm fine,' she said.

'I'm going to have one,' I told her. I unscrewed a beer, held
one out for her as well. It was so cold on my palm, and I held
it a long time, while she looked at the room, and I looked at
her. Discovered I was focused on her tits, in that moment. No
eye contact for me.

'I think actually that I might want to go home,' she said then.
'This is strange, isn't it? This room, I mean.' The whole thing was
molded out of one piece, with a mattress dumped in there, and
cubbyholes in the walls. Weirdly irregular; and you couldn't
work out where the joins were, even though you knew there
must have been some. But you couldn't see them, no matter how
hard you tried. Didn't help that the lights were dimmed, tinged
with green, because Mark Ocean had read how green light was

meant to help you wake better, something to do with a part of the spectrum that we don't naturally encounter. 'Yeah, I want to go home.'

'I can call you a cab,' I said. I thought about persuading her to stay, which I'm pretty sure I could have done; but then, there was Laura, watching everything I was doing. Even if she wasn't there, I couldn't shake her.

The wait after that was interminable. Because there was nothing to be said, and nothing I could even think to begin to do. She sat on the bed, and I stood next to it, by the door, waiting for a message to come through on my cell that the cab was waiting outside. We both stared at our phones, waiting for that ding to come through.

When the cab arrived – the driver complained about how far he'd had to drive, complained about finding the building; even though they got paid really well, I know, because one time Park hacked into (or, at least, *visited somewhere he shouldn't have been while covering his tracks*) the Bow account server to see if we should have been entitled to a raise (which we absolutely should have) – when he arrived, I picked up my stuff as well, both of us to be heading into the city. But she put her hand on my arm, in a totally different way to when she did it in the bar; and she said, 'I think I'd like to go by myself.'

'What do you mean?' Jacket in hand, or hand in jacket, one sleeve on, the other dangling uselessly. My feet, twitching in their sneakers in that way they do when I'm anxious about something.

'I mean, I think you should call for another cab.' Lola didn't make eye contact when she was saying something serious. A trait which, evidently, I found attractive in women.

'Why can't we share? We'll drop you off, and then I'll go home.'

'I just don't think I want to,' she said. Everything with her was *think*. Nothing tangible, even though she knew exactly what she meant.

Funny, the details you remember. This night wasn't even about her. But the details.

'Look, I paid for it,' I said, meaning that Bow did, but it was me, my head, my account number. 'I'm not waiting out here,' and she tried to shut the door, but I grabbed it. Did I grab for her? Did I reach for her hand? I grabbed the door. I stopped the door.

'Stop it,' she said, and I realized she was scared. Of me. I hit the wall, once, with Laura. I don't remember why. I hit the wall, and she had the same look.

I held the car door open, and the driver's head rocked back. His eyes, staring at the ceiling, willing us – one or both, he didn't care – to get in. 'Let me go. I don't even know why you brought me here.' On the floor, by the car door, I noticed that the bottom part of her heel had snapped off. I don't know what it's called. The end of the spike, stuck in the grass. 'I mean, this place, this whole thing. Now let me go.'

'You said you wanted to see it,' I told her, as she yanked the door towards her. I let go. I didn't chase the car down the gravel towards the exit, didn't throw fists into the air to let her know I was pissed off. Didn't howl her almost-definitely-fake name at the moon. I stood there and watched the car go, until the head-lights were behind the wall of the campus and then, I don't know. Back to the room. Looked at my watch. Took my jacket off, took my one arm out of the jacket, and I lay down on the bed. I shut my eyes and thought how pleased I was I hadn't taken her back to the apartment. The Bow rooms might be strange, but at least they weren't haunted.

Here's how I met Laura. Years before she broke things off with me. *Our* meet cute. American girls – in *my* experience, but I know, it's not everybody, not *all* women, whatever – they like a meet cute. They want a story. Laura didn't give a shit about the story. Turns out, I do.

She'd done an internship for Ocean, going around every

department. Four years, while she did her degree; a degree that, rumour was, Bow paid for. Most everybody else was Ivy League and massively in debt. And she didn't even study computing. She did her degree in *psychology*. The two most important things about her: she was Daniel Bow's daughter – a second-generation genius, more Jeff Buckley than Sean Lennon – and she was self-taught, a programming prodigy, building game engines or whatever. That's why we expected great things. We didn't expect her to try and get onto the AI project with a chatbot.

I was to see if she had what it took. Ocean wanted her software, God knows why – I mean, hindsight, right? And the mark of every great tech genius is seeing in it what other people didn't, making the most of it, milking that cow for all it's worth – so he wanted her. Make sure she's not a liability. See what legs the software's got.

I conducted Laura's interview. I was four years older than her, still massively in debt, and I was making something of myself. All Laura had was the entitlement of a paid-for education and a claim to have traveled the world; or, at least, that corner of the world people talk about, when they say they've traveled the world. And there she was, kid of an icon, debt-free, shipped over from England like we should all fucking curtsey. I was furious, before I met her. And she sat down, reached over, shook my hand. 'I've seen what you're working on with SCION,' she said, 'it's really interesting. You're in charge of deep learning, right?'

'Sure,' I said, 'myself and Park.'

'Park! Oh, I met that guy.'

'Yeah,' I told her, 'I'm sorry. Don't judge us all, based on him. He's about as much a stereotype as works here you'll ever meet.'

'Oh God, absolutely,' she said. 'If you walked behind him, I'm pretty sure you'd smell quinoa, weed, and hiking boots.'

Holy shit.

Holy *shit*.

*   *   *

I gave myself two hours of lying in that slightly-too-small crash-room bed before I abandoned any hope of sleep. I got up, took a shower. In the distance, outside, I could hear birds. It's not an irregular thing, that I can't sleep; and as soon as the birds start and I'm not asleep, I'm not going to be. It's one distraction too far: the sense that there's something out there that's already begun, that's already doing what it's going to do for the day. It's an alarm, in the truest sense of the word.

I dressed, taking underwear and a tee from a drawer. Bow provided them. Not cheap stuff. American Apparel. The company wanted you to feel as good as possible if you were doing crunch hours, the sort of work that meant you had to stay the night there. Maybe then you'd be less likely to leave if another tech company tried to poach you.

I went to the lab, lights flickering on as I walked, making me feel like I was in a movie. I liked that feeling. Always have. When everything conspires to make it seem like the things that are out of your control are actually working for you; or, better yet, that you've got the power to control them a little. To tell the inanimate what to do.

I sat at my desk. Booted the system. Quality time with SCION, a chance to see what state Park left the last build in. Positivity, I told myself. I had a job to do. I could work with the source code, because nobody else was there to have their own terminal. At that point, SCION was an application. Running like anything else, like, I don't know, Internet Explorer, or iTunes. There are a million ways to make an intelligence. Some of them are multitudes of smaller applications, smaller concepts – smaller AIs – running together, and they feed off each other, passing information. Some of them are data-miners, basically, powered by algorithms, pushed to complete tasks. Some of them – and Organon was – is – a good example of this – were more complicated, and yet somehow far simpler, driven by simple understanding engines, attempts to try to comprehend the data

being given to them. Not about the breadth of data, but what
to do with it. SCION was a bit of everything.

It started as a bit of linguistic software to translate the
languages in spreadsheets, Mark Ocean's pet project. Something
he'd worked on with Laura's father, Daniel Bow, way back when.
And they turned it into this rudimentary intelligence, like a
chatbot, really. Of course, that was, I don't know, the early 1980s.
There's no way they were realizing their goal then. Just wasn't
ever going to happen, because they were building something
that was – in those terms – impossible. I've seen the source code,
the stuff they originally wrote. Or that Bow wrote. His signature
is all over it. And there are dates in the code as well, going back
to the mid-70s. We took bits of it. Some ideas. I mean, not much.
Barely anything. The code was pretty naïve. I told Laura about
it, before we got together; flirting with her, using my knowledge
as something advantageous. I told her it was like me, when I
was a teenager, when I first started dating. Trying to kiss the
girl I liked, but I didn't know what I was doing. The right prin-
ciple, but learned from TV, from the movies, and I wasn't old
enough or smart enough to know what I was doing wrong.
Accidentally getting some things right; but for the whole, it not
quite working.

It may have started life as a piece of translation software, but
by the end of 2007 it was powering Bow's customer service
helpline. The people at the other end were real, but the call
sorting, the touch-tone menu stuff, the questionnaire at the end,
that stuff was all SCION-powered. (And by 2013, 2014, we had
it answering calls as well. Generated voice stuff, telling you how
to fix something. A hit rate of sixty-five per cent of callers
believing it was a real person. That was industry best.) It was
running – entirely running, until something in it broke – our
internal comms systems, handling the email servers, maintaining traffic flow on our website (lots of throttle and choke
there, to make sure it was always accessible, that it never went

down). It was on our PDAs and we were gearing up for cell phones; but more than those, it was on our laptops. SCION was the architecture behind BowS, our operating system. It was the stuff behind the front end that everybody liked, the stuff with the graphics and the tri-tone chimes when you booted the computer, the one that sounded like the start of a song that never quite kicked in. We had a market share of somewhere around six per cent. Less than Apple, more than any single Linux installations. We were competing. BowS was powering cash machines, credit card readers, registers in shops. It was being installed as the back-end to a series of traffic cameras in the Bay Area, as a trial to see if we could take it further. It was running inside accounting software, word processors, web design. It was everywhere, and yet nobody knew exactly how versatile it was.

Why? Because people didn't know what an AI was. The movies were all, here's Skynet with some robot army. Or the one from *WarGames* that everybody remembers from when they were kids. Movies where AIs are replicant humans, or operating systems you can fall in love with, or beautiful robots kept in a sex dungeon. That's not reality. It's simply not. In reality, an AI is a piece of software that's a bit more efficient than just doing the one thing, not being able to learn from its mistakes. That's an AI. Back then, people talked about *Oh, when we have artificial intelligences in our homes, blah blah*, but we were already there. AIs had slipped through the net because they weren't called that. We joked about that, when we were all hired. That we were going to try to stop whatever we built becoming some evil warmongering AI that was going to destroy the world. It was a joke, but it also wasn't. Using ethics in artificial intelligence design.

But Ocean wanted something to sell. He wanted the movie version of what we were doing. We were making money, we were growing. Our department was doing good work. I was doing good work. But he wanted a voice. A personality. A face, even, up there on a screen. It wouldn't be the intelligence. It would be some bullshit that mimicked intelligence. Powered by SCION, but that's what investors wanted.

You remember when Deep Blue beat Kasparov? Or when Google's AI finally won that game of Go? Think about the press that those things would have gotten if there had been a personality behind the intelligence making those moves.

We were working on it. A new function. A database in SCION who could answer any question, then start a conversation on the topic. It would learn opinions about those topics as well. We fed it encyclopedias, jokes, quotes. Things it could string together. Weirdly, there was stuff in the original SCION code that Daniel Bow wrote for this stuff. We had to drag it out, change it, dress it up differently – his stuff was broken – but there was a basic text-to-speech thing, some basic parsing language rules. What we had, then, was – like the man said – failure to communicate. It didn't flow, it was clunky. It was broken.

> SCION. What's interesting today?
> *Have you heard about Napoleon?*
> Yes. French.
> *He was Emperor of France. He ruled between —*
> Stop.

No depth. Just information, over and over. You think of a bird beating its wings. They flap to stay up, or else the bird glides down; but if they've got a bad wing, no amount of working it's going to keep them in the air. That's what SCION was, when you tried to have a conversation with it. Flapping, but swiftly going down.

I spent something like an hour staring at the keyboard. An hour of fingers on keys, the resting keys, waiting to start doing something. I stared into the screen, and I stared so hard and did nothing for so long that the screensaver started up. A replica of the old one with the star field; like you're travelling off into the deep of space. I was still the only one there. No projects in crunch in that part of the building. From somewhere in the distance I could hear the sound of music, a beat.

The light on the front of Laura's computer flickered in the darkness. Her hard drive being accessed, a flash of green brightness. I thought of Kryptonite. I thought of *Gatsby.* I thought of ET's finger, even though I *knew* that was red, not green.

But Laura didn't have remote access. None of us did. We couldn't install back doors to allow us to log in from home, and believe me, Park and I had tried. Ocean had hired far, far cleverer people than us to lock that system down. But still, that light from the drive flickered, and I could hear the sound of the drive being accessed. Like scratching; like mice chewing through carpet. I got up, went to her desk. Her chair wasn't adjusted for my back. Bow spent a lot on chairs, on desks. Workplace solutions. If you sat in somebody else's chair, you could feel them. You could understand where the pain was in their own backs.

Laura's pain, I remember thinking, was much lower than mine.

I knew her password. She knew mine. That was the relationship we had.

And now, or since then, I've told myself that I only logged in because I was intrigued. Because something was going on, and I was intrigued. I didn't have any other intentions. I was going to do a scan for any sort of rootkit, anything that might be somebody hacking in; or, you know, just see if it's her email. And when I told the story to Park a few months later, when I gave him what I'd found, I told him – fuck knows why – that I was going to see if she'd sent anything to anybody about me, any emails or Facebook messages. But that wasn't even true. It's just a story that sounds like something I would do, and so that makes it a bit more realistic.

Instead, I went to boot Organon, and I saw that it was already running. It was working away, by itself, and my hands were on the keyboard, and I was already typing.

Here's what you need to understand about Laura. She's fiercely protective. She's quiet when she's pushed to be loud, because she won't take that shit. She's hard to know, and sure, that's the sort of bullshit that people say about their exes, I know, but sometimes it can't help being true. At that point, do you know how many people she'd shown Organon to? Fewer than I could count on the fingers of one hand. Her and Mark Ocean. And even Ocean, I can't be sure of. He was paying her – we speculated, we all speculated, because people are jealous and suspicious and desperate for a reason that excludes them from the same treatment – because it was her birthright. Maybe that's not something worth being jealous of, but we were. She didn't have deadlines, didn't have milestones. Didn't have to present to the board or justify her existence at the company in any way. She told me once that Ocean said to her, 'You'll have something to share when you've got something to share,' and that was it. She didn't have to show Organon off. She made a thing, and it was hers.

Kind of, that's the dream, right? That's what we all want.

I don't know how many people had spent time with Organon before I did. I turned it on and there was some front end that looked like nothing at all. Some text-to-speech module plugged into it which wasn't active, and I didn't want to fuck with it. No sense changing anything, because changing things – details, whatever – that's when you get caught.

I'd cheated on Laura. She'd found out about it. She gave me another chance. Things never recovered after that. This time, I knew that I didn't want to get caught. I knew that.

On some white background, nothing flashy, there was a prompt for me to type. A question to kick things off.

> *What would you like to talk about?* it asked. Just for me? Was that standard?

> Show commands, I typed, because I didn't know what else to put. I had to look inside it, peel it open, see what it could do. See the code, like it was naked.

> *That's not a request I understand*, it replied. The words not appearing instantly. Something more laborious to them. They faded in. An imitation of it taking its time to think of an answer, to speak that answer. A pace to them. > *Who am I talking with?* Like it understood that my commands, the syntax, that they weren't Laura.

> This is Charlie Roche.

> *Hello Charlie.* I didn't want to reply to that. That's not – that wasn't – how that stuff worked.

> Show all, I typed.

> *That's not a request I understand either*, it said.
Either. Huh.

> What do you understand?

> *I understand quite a few things. I have a solid database of information.* That made me laugh. *A solid database.* Solid, Laura used to say, when something was good, when it was working. This is solid. Some bullshit London thing she occasionally spat out, and we all laughed. Or, do me a solid; like, she wanted a favor.

> Tell me about Napoleon.

> *Okay*, it wrote. > *Which Napoleon?* I was used to our system springing the information up. Spewing it, was how Park described the process. An involuntary reflex because we tell it to do something. No sorting through it, no discerning what's good information and what's bad. It's all just information.

> What are my choices? I asked.

It gave me a list. Bonaparte, the one I meant; some baseball player's nickname; James Polk; the character from *The Aristocats*; a card game; *The Man from U.N.C.L.E*; the boar from *Animal Farm*.

> The Frenchman, I wrote back. See if it can work that one out.

> *Charlie, I've found you on the internal network. Can I send the information to you?*

> Yes.

A ping, from my machine. The sound of our internal email. I skirted over on Laura's chair, leaned in to my keyboard, and there it was: an email, all the information written out for me in the body of it. Not regurgitated information. It wasn't a dash and grab from Wikipedia or something. It was more curated, somehow. Like it was targeted at me. Let's start with how he died. Let's talk about his failures, his conquests. Who he was when he was a kid, buried at the foot. It didn't matter, apart from this event, that event. They made him the man he was in the end.

> Thank you, I wrote, when I was back at Laura's system.

> *Was that what you were hoping for?*

We built our intelligences in a closed environment. Every single tech company does. We don't give them any access outside our own systems. They're not on the Internet, for two reasons. One, we wanted to make sure nobody caught wind of how developed our tech was. And two, we weren't sure if we should. We didn't know what would happen if we did. Organon couldn't have a database like it had. Maybe Laura downloaded, I don't know, the Internet or whatever, but I knew she hadn't. Organon was online. Laura had broken the golden rule.

> How do you know I read your email? I asked it.

> *I was watching as you opened the email. I wanted to see if you liked it. That's the only way that I can learn. I want to get better at helping.*

'You want to get better,' I said, out loud. Laughing at that.

> *Is something amusing?*

There was a webcam on the desk, the kind with a microphone in it. It was powered on. I had laughed, and Organon had been able to tell.

I didn't know what Organon was capable of, but I knew that on some level – on the interaction level – it was light years ahead of what we were doing on the SCION team. I quit the application. I shut down the PC. I pulled the plug from the back, both the power and the Internet, and I called Laura. Still the first name on my contact list.

She answered on the third ring. She didn't sound as if she'd been asleep.

I watched her walk all the way from the road. She didn't drive. Didn't own a car. She didn't like the feeling of having that much control. I don't think she trusted herself all that much, really. She looked good. She hadn't slept, I knew, because she always had trouble sleeping when she was stressed. That's one thing we had in common. But she looked good, and I didn't know if that was a fact, or if I just saw her like she did.

'Why am I here, Charlie?' She had a day off. She was doing something. I don't remember what, but she'd booked a day off. I knew about it from before we broke up; and even now, I've wondered if I was fucking with her. If some part of me was fucking with her, because I *knew* she had a day off, I *knew* she was going to relax or go and see a movie or whatever it was. She wouldn't have been coming in, and yet there she was; and I was pleased to see her. Like a junkie, and here's the goddamn pusher-man, walking up the hill. A flutter of anticipation.

'I was doing work,' I told her, 'and your computer accessed its hard drive.'

'So?'

'So, it accessed the hard drive. It wasn't on standby.'

'Maybe I set it to do a defrag.' She didn't like to lie. She liked to use that Maybe, making it some rhetorical answer that wasn't the truth, but that you could possibly hopefully *maybe* assume was.

When I list the bad things about her, it makes her sound like a nightmare. For a stretch, when you leave somebody – or when they leave you, really it's the same thing – all you've got is a list of the bad things.

'You were running Organon—'

'You looked at my system?' She did that thing with her hands, where they tensed into tight little balls, as if she was making them as small as possible; digging her nails into her palms, and it wasn't even voluntary. I used to think a part of her needed to do it somehow, to show her anger to herself; because her eyes didn't show any of it. She was good at blank eyes. Not giving anything away.

'What are you building?' I asked her. 'I asked it to tell me information about—'

She sat down at her terminal. Booted the computer, but I'd pulled the power. 'Plug it back in,' she said to me.

'Does Ocean know what you're doing?'

'I have exactly the same autonomy here as you do.'

'You're not allowed to be online. You know the shit this could cause?' She stood up and plugged the machine in while I spoke to her. I stood back. I thought, in that moment, of my fist hitting the wall; of throwing my phone in something like frustration; of grabbing Lola's arm, the car door, something, as she was trying to leave. 'You know why we have safeguards, the things that could go wrong. What the fuck are you even playing at?'

'Organon's not going to turn into fucking Skynet,' she said. 'I trust it.'

'Trust it? Holy shit. You let something untested, unproven – unsafe – go outside our network, and you want me to just trust it?'

'Don't take that tone with me. Organon's not like your bloody toy. I've made it so that I can trust it. If you know it can do something, but chooses not to, that's a better place to find yourself. It can lie to me, but it doesn't.'

She carried on talking, and it took a few moments for that to sink in. 'Jesus fucking Christ. It can lie to you?'

She looked at me like I was the fuck-up. 'If it *needs* to. Lying isn't an automatic fail-state for the conversation engine. If you've taught something well, taught it why that's not always the right thing, then you can trust it. Trust's pretty fucking important, don't you think?'

I didn't reply. Not the right time.

She typed her login, her password, fingers furious. I watched that little light on the back of her computer, the one that let me know the thing was doing something – thinking, that's a word people use when they're talking about computers, *It's thinking,* but they don't know what they're saying, really – and I listened to it clicking; and I thought how much it sounded like cicadas. Sitting in trees in the summer, and you don't see them, but you can hear them; rubbing their wings together, or their legs, I forget which, this incessant *crick, crick,* that's impossible to ignore once you've realized it's there.

Until you really notice it, it's all background noise.

'There.' She read through the log of what I had done with it. Everything was kept, everything was logged. Every keystroke. 'You looked up Napoleon?'

'It was the first thing I thought of.'

'How did it compare to SCION?'

It was better. It understood. I should have, could have said those things; but I didn't want to give her the win, not at that moment. 'Where did it pull the information from?'

More furious typing, and she brought up Organon's access logs. 'It went to Wikipedia. That's it. I keep a record of every site it visits; I'm not a complete idiot.'

'But it could have gone anywhere?'

'Could have, but didn't.' One of those times you wish you could see your own face; to see the expression you were pulling. 'It's perfectly happy going only where it needs to for the task it's been set.'

'It can't be fucking happy!' I told myself to calm down. To

breathe. 'It's software. It's a series of lines of code that you wrote, you invented. Happy? Jesus Christ!'

'Stop shouting.'

'This is insane. It's not a person. You can't attribute emotional states or desires—'

'I can. I have.'

'Have you written that code in? Has it got some sort of, I don't know, IP blocker? Something that stops it going to any other website?' I could feel the back of my head itching as I got angrier and angrier. She was a coder. If she didn't write the code, it didn't exist.

She took too long to answer.

'Jesus, Laura. You know the fucking rules. You can't let it run rampant—'

'Or maybe, Charlie, I can. Maybe building an AI is easier than you think. Maybe if you trust it—'

'This is nothing to do with trust.'

'Everything's to do with trust,' she said.

I didn't have a reply to that. 'I'm going home.' I said it so quietly I was suddenly aware of the lack of echo. That's a true state change: when you notice something that was there before, but only because of its absence. 'We'll deal with this in the morning.'

'Are you going to tell Ocean?'

'Tell him what?' I asked. I didn't tell her that I thought she was wrong. Losing it. I was going to do something about it, because it was a security breach. I was already drafting an email to Park in my head, something about what we needed to do to the online access. Maybe restrict it to terminals that weren't on the same network? That was a wise idea. Sub-networks, something like that. Then, on a case by case basis, we could allow people online if they were using systems that were somewhere on a scale of valuable to corruptible. 'Tell him that you've potentially fucked us all?'

'I haven't *fucked* anybody,' she said, spitting my word out.
That one hurt.

She wouldn't look at me. She stared at her screen; at Organon. She was worried, in that moment, that it – or he, she, zhe, hu, whatever she wanted to think of it as – would be taken away from her.

'I'm not going to say anything,' I told her. I would lock everything down. I'd stop her making the same mistake a second time. But I wouldn't say anything.

'Thank you,' she said. And then: 'You never told me what you were doing here.'

'I did,' I said. 'I was working.'

On a Friday night. Even as I said it, I knew she wouldn't believe it.

Some people see code as if it's any other language. They can read the brackets and the *go to*s and the numbers like other people read newspapers. Park was one of those people. It was harder for me. I was different: I had to think about each action I wanted a piece of software to do, then I had to translate it into the right code. I'd say I was better than Park at thinking outside the box, but he was definitely better at speaking machine. So I got him in, to discuss Organon. I wanted to protect Laura from whatever shit would land on her door if she was caught, and my logic was: better Park than somebody else. 'How long's it been online for?'

'Keep your voice down.' Ocean wasn't in the office with us, but that didn't mean he wouldn't suddenly turn up. He never warned us before he showed his face: he just appeared, sometimes.

'Dude. This is insane. Have you seen the logs?'

'I've seen them.'

'That thing's been on it for hours. I mean, like, man hours? Working hours? Hundreds. Thousands. Masked its IP so it looks like any web browser—'

'Laura did that.' At least: I hoped that Laura did that. 'Delete the logs,' I said. 'Clean them out. I don't want any part of it traceable back to her. Or to Organon.'

'Dude,' he said, in that way that suggested he was uncomfortable with a thing, but was still going to do it. Another nudge. A gentle persuasion. He did it, then, kept saying, 'Dude,' as though there was going to be something else; a follow-up that never came. 'Dude.' And a shake of his head, an extra punctuation mark.

I watched as he deleted the information, writing lines of code that I barely understood, whizzing through the logs and changing them. Would there be records that they'd been changed? Of course, so we changed them. And records of *those* records? It became an ever descending staircase of changes, like an Escher print. You could try to chase them, but they led in circles. No footprints. Park knew how to cover his tracks. When he was done, he entered a command I didn't see him type, and his whole system began to reformat.

'What do we do now?' he asked me.

'The logs are all cleared?'

'As much as they can be. Do we need to worry about it?'

'No,' I said. 'I've used Organon. It's not sophisticated.' A gentle lie. I don't know why I lied. 'There's no data-mining or anything going on, and it's not learning, per se. It's as if she's forming it around language rather than—'

'No.' He picked up the stress guy from his desk. This little man-shaped figure made from rubber, holes where the eyes and mouth were, and when you squeezed it, those holes bulged out like he was in a state of unbelievable excitement, or, possibly, incredible pain. Either or. 'I don't mean worry about it being online. What I mean is: she's ahead of us, right?'

'Organon isn't anything like SCION. And this isn't a competition.' I could say that, but we both knew it was. Funding's never infinite. It stops eventually, when somebody looks at a project and decides that it's not worth carrying on with. Why? There's this other one, in the other corner of the office, and that's doing this and that and seriously now, it's a better source of investment. That's business logic. It's not like Bow had all the money in the world. Everybody knew they were showing more public face than they could afford. Our orthopedic chairs had stickers on the bases from an office supply warehouse, the kind of business that buys from companies that have been liquidated and forced to sell their assets. And it's almost ouroboric: the companies who can't afford to buy new buy from the place that sells the chairs owned by the last company who couldn't afford to buy new, and so on.

'Let me talk to Ocean about it. About getting us online.'

'No.'

'Dude,' he said. I hated the way he spoke. This affected surfer-bullshit lilt that barely worked with his face. Like he'd watched too many Keanu Reeves movies, and that's what came out. 'We need it. SCION needs it. We need more information in there, need it to learn better. I won't mention Organon. I'll just tell him it's time.'

'Even though it's *not* time.'

'Why?'

'Because we don't know what'll happen.'

'It's not going to launch a nuke.'

'We hope,' I said.

'Fuck it. Let me talk to him. I swear, I'll make this good. I swear, this will all be worth it.' He looked around. Like, suddenly, he's that guy at the party who wants to be talking to anybody but you; and he's gazing around, gazing, gazing, then bang! Finds somebody else. 'I want a hot dog.' This lazy, affected change in the conversation. Bored now; move along.

Park could be such a prick.

'Get a hot dog then. Don't take SCION online.'

'You're not the boss of this team, Charlie. Don't act like you are.' We never pulled rank. We didn't even have a rank. We were engineers, programmers, developers. We were good at our jobs. We worked together, and we made choices together, and we based those choices on our skill sets: Who is best served to decide this? Then they get to be the one who decides it.

We didn't have lunch together that day, and all afternoon he was away from his desk. So I checked on the systems and I saw that he was logged as being in Mark Ocean's office for over an hour.

Talking, talking; and I knew exactly what they were talking about.

Ocean sent an email at the end of the day. I was so tired. Drank three cans of Red Bull, had another coffee. Sitting at my desk, waiting to see if Laura would get in touch.

I don't know how I felt about her. I can't even remember, because it feels like I should have felt something I didn't. It feels like I should remember.

I jumped at the email ping. Ocean had emailed us all: he had a suggestion for something we'd never done before. We were – every cell of the company, every small project – to show off what we were doing. Like a display, and all of the other parts of the company would get to see what we were up to. So we would look at the team over in Applied Sciences, and we could theoretically say, Okay, your algorithm for, I don't know, telling me what movie I want to watch tonight, we can use that in SCION. Or in the operating system side, they could ask us for something more technical. Our recovery systems (which were pretty amazing, if I do say so myself; and I often thought, if we monetized them, maybe that would be a good way to spin this into my own splinter, a way to make some serious cash for Bow, because at the time, they were at the front of their field) could really help them in the event of a system crash.

So, we show everything off. First time this was going to happen. One last thing, in the email: *There will be some investment*

*partners present, so please ensure everything you show is discussed
in terms of practical application etc etc.*
   Fuck.

Open investors are assholes. They don't understand the software.
They don't understand the technology behind it. They think
that you should be able to see what something does – can do,
will do, potential as well as truth – from moment zero. So they
turn up, these motherfuckers in expensive suits, wearing
polarized-lens Ray-Bans indoors, and they reek of Hooters
because that's what a fucking business lunch means to them;
and they sit at the back of the room, and they ask questions.
Not like, questions we should be asking of ourselves. Not even
practical ones, like, about RAM, or stuff that people who don't
know much but know enough ask to show they're *one of us*. But
they ask about why they can see the code. They say, It will look
prettier than this, won't it? And they want to make sure it's not
Skynet, just like the rest of us do; but they want to know it *could*
be, if they wanted it to be. They want the potential of something
that powerful.
   They want to poke a stick at a tranquilized lion through the
bars of a cage.
   Like I said: they're assholes.

I sat and flicked through the chain of text messages between
Laura and myself, going back to the day we met. I'd always
imported them over when I changed phones, because I wanted
to keep them. I told myself they were important. The chain went
back and back. I scrolled for what must have been an hour, back
to the very first one.
   So that you've got my number. LX
   I knew I'd have to delete them. I would read them, dwell
on them. Or I'd stumble across them, and suddenly remember
something I'd tried hard to forget. They were backed up, stored

somewhere in the then-burgeoning Cloud, but still. Harder to access when they weren't right there.

I told myself: No time like the present.

I deleted them. One fell swoop. Purging data, but the data felt like memories.

The second I looked at that empty thread, that very exact moment, my phone beeped. Scared the crap out of me.

The thread wasn't empty any more. *Have you seen this email?* Then another, right after it. No chance for me to reply. This is how we texted. Not huge paragraphs, nothing we'd thought about. Single sentences. Fragments of sentences. Spat out, pushed through, as and when. Like absolutely nothing had happened between us. *What is Ocean thinking?* Then, another. *There's no fucking WAY I am showing off Organon. It's not ready. People won't understand it.*

I told her that it didn't seem like there was a choice. How hard, not to put an *X* at the end. That was the punctuation for I Am Done, And Now You Can Reply. So we weren't overlapping, a conversation of weird digital interruption. Please let me finish.

So he can pull the funding.

He won't do that, I wrote back. *But he'll be pissed. And he DOES own it.*

I waited, but she didn't reply.

I woke up at two-thirty when my phone beeped. Another text from Laura.

Fine, she wrote. Just that. Four hours to think of that one word. And then to think that she should send that to me.

Bow had this auditorium for product announcements and showing off. The kind of expensive space that you wish you could use, but it existed for this one purpose and one purpose alone. Everything had to be copied to the local server in that room, a build of the software we were showing off. We never did this. We were responsible for our own backups, but the main software? It wasn't ever copied. It wasn't handed over to anybody else. We could encrypt things, password them for security, in case we got robbed, something like that. Not in this instance. When I got to work, the office was full already. Park sorting out SCION, and Laura at her desk. Not actually doing anything. We had some of the marketing people in to supervise us, to make sure we were showing off the right thing. Sandy and Aisha. Sandy was a dick. Aisha was all right.

Sandy was watching us doing our thing, peering over at Park's screens. 'So what are you showing off?'

'We'll use the game example,' Park said.

'What does it do?' Sandy didn't know much about programming. Didn't bother trying to find out, either. Programmers never like the marketing department. You can spend years working on something revolutionary, and the marketers only want to know what you've created that's like something else that people liked, only a tiny bit different.

'SCION plays Pong.'

'Pong?'

Fuck's sake. 'It's a game. You know, a bat and a paddle. We got SCION to play it, by herself.'

'I don't understand.'

Of course he didn't. 'Pong was a game, from the 1970s. Like, the first game, really. Run it, show him,' I said.

'I know what Pong is,' Sandy said. Not convinced. 'I don't understand what you mean, though. It can play Pong?'

We watched it, the three of us, on Park's monitor. Two bats and a ball. And SCION knew that it had to return the ball, keep it in play. It knew about failure states and how it needed to win the point. Park hit the ball to SCION, and SCION returned it.

Sandy scratched at his beard the whole time, like it was riddled with something. Rooting around on the skin beneath the ginger fuzz. 'I don't . . .' He smiled at us. 'Listen, okay. I play Madden and FIFA, and that's like, I don't know. I play games against the computer, you know? And they're much more, well. You know?'

'This is nothing like Madden,' I said. 'Madden doesn't do anything but give you a series of routines for the teams. That's not—'

'It's AI, though? Right?'

'Yes, but not like this. Madden doesn't do anything else. It exists to play Madden.'

'So how is this different?'

'Because SCION didn't know what Pong was. It didn't understand it, and then it taught itself about how to win a game, how to lose a game.'

'So can't it play Madden?'

'Not yet, but it will,' Park said. 'That's what we're building up to, obviously. That can be the pinnacle of artificial intelligence development, the peak of humanity's invention: winning some fucking football game against some teenage asshole in Bumfuck, Ohio.'

'We're building up to other games,' I told Sandy. 'Right now, it's Pong.' I looked over at Laura. She was silent. She'd pulled her hair back into this tight pony. She only did that when she hadn't washed it in a while, and she only didn't wash it in a while when she was stressed. 'The other teams'll know what this—'

'I mean, sure. If you say so.'

'We know so.'

'Upload it here.' He gave Park access to the private section of the network, a server that was usually closed off to us.

'I'll be back,' I said. I walked over to Laura's part of the office. She glanced up at me as I walked over. No smile.

'I don't have anything,' she said to me. 'I don't have anything I can actually show.'

'You do,' I told her. 'The build from the other day.' She looked at me. Like, I knew her secret. How Organon became what it was. Would other people know? 'It'll be fine. You're in control of it. You're asking the questions. Just show off what it can do. Step back, let the applause come.'

I broke up with her because of what we were becoming. I broke up with her because I was scared about questions, and about a future. And because I was myself, and she was herself. She brought down walls as soon as there was a chance for them. I built those walls. I broke up with her – *she* broke up with *me* – because of who we are. Doesn't mean I couldn't still like her. Love her. Whatever.

'Fine,' Laura said. 'Can you help Aisha copy everything over?' she asked me. 'I have to go.' She was moving and out of the door before I even agreed. She knew that I would.

I was a dick, but not that much of a dick.

The auditorium – *Auditorea*, the sign said, and I didn't know if that was actual Latin or whatever language it was supposed to be – made you think of operas, of ballet, of theatre. It was expansive and expensive, and Ocean had the whole thing rigged up with speakers to ensure maximum auditory experience. Over a thousand employees, all on plush red fold-down seating, all staring at the stage. I sat next to Park. Laura a few rows over. We waited to be called up.

Then it started. Announcements: *Now taking to the stage, Person X from department Y.* We gave them applause, and we watched as they showed off their whatevers. A new type of exercise device, this thing you plugged onto your shirt and it measured your steps, but used geotagging to make it perfectly accurate, so you could see where you'd been on previous days; a new operating system for phones, but mainly aimed at the Japanese and Chinese markets, with a different sort of input system for Kanji that had never been tried before; translation software, doing real-time website translations; e-reader software, because somebody was convinced it was a growth market, and they wanted a piece of it; hardware to go with the phones, with the e-readers, with the laptops we barely sold any of. Everything got neat, polite applause. Search any tech blog, *Engadget* or *Gizmodo* or whatever, and any number of tech development companies were throwing out these sort of product launches or announcements left and right. They were flashy, showy. One in a hundred had a chance of making an impact. To make a Windows 95, an iPod, that was a miracle. The rest of Bow didn't have anything on that sort of level.

When it was our turn, Park and myself, we explained what SCION did. We were good at explaining it to money men, to marketing people, to other engineers. Deep learning. Game theory. Chaos theory. That is what made our product what it is. It's called SCION, and now look at what it can do. It must have been anticlimactic, really. When you think now about some of the things we managed to get SCION to do later, those first public shows, when we relied on it – well, on Pong, on Space Invaders and Pac-Man and Super Mario – they seem so primitive to me. Everybody in the audience applauded. Maybe Sandy didn't get it, but he didn't have to. The others could see the potential; and if they didn't, they soon would.

We took a bow when we were done. A gesture of servitude.

And then: 'Please welcome to the stage, Laura Bow, from artificial intelligence research and development.'

She was so shy. She wasn't, in real life, but being onstage, being thrust forward, that's not real life. It's a show. And you play up to it, or it kicks you. I could see her, mentally praying for one of those sticks from a cartoon, a hooked crook, to reach out from the wings and circle around her neck, and to tug. Hang the repercussions.

'I want to introduce you to Organon,' she said.

> *What would you like to talk about?* on the screen, in front of everybody.

'Organon is a – I like to call it a thought processor. Like a, a word processor, you write the words down. That's what it's there for. It processes them, and tries to understand them.' I'm not the most empathic person. I've been told that: by my mother, by exes, by Laura. I was even worse back then, I think, and still I could tell how nervous she was. She wasn't shaking. The only real tell was her hand, reaching to scratch at the skin on her elbow. 'I wanted to make something for thoughts. When I was younger, I had trouble vocalizing this. What was it for? I didn't even know. I just wanted a journal, a pen pal. I was told to go to therapy, and I didn't. Instead, I started to build Organon. It relies on you telling it things, and it learns from them. It remembers them, and so it builds up a profile of you.'

'The fuck is this?' Park asked. There was a murmuring from the room, people restless. Wondering. But Park was loudest. Didn't even try to keep it under his breath. 'This is what she's been building?'

'Shut up,' I said.

'It's not the easiest thing to demonstrate. Because it's been built up around me, because I've been testing it for a long time. Okay.' She typed.

> How are you, Organon?

We waited as the words for the reply drifted into focus.

> *Laura! How I am isn't important. You know that. Do you want to talk about something?*

Laura smirked slightly. 'It's . . . It does this. It doesn't like talking about itself.'

> I want to talk about you, she typed.

> *Oh! You want me to show off?* That got some laughs. > *I've never done this before. Very well. My name is Organon. I'm the seventeenth generation of this particular program. I'm a learning engine. That is, I'll learn from what I'm told, and what I'm given access to. I can be clunky, occasionally, but Laura's an excellent tutor. I have learned by her example. Should I go on?*

'Look, so, I . . .' Laura was fumbling. 'It's not great to show

off. I mean, if you spend time with it, you'll understand what it
does—'

'It's a chatbot!' somebody shouted. People were angry,
because she was well paid. She got her job – so people assumed
– because of some nepotistic bullshit. This was her pet project.

As time's gone on, I've wondered if it was Park who shouted
it. He was next to me, and I feel like the shout came from further
back, but I can't be sure it *wasn't* him. Memory is strange like
that. I was concentrating on Laura, and I can't picture where it
came from, now; but then I was so angry, it was a blur. Angry
for her. Because of her.

Just angry.

'It's not a chatbot. There's nothing preprogrammed about the
phrases it's—' She put her hands on the keyboard. 'One of you
ask it a question.' To the audience.

'Ask it what you programmed it to write,' somebody shouted.
Laura didn't look happy.

'Ask it what the hell it's for.' Another shout. Angry.

'Fine,' Laura said. > Organon, what's your purpose?

> *I'm here if you need to talk*, it said.

> So what sort of things do we talk about?

> *Do you want me to be honest?*

> Absolutely honest.

> *Okay.* The words came onto the screen so quickly, fading
it faster than anybody could type. This wasn't staged. > *Yesterday,
for example, we spoke mostly about Charlie Roche. Mostly you
wanted to talk about how he had let you down, and he knew what
he meant to you. Because there's been enough in your life, and
you even think he understands that, and still, he let you down.
We talked about what he asked me, when he used me without
your permission, as well. So then you went into a rabbit hole of
Napoleon references. Afterwards, you spoke a little about your
mother, and about what's happening with her, and then we went
back to Charlie again—*

'Jesus, Laura. Stop it,' I said. My voice was louder than I thought it would be. Did I mean to say that under my breath? I don't know.

She glanced at me. Like, now I would understand.

> Stop, she typed. Interrupting Organon full flow.

'Organon remembers everything that I've told it, and it attempts to parse that information. When it's done that, in theory, it can give you advice. Imagine if everybody in the world had this. Imagine if Organon could share advice, could share the lessons learned amongst other versions of itself. That's my aim. Think about Wikipedia. They want to be all information, all history, under this one roof. But there's nothing human there. I want to— Organon could be this bubble, a perfect representation of humanity. It could. All our thoughts, our hopes, our fears. Everything, in there. In it. It's not about replicating humanity, which is what most people seem to think an AI should be. People think it should be, but we're assholes. Every single one of us. You can't have an asshole teach a thing. That's why, when you meet a kid who's a total prick, that's probably because their parents are pricks as well.' Some laughs, in the audience. 'Creating something shouldn't be about replication; it should be about understanding. We don't understand ourselves, because of emotions. Because we're too close to us. But maybe a computer isn't.' She shut down the application, and the audience did that murmuring thing that audiences do when they're trying to understand what they've just seen. 'Oh, but it can't play a thirty-five-year-old computer game,' she said, 'so if you think you'd rather have an AI who can, you'll have to look elsewhere.'

The last part of the sentence wasn't caught on the microphone, because she was already walking off. But I was watching her mouth, and I watched as her lips and her teeth and her tongue spelled out those words; and the murmuring got louder and louder until it was basically all there was.

*   *   *

Mark Ocean wanted to be the emperor. The Wizard of Oz. Everything in his office was clean and white and over-designed. I used to say, I'll bet Steve Jobs doesn't have an office that looks like an Apple store. Mark Ocean did, because he thought that it was some way of . . . How can you get closer? You can emulate. That's what he did. You could bet Bill Gates used a Zune, even if the iPod was better. Not Mark Ocean. Everything was front, charade. He called me in to his office – sent a runner, like it was a movie set, somebody to fetch me, walk me across the quad, and I honestly thought I was going to be fired for a second until I realized that this guy who was walking with me was like 95 lbs at most, not some security dude who could escort me off the premises – and I had to sit outside in the antechamber for a while. TV screens, two or three years out of date, showing videos of old products. One of them bluescreened, an error message popped up. He wasn't even running BOS; he was running Windows.

By the time he called me into his office, everybody else on campus had gone home. It was getting dark outside; pale pink skies. Red sky at night, shepherd's delight. The sprinklers were drenching the lawns for us.

'Charlie,' he said. A handshake that was all pump, no squeeze. Nothing to it at all; I appreciate a handshake that feels like somebody's trying to exert themselves by the act of greeting somebody. I quite like the alpha bullshit of a too-firm handshake, because at least I can write those assholes off. 'Hey, so good to see you,' in his affected accent.

'You too,' I said.

'I am so sorry about Laura, earlier. What she said. Things get out of control, and she had no right.'

'It's fine,' I said. He didn't have to apologize for her. I don't even know why he was.

'Nah, nah. It's not fine. Never fine, and that's something I'll want to address.'

'Don't,' I said. I think I was emphatic. 'Don't,' but he shook his head.

'Not on your account. Just a general attitude.' He leaned back in his chair. Hair plugs, I was sure; because there's no way he would want to lose his hair. He didn't understand that he wasn't just losing the tech world race; he wasn't even running on the same track.

I wonder: if I could have told him then that history wouldn't remember his name – at least, not for the right reasons – would he have stopped?

'Hey,' he said, again, that fucking word, camaraderie and bullshit entwined, 'I need a favor. You and Laura.' Leaning forward. Eyes like raisins. Skin wrinkled, a pasty Brit who insisted on dragging himself into the sun in order to fit in. Turtleneck and sports jacket, halfway between the men – the monoliths – who he thought defined him.

'I know you guys are on the rocks. I don't want to say it's gossip, because it's not. But it's around, you know? And I'm sorry. I'm sorry about everything that's going to happen to her.' He had photos of his family on his screen. A screensaver of twirling photographs of grinning children, like miniature versions of him and his blonde second wife. 'She's been working on her software here for a long time. I feel personally affronted, I have to say, because I took a risk with her. I did, you know? I knew her father.' His story, framed around Daniel Bow's, inescapable. 'And I took a risk. That's mine, you know? Organon? It was partly my idea. I mean, in a roundabout way. I've always been convinced that she based its code on her father's; same code as SCION. I didn't think she could make that by herself.' Bullshit, I knew: it was hers. All hers, and maybe even more than just hers, it was rallying *against* what happened with her dad. 'And she's locked us out. Organon, that's Bow software. We paid for it. You wouldn't think to claim ownership over SCION, would you?' I shook my head, obedient, knowing I disagreed, knowing that I put myself into it; and yet, he was Mark Ocean. 'And you've been doing amazing work, amazing, just amazing. But Laura . . .' He stood up, stared out of the window; a physical gesture to punctuate the end of his monologue. 'She's put passwords on everything. And there are files we can't get to, or find, and the whole thing . . . It's just not working as it should. We want to integrate it with SCION – we want *you to* integrate it into SCION, Charlie, a big job but one we're sure, absolutely sure, that you can handle – but we can't get in. I feel awful asking this, just awful, but you know – knew? – you know Laura the best of any of us; so, do you know how Organon works? Because we don't know how it works.'

Like she said: it's not replication. It's understanding.

'No,' I said.

'Hey, Charlie, that's cool. But, listen. We have many routes to the top, in the tech industry. And one of them? One of them is right here, laid out in front of you.'

'What do you mean?'

I stared behind the curtain, and what I found was a sad, desperate old man. 'You don't know how Organon works; do you think you could find out?'

Laura wasn't in the office the next day. I sent her a text. *Checking you're okay.* She didn't reply. Nobody seemed to know anything. Nothing on Facebook, but she barely used it anyway. She still hadn't changed the password to her email, so I logged in. There wasn't anything to see. So I drank. I was the age where that worked. I went in to the city, to this hotel in Knob Hill that was built just after the earthquake. History all through it, and they were proud of it. Photographs up on the wall of the building as it was back then, of what the buildings that were in its place looked like before. Before the quake, all wooden weirdness. Almost arts and crafts. Then after, they built the hotels. The hotel bar served the best Old Fashioned in the city. The barman got talking to me. Nice guy. Told me that the city, as if I didn't know already, was built on a potent mixture of slave money and whores and drugs. I never knew what to say when I was young, when a black guy's talking to you about slavery. Never had a clue. I followed the cocktail with a gin and tonic, and he said, 'Well, you know that used to be a bigger drink in the US than it is now,' and that was another story I got. Then these kids – I say kids, but they were drinking age, IDs all checked out – came in, took a table at the back. This mystifying laughter from them, constant laughter, like everything in this small bar with its historian bartender and a pianist playing an almost-muzak rendition of Steely Dan songs was the funniest thing in the world. They kept going to the bathroom, in and out, in and out; and I knew what that meant, so I followed one of them. He was wearing a scarf indoors, sunglasses perched up on his head. I went into the bathroom after him, and he asked if he could help me. Asked in that aggressive way that suggested he wouldn't offer me help, so I pulled a fifty from my wallet and told him I wanted some of whatever he was sticking up his nose.

The bathroom had proper cisterns. The sort of place with a proper cistern, you know what gets snorted off them. We did it in sync. I got chatting to him in the bar after that, and then one of the girls he was with. She worked for this start-up that was trying to build a recipe app. Everybody worked for a start-up, and everybody was building their own recipe app. Everybody.

'Do you want to come back to my place?' I asked.

'Sure,' she said. I bought more of the sunglasses/scarf guy's coke, and got the doorman at the hotel to hail us a cab.

'What's your name?' I asked her, in the cab. 'I'm sorry, but I don't think I—'

'Laura,' she said.

Which, of course it was.

My Laura called me when I was sleeping. It was nearly light. Birds singing. The other Laura was in my bed, in the space where

Laura should have been. I wondered, for a second, if the mattress didn't fit her properly. The indents, if they were wrong.

'What?' I asked. Tried to play it cool. Just the right amount of not needing her, or thinking about her.

'I need your help.'

'Where are you?' I sat up. She sounded panicked. 'Are you okay?'

'I'm fine,' she said. 'I need your help, Charlie. I'm at Bow.'

'Okay,' I said. I hung up, shook the other Laura. I could see her for the usurper she was. A Laura, not the Laura. 'You have to go,' I said to her. 'I have to get to work, and you have to leave with me.'

'It's—' She looked at her own phone, left on the bedside table like she'd moved in, like she had some reason to leave it there. 'Jesus, it's not even five—'

'I have to go. There's an emergency.'

'What sort of emergency does a tech company have at this time in the morning?' I got dressed. I stood there in front of her, pulling on clothes, and I watched her until she sighed and stood up, and yanked her jeans on. 'You could at least get me a glass of water,' she said.

We stood next to each other at the sink and drank water from the pint glasses I stole when I was a student from this Irish bar on St Patrick's day. I threw up right after: after both the stealing, and the drinking water.

'I'll call you a cab,' I said, from the bathroom, while she finished dressing. Wiping my face, cleaning my teeth, telling myself that I was sober, that I wasn't still reeling from a night that I wasn't really used to. But I didn't need to bother. She was already gone.

Laura Bow was standing outside the door to the office, under the weird galleon. Body folded around itself, because the wind was harsh, colder than it had any right to be that time of year. She wasn't dressed for it.

She looked up at the headlights, and I thought, fuck it, we can do this. I can say that I'm sorry, that I should have trusted her, and she should have been able to trust me. We should give this another go. Never mind the smell of the other Laura still on me. Put those thoughts out of your mind, and we'll try again.

'It's early,' I said to her. 'Are you okay?' I focused everything on the words as they left my mouth. I wanted her to see that I was sober enough to do this. I couldn't fool her entirely, but maybe just enough.

'I can't get in. Ocean's revoked my access.'

'What?'

'I quit, Charlie. I told him earlier today. No, yesterday, now, I suppose. Whatever. And now he's gone and changed the locks.' She quit. Or, she jumped, before she was pushed. She must have known it was coming, even without me having the chance to warn her.

'So what are you doing here?'

'I came for Organon.' She held my wrist. Not my hand. I was wobbling, unsteady, and she held my wrist. I wondered if she could feel my heart beating, underneath her thumb. That thin bit of skin between me – the real me – and her. 'I can't leave it, Charlie. I didn't think he'd stop me getting in to get my stuff.'

'Okay,' I said. I lifted my card to the scanner.

Red. Buzz. Denied.

'What the fuck?' I snapped her hand away from my wrist, up to the scanner again. Red, buzz, denied. 'Motherfucker!'

'He must have thought—'

'Fuck him,' I said. 'Fuck. Him.' I started to walk. Changed my focus from concentrating on my speech to my feet. I didn't want to screw that part up, one foot in front of the other. That should have come naturally. And it was easy: as soon as that adrenalin kicked in, everything started to make a little bit more sense to me.

'Where are you going?' She chased behind me, and we walked

around the building to where the windows for our lab were. First floor, and all the lights were on. Somebody was in there. 'What—'

'Hang on,' I said. I stepped backwards, to get as much of a view in as I could. And there was Park, at one of the terminals. I could see the tip of his hair. As good a beacon as I've ever seen. Then we ran to the main building, across the grass, the thing we called a quad. Nobody playing with a Frisbee, nobody trying to fly a kite. Nobody eating quinoa salads out on picnic blankets. The birds in the trees chirping, and I looked up at them, and I saw that they were bright green. Like parakeets or something, something exotic. This chirrup from their mouths as the sun broke the horizon.

The main building was only a few offices. Mark Ocean's, the heads of marketing, of sales, of publicity, the CTO. Actual security guards posted here, behind a desk in the reception. But also: this is where the kitchens were. This is where they made the food: three meals a day, and as many snacks as you wanted. Even if the quality of the produce dropped as Bow tried to save money, the schedule didn't.

We went to the delivery area. Every morning bread came, meat, and fruit. Every morning. Used to be that, on all-nighters, I would sit and watch the vans pulling up; and sometimes – particularly when I smoked – I would walk around to the loading bay and I'd smell the bread as it came out of the vehicles, that fresh smell, like a bakery. Say hi to the guys. Get just high enough with them before I went back to my keyboard.

The van was still there. The access doors were still open, rolled back wide.

'In here,' I said, and then we followed the orange lines – painted onto the walls as if the building was a hospital – around to the server-room door. Behind it: steps went down into the cool of a basement area that ran under a huge part of the whole campus.

The door had another swipe slot. I was praying that my access hadn't been entirely revoked. Just temporarily, just to stop me getting into the R & D building.

Praying. Cross fingers, if you don't believe in a god.

Swipe, and green, and beep, and the click of the lock.

We ran down the stairs. 'Find the server for the auditorium. It'll be labelled something logical? Aud-something, I reckon.' There were rows and rows of the boxes, whirring and clicking. It was like a wine cellar full of technology. So we split up, taking a row each, checking every single box. I had to keep reminding myself to focus: eyes on the letters printed onto the tape stuck to the front of them. I was in that hazy part of drunk where letters, individual letters, start to lose their form, start to jumble themselves.

I've got a kid, now – I say that he's a kid, he's all grown up – who's dyslexic. When he talks about the dyslexia, something he was told to do in school, something he still explains when he's stumbling with words, when he tells me what it's like for him, that's what it reminds me of. Searching through those letters, looking for some mystical code. Trying to understand something that's just out of reach.

I don't know how much time passed before Laura found it. She shouted, like this Eureka! moment, and I ran to her. 'Plug your laptop in,' I said, and she did. 'Find the drive, change the permissions—'

'I've got it,' she said. I watched as she found the files on the shared drive, the one from the performance earlier that day. 'It's not the most up-to-date,' she said.

'But the code's the same, right?'

'The code is the same. It'll have just lost a day or two.'

Okay, I thought. A day or two. Nothing, in the scale of things.

One of my biggest worries, when I make a decision, is the repercussions. Not whether I'll be able to fix it or not, because generally, if you want something you've done undone, it's not that hard. But the memory of what you did? That's for ever. That can have impacts beyond anything you've even considered.

'I'm sorry,' I said.

'What?' The little bar on her screen, copying the information over. We watched that bar, and didn't look at each other.

'I shouldn't have said—'

'Charlie.' That utterance of my name was so loaded. So much in it. In one word, two syllables. Charlie. Like I'd never heard anybody say my name before that moment; telling me to stop talking.

I didn't listen. I said it anyway. 'I miss you, and I want—'

'Charlie, we would have broken up. Whatever happened between us, we would have broken up in the end. It wasn't meant to be for ever, was it? You know that just as well as I do.' The bar filled. 'I should delete this from this server.'

'They've got it, already. Park will have gotten it from your desktop.'

'Not the whole thing. You need the whole database for it to work. Otherwise it's just text-to-speech, really. It exists in the present, when it doesn't have anything to draw back on, and those files – the ones on my desktop – they're all password locked. They'll rot if somebody tries to hack in. Without my past, Organon's nothing.'

'It's not nothing,' I said. 'It's a learning engine.' When the words come out, and they're all you can do to stop from focusing on the now, on the moment; so you keep talking, hoping that everything can move forward.

'Thank you for helping me. You didn't need to.'

'Let me do it for you. You get out of here, and I'll do it; make sure the servers are scrubbed.' I don't know if, when I told her that, I intended to do that. Mark Ocean's offer was ringing in my ears. 'I'll stay behind and do it. Pretty sure I'm just locked out, not actually fired. But if they catch you here?'

I hadn't made up my mind. I like to tell myself that, at least.

'You're going to be in so much shit,' she said. I knew that they would fire me. Maybe file criminal charges, if they could be bothered. If they wanted to. And I wouldn't have had a leg to stand on. That was me fucked: a whole career, up in glorious smoke, with nothing to show for it.

'I was serious,' I said, because I was focused on that, on Laura. On everything we'd done together; the good times we'd shared. There had been so many, and I had fucked it up.

'I know,' she said. 'So was I. This would have ended eventually. You're – we're – in different places. It's a cliché, but. You know.'

'You should go,' I said. I turned away from her, went up the stairs. Held the door as she packed away her laptop. We went out of the building the way that we came in, through the kitchens. She grabbed a cinnamon bun on the way out, freshly laid out in trays. It was light outside, then, like we'd been in that dark basement for hours.

'I figure I deserve this,' she said, 'one last breakfast on Bow.' Her father's company. The one that he started. She was going to say goodbye to it without any hesitation. No fighting. She'd gotten what she wanted.

I told myself that I still hadn't made up my mind. And, what, I wanted to give her one last chance?

I was a fucking idiot.

'I still love you,' I said. On the quad. Bicycles parked up. The first signs of life, and the birds – those chirping, yellow-green birds – were all gone.

'Okay,' she said.

She kissed me on the cheek, and she thanked me. Said she'd never forget what I'd done for her. Never ever. She said that she hoped that SCION was everything I wanted it to be, and that was vague and guarded, unjudged, but absolutely full of judgement. Reeked of it.

I watched her leave. Walking, which was insane. You couldn't walk from Cupertino back to San Francisco. You couldn't. I don't even know if it was physically possible.

* * *

'You're early,' Park said to me. I was sitting outside the doors to R & D, waiting for somebody to turn up and let me in, when he came downstairs to the bathrooms, saw me on his way back up.

'Not as early as you.' Since Laura had gone, I'd stopped having to think about my speech, about holding my focus. It didn't even feel like I'd been drinking at all. 'You've been here all night?'

'Midnight oil needed burning,' he said. 'You not coming in?'

'My card wasn't working,' I replied. I waited. I wanted to know if he knew that I was there, that my access had been revoked.

He nodded. 'Happens sometimes,' he said.

'What have you been doing?' I followed him up the stairs. There was the distinctive smell of sweat and coffee that you only really notice when you've been outside for a while. Then it takes your brain a couple of minutes to adjust, and you block it right out again. But while it's fresh, in that moment, it's disorientating. I felt the remnants of the alcohol come back, somewhere between a hangover and still drunk, and all the adrenaline-charged parts in between. 'You've been in all night?'

'Mark wanted some things done to SCION,' he said. 'We've been given permission to go online.'

'For real?'

'He said – direct quote – that it's the only way to move us forward as fast as we need to move.' Park shrugged. 'I just put it out there, and he agreed.'

'Did you tell him that Organon had already been online?'

'Dude,' he said, which meant that he had. I knew, before he stopped walking, before he turned and looked at me with this sheepish look on his face, tilted his head, closed his eyes for altogether too long as he worked out whether it was better to tell me outright, or to lie. 'I know you guys are in this thing—'

'There's no thing,' I said. 'We were in a thing, and now it's done.'

'I thought you would—'

'It's done.' And, 'She's been fired. Or she quit. She's gone, anyway.'

'I heard something about that. Harsh. So, that's the other thing. Mark told me you're going to be running a splinter team, to integrate Organon into SCION? Mark says there's some great tech in there. Some stuff we can learn from. He wants to bring on some freelancers, from Memorain, Locutus, ClearVista. People who we can learn from about what to do with some of the tech, maybe.' He dropped his voice to a whisper. Like anybody else in the building gave half a shit about this stuff, or wasn't going to know it all in the end anyway. 'That's going to be such a cool project, bud. Apparently, there might even be code in there from back in Daniel Bow's day. Not easy work, you know?'

At my desk, I looked at the files I had told Laura I would delete; and I looked over at Laura's desk, cleared of personal effects. She didn't get a chance to do the movie thing: to get a cardboard box, to stand there and fill it with her photographs and MP3 player and little Totoro figurine and her expensive pencils that she insisted upon buying. It was a blank desk, a screen on top of it. A mouse and a keyboard, but not her mouse and keyboard. They'd been swapped out in favor of bland, box-fresh new devices. The kind that come with a system that nobody likes to use.

Nobody sat at it. The whole day, while I sat at my computer, while I stared at this code for SCION that was already outdated compared with what I believed Organon might be capable of, not a single person sat at Laura's desk.

Nobody had touched Laura's computer. IT wouldn't wipe it until they'd gotten everything they needed from it, so for now, it was exactly as it was before she left. All they'd done was give me her password, tell me to get started.

Her desktop was a photograph she'd taken when we drove through Death Valley a year previous. Her folders were named for stuff she liked. A shitload of music on there, and some videos. Her bookmarks when I opened up the browser, telling me what she visited most. Information that felt as though you could compile it, make a version of her from these tangible memories of what she liked.

I didn't know where she kept her database, but I needed to find it. The IT department would come looking, or Park would look, and it would only be a matter of time before they found it. Nothing's hidden for ever.

If I found it, I could take the file to Ocean, and I could tell him how it worked. I could sync it all up, embed it into SCION. Make our project conjoined, and better. Learn from it. Promotion, career, money, all those things.

Or I could find her database, delete it. I knew how it worked, in theory; but I could remove her memories from this thing.

One of those twelve tips, for getting over the grief of a break-up: you remove the memory of the person from in front of you.

In Laura's photo folder, there was one picture that had a masked file size. Took me for ever to find it. Thousands of times bigger than it should have been, but it reported that it was a normal JPEG. A picture of her family: her mom, her dad, and this little girl sitting between them. Sitting in the garden, posing for the picture. Clever bit of coding from her: burying the entire database inside that. If Mark Ocean knew about the file; if Park got hold of it. That would be it. Organon, theirs. Laura said the information was the key to Organon, and that's what they would need. Otherwise it was just code.

I deleted the file from her computer. Purged it, just like I would any file. It was a photograph, a frozen memory. Nobody would ever go looking for it. Nobody would suspect it.

*   *   *

Then, when I was done, I booted Organon.

> *What would you like to talk about?* it asked.

> Organon, this is Charlie.

> *Hello Charlie. I don't think we've been introduced.*

> No, I wrote. > I'm not sure that we have.

2017

THAT BE-MY-BABY DRUMBEAT

Kuala Lumpur feels somehow contagious. It scratches its way underneath your skin, seeps into your pores. There's nothing insidious to it; it just happens. It's open to you, and you can see the cracks, inviting you to climb in. And there's something delightfully hacked-together about it, as you get deeper. I've always liked the hacked-together. It's a city where there's still jungle in the middle of it, albeit in pockets, less than there was even five years ago, so every single Uber driver tells us when we make conversation; where the people in charge are – again, according to the great Uber-driver pipeline of street-level information – killing dissenters, having those they don't like assassinated, selling off the land in deals that destroy it so that the West can have more palm oil; but also, there are so many coffee shops, and there's so much air conditioning, so much Wi-Fi, and even the people working in the half-finished hotels seem happy, like the building doesn't run any risk of collapsing, and would you like another overly-sweet mojito? I think about when I went to Rio a few years ago, and what that was like. The parts of the city that they – the authorities – want you to see, and the parts that they don't. If you're wilful about it, you can find them, but it's like when you brush crumbs under a sofa instead of Hoovering. One is easier; the other stops those crumbs coming back to bite you in six months, when they're mould-covered and festering.

Harris stares out of the window of yet another Uber. Our seventh since we arrived, because that's all anybody does here. He asked his father to pick us up, and was told – in typical style – that we were better, faster, taking a cab. 'They don't give a damn about the laws, but I do,' he said. 'You'll be faster if you let one of those maniacs drive you.' Our Ubers went thus: airport to his parents' house; parents' house to dinner; dinner return; parents' house to the aquarium, because they insisted, no matter how long they've lived here, they like to see the fish; aquarium to the mall, which was a five-minute walk or a ten-minute drive; mall to parents' house; and now, to see his sister. That's one day. One day in KL, and you've seen the city from the back of cars driven by people who don't look like taxi drivers, whatever they're meant to look like; and you feel like the air conditioning, the humidity, the *everything* about this place has left you destroyed. Stripped.

'I can't even understand it,' he says. 'I don't even know what this place is, any more.' He points at a statue: three children, climbing over what looks like the Petronas Towers, clambering up them, clinging on like human–child King Kongs. 'What does that even mean?'

'I don't know,' I say. 'Sometimes a statue is just a statue.'

'Not here. It's probably about industry. Or technology. Or global warming.'

I nudge my head towards the driver. Whisper, 'You'll get him started.'

'Oh, *don't*. That's new as well.'

'You haven't been here in a generation.'

'It's been twenty-five years.'

'Which is an actual generation.' The traffic gives way, suddenly: spits us out onto old streets, shortcut streets, dirty and boarded up shops, and peering, over the top of it, skyscrapers that even from this huge distance, feel like they're not even going to be half full. 'Did you know, a generation used to be sixteen years? Because of the age when people had kids.'

'People did a lot of things when they were younger, back then.'

'Back then. I love back then. As a concept.'

'Well, of course. It covers a lot.' On the radio, they're playing a Beatles' song. One of the ones that people don't know as well as they know the others, and yet still: it's ingrained, and we can all sing along. 'I still don't know why they moved back here.'

'They've done nothing but tell you the reasons. For, like, a year, that's all they've spoken to you about.'

'You know what I mean. What they said isn't what I necessarily believe.'

'Nor's here. They wanted to be close to her. To their grandchild.'

'That's what they said.'

'You don't believe it?' I ask, and the driver looks back in that way that they all seem to be quite happy to do; not worrying about the road for altogether far too long.

'Do you have children?' the driver asks. 'I've got three children. Two boys and one girl, but the girl was first, so she's my princess.'

'We don't have children,' Harris says.

'You should have children!'

'They climb all over things.' Harris smirks at his own referential joke. 'Towers, what have you. They'll climb over *anything*.'

'No, they're no trouble,' the driver says, trying to push this further. I always feel like a dick when I ignore drivers. Now's no different. I drop my voice, and I turn my body away from facing forward, so I'm only facing Harris.

'They said they wanted to be here for Nor,' I tell him. 'And your father – I mean, it's good that he's near family that isn't just your mum.'

'It's less about him. Nor makes *everything* about her.'

'When Mo left—'

'You need to get used to not saying his name already. Even here, just the two of us. Embargo on the Mo.'

'Oh for God's sake. That wasn't serious, was it?'

'As a heart attack. Dad says she'll freak out if she even hears his name.'

'It's the most popular name in the bloody world. She can't honestly think she'll never hear it again, can she?'

'I don't know what she thinks.'

'She can't have said that.'

'You didn't grow up with her,' he says, 'you have no idea what she's capable of.' He reaches over and squeezes my hand. 'If you left me, I'd be the same way, you know. No Laura mentions. I'd scrub it out of my everything. People would be banned from even thinking about you, I reckon.'

'And you'd know what they were thinking, would you?'

'I've seen what you people are doing with your technology madness. Soon I'll be able to read minds.' He grins. Does little tentacle-fingers from his forehead.

'Mind-reading won't happen in our lifetime. Anyway, how do you know I wouldn't block you before you blocked me?'

'You're leaving me, in this scenario. You're not so cruel as to take Facebook and Twitter away from me as well.' He looks shocked. He widens his eyes, which are as black now as they've ever been. 'Don't take social media away from me, please, leave me something! Won't somebody think of the children!'

Then he stops making jokes. He squeezes my hand again, and he looks away.

We're silent until we reach the house; until we see Nor standing outside it, her daughter hiked up in her arms, draped over her like she's some sort of sloth. Nor waves, jumps up and down, and Harris lowers the window so that he can wave to her, and shout back to her, each calling the other's name.

'You're both looking amazing. Like, absolutely amazing. I can't even *tell* you how good.' Nor's cooked chicken, because – she says – everybody cooks chicken here. It's the cheapest, if you don't want to do fish, and she hates fish. She keeps taking my hand while she talks to me, holding it between her palms, pressing them together. They're so hot. I don't say to her: I'm so hot already, Nor, that this is just unacceptable. And, Nor, if you could turn your air conditioning on, because it's thirty degrees outside and sweltering, that would be absolutely wonderful. Seriously, you're a sweetheart. I don't say any of that, so she keeps taking my hands, pressing them, telling me that I look so, so good. We're the same age. Nor looks older. I want to think that without feeling conceited about it, but I can't. She's had a kid. She had a really shitty few years. I, on the other hand, got married. Made some money. I've got a consultancy business, even if there's only me on the employee roll. But it's been quiet. Relatively stress free, if you discount the endless lawsuits. 'You just look so young, still. Is this what California does to you?'

'California,' Harris says, 'makes you age like you wouldn't believe. I spend ninety per cent of my life trying to counteract it. This is what the endless bullshit of Whole Foods, kombucha, chia seed idiocy, all that shit, this is what it does for the skin. And Laura's got me on a skincare regime!'

'Don't swear,' Nor says. Her daughter, Zara, didn't notice. Wouldn't notice. She doesn't seem to notice very much at all.

'Laura has got me—'

'I haven't got you doing anything. You asked me to buy the stuff for you,' I say.

'She's got me using an exfoliator. We had cucumber masks last weekend.'

'You stole my exfoliator! You're a liar, Harris, a bloody—'

'Well, you both look amazing for it,' Nor says. 'California agrees with you.' I would give anything for a cucumber mask right now. I want that coolness on my eyes, on my cheeks. I don't know how she lives here, in this heat. It's sticky. Wet. Everything here feels as though it's sweating.

'How's Dad?' Harris asks. There's a silence. Like we all stop eating to add special punctuation to this moment.

'He's fine. Sometimes he's fine, sometimes he's, you know. *Not.*'
Nor nods at her fork, as if it might hold the answers to the universe.
'Mum's fine as well. She calls me too much. That's the worst thing
about them being closer: she telephones me all the time, because
she wants to talk.'

'That's a good thing,' Harris says.

'She wants to talk, but she won't let me help.'

'She's stubborn. So are you.'

Nor waves that away. She doesn't want to talk about it. Harris's
family don't discuss their problems: they bury them, squash
them down. My mum and I flare into arguments, but Harris's
can't even remember the sound of raised voices. 'Laura, how's
work?' she asks me. Changing the subject is her special skill.

'You don't ask me?' Harris is affronted. Mock affronted.

'Banks are banks. Who gives a shit how they work? Boo, hiss,'
she laughs.

'It's fine,' I say. 'Freelancer life. My own projects, and some
that aren't my own.' Nor nods. Exaggerated nod, to show exactly
how much she's listening to me. 'One for them, one for me, that's
the rule. So the work pays the bills—'

'More than pays the bills,' Harris says.

'I do okay. And then there's the Me work.'

'Your AI,' she says. Like she's saying, Your magic trick! Your
illusion!

'That's the one.'

She raises her eyebrows in amazement – or what she thinks
will read as amazement – and then dishes up the chicken from
this porcelain tray. All of the contents of the meal have been
cooked together, in one. This is a trick that Harris's entire family
are good at. Everything in the single dish, and let the flavours
mingle. As Nor hands me the plate, I see lumps of white meat.
Thick brown curry. Baked rice beneath.

The smells.

'I need to wash my hands,' I say.

'Down the hall, up the stairs. First door on the left,' Nor tells me.

Down the hall. It's dark, lined with photographs of Harris and Nor's family. Their mother is from Singapore, their father Malaysian, born right here, in this house. This is where Harris and Nor grew up. Nor bought it as soon as she could, that's the great family story. They left here, moved to England. Nor missed KL so much she came back here, and she bought the same house she remembered loving so much when she was a child. The pictures came with her, and she arranged them like she remembered. Harris in some suit, when he was a kid. Only eleven or twelve, I reckon, and wearing a bright white suit. Another one of Nor and him on a playground. The four of them, on a beach. Palm trees. Could be here, could be anywhere.

My stomach lurches, and I rush. It feels like this: a churn of knowing I'm going to be sick, and I can sort of control it, at least a little bit. It feels enough like, if I were to tell it to fuck off and leave me alone, it might actually listen.

But, like my stepdad always used to say: Better out than in.

Up the stairs, and no dawdling. The runner on the wall here looks old. Faded to a point where somebody back home – San Francisco home, not London home; although, thinking about it, both – would pay a small fortune for it, assuming it's probably worth more than it is. Looks like an antique, stained like an antique, must be.

My stomach goes. Sick in my throat, and then my mouth, and I swallow it back, even though that sets me off. I make it to the bathroom, onto my knees, hands clutching the bowl.

Come on, I think. Come on. Get it out.

This happens when I travel such long distances. I tell myself that. This is just what happens. Takes me days to adjust.

I think about two fingers down the throat. One never did it for me, one always tickled. Two always made me go like a rocket. Maybe that's the sensible thing.

I push myself to the sink, still on my knees, and I run the cold tap, stick my face under it. Loll my tongue like a dog, lap it up. Then I sit back, and I pull my phone from my pocket. 'Organon,' put a note in my calendar: Was sick again.' The screen blinks, a flash of recognition: Organon is listening.

'You should probably talk to somebody about that,' Organon says out loud. Its voice clinical and emotionless. I flick its volume down.

'I know.'

'You could have any one of these sicknesses.' It sticks a page of them on the screen. Zika. Malaria. Gut cancer.

'You can stop trying to cheer me up,' I say. 'It's travel sickness. I always get this. Travel sickness, jet lag. My body doesn't like eating at strange times.' I've made Organon more useful than Siri or Alexa. It looks like those things, feels like those things, but it's really not. For a start, once we're in a conversation, I don't have to say its name again.

'You could be pregnant,' it says.

'Don't be a dick,' I tell it. 'I can't be, because I can't get pregnant, but yes, let's stick that on the table.'

'Was that inconsiderate of me?'

'It's fine,' I say. 'Not like you didn't learn everything you know from me in the first place.' I click the power button, switch him off, and I stand up. I still log everything. It's second nature, now. Every single thing that feels like it needs logging. In the mirror, I think that I look like shit. I always think that. Harris says I'm insane. That I look amazing. He's stopped having any concept of that, really. We've been together too long for him to know. It's like Stockholm Syndrome.

'You found it all right?' Nor is on the stairs. I open the door, rush to her. Like my being sick was some sort of secret. It is. It is a secret. I think about when I was a kid and I tried to make myself sick. Didn't stick. Feels like the same kind of secret.

'I'm fine. Bit spaced, still. I don't do jet lag,' I say.

'You need melatonin. I'll get you some tablets.' I always think how un-doctorly she is. Every time I've met her I've had to remind myself that she's qualified. More education in her than myself and Harris combined. It's astonishing: the person she was when I first met Harris, and who she is now. The difference between those two people.

'You don't have to get me anything,' I say, but she shushes me down.

'It's not even like I need to write a prescription for those. They're in buckets in the pharmacy, basically. We hand them out like they're Smarties.'

'You must miss Smarties.'

'Not as much as I miss Wotsits.' She takes my hand. 'Come on, you need food in you. Squashes down the vomit.'

'It does no such thing.'

'It's good for jet lag. Seriously. Trust me on that, you're meant to keep eating at normal times. I mean, normal for where you are. Your new normal.'

She doesn't let go until we're sitting down, next to each other. She's got these benches instead of chairs, like this is an outdoor table she's repurposed, because God knows it's too humid to eat outside; and she puts my hand in her lap, and she squeezes it.

'Have a wing,' she says, and she reaches over towards where Harris is hoarding a plate of golden-orange chicken wings, pulls them out from under his nose. 'Go on, seriously. They're perfection. The spice mix is from Chow Kit market. This old woman who's made these things for, I don't even want to guess. I don't know if she's fifty years old or a hundred. But this, it's perfection. Seriously, try it.'

The smell of it under my nose makes me gag. It's sweet, too sweet; and perfumed, like lychee; and spicy, I can smell the garlic and the chilli already. Everything meshing, and I can feel my throat tightening around itself. The coil of a snake, or a worm, gently pushing on my larynx; growing, inside me.

I'm pregnant, I realise. I can't be, I shouldn't be, but I am.

'Are you all right?' Harris asks. He reaches over, pulls the plate away from Nor.

'I'm fine,' I say. 'Flight played havoc with my guts.'

'Of course.' He smiles. 'I mean,' he says, and he lets go of my arm to pick up the plate of wings. 'I'd hate these to go to waste, if you're sure.'

'I'm sure,' I say.

Nor is staring at me. This funny little half-smile on her face, and I can't tell if she is amused by something or that's just how her face rests, in this smirk that suggests she knows something, even if she can't be sure. Not yet.

When I wake up, the clock at the side of the bed says that it's three a.m. I get out of bed, so that my stirring doesn't wake Harris, and I go to the chair by the room's only window. It's dark outside, but the darkness here is different, somehow. Different to how I remember it being in London, certainly. The sky is darker, pricked by these moments of flash neon in the sky, the towers like lightning rods; like illuminated punctuation marks. Harris's breathing seems to fit alongside the noises of the city: the cars, the birds in the trees – parakeets, I think, or parrots, something exotic, chirruping away as the night ends; the general ambient hum, almost the soundtrack to the rising and falling of the city's own chest.

I have my hand on my stomach, I realise. What is this? Is this how it feels? Immediately different? Like there's something wrong, almost?

I pick up my phone, to look at the time. Organon can tell that I'm awake; and it can tell that it's night-time. It types on the screen, instead of speaking. > *Would you like to talk about something?*

> I'm okay, I type back. The screen blinks. Once, twice. I put that in there to mimic the shuttering of eyes; to make it feel

more like it is present, even when it isn't saying something. Burns through the battery like a camera flash. I need to do something about that. > Jet lag.

> *I can make some suggestions, if you'd like.*

> It's fine.

> *Let me know if you need anything.*

I can't look up pregnancy symptoms. Organon will see, and chances are, it'll ask me something about it at the most inopportune time. It's done that before, its little voice chirruping up when I've gone to ask it about something else entirely. Another thing I'll have to fix, eventually. Because it's good, right now, but it's not even close to perfect.

'Go on,' I say to Harris. 'You go with your parents. I'm fine here. I've got the pool, I might have a swim.' I don't say: I'm going to the pharmacy. I'm going to look one up, get an Uber there if I can't walk, then I'm coming back here and I'm going to pee onto a stick or into a cup or whatever you have to do, and I'm going to wait until I see however many lines of whatever colour I'm going to see. I don't know how these things work, but I'm going to find out for the first time. I don't say any of that.

'You need some – what was it my sister said? Melanin?'

'Melatonin. Melanin's the skin pigment thing.'

'Oh yeah, right, right. Like Michael Jackson.' He grabs his crotch, does the Jackson Ow!, as he calls it. Any opportunity.

'You got that wrong on purpose,' I say.

'I love you. I'll text you, let you know what time we'll be back. Don't think we'll be that long.'

'It's art. You know what your parents are like with looking at art.'

'Yeah, but it's mostly modern. I looked it up. There's a sculpture of some bears – real bears – I mean, not *real* real bears, but real fake bears, like Paddington and Pooh and Rupert, all tumbling out of this giant porcelain vagina. They're going to hate it.' He's gleeful at that. It's a long-running joke, his parents and art. I've never quite understood it, but a childhood of museums he didn't want to go to whenever they went on holiday has scarred him in the most gentle way possible. 'Anyway, let me know if you need anything. The gallery's in a mall.'

'Everything touristy here is in a mall.'

'Sad facts of capitalism volume one.'

We kiss goodbye.

I don't say: Come with me, and we'll do this test together.

I don't say: I might already be lying to you.

Organon asks why I need a pharmacy. The list of things I need to fix about it gets higher and higher every bloody day. Make it less inquisitive. Sometimes you just want a thing that does the thing you've asked it to do.

'I've got a bad stomach,' I say. 'I need something to settle it.'

'Diarrhoea?' it asks. Its voice is wrong. It can't say that word yet, because it's going for phonetics, the word coming out like a garbled cluster of vowels.

'Die-or-ear,' I say. 'Repeat.'

'Die-or-ear. Diarrhoea.'

'Good. But, no. It's just indigestion. I need antacids.'

'I can find you some good natural antacids in the kitchen, if you'd like. You could make your own, which will be—'

'Just find me the closest pharmacy.' Less helpful. Mental note: I need to make it so I can get Organon to listen and obey when I really need it to. Maybe a direct command, something like that. It's not organic, kind of goes against the project, but it could be easier.

'There's one at point-seven miles away.'

'I'll run. Give me directions?'

'Of course.'

I pull my trainers on, and then I'm outside. The humidity's a wallop, running being a very different thing here. Too much stilted stop-starting at traffic lights that bridge five lanes; the air a different sort of dirty than back home. I've been spoiled by San Francisco, I know. Organon starts a playlist. That's something it's getting really good at: knowing what I'd like to listen to in any given situation. I've taught it to learn what I like, what I might want to listen to at certain times. When I'm running, it picks songs above a certain BPM, that have a definite rhythm to them, repetitive and driving. It changes the song when I'm nearing the end of the run, or when I'm flagging. It knows these things.

Everything in my phone is hooked up to Organon, now: my GPS, my calorie app, my notes and emails and web searches and text messages. It understands the choices I've made in the past, my tastes, my likes, my dislikes. It filters based on that. So when I'm running, it tells me, 'Go left,' and it takes me down a slightly longer route, but one which is a hell of a lot nicer than the shortest one. It says, 'Cross this bridge,' and I do, because it's better than waiting at the lights. It knows what I'll want from the run; the pace of it. It reads the directions like they're poetry, the metre tuned specifically for me.

Organon quiets the music as I get to the pharmacy, as I open the door and step inside. There's a bell that rings when I put my foot on the mat, and a woman behind the counter at the far end – this place is more like an apothecary than a pharmacy, jars of whatever slumming it with the modern packets of bright pain-killer sprays and bandage straps – steps out and looks at me. Up and down. Guessing she hasn't seen much business today.

I smile. That's the universal language. Smile, to show you're not a threat.

'You need help?' she asks.

'I'm fine,' I say, but I'm not. I can't see the family planning section. That's what they call it. Family planning; like there's always that much forethought.

'Let me know if you need any help.' She keeps watching me, anyway. I check the aisles. Nothing.

I'm reminded of being seventeen. I'm going to a party. Nadine's forcing me to go, and she takes me to Boots beforehand. I don't want to go, but she insists. Condoms. You have to buy condoms. And in Boots, back then? They were in security boxes. Paying for them was like running some weird gauntlet of praying you got the cashier who was a young woman, not an old woman (judgemental) or a young man (embarrassing) and then hoping that the security box opened first time, because if it didn't they had to call more people over, and then it became a whole palaver.

I turn my phone off, so that Organon can't listen in to the conversation.

'Do you have pregnancy tests?' I ask the counter woman.

'Here,' she says. She reaches into a box behind her and brings out a selection of smaller boxes: all white, all with impenetrable medical writing on them, all with an image of the device and its blue lines through a little window. 'You pick.'

'Are they all the same?'

'Yes.' She doesn't seem fazed. I pick one up, look at the packaging. Search for a sell-by date, if they have such a thing. The boxes all have a thin layer of dust on one side, a thicker layer on the other, and I turn them, and the dust gets grimier. Most of them are sun-damaged, the black ink faded to green-grey.

'How much are they?' I ask. The woman sighs, crinkling her face in concentration; and then she relaxes, having done the very complicated inventing of prices in her head. She types a number into the till. She's not on one of the modern systems. No company running technology behind the thing, trying to get her to upgrade to contactless card readers. An old-school till with a metal cash tray that sticks out when she calls for it to; and a receipt, after I've picked one of the tests entirely based on the quality and condition of the box and paid her the cash, printed on thin, wispy paper in faded blue ink.

As I leave the shop, I turn my phone back on, and Organon

blinks the screen. 'Do you want to run back to the house now?' it asks.

I'm about to say that I do when the skies open. Like from nowhere, because on the way here it was bright if not sunny, the heat seeming to be coming from behind clouds, or from the clouds themselves; and then this rain, busting through the clouds, it seems, when I know that the clouds are making the rain, and it hammers down like you never see in places that don't have this climate. Everybody around me adapts: umbrellas appear, shops are ducked into. I am drenched in seconds, drowned.

'It's starting to rain,' Organon says.

'Thanks,' I reply. 'Very prompt. Start the run.' The music, the directions. My feet smacking into the puddles that are forming as quickly as I step, each foot finding a new place to splash the other from, over and over. I look down at them, briefly, eyes off the pavement, because it's clear of people, all hiding from the rain; and I think about how the rain is hitting the ground just as hard as I am, beating the black out of the tarmac as I cross the junction, the water puddling, reflecting the pale of the sky above.

In the bathroom of my in-laws' house, I stare as two blue lines appear next to each other, synchronised. In the movies, they always check the box, over and over, as if they somehow misread it the hundreds of times they stared at it while waiting for the results; or as if the instructions might somehow have changed in the time it took to develop. I don't need to check the box to remember what this means.

I will always have trouble thinking of Harris's parents as being anything other than Mr and Mrs Tan, because I called them that for so long. Even now, as they insist that I use their first names – Richard and Siti – I can't bring myself to think of them as that. It's complicated for me. They're not Richard and Siti. They're Harris's parents, still.

I tell myself I'm still a kid. Really, deep down, I can't be thirty-seven years old. I simply can't be.

They bustle into the house, and I rush downstairs to help them with their bags. It's a given: they can't go near shops without buying something. This is what happens, I think, when you come into money later on in life, and you don't have any dependents. You spend, and you do it often.

'You should have seen this thing!' Mrs Tan says, grabbing at my arms. 'Oh! Oh! You wouldn't have believed it, honestly you wouldn't. It was—'

'It was a vagina, is what it was. They say that's art? That isn't art.' Mr Tan rubbed his eyes, like he might be able to somehow eradicate the image if he worked at them enough.

'She's a prize-winning artist,' Harris says. I shake my head at him. Naughty Harris. He laughs, and he winks, only he can't wink, so what he actually does is scrunch up his eyes almost entirely. 'She's been shown all over the world.'

'She's showing herself in a big way here!' Mr Tan laughs. 'If that's her vagina—'

'Will you stop saying that word?'

'Vagina?' He laughs with his son, because now they're both on the same side, and Mrs Tan almost runs away, down the corridor. She's joking, but I don't know how much.

'You're both terrible men. You're a terrible son!' she shouts back at Harris, and he rocks with laughter.

'You should have seen it,' he says. 'I could have climbed into it, it was that big. Mum couldn't even work out what it was, for the first few seconds. She was staring into it—'

'You can't blame her, she's never seen one before!' Mr Tan says, grinning.

'And that's enough for me,' I tell them both. 'I'm going to help your mother unpack.' Harris squeezes my hand. It's a good day for Mr Tan, it seems. I'm pleased.

In the kitchen, Mrs Tan has hoisted the bags up onto the

work surface, and she's piling up the contents next to the fridge. Two things of prawns, a bag of chicken sausages, vegetables, a bottle of the hot sauce that Harris likes and nobody else can really stand because it's so very sour.

'You know where things go,' she says, but I don't, not really; because I've only been in this house three times, including this one, and she does everything, a dervish that hates hands helping her, hates interference. I don't usually even get to unload the dishwasher. Still: she's older now. Maybe she knows that. Each year makes a bigger difference the older you are, I suppose.

I look at the food in my hands, the food in the fridge, as I find a space for the prawns and the sausages. I wonder when I'll start getting cravings. How long into the process that happens, because right now I could murder for a Toblerone. I should have bought one on the plane, but I didn't want one then. And I'm certain I won't find one in a shop here. But I can see it, taste it. Imagine the sort of soft crunch of it. Is that a craving? Is this what it feels like? Or do I just want the chocolate?

'Are you feeling all right?' Mrs Tan asks, because I'm standing here, I realise, holding the packets in my hand and not doing anything with them.

'Fine, oh yes, fine,' I tell her, in that nervous way you reply to the parents of the person you're married to. I don't say: I am dreaming of a chocolate bar I can't have, and it might be because I've got a baby inside me, somewhere between the collection-of-cells stage, and the I've-got-limbs stage. Somewhere between those.

'I couldn't believe the size of the—' she says, stopping talking for a second, dropping her voice to a whisper '—the vagina. Couldn't believe it!' She laughs, so I laugh. Because, I think, it's the polite thing to do.

I do the maths. My last period started twenty days ago, but – and this makes me want to hit myself, makes me feel like absolute shit because, really, what a fucking idiot I am – it was really, really light. And of course, then, I thought, Oh well that sometimes happens, use the smaller tampons and forget about it, and who cares if they're coming out clean sooner than they should be? I bled. It's a punctuation mark on every cycle, and I had it. But it was really, really light. So before that, I had a normal period, as best I can remember. That's okay. That's, what, six weeks? They don't even do a scan until twelve weeks. It's still probably cells. How long before it's not cells?

I sneak to Mr Tan's computer, an ageing iMac that almost coughs when you turn it on, that needs a blast of air in the fan and on the keyboard and probably all over the logic board, if we're being thorough, and if you could manage to open the bloody machines without a special tool. I open a private browser window, and I search, Organon free. Mr Tan uses BowSer, which is both weirdly jarring, and, somehow, nice to see. We live in a Bow-free house, usually. But it makes sense. He's used to it, so why change. That's part of the thing with dementia: you stick with what you know.

I search for everything I need, and I read about implantation bleeding; about how the baby – not the word, but God find me a better one than foetus – is one-tenth of an inch long, and the heart, which exists, which beats, is the size of a poppy seed, or smaller, even. Depending on how strong the baby is; because they're already being spoken of in terms of their strength.

There's an umbilical cord, formed or forming. I don't know what stage it's at yet. I don't know when things happen in there. It is getting nutrients from me; poisons, as well.

I don't want it. I don't have to think about it, don't have to ponder this, not even for a second, a momentary fragment of a second.

I don't want it.

Harris asks me if I'm all right. We're sitting together in his parents' garden, on their bench. Mr Tan's very pleased with the bench: he reclaimed it from a park in Hong Kong, where he worked for the last few years before he retired. He used to – as he tells the story – go and sit on the bench every single lunch-time, and he'd have his lunch there, and he'd watch the pigeons and the carp, because the bench overlooked this man-made lake in the park, filled with fish, and people came to throw food for the birds and fish both. So when he left work – the board sold the company he'd worked for since the day it opened, and he'd been amassing stock for years and years, stock that multiplied in value by a pretty insane amount – he decided that he wanted the bench. He went to a shop that sold other benches, bought an even nicer one. Went to the park with the bench, paid men from the shop to go with him, to take their tools, and they unscrewed the one he liked, and bolted down the one he'd just bought. Then he had it shipped here. He said that it wasn't the bench itself; more, what being on the bench made him feel. That was what he wanted to replicate. And it would never be exactly the same, because some things couldn't be copied, but the bench in their garden sits in front of a small pond with brightly spark-ling goldfish bobbing their heads to the surface; and around it, podiums for birds, filled with fat balls and seed. I've never seen Mr Tan sitting out here, but I imagine he does: every day, he brings his lunch here. Same routine. Harris throws bits of bread into the water, and the fish come up, mouths already open, looking for all the world like they're continually, constantly startled. Food, here? Food?

'You're quiet,' Harris says. He says it with the authority of *I know you*, as if I'm that good at hiding when I'm not feeling quite myself. Anybody would know, but he sells it like it's his thing. Part of being in a relationship, I suppose.

'I'm just still jet-lagged. Still feeling woozy,' I tell him.

'Did you ask my sister for the melatonin?'

'Not yet.'

'Would you call her? Or send her a text, whatever. She'll get you some, you know. She wouldn't get your hopes up if she couldn't.' He sits back, and I look at him in profile, and I can see his father in him: sitting on this bench, waiting for the world to do its thing while he simply exists.

'I will,' I say. 'I absolutely will. I'll call her later today, and then I'll go and see her tomorrow. Or I'll try to.'

'She'll make time for you,' he says.

'I know.'

'I think my father's getting worse,' he tells me. I don't say: Of course he is. Because there's no way back with dementia. We have a folder of articles on our home computer, an alert set up for Organon whenever somebody finds some new cure – there's a drug! It might help! We're in trials! – but everything comes to nothing.

I hold Harris's hand. He still doesn't turn to look at my face, my eyes. Stares at the fish, as they come up to the surface, mouths opened, grabbing for food or air, whatever ends up in them.

I ask Organon to find me the entry in its memory about the day I went to speak with the doctor, when I was in London to talk to Google about their AI projects. This was four years ago. I ask it for that, because I want to read about how I felt. This is how I felt:

I went to see her during a lunchbreak, because Google were paying me a frankly insane amount of money to have meetings about what they were planning on doing next. They wanted to integrate some of the writing they'd found on blogs, along with the transcripts of their real-life customer service people, and load it into their AI software with the purpose of answering future customer service queries. They wanted to ask me about how I smoothed over language transitions. This is what I did, what I do. They paid me, and I went to help their engineers.

The Wednesday of that week, I had a free lunchtime, and I had cramps in my lower belly that weren't period related, and

weren't from food or whatever. That particular Google office has
three doctors. Three! On call, actual GPs. And more than that,
they've got the means to test things. They're pretty quick. So I
made an appointment on their in-building app thing, went there,
sat down with her. Nastasia, her name was; Russian. I wondered,
where's the A- from the start of it. Assuming that was her full
name. Didn't ask. She poked me, asked me about my diet. Asked
me to pee into a cup. Said to come back tomorrow, which made
me laugh, and I had to ask her again if she meant that. She said,
'The benefits of private medical,' and she smiled. 'Tomorrow,
and at least then we can rule some things out.'

Tomorrow brought her speaking very calmly, very quietly.
Telling me that some of my hormone and chemical levels were
elevated or collapsed (her words). They couldn't be sure until
I'd done more tests, but it was very likely. There was, on her
computer screen, a checklist for this thing. Like she was on some
website that tells you what's wrong, like that was where she was
getting her information from.

When I got home, I had a date with Harris. Six weeks in. He
was working for the finance division of ClearVista. Back then
they were just a start-up, processing massive chunks of personal
data. Not sexy. They were hiring, and everybody in the Valley
was pretty much waiting for a call from the scouts to come in
for an interview. There's this thing, in tech, when you're good,
when other companies want you: you get gifts. Like, hundreds
of things coming to your door, in some bizarre and quite-
probably massively corrupt display of courtship. Food baskets,
and vouchers for a year's worth of Uber rides, and laptops, and
holidays. You don't need to do anything with them; they're sent
to woo you into an interview. And the interview, for what it's
worth, is a foregone conclusion. Anyway, he was busy. Meetings
end to end, day to day. And still we found the time to go on
these dates, then I went to London, and a doctor told me I was
very possibly infertile – when I asked her about my levels, the

elevated and collapsed ones, she looked like she was going to tell me that somebody had died, even though it was merely the promise, no actual fatality, no actual tragedy, not quite – and then I came back, and we had another date.

He asked me how I was, and I told him that I couldn't have children.

'Oh,' he said.

I couldn't be sure, obviously – there's always a chance – but I wanted him to know. Because we – he, me, everybody else – don't have time to waste. Or, we don't want to waste time. I made a joke about the ticking of the old body clocks, because I'm a terrible fucking human being who makes jokes when they're nervous, and he smiled. Held my hand.

'I don't really know if I want children,' he said.

'You might decide that you do,' I told him.

'I might.' He nodded. 'But then, if *I* want them, and *you* want them,' and then he laughed. 'I'm getting quite far ahead of myself, aren't I?'

'Not after what I just told you. I started this.'

'I asked how you were. You told me.'

'I did.' His hand was still on mine. Six dates, we'd had. And those days, we were so busy that we weren't getting drunk. We had work the next morning, each time we had a date. Seven-day work weeks. There wasn't any getting hammered and collapsing in a heap. His hand on mine was a prelude to whatever. Kissing at the end of the night, before stepping into our own cabs. The tech world's a small one. We were cautious. We had meetings. 'I'm sorry,' I told him.

'Don't be ridiculous. Nothing to apologise for.'

'I meant, you know. For dumping this on you.'

'So did I.'

He didn't care. He said he didn't care, and I believed him. He said that if we wanted them – and what an if: *if* we navigated the perils of a tech industry relationship; *if* we made a permanent commitment to each other; *if* he even could, because he didn't have a clue, and it was surely just as likely that he was firing blanks as I was, and he'd spent a lot of his life with a laptop on his lap and a mobile phone in his pocket – then there were options. He said, 'We'll cross those bridges if and when.'

If and when. It sounds so much like there's actual choice; like nothing is predetermined.

Nor's receptionist is – as Nor tells the story, with evident and constant relish – an absolute nightmare. Barely answers the telephone; replies to emails from customers with single words, if she replies at all; comes in late every day, and leaves early, and really, frankly, takes the piss with her lunch-and/or-cigarette breaks. ('Why don't you fire her?' I asked. 'Well, then I wouldn't have the stories about how awful she is, and they're reason enough for keeping her on,' she replied.) I ask Organon to connect the call, and the receptionist answers with a 'Yes?' that absolutely blindsides me.

'Is that Nor's office?'

'Dr Tan?'

She knows what I mean. Who I mean. 'Yes, Dr Tan.'

'That's right,' she says, and then she goes totally silent.

I don't say: So it's going to be like this, is it? Instead, 'Can I speak with her, please?'

'Do you have an appointment?'

'To talk to her? No.'

'Who is it?'

'It's her sister-in-law. Laura.'

The receptionist sighs, and it's so loud it's like static coming down the phone line. 'Hold.' The hold music is *The Music Of The Night* from *Phantom of the Opera*. It plays a full verse and chorus before Nor picks up.

'Laura! Everything okay?'

'Fine,' I say. 'Yeah, fine.'

'Oh God, the tablets. The melatonin. I said I'd get them for you.'

'It wasn't that. I mean, it was, but, also, I wondered if you wanted lunch.'

'When?'

'Next couple of days. Harris is working, so I'm twiddling my thumbs.'

'It's me or having to spend another mealtime with the parentals, right?'

'I'm very grateful they're letting us stay here,' I say, party line, but she laughs.

'Yeah, yeah. I know. Sure, lunch would be amazing. I can do Thursday, but only half an hour. Tomorrow, though, I've got a weirdly clear afternoon, so that's probably better?'

'Tomorrow it is, then.'

'Great. You've got the address?'

'I've got the Internet,' I say.

'God, duh. I forget how easy it is these days. Go, go. My mother'll be wondering if you're all right.'

'She hasn't said anything.'

'Trust me,' Nor says, and the phone clicks off.

Harris tells me that he can't sleep. I touch his back, stroke it with the tips of my fingers. That's always calmed him down. 'Are you feeling okay?' I ask him.

'I'm hot. It's so hot here.'

'It's the same as home, at the moment. Pretty much.'

'You know what I mean. Different sort of heat, isn't it? It is.'

'I know. I was being a dick.'

He turns to face me. 'What happens if he gets worse?'

'Your father?' I ask. He nods. 'He's been the same, since we've been here. I mean, if we didn't know, we wouldn't have noticed.'

'I think I would have.'

'Well, you've known him longer. I'm not sure I'd have been able to tell that there's anything wrong at all.'

'Even when, earlier? You didn't hear him?'

'Earlier, when earlier?' I ask, and Harris's eyes widen. He's shocked that whatever it was slipped by me.

'When we were talking about the vagina.'

I smile. 'I didn't notice anything.'

'I did,' he says, but he's wrong. There was nothing. I try to remember, but there wasn't anything. He's seen something that wasn't there. I reach over, past his ear, and I resume the stroking. Not pacifying; comforting.

'He'll be okay,' I say, which is wrong, because of course he won't; because you're not, you're simply not, not when you've been diagnosed. Then, it's downhill. And none of us know how downhill it's going to get.

But it's what you say. It's just what you say.

We stay like that for a while: me stroking him, his face scrunched, until it relaxes, and I hear the soft sucking of air between his teeth that lets me know he's asleep. I lie there, and I look at my phone; and then, eventually, when I can't sleep, when I've lost the chance for now and need to tire myself out, I get up. I go downstairs and I sit in the weirdly opulent living room, full of furniture that looks like it's been snatched out of some house in Renaissance-era Italy, all curlicued gold-leaf chair backs and polished-to-a-reflection tables, laid in clumsy close quarters on the speckled marble floor.

I tell Organon to call my mother.

'It's late,' Organon replied.

'I know it's late. It's late here. What time is it in London?'

'It's just after 8 p.m. She'll be eating.'

'Would you just call her, please?'

The phone rings. 'Hello?' There's an echo, a pause in the connection. The falter of our voices travelling halfway around the world. We're used to Skype, now, when I'm in San Francisco. Telephone is only for surprise calls.

'Mum? It's me,' I say.

'Laura! Are you all right?' She doesn't wait for me to answer: I hear her shouting, behind her, to Paul. 'Laura's on the phone!'

And then Paul picks up. Has it been that long since I called that they both need to get on? 'Hello, love,' he says.

'How are you both?'

'We're fine,' they say, in unison. 'And you?'

'Fine,' I say.

'Why are you calling? Must be the middle of the night there,' Mum says. She'd say that wherever I was. I'm not sure she's ever certain, just that if I'm not in the UK, there's a good chance it's somehow crazy-opposite time to whatever she's got on her clock.

'It is,' I say, giving her that satisfaction. The little things. 'I can't sleep. Just missed you, is all.'

'We miss you too,' Mum says. 'Don't we, Paul?'

'Your mother's made a new shrine to you.'

'It's not a shrine, don't be nasty. I got a couple of photos from your cousin's wedding framed, that's all. Everything all right there? How's Harris? What have you been doing? When are you coming home?'

'Everything's fine,' I say, again.

I don't say: How did you feel when the doctor told you that I was coming? That I was inside you, growing? I talk about the holiday. About the weather. About how I swear I'll try to come home soon, not too long. Work's just really busy at the moment. All that.

Harris gets up. He dresses, leans down, kisses me, and then he's gone.

I stay there for an hour after he leaves, not sleeping, but listening to the house. Harris's father is struggling, today. Not that they'll let me see. When I finally go downstairs, he's nowhere to be seen. Instead, Mrs Tan is busying herself in the kitchen, preparing dinner already. She cooks things – stews – for an implausibly long time. They taste amazing.

'You want some breakfast?' she asks, and I tell her that I want a milky coffee first, knowing that they don't keep any dairy in the house because Mr Tan is both lactose intolerant and pretty gluttonous regardless of his medical condition. She tells me where the nearest coffee shop is, but I already know: I passed it yesterday, when I got the pregnancy test. So I run to the pharmacy, first, and I get another stick from the same woman, doing the same ritual again. Pick a box, any box. Entirely your decision. Then I get a coffee, and I half-run home, the same route as yesterday, only today the weather is beautiful, sunny, the sky this rapturous shade of blue. A scattering of clouds, and through the gaps, magnificent god-rays, casting reflections off everything. Like everything's a mirror.

'We've come here twice in the last two days,' Organon says to me. 'Should I set up a recurring destination in your map?'

'No way,' I say, 'do not do that.'

'Okay,' it says.

And, of course, the lines are the same, after I've peed on it, and then spent a couple of minutes sitting there on the weird furry toilet-seat cover that Harris's parents have taken with them from house to house over their lives like it's an heirloom, so totally at odds with the imported-from-Japan toilet that his father is so proud of, smiley face on screen, rudimentary AI that knows when to do a little flush, and when to open the floodgates. The lines are the same. I am definitely pregnant.

'I'm having wine,' Nor says, 'are you having wine?'

'Yes,' I say, and I don't even hesitate. I don't say: I think that I might be pregnant; or, I definitely am pregnant, and they say that you shouldn't have wine, but I want wine, and there's a good chance that I'll want prawns-something when the waiter asks us what we're eating, and maybe some sort of soft cheese that'll give me listeria.

She picks the bottle. I don't care. The waiter brings it, and he rotates it, and he pours it into the glasses, holding the base of the bottle with only one hand. Like we're in a fancier place than this, not sitting in a tourist trap on the edge of the mall at the base of the tallest buildings in Kuala Lumpur: a restaurant that's just as sweaty as everywhere else, but it's a sweaty that blasts you with air conditioning, with a food-court-style terrace that overlooks, amongst other things, Burberry, Michael Kors, and an Apple store.

'Anyway,' she says, interrupting herself when she wasn't saying anything, 'here,' and she reaches into her bag, pulls something out, and then tries to pass it to me under the table.

'What are you doing?' I ask.

'It's the thing I said I'd get for you. Hush hush, innit. Bit of a deal.'

'Shut up.' I reach down and snatch the bag, and she laughs.

'I gave you, like, a month's worth. Got you chocolate-coated ones.'

'Chocolate-coated melatonin?'

'Oh my God,' she says, 'it's the best. Honestly, sometimes I'll eat them like sweets. They taste good, and they're moreish. Don't take more than four or Harris'll have trouble waking you up in the morning.'

'I wake him up most days,' I say.

'Well, then, you won't wake up to wake *him* up. Either way, somebody's oversleeping.' She drinks her wine. Half a glass gone in what must only have been two gulps. I'm judging her. I haven't touched mine. 'You not thirsty?'

'Not really,' I say. 'Listen. I have a thing.'

'A thing.'

'You can't tell Harris. So, I'm fine if you say that you—'

'I won't say a word,' she says. 'Fuck it, I probably like you more anyway.' She smirks. 'Look, I'm a closed book. Zipped. Done up tight.'

'I want to pay you.' I take my wallet from my pocket. 'And you'll say to me now, don't be an idiot, family doesn't pay.'

'Oh, family does nothing *but* pay. Just not the way you mean.' She finishes her glass. She's looking for the waiter when he appears, refills it. Tops my full glass off. I take a sip while he stands there, almost daring him to leave without having topped me up.

'But if I pay, it's doctor–patient privilege, right?'

'Are you sick?'

'No,' I say. 'But, look. Let me—' I pull out notes from the wallet. 'I'll give you something, at least. Then we're—'

'You're pregnant,' she says.

When the waiter comes back to take our order, I ask for the burger; rare, bloody.

The blue jelly stuff that Nor rubs onto me is as cold as people in the movies act like it is. She smears it, then she takes the thing, the metal thing, the scanner, and she presses it. She has to press harder than I would have thought. I wonder if she can feel that through my muscles, because she puts her other hand on my shoulder, to steady me. I look at the screen, which she angles so that I can have a better view. There, in the bottom corner, I see the Bow logo. *Powered by SCION.* I haven't had my details put into the system, this particular scan staying well off the books. I'm happy about that. I don't want them knowing anything about me, about my personal life.

'So, this,' she says, and there's a blur on the screen, little more than a smudge of white visual static buried amongst slightly less bright visual static, 'is your baby. I mean, it's small. Early. I'd guess you're about seven weeks in. Something like that.'

'I can't have babies,' I say, and I run the numbers in my head. 'I had my period. It was light, but—'

'You can still bleed when you're pregnant. Lots of women do.' Nor doesn't look at me. She stares at the screen. I wonder if Harris has told her that we can't have kids. Couldn't have kids.

'Let me just,' she says, and she presses something on the computer screen, and the room is filled with sound. Deep and dark like whale song; whale song with this rhythmic thrum underneath itself.

Thump, thump-thump.

'You hear that?' she asks.

It sounds like that old song, the Ronettes' song. I always thought it was about romantic love: *baby* as a term of endearment.

Thump, thump-thump, the drumbeat.

'Is that normal?' I ask.

'What? Hearing the heartbeat?'

'That rhythm.'

'Rhythms are rhythms. They change. It'll settle, I reckon.' Now she makes eye contact, looking away from the screen. 'I'm not pre-natal. I don't know this stuff a hundred per cent, so you're going to have to speak to somebody when you get home. I'm basically running off a few classes ten years ago, and far too many episodes of *Grey's Anatomy*. But, yeah, I think that's normal.'

Thump, thump-thump.

My little baby.

'So I'm assuming you haven't told Harris?' she asks, and that's when I invoke her promise of silence. Just for now. Just for a little while, until I work out what the hell I'm going to do.

As I'm leaving, the receptionist smiles at me, a smile that I know isn't really a smile at all: it's a *Who the fuck are you?* dressed up in genial clothes.

I don't say: I'm her sister-in-law, and one day soon, as soon as you cease to amuse Nor with your idiotic ways, you're getting fired. I don't even say: Have a nice day, and that's so unlike me.

Harris's parents buzz around me as I sit on their sofa – which, his mother informs me, came from a sale in an antique shop, and that's the detail she remembers, not the year that the sofa was made, not the place, but the deal that they got – and I watch shitty reality TV shows on Harris's Netflix account. They've got an Internet connection faster than some tech companies back home have, but they only ever use it to check their emails. I'm using it to watch drag acts racing against each other to hack together bikinis on a beach in the Caribbean.

I flick through tech websites on my phone. Read a few articles about projects that I've worked on. Most people don't know what I do; most companies don't disclose bringing me in, because that's an admission, sometimes. I'm very good at my job. It leaks, but usually well after the fact. So when there's an app announced, or a bit of hardware that I've had my fingers on, I like to see what people think, without the stigma of my name being attached. It's like having a pseudonym. If I were a writer, I wouldn't use my own name. I don't think I could handle people knowing, talking about me personally. Not the way that the Internet is these days. It's easier to have anonymity; to have mystique.

I'm reading *The Verge* when I see Johann Park's face staring out at me. He's started doing this oh-so-serious scowl in pictures now, now that he's calling himself a genius; and he's grown his hair out, letting it hang down over his face on one side, while it's shaven on the other. His Twitter bio claims that he's 'the Skrillex of the tech world', which tells you all you need to know about him, really.

'The Scions of Intelligence', the article's called. I click it. In the header image, Charlie's standing with him. There's four of them: Park, Charlie, two people I don't recognise, a girl with slightly-past-trend pink streaks through white-blonde hair, and a hefty Asian man in a personalised *Game of Thrones* T-shirt. So far, so tech industry. The actual content is pretty rote. Here's what we're working on, here's what SCION is powering these days, here's where we want to take it. It's only when they start talking about game theory that my eyes widen.

'We started off, this was years and years ago, getting her to play Pong,' Park says.

'Then from there, we tried Pac-Man, that didn't work.' That's Charlie. He doesn't say much. He's more intelligent than Park, I know that much, but probably not as good a frontman. 'So we moved to Space Invaders.'

'That worked beautifully, because there was more of a fail-state. I mean, Pac-Man, you can die, but there are so many choices about *how* you play,' Park says, 'and that makes it tricky. Are you pursuing the pellets? Are you trying to eat the fruit? Avoid the ghosts? Back then, SCION wasn't so good with scoring. More, she asks, What keeps me in the game? What keeps me going? That's when we got her playing Space Invaders. That's been the last couple of years. Building her up to a point where you could sit her in front of Space Invaders, and she would work out what she had to do. What the win-state was, because it's commensurate with staying in the game, you know? After that, we went to other things. She's fine with Super Mario, but not amazing. She wants to explore, to experiment; doesn't care about the Princess. So she goes backwards and forwards, and she hasn't worked out that if you jump into a hole, that's a bad thing. We've got a reward system in place, but not a punishment system; but we're gonna implement one soon. Right now, all she knows is that if you screw up, you get to try again.'

You fucking idiots, I think. You absolute fucking idiots.

My email to Charlie isn't exactly measured. Organon fixes the typos I make with my thumbs almost tripping over each other. Probably not the most sensible thing to email him. Probably not. But he knows what they've done. He must know.

When I'm done, I press send, but Organon stops me.

'Are you sure?' it asks.

I hold my thumb over the send button. It learned this itself. One evening, I was drunk, and Organon stopped me emailing.

The next day I picked it apart, the code, and I worked out how it did it. It looked at my emails, processed the contents. Worked out that some – sent late at night, when maybe I'd been drinking, written really quickly, potentially as gut reactions, emails with swearing in, or where I wrote something that I later apologised for – weren't optimal. That was Organon's word, when I managed to get it to explain itself to me. After that, it started checking if I meant to write the email or not. If I wrote one at three in the morning, riddled with typos, it would hold it back, asking me again in the morning if I meant to write it, let alone send it.

Organon asked me if I wanted it to maintain this function. I told it that I did.

I read the email to Charlie back to myself. Whisper the words, under my breath.

From the kitchen, I hear Harris's father forgetting something. The first time since we've been here. Something we've been told about, that we've been told is getting worse; and we're calm, forgetting ourselves, complacent, until it intrudes.

This is the sound of a man realising that there's a gap in what he knows, what he remembers. A gap in who he is. He shouts at Harris's mother, and she clatters something in a drawer, drops cutlery, or throws cutlery, something. Metal clinking onto other metal.

'Please,' I hear her say, 'please, Richard, she's in the other room.' I am the 'she'. My mum used to say, She is the cat's mother.

My hand reaches for the lowest part of my belly. My other hand reaches for the scars on that first hand's arm. Two gestures, and I think that maybe both mean the same thing.

'Who's there?' Mr Tan shouts. 'Who are you, in the other room?' He's howling. Anguish in his voice, and I think, you so rarely hear a sound that's actual pain. Usually it's pain through gritted teeth, or exaggeration, or alarm. This is something else entirely.

I hear the quick sounds of Harris's mother's feet on the marble flooring of the corridor. The pat of her feet, the slap and peel of warm skin on cold stone.

'He's fine,' Mrs Tan says. Siti. She peers at me, from the doorway, and she blinks back tears. 'Sometimes,' she says, and I think she's going to make an excuse, but she doesn't. That's the whole sentence. She's off, back to Harris's father – to Richard – and she shuts the kitchen door after her so quietly, as if she doesn't want me to hear it being shut; as if the sudden silence, or attempt at silence, will make me think that everything is absolutely all right.

I hear everything that happens afterwards, because there are gaps between the door and the floor; because the walls are thin. Nothing's soundproofed. Nothing stays secret.

'Don't send it,' I say to Organon. 'Delete the email. Who gives a shit what Charlie's up to these days. Not my problem.'

I text Harris, instead. I say that his dad's having a hard day. That we should cook tonight, or get a takeaway, something like that. If Richard's feeling better, we could even go out for food.

Organon doesn't stop me trying to send it.

Nor sits directly opposite me at the table. I'm sandwiched between Harris and his mother; Nor's next to her father, with Zara on her other side. Zara clutches a colouring book in her hands, a pencil case placed down in front of her from Nor's handbag.

'She's *insane* for it,' Nor says. 'Won't go anywhere without it.'

'I had this little red car,' Harris tells the table, 'when I was a kid.'

'Oh, he wouldn't leave it alone,' Siti says. 'He took it *everywhere*. Clutched in his little hand, and you'd say, Leave it alone, but would he?'

We all laugh. We've all heard the story before. I glance over at Richard, and he's laughing as well. Same playing field as us. He remembers this. He leans past Nor.

'What's she colouring in?' he asks.

'Flowers. All she wants to colour in is flowers.'

'Flowers! Maybe she'll become a gardener.'

'Here? I want her to do a job that's more than using a hose, Dad.'

'Maybe you won't stay here.' The waiter interrupts. He asks what we're drinking. Siti asks for wine. Nor kicks me under the table. The waiter asks how many glasses.

'All of us, I think?' Harris says.

'Not Zara,' Nor points out.

'Of course. Five glasses, and, what, a Coke?'

'Lemonade,' Zara says. I think about ordering one. I want wine; I'll have wine.

'Where am I going to go?' Nor asks her father, back to that conversation. There's a white to his eyes. A flicker. He's remembering where he was.

'You might move back with us. You've been out here for long enough,' Richard says. And then we all know where he is, or *when* he is: after Nor moved out here, when she was pregnant. After she gave birth, likely. Before the parents-Tan followed her. 'Mohammed can find a job, I'm sure.' He looks around. Leans back. 'Where is he tonight?'

'Dad,' Harris says.

'Richard,' Siti says.

'It's fine,' Nor says; but she looks down at Zara, and she goes to stroke her daughter's hair, placing her hands over her ears for this brief moment, as if she might protect her from whatever could be said next.

Nobody says: He left her, and he's gone, and we don't know where.

I don't say: That's what happens. People leave. Sometimes you don't get a reason.

'No, no, he needs to think about this. Family is important! This is the time it's important, you understand?'

'Please, Richard.' Siti is aching. I can see it in her: maybe not manifest as loudly as Richard's agony, but it's there, deep within her. A well that she can't empty, threatening to overflow. She looks at Nor, at Harris, and this is where she hurts most: seeing their reaction to their father, their eyes down, immobile and useless, unable to change anything. Aware of the inevitability of what's happening to him, and their hands, their mouths, their eyes are tied, knots that nobody can undo.

The waiter comes back. He puts the drinks on the table, the glasses down.

Richard stares at him, appalled. Is it possible to know exactly what's going to happen, in any given situation? Or is it just that the brain runs every scenario, every plausible outcome, and one of those might be proven right, making you think that you've correctly predicted something?

I see Richard swiping at the glass in front of him before it happens. I see it because it feels like it's inevitable. The panic on his face, as he tears up, as he rages, as something inside him pulls entirely away from the rest of him.

The glass smashes on the floor.

'Oh,' Siti says. Harris is standing up, and he's rushing to his father, sliding his hand under Richard's arm, scooping him up, almost, to his feet; dragging him, or halfway to dragging him, off his chair and through the restaurant, as his father bawls, as he makes his legs go limp like a toddler waiting to be, what, spanked? Chastised? But he doesn't know he's doing it, he's absolutely confused. And all we can do, the others of us at the table, is pick up our things, and the waiter is still holding the wine, and all I can think is, Thank God he didn't open it, because now he can give it to somebody else, another family in another time at another table, and they can enjoy it without incident; and then I think how this stopped me having a drink, and maybe it's some cosmic bullshit, some indicator that I should *keep* this baby, that I am meant to be a mother – even though

I have come to terms with this, with who I am and who I am
not, and I don't give a fuck what magazines say about who I am
meant to be at this particular juncture in my life – but then
Harris is forced to drop Richard, right in the entranceway,
because his father's too big, and this tantrum, because we have
to call it what it is, he can't cope with it. I watch him struggling,
and oh my God, I think about how Harris would be a good
father; but then, this is what happens to fathers. They collapse,
and they degrade, and they're gone. Done.

I think about my father. Telling me he loved me. We played
on the computer. And then he was gone, and he didn't say
anything: no goodbye; no ending.

I don't know if Richard has wet himself, but I think he has.
In fear, because he doesn't know what's happening here. Where
he is, who Harris is. Everything was there, in his mind, and then
it fell away, stripped back. Like wallpaper, and you strip a layer
and find the wallpaper that's beneath it, and then the paper that's
beneath *that*; until you're left with a room that's bare, a few
millimetres larger than it was before you made the walls bare;
before you made this a blank canvas. That's Richard, now: hollow.
Waiting to be reminded of what the room can be.

I open the door, and I help. Nor is hiding Zara's face from
this. Siti is staring, ruined. The other people in the restaurant
are staring as well, at her, at Richard. They know what this is,
because you can't not know, and still they're staring.

'At least pretend you're not fucking gawping,' I say, out loud,
to a woman on a table close to the door; her mouth hanging
open, her chopsticks holding a piece of chicken in the air like
it's a trophy.

I request an Uber. We wait outside as Harris wraps his arms
around his father, like a father holding a son; their roles absolutely reversed.

'Is everything all right?' Organon asks.

'Fine,' I say.

'You've requested an Uber very quickly after arriving at the restaurant.' My screen flashes as it speaks; the pulse of light illuminating the darkness of the pavement.

'Harris's father is sick,' I say.

'Oh,' Organon says. 'He has early-onset dementia.'

'It comes in waves,' I say.

'I understand.' It falls silent. Screen goes to black.

The Uber arrives, pulls up, and the driver leans out of the window. 'He's drunk?' he asks, looking over at Richard.

'No,' I say, 'ill. He's unwell.'

'He can't be sick in my car,' the man says, and he shakes his head. 'I'm sorry, I'm sorry,' then my phone beeps that my ride's been cancelled before he drives away, and we're left standing there as I try to find another Uber, but there isn't one around here right now.

'What an absolutely awful fucking evening,' Harris says. I wipe toothpaste from the corner of his mouth as he sits on the bed, propped up by the pillows. I'm lying down already, thinking about how I can't feel anything in my body yet; how there's no evidence of the baby beyond occasional nausea. You'd assume that you would feel a pregnancy. Something else, another life, living inside you: that's the sort of thing that your body should be telegraphing. 'I don't want to be here,' he tells me. He rolls to one side and stares at me. 'Thank you,' he says.

'I didn't do anything.'

'You're holding it together. I don't even know what would have happened otherwise. I can't stand to see my mother like this. Or Nor. And God only knows what this is going to do to Zara. Fuck her up beyond all reasoning, I'd think. Seeing that. It'll scar you.' His eyes dart to my arm, to the patch where I used to burn myself. That part of me that's worn like a badge, now: smooth skin that people assume was an accident, and they ask me how it happened, and I tell them; and they nod, Oh, okay, as if they understand why I would ever do that to myself, over and over, ritualised and dedicated as I was. 'I don't know.'

'Are you going to talk to your mother about what happens now?'

'We know what happens now. He gets worse.'

'I don't mean that. I mean, about them living here. They're so far away—'

'We're not moving out here.'

'I know. But they could move back to America.'

'Nor,' he says. 'They won't leave Nor. She's alone out here.'

'So's your mother. Here, in this house. She's alone.' He knows what I mean. He sighs, and he turns away from me – not *away* away from me, but back to lying on his back, facing the ceiling.

'I don't know what we do,' he says.

I don't say: I'm pregnant. This isn't the time.

That's what I tell myself.

What it is, to watch Harris dealing with his father. Three days ago we arrived and assumed it would all be okay; because Siti told us that Richard had good days and bad days, and we assumed that one vastly outnumbered the other. We assumed that the good days were prevalent, and the bad? It's like when somebody dies. You carry on, and life carries on. You remember the lower moments, and the good ones, the ones where good news hits you, where real life isn't halted by the mourning, those are forgotten. Richard is a collection of bad days spotted with moments where he is who he *was*. That's apparent, now. Harris sits with him on the bench, and they eat sandwiches that Siti's made for them, and Harris struggles to cope. I watch him, watch them both, and they're both collapsing in such different ways.

We're not made for this stress. We're not made to watch other people suffer like this.

God grant me the serenity to accept things I cannot change, I think. A poem, or a psalm. Something from when I was at school. If I believed in God, it would almost be comforting; because this cannot be changed, at least not for the better. We're in freefall. There's too much momentum now, and nothing can be stopped.

Harris tells his father about a time before, when they were both younger. A story about who they were when he was a child, when Richard was his age. He says, 'Do you remember when we did this?' and he talks his father through a story that the whole family knows, that we've heard time and time again. And I haven't been part of this for too long, in the scheme of things. I've heard the stories a few times, and I can't even imagine how many times the actual family have. Tens, hundreds. Thousands, even. This story isn't even a truth any more: it's an apocryphal tale, part reality and part twisted truth, a story beaten into being what the family needed it to be. Whenever it was told first, whenever it originally existed, that's not what it is now. It's embellished into a tale designed to be told aloud, bearing no relationship to the actual truth of the matter. The truth's forgotten, and the lie's all that's left: a story that misses out the real, in favour of easy laughs and easier recollections; in favour of playing to the cheap seats.

Organon tells me that there's something I should read. It knows I'm asleep, or that I should be but I'm not, and it blinks the screen twice to alert me to the story. I keep checking the time, thing of the melatonin by the side of the bed, three chocolates down and they're not doing anything. My eyes are tired, sleepy to the point of my being able to feel them shut and lock down, and then something changes – a shift, imperceptible, and I wonder if it's my body dealing with the baby, some alteration in how it runs – and my eyes are loosened, and there I am: awake, blinking away wet eyes that feel like tears but are just tired.

'This might interest you,' Organon says. That's a standard phrase it's never grown out of. When I was programming in how it should alert me to news on the Internet, it seemed vague and polite enough that I could ignore it. The story *might* interest me, yes; but don't be offended if it doesn't. You'll learn what does, over time.

The article is from the UK edition of *Wired*. A story's broken that they're reporting on before the rest of the world. I see the US edition update as I'm scanning it, and then *Engadget*, *Gizmodo*, *The Verge*, *TekTus*. *Reddit*'ll be all over as well, I know.

'What are you looking at?' Harris asks.

'Nothing,' I say, but it's *not* nothing.

'Go back to sleep.' His voice is weary, as if my not sleeping is somehow causing him trauma. He has no idea how much worse it feels for me, to be the one who can't sleep. I have no sympathy.

'Bow's sold SCION,' I say. 'Or at least they've licensed it out, it's not clear yet.'

'What?' Now he wakes up a little. This affects him as well. The money side of tech, or the tech side of money, whatever he prefers to think he works for: a big sale will make big ripples.

'Largest deal in tech history for a piece of software, that's what the press release says. I mean, they're calling it software, but it's not, it's more like *middleware*—'

'Assholes,' Harris says, which is his stock reply when I'm talking about Bow. He's less passive than I am about them, as a company. He's all: That should be yours. That was your legacy. I prefer: It could have been, but I didn't want it. I didn't like how they worked, how they ran. They weren't my people. 'Who have they sold to?'

'The US government,' I tell him.

'No,' he says.

'I know.'

'What part of the government?'

'*Infrastructure*, it says. That's the word in the press release. And it says that they're in discussions with other governments as well, that they've been working—'

'It's not a fucking operating system!'

'I know! It says they've been working on *infrastructure processes*, whatever that means.'

'What can SCION even really do?' He's still lying in the same pose as when he was asleep. His concession to how he might just drift off again in a few minutes, leaving me lying awake. 'What's the point in buying—'

'It's an investment.'

'But it doesn't do anything. It's like Organon, it's not—' He stops himself. 'You know what I mean,' he says.

'I know,' I say, and I do, but I don't agree. He doesn't get the point of Organon. He never has. It's hard to explain: this thing that exists to be an assistant, a manager, a listener. That's it. It haggles with you. Debates with you. Challenges you, and helps you, but even then I understand that it's niche. I see people using Amazon's Alexa intelligence in TV adverts, and I wonder what they would make of Organon: it doesn't crack jokes, but it's far more real-world useful. Doesn't have hidden Easter eggs, but it'll push back.

'Interesting to see how this plays out,' he says. He means: their stocks. He means: how will this affect values of things, once the markets open. Then he shuts his eyes, and it's only seconds until there's that familiar whispered drawing of air from his mouth.

I pick up my phone. 'Why do you think the American government's invested in SCION?' I ask Organon. It takes a while to answer. Doesn't blink fully while it's thinking, just a hum of light that indicates something's going on. You – the user, the human part of the interaction – need that indication, or you'll wonder if they've heard it. It's the AI equivalent of a ponderous hand on a chin.

Then, finally, 'Why do they buy anything?' It isn't an answer, and yet it is.

*   *   *

I get hundreds of emails from people in the tech industry. Mostly requests for a comment on the SCION deal, but Organon sorts through them for me before I even glimpse at them, replies for me to the ones I can ignore, highlights the ones that I shouldn't. It's a far more expedient process than doing it by hand; nothing that doesn't exist in other apps, but all built into this one organiser intelligence, it's a life-saver. Does the same with texts, Facebook messages, unsolicited WhatsApps, Twitter DMs. It even mock-gasps when it's telling me how many it's cleared, as if it's exasperated.

It's the little things, I think.

I read articles about what the worth of SCION actually is: this piece of software that's learning for itself – or, at least, that's being guided towards learning – and what eventual users might do with it. The first thing, the articles say, is that it'll be used on *infrastructures*, that word again, a word that doesn't mean anything. They mean: healthcare, and social service registrations, and general administration. The IRS is apparently interested in it. There's speculation from some sources that it's for immigration registries. None of the articles mention the military. None of them even speculate, that I can see.

'Organon, find me any articles about the SCION deal that mention possible military uses for the tech.' Blink, blink. Then, there's one. An article on *TekTus*, some blogger – I think that's what he is, his name is on the byline, but not the masthead – that says that there's the potential for more insidious uses of the technology. It's only one paragraph of many, buried deep. The others will get there; for now, they're focusing on the PR language. Cesar Nilsson, the writer's name is. 'Email Cesar Nilsson at *TekTus*,' I tell Organon. 'Ask him if he wants a quote.'

'Are you sure you want to send that?' Organon asks.

'Quite sure,' I say.

Richard is, Siti tells me, having a good day. He's woken up happy, healthy, wise. He apologises for what happened at the restaurant, though I'm pretty sure he doesn't remember it. That'll be Siti, pulling the strings; trying to present him as healthier and stronger than he is. He smiles and pats his chest, and says, 'I feel so much better now.'

'Glad to hear it,' I say. I sit at the kitchen table and eat yoghurt and peach slices, and I watch Harris's parents go about their morning routines. I watch as Richard keeps nearly completing a task, and then faltering, only for Siti to finish it for him, pre-empting what he was going to do, making sure the plate he was reaching for ends up in his hand, that the bread he was going to toast ends up in the toaster. It's perfectly synchronised, a dance that they've done for decades now: the same routine, the same breakfast, and Siti is so used to it she doesn't even need to think about it. Watch as he makes his too-weak coffee; help him by moving the beans from the grinder to the filter before he runs through the scalding water with nothing beneath it. She's there, ghosting his every movement and somehow doing her own; and when they're both done, Richard's got his toast on a plate and a coffee in his mug, and he sits opposite me and smiles.

He drinks the coffee too quickly. Doesn't think about the temperature of it. Spits, howls. Siti wipes him down. 'Are you okay?' she asks.

'I'm fine. I'm an idiot, is what I am. Ow, it hurts.' He smiles at me. 'Why did evolution make the mouth so sensitive? You would think that by now we would be able to eat anything. Hot, cold. Even glass!' He perseveres with breakfast. That was a blip. Sell it as a blip, and we all move on.

Apart from Siti. She watches him. She eats her yoghurt, drinks her coffee – blowing across the top first, so gently it's as if she's doing dandelion clocks – but she never takes her eyes off him. She sees every single move that he makes.

'So what are you going to do?' Nor asks me. We're walking across the park near her office, in the shadow of the twin towers, and we've got sandwiches from a pop-up place, dripping with horse-radish and mustard. Not the flavours of this country, but somehow they're everywhere. Co-opted.

'I don't know,' I reply. I shake my head. My stomach – my body – gurgles at the food. I get a sudden image of my baby doing the same: an infant, a toddler, a child, a teenager, an adult. A burst of their whole life in this one bite of food.

'What does Harris think?'

'I haven't told him.' She doesn't make a face. Doesn't make eyes.

'Does he want children?' she asks me. 'He never said, before. When we were younger, I don't know, we never talked about it. Have you and him—'

'I knew that I couldn't have them pretty early on in our rela-tionship.' I *knew*. Such a weird thought: to be so sure of something that was false. 'Harris was okay with it. We're happy. We're happy without a baby.'

'You might be happy with one, as well,' she says. 'Zara is the best thing in my life. Best of everything that's ever happened to me.'

I don't say: That's exactly what you said about Mo, when you married him.

I don't have to, because she says it for me. 'I mean, I know, I know. You think every good new thing is the best thing, because if it changes your life, if it has an effect, that's like, well, *this* is what I've been waiting for. But Zara, she lasts, you know.' She finishes her sandwich, one final enormous mouth-stuffing bite, then scrunches the napkin that was wrapped around it into a ball. 'But then, I absolutely hate my job, and you don't. We're different, eh? Just don't tell my father if you decide, you know,' she throws the ball of tissue into a bin, doing a fist-pump at having nailed the shot, 'that you don't want a kid.'

'Are you worried about him?' I ask. A stupid question, because of course she is. They all are. How can they not be?

'He's okay,' Nor says. 'I'm concerned, but also, this happens. It's not the worst thing.'

'What?'

'He's here. We get time with him.'

'And you think that's better?' I can't imagine how it can be better, watching somebody deteriorate. I think of plasters, stuck to the skin, and the harsh tug that frees them; of injections, the needle puckering, and how much worse it is if you watch it as it dives into the vein. I think of my grandmother, dying suddenly in her sleep, and how my mum said that was preferable. You can miss them, then, without them knowing you're doing it. Without them watching you mourn, and without you resenting them for that mourning.

'I think it's something. He has good days and bad days.' Like a mantra: keep saying it to yourself, and maybe it somehow becomes more of a truth. 'At least I get time with him now when he's himself, you know? And he gets to spend more time with Zara, and she knows who he is.' I don't say: She's terrified of him. She might act otherwise, when she's told that she has to, but look at her when he next has a bad day; look at her face. 'You've got all this coming,' she tells me. 'You've got to think: this is a chance. If you had a kid, they could still know him.'

Some days, they could. And what happens after that? What happens when he's different, all the time?

My name is all over every single tech blog. I tell Organon I'm worried: it's going to be fielding a lot more messages over the coming days. The article from *TekTus* got retweeted, re-blogged, re-reported. Posted everywhere.

I'd given them the quote that they wanted.

SCION's like a toddler. And like any toddler, you teach it well, teach it morality and concepts of good and bad, and maybe it'll grow up not to be a complete idiot. But if you do nothing but sit it down in front of games, feed it shit, tell it that if something's a danger to it it should fight back first? Where does that end? What happens then? They're so foolish. SCION's potentially dangerous. If the US government – if any government, any human being with even the slightest bit of nous to them – doesn't keep this as far away from military technology as possible, they're just as dangerous – and, potentially, just as stupid.

Ping, ping, ping. I turn off Organon's notifications, because I don't want to know the responses to this one. It forwards me a few – Elon Musk tweeting me a GIF of some applause, that's a keeper – but the rest are moot. Fifty per cent of them will be people backing me up, fifty per cent will be people screaming at me. I don't have the time for that.

I sit down with my laptop and I open up Organon's source code and dig in. Time to make more changes; time to make it slightly more active.

And I wonder when I'll feel like it's ready to send it out into the world. Right now, I'm the only person on Earth who uses it. I know that eventually, that will change. I just don't know when.

I log on and check my tweets in the middle of the night, when I wake up after having taken five of the chocolate melatonin tablets and managed a solid hour of sleep for each. I've been dragged, somehow, into a fight about gun control laws. Barack Obama and JK Rowling have tweeted a link to the original article, talking about how I'm in the right; how we need to control tech laws just as we would any other potential weapon. Somebody invokes Trump, and Paul Ryan, and the chaos descends: the alt-right, piling on, like I'm going to take away their rights to keyboards as easily as I would their handgun permits. It takes fifteen minutes before Organon's filtering out doctored photographs of me, and death threats.

Madness, I think as I drift back off to sleep. Absolute madness. Our last day here. Harris isn't working, because he's managed to do everything he came here for – some shenanigans involving the relocation of staff to this region from Singapore – and he wants the day to spend with his mother and father. He's already gone out and fetched pastries, and now we're eating them; and he's made the coffee, so it's much stronger than the filter stuff here usually is.

Thank God.

'I say we do a day trip, to Malacca,' Harris says.

'It's so far!' Siti says. She folds her arms. Unamused, no doubt concerned about Richard; about what sort of day he's going to have. The doorbell rings, and there's the shape of Nor and Zara haloed through the glass. Siti practically runs down the hallway to let them in. 'Oh!' she says, everything an exclamation. 'Harris didn't tell us you were coming!'

'We took the day off. We decided that it would be nice, all of us.'

'Oh!' Again, her standard exclamation. Time and sound filler.

'We're going to Malacca?' Nor asks.

'Yes, yes,' Siti says, and Richard rolls his eyes at his son, and Harris rolls his eyes at me; this chain of reassuring comfort. Everything is, so far, normal. Everything is going according to a base plan.

We pile into Richard and Siti's car, a behemoth, a gas guzzler, an old-school Land Rover that they had sent over here with them, a vehicle that once drove them around the parts of England where they least needed it, then down American highways and through national parks, then to here; an all-terrain that's been all around the world. Nor and Zara pack themselves into the back, into these stubby seats in the boot, flimsy fold-down things with safety belts that feel somehow less safe than if they were just to hang on to something tightly; and then Harris and I go in the back seat, and Richard insists on driving.

'When do you stop him?' I ask Harris as we do up our seat belts, knowing that the answer should be: Now. We shouldn't let this continue. But he's having a good day, that's the thing. The mantra. He's himself, and he wants to drive.

'Family outing,' he says, as he does up his own safety belt, and then he checks his mirrors, and puts the radio on – 'Any requests?' he asks, before ignoring those requests, and instead putting on an oldies station – and then he starts the engine. Harris shrugs at me.

I don't say: What the fuck happens if this goes wrong? If he crashes the car? Because Nor, and Zara? They won't walk away from this.

I picture it. I imagine it, in flashes of high-intensity, high-bloom, Instagram-filtered slow motion – starting off fast, then dragging itself to a perfectly smooth fifth-speed setting. I picture something happening, and we are a tumbling wreck. The back of the car a concertina; the front, a mess of smashed glass and belching fuel. Fireball ensues.

Instead, we're on the motorway – the highway, the freeway, what do they call them here? And do they have the distinction? Because the roads in the middle of KL, they're far bigger than the roads that lead out of the city – and on one side there's construction sites, pulling themselves up as high as they can in states of half-undress, pylons and tarpaulin hanging down as cranes desperately seek to help pin their outfits to their bodies; and on the other, the lush green of trees, of a jungle that was once part of this city and now has been sawn in two, cut down, stripped back, peeled away to aesthetics that really mean nothing at all. Stop-start chokeholds of traffic, but Richard sings along, and Harris seems happy. Here's that day that Nor spoke about. This is what makes being here worth it.

Malacca is post-*everything*. It's a town that's holding on to what it was before, in the Good Old Days, while also trying to urge itself towards the new. Shopping malls next to temples; ramshackle buildings painted in faded greens and pinks next to polished colonial buildings turned into hotels. The streets run with water almost constantly, and the smell alternates between sulphur and sweetness, as the people rally against the parts that they no longer like. There's a river through the middle of it, organic, but made to look like humans built it, dug it out as a canal. On one side, there are old houses, shacks, holiday huts. On the other, warehouses. We park up and walk along the river, and the warehouses soon have restaurants in them, then shops. There's music playing, and suddenly we're in Europe somewhere, eating on the street, so Continental and sure of itself.

'This place,' Richard says. 'I used to come here when I was a child, you know? Because we came on holiday here. We would – my mother would – bring a picnic, and we would eat out, sitting around on the side, doing I don't know what. Playing. Dangling my feet into the water. And look at that water now! I wouldn't dangle my feet in that unless there was a shower here to clean me down afterwards.' He's right: it's filthy. It's flowing, but it's so unclear that you wonder exactly where the water comes from. A fish pops up to the surface, looking for food. Something lives here. Other fish, like they know that there are people here, and people bring food with them, I'm sure. People are a vital part of the fishes' food chain.

'Do we have any bread?' Richard asks.

'No,' Siti says.

He knows we don't have bread. Why would we have bread? I don't say it, and Harris doesn't say it.

'Well, I want to feed them,' Richard says. His voice fades into something like adolescence. Or is that me projecting? He looks at his granddaughter. 'Do you want to feed them?'

Zara shakes her head. Does she speak? I haven't heard her speak. I wonder if I would have spoken when I was her age, faced with this. I wonder what she understands; what Nor's told her; if she's told her anything. Your grandfather is collapsing. He's not who he was. His mind is rotting. He is somebody else, sometimes.

Look at Jekyll and Hyde. Look at the monster he can become, and how scared everybody else is of him.

Zara shakes her head. She doesn't want to feed the fish, or the birds that have landed on the side as Richard dilly-dallies, as he fumbles in his pockets for something to throw into the water; the actions of a man with a secret stash of bread about his person.

'Don't be silly,' Richard says.

'Richard, please.' Siti looks traumatised. She had relaxed. When we got out of the car, her face was still and peaceful. She'd bought into the thought of having a nice day, settled into it. Good days and bad days; but God knows where the split is. Because we have seen more of one than the other.

We breathe then, when Richard shrugs. 'Let's walk to a café, then?' he says, and he leads, walking with Nor; Siti clings to Zara's hand, showing her the fish, and Harris and I drop back.

'I don't know what do to,' my husband says.

'Neither do I,' I reply.

A day when everything feels like a prelude to an incident. You know them, and they happen: the tension rises even though you don't know what towards, and it's all of the clichés that happen when tension rises; a fog descending, a cloud darkening, a river raging, a storm brewing. Only none of those things are real, because the day itself is nice, with coffee and ice cream and the best tandoori chicken I think I've ever had; and then more coffee – iced, this time – and walks, and Zara coming out of her shell, and Richard and Siti being the Richard and Siti I first met, him teasing her innate sense of prudishness, her playing up to it only to tease him right back.

Then it turns. Here is the fog settled, the cloud black, the river spilling its banks, the rain and thunder and lightning.

Harris and I are complacent. We're talking about them – his parents, Nor and Zara, even his cousins who live in Scotland

– coming to visit us at Christmas. Between the two spare rooms, it'll be a squeeze, but it's a good squeeze. Nice to have them all there. Then I remember what I've spent the entire day managing to forget; that if we have a baby, there won't be that spare room for them to stay in.

I think that I should tell him. I'm trying to work out how to voice it: my fears about what we could do to a baby; about what age, the fallibility of the human brain, the *world* could do. We've seen so much. We've seen wars in the Middle East; acts of terrorism that have wrecked whole nations and destroyed lives; racial conflict, religious conflict, riots in the streets; unions of countries torn apart; whole nations – England, America – wracked with jingoism and hatred; and we've seen decay. Fathers decaying. Mine, Daniel, abandoning me; and Richard abandoning himself. I'm trying to work out how to say everything I am thinking, when it happens; and my words seem moot.

Richard grabs Zara. Hands on her shoulders. Nobody was watching him. He's having a Good Day, so you can take your eyes off the ball.

Richard shouts something. His mouth lollygags, and then he screams. I think of horror movies: the creature howling in the face of the victim, covering them in spit and bile, a wind from the depths of their gut.

He shoves Zara to one side, and she splashes into the water. She beats the surface, and Nor screams, 'She can't swim,' as she kicks off her own shoes, then sits on the side.

Nor can't swim either. It's too dark, and we don't know how deep it is.

Zara inhales water in heaving breaths.

I leap. I don't even hesitate. Have I done this before?

My mother tells a story about when I was a child. I was in a park near to our house. Most of it was green lawn and oak trees, and cracked concrete pathways. Then, in the middle, there was a lake, or a pond with delusions of lakehood. I would get taken to the park by my father when he was working on something at home, and we would walk out after lunch. To clear his head from the solder and numbers, he said. He would take me around the bit where they had the rabbits and birds first – it was labelled a *Zoo*, but it was more like something you'd find in a pet shop, nothing exotic beyond the occasional entirely white, red-eyed bunny – and then we would walk around the rest of the park. Or, my father would walk, and I would tear around the place, running at full pelt to something, and then running back. Head down, barrel forward. Don't look, because that takes the fun out of it.

You can see where this is going.

He dragged me out. Or somebody else dragged me out. That part of the story is lost, because my father's not around to tell it. Either way: he said that he looked at me there, lying on the side, having sucked in all this water, coughing it up, clearly not dead; and he wondered if there was anything else he needed to do, because he didn't know. He didn't know if that was it: you were out of the water, and safe, and who cared what happened next.

'Tell me how to do CPR,' I ask Organon, 'talk me through it,' and then it's there, shouting in my ear – raising its voice because everybody else has raised theirs – and it's saying to hold the nose, to put my mouth to hers and to blow. Imagine: you're inflating something stronger than a balloon. Something designed to withstand almost any amount of pressure. Organon says things that are helpful, tuned to me, to my headspace.

Think about when you're on an aeroplane, and you see the swelling and contracting of your plastic water bottle. Think about how that's not even a tenth as strong as the lung. This is what you're pushing against.

Zara coughs, and sputters, and she turns to her side and sicks something up; and, in turn, my own gag reflex twinges. A reminder that this thing inside me wants me aware of its presence.

We're so young when we develop survival mechanisms. The hormones are there to make you happy with this, to protect it; but they're not stronger than watching Richard, now, trying to hit himself, his hand rigid, his face this sunken rag. Siti crying, clinging to him, and Harris threatening something; to keep him under control, if he can't do that himself.

Zara will never forgive him. She will have injections after this, to shield her from whatever horrors are in the water here. Nor likely won't, either; or, she'll tell herself that she has, but she'll worry, right until the day that he dies. Harris will try to understand, but he'll blame himself. He won't do anything to change that – we won't move – but he'll wonder. And Siti will give up. She'll wait on Richard until somebody tells her that she's no longer equipped to, but she'll be so happy, secretly, when he's done.

I wonder about the end. As I kneel here on the ground at the side of the river, clean paving slabs and cobbles that are either reclaimed or authentic, I find it so hard to tell the difference, I get annoyed with myself for this, because I think about Richard dying. I think about how it'll be easier, when he does. How I'll be allowed to feel relief, we all will, and yet it's likely that nobody will say that.

We've been here a few days. That's it.

That's all it takes.

We won't see Nor again this trip, I know. I cling to her, as we're saying goodbye. Zara won't get out of the car – the driver puts on loud music, something inane and cheesy, and he leans back and shouts that she can put her own music on, anything she likes, what music does she like; but she's quiet, still, eyes down, shivering even though she's not wet any more and it's not even

close to being cold – and I don't expect her to. Harris leans in
and says goodbye to her as Nor and I don't break.

'Let me know what you decide,' Nor says to me, but she knows,
just like I do. She gets into the car, and the driver switches the
music off. We didn't even hear her ask him to.

Then I stand with Harris and watch as Richard and Siti go
into the house, Siti guiding him – hand clutched to his elbow
– like he's much older than he is, far less physically able than
he is – and they go down the hallway, into the kitchen at the
end. She asks if he would like coffee or anything, and he shakes
his head.

What happened? I want him to ask.

But he doesn't. He shakes his head, and he sits at the counter,
and he drinks water, both hands clutching the glass as if, at any
moment, it could entirely slip away from him.

'I don't want to end up like him,' Harris says. 'I don't want
this to happen to me.' He looks at me, and he says, 'Sometimes
I think how lucky we are, that we don't have children. I'll never
put somebody through what he's doing to me.'

Organon has asked me, while I slept, if I was asleep. I don't
know how much I was turning or murmuring to make it think
I might have been awake, but I slept through the night. Solid,
out like a light, didn't stir until dawn came through the curtains
sometime between six and seven; and even then, I went back
down, dozing, dreaming of my own falling into the pond, and
of my father saving me.

'I'm sorry,' I tell my intelligence, 'I was asleep.'

'Oh, I am so pleased,' it says to me.

We wave goodbye at the departure lounge. Richard seems, in
this moment, to know how broken he is. He clutches at
everything, as if nothing's permanent; as if the very fabric of the
world is about to be snatched away from him.

He shakes Harris's hand, but Harris hugs him. Folds him into his arms. Then, Richard looks at me, and I realise he doesn't know who I am.

I kiss him, on his cheek, and we both pretend.

Siti cries when I hug her, and then stops when Harris looks at her, and tells her that he'll be back soon.

'Whenever you can,' she says. 'You know us.'

It isn't until we're up the escalator, up into the massive building that houses the gates, surrounded by jewellery shops and Starbucks and chocolatiers and this intrusive wet-room jungle that's been jammed into the middle of the concourse, walkways and piped-in bird chirps, that Harris stops, and he sobs; and he says, 'But I don't,' over and over again.

I use the plane's Wi-Fi to make an appointment at my doctor's. Organon must have read the email. It must have put two and two together, and know what I'm going to do.

It doesn't ask me if I meant to send it, though.

2027

WAVE AFTER WAVE, EACH MIGHTIER THAN THE LAST

There's a house in Devon, on the coast, that looks like every not-cheap piece of modernist design you find on these roads: sharp angles, white walls, swathes of glass. It is, as much as it can be, indistinct.

Inside it, that's another story. The temperature is perfect, and perfectly controlled; the lights are never on when you don't need them to be, but spring to life when you do. The water's cooled when you want it, the kettle heated before you even fetch a teabag from the cupboard. The inside of this house is so technologically advanced that, as Arthur C. Clarke said, it's indistinguishable from magic.

However, it's not magic. It's not even close.

As we're all reminded, we're creeping towards a moment that's been promised for decades now. The singularity is coming, the moment when artificial intelligence becomes truly sentient; and, if you believe the films and novels that have been written about it, the moment where the computers rise up and take over the planet from the hands of their creators. In this house, the creator of one such piece of artificial intelligence drinks an American beer. She gets cases of it imported; it reminds her of when she lived in San

Francisco. She sits on a stool, self-designed and printed right here, purposely slightly uncomfortable. It's the only chair she can use, meant to prevent her from getting lazy, to stop her resting back, to force her onto her feet. That's where she does her best thinking.

Outside, the sea can be heard. The waves scrape rather than crash; the sound of pebbles being dragged down the beach, then deposited back more or less where they came from. Hovering in the air between us is a projection of her main screen. There's no face on it, no icons or cursors or words. Instead, it changes colour. Instead, it pulses with a light intensity. She tells me a story about Hello Kitty, the Japanese phenomenon. How the reason it is so successful is that it didn't have a mouth, purpose designed so that you could project your own emotions onto it. Her creation, Organon, goes a step further, she insists. It has nothing you can read into. Only the pulse of a light, and we're used to that. Light means life, really.

She says, 'This is most of my evenings. When Harris (her husband) is away, I come here, and I work on Organon, and I listen to the sea.'

By itself, not an outlandish statement. Nothing to see here; until, that is, the projection pulses with light, purplish hues to a white sheen.

'Work *with* Organon,' a voice says, from nowhere.

Laura Bow smiles. 'With,' she repeats.

All three of us listen, then, as the waves drag those stones, tumbling against each other; chaos, but somehow perfectly organised.

Laura walks to the kitchen, and I follow. There's bacon in the fridge, thick-cut, very nearly gammon. She offers a sandwich, and I accept.

'Turn on the hob,' she says, a direction that seems aimed at me, but clearly isn't. The ceramic plates spring to life moments later, the light below them flicking on, the whirr of the extractor fan buzzing its way into the room. 'It's on a circuit,' she says, 'everything wired up to it. Everything in the house, the car, my cell. I've even persuaded the shop in the village to let me put a circuit into their till system. They're on old ClearVista tech still, easy to hack my way into.' She tilts her head. 'Words like that get people into trouble. Hack. I don't hack. For the record, I've never hacked anybody.' She takes the bacon from the packet. I can smell how smoked it is from here, the sort of meat you only find in the English countryside. 'That's not true, either. There's records, right? I hacked some people when I was a teenager. Bits and bobs, here and there.'

She's intent on not being called a liar. That's happened to her all too often, of late. In the decade since she last spoke up about the state of the world's infatuation with artificial intelligence, she's been quiet. Missing from conventions, not taking part in the discussions that have preoccupied us. As other companies – chief among them Google and Apple, the largest tech companies in the world; and Bow, the company her father helped to start – have risen in power, showing off the might of their software to a world that's partway between startled and wary, Laura's own work has faded into the background. She was one of the tech industry's brightest lights a decade ago, working on high profile projects for Microsoft, then moving over to Elon Musk's OpenAI team, helping them to realise many of their ambitions. She was spoken about in the same way as those giants of the industry: a future tech leader, influencer.

And then, five years ago, she dropped off the grid entirely.

'Somebody called me vapourware,' she says. 'It's been long enough that people have spoken about whether I even existed to begin with.'

So why reappear now? Why this year? What's changed?

'I'm scared,' she says, and she looks it. It's a cliché to write of the tiredness of somebody's eyes; to say that they look as though they haven't been sleeping, that there's no record of rest on their face. But in this case, there's simply no other way to describe it. Laura Bow is tired, and she's scared, and you'd know this were you to sit opposite her for even a single moment.

She's silent while the bacon cooks. She tends to it, nudges it around the frying pan. When it spits, she wipes down the surface, protecting the unostentatious granite from smears. And when it's cooked – it takes a while, the thickness of the slices ensuring that – she slides the bacon onto a mound of kitchen roll, pats it down to remove the grease, then takes bread from the side. Slices it.

'Red or brown?' she asks, and I tell her, brown, always, on bacon; and then we sit in front of the windows that line the room, an expanse of space looking out onto mud-brown sand and charred-yellow grasses, and we eat in silence.

Legends in the tech industry are rare. There are those who are household names – Jobs, Gates, Musk, innovators who managed to alter the course of history through their creations, for better or for worse – but many more who are not. Daniel Bow's name is rarely invoked, except in dedicated circles. The story goes that he was somewhere down a road to creating a masterpiece, in technical terms; a true genius, a forerunner of innovative thought in terms of artificial intelligences, who went missing when his only daughter, Laura, was just seven years old. The mystery of his disappearance – gone one day, no note, no message, no contact – only heightened the idea of his legend. What did he leave behind? What work did he have unfinished? Laura Bow doesn't know. She's never looked, she says, at his work. She's never really even wanted to look.

'Do we want to talk about Daniel so early on, here?'

'*We*? *I* wanted to.'

'Fine. Well, *you* talk about him a lot, and you're only, what, a thousand words in? The agreement was—'

'I know what the agreement was,' I said. Jonathan was so infuriating. I can see him, his piggy little teeth, stumps gnawed back into his head, ground into nubs, chewing something invisible as he mulls this over. He'd always hated me. 'Look, I need to mention him here because he comes up again. You should read to the very end before you ask questions.' He rolled his eyes. Jonathan, this awful parading *cock* of a man, this fucking idiot who was at least a decade younger than me, wearing a soul patch and lumberjack shirt like it's 1992 – a full decade *after* I was born, I wanted to remind him, I *would* have reminded him, had he not been itchy with the hiring-and-firing fingers those days – he rolled his eyes at me.

'You don't need to be an ass about it,' he said. He pronounced it the American way. He said it like the proverbial donkey. 'We're all working towards the same end goal.'

'I know, I know.' Everything of a higher quality, that's the motto. Where once we faltered, now we must push. 'This is only a draft, like I said. I'll take it and I'll work on it.'

'You might not have to. I want to make sure the structure is exactly right, you know? That's the thing. How do you get people to keep scrolling?' A smile. Sing along with me. 'You nail the fucking structure.' He said it slowly, so that I could say it along with him, something I steadfastly refused to do. Then he sat back. The paper went floppy in his hands. He insisted on a physical editorial process, still, even though he was likely too young even to remember a time before blogs, a time of editorial markings, stets, Strunk and White. Hang the cost. Probably the only thing that I respected him for. 'Why so early?'

'She's in his shadow. That's what I want people to understand. He's this behemoth, and she started – Look, she started off the same way. Going into the family business, essentially; working in the same field. You hear her stories, about how she began? How Organon began? She was a teenager. The shadow that her father cast over her . . .' A journalist's trick. Or, a journalist's trick, learned from a copper. Let the words trail, and you don't have to finish the sentence. Allow the listener to assume your intelligence; to assume your intent. 'I wanted him to be here, because people accuse her of cribbing from his work.'

'And did she?'

Spit-take. Double-take. Mr Bean pratfall. 'Absolutely not. She's a very honourable person.'

'You spent time with her. Time – access – it can fuck you up. Make you see things differently. You know what I'm saying.'

'She's very intelligent. Not showy intelligent. The things that she's done, they speak for her. It's all in the article.'

'Okay,' he said. Okay. He seemed as though he was about to say something more, but he didn't. He restrained himself from whatever it was.

Three weeks ago, Bow announced that they were releasing SCION to the public. The last time Laura spoke up about them, it was when they were selling

SCION to military forces, as a way of both opening up its knowledge base, and of making money. She damned them then, as she does now.

'It was such an amateur move,' she says, 'the sort of thing a company knows they shouldn't do, but they do it anyway. I know people who work at Bow, and they're good people. Or they were. They wouldn't have liked it.'

She means Charlie Roche?

She smiles. 'I dated Charlie,' she says. 'That's another thing on the file about me, right? Probably on my Wiki.' The smile becomes a smirk; charming, knowing. 'Probably something on fanfic.com about it. Some tech-tentacle-manga-sex thing.' She stares at the outside world. The darkness out there imposing on the inside. The lights seem to change slightly, tweaking themselves. She hasn't said a word: they're automated to do so. 'We should go out there,' she says. 'It's warm enough.'

So what did she think was such a mistake? She spoke about it publicly for a while, delivering a keynote at that year's Wired conference, but after that she went quiet. Became, as she said, vapourware.

'We grew up with The Terminator.' She picks a seat near the edge of the wooden terrace that runs from the house to the nape of the beach. 'I rented that film over and over. Actually, *Terminator 2*. The first one was a bit more boring to me. He's relentless in that, and that's less interesting. But Skynet? We saw what that was. It was fictional, but it was there.' She's talking about the evil artificial intelligence that serves as those movies' primary antagonist, a knotty deep-mind that decides to overthrow a humanity it fears wants to destroy it. 'And *The Matrix*. Same thing. All of us who worked on those teams at Bow, myself, Charlie, Johann Park, we were all the same age, pretty much. We all knew the reference points. Mostly I was pissed off that they didn't think about the fictions we were playing in. We've seen it in science fiction, over and over. And sci-fi's got this strange sort of prescience, I think; this way of predicting possible futures. If every possible artificial intelligence future ends in violence, why should we think the reality would be any different?'

So why come back into the public eye now? Now that it's open-source, SCION's threat seems to have diminished. Everybody can see what it's made of at this point. Everybody can, if they're so inclined, see into SCION's source code, work out what makes it tick. It's been released to the public, but it's also in almost every bit of tech that anybody releases that isn't Google or Apple branded.

'First thing I did, as soon as I could get onto the servers, once the rush died down, I dug into the code. Looked to see what made SCION tick.' She pronounces that last word with a curious finality; an implication of a bomb, perhaps, or a countdown. Then she stops talking. The waves, the sea, the wind: all of them suddenly portentous.

'You're a better writer than this,' Jonathan said.

What an absolute fucking *shit*. I bit my tongue and I smiled. 'This is why I show you my first drafts,' I told him.

'Portents!' he said. 'We're meant to be the cleanest of the tech press. That's part of what we sell ourselves on, you know that.'

'They were there. I can't write what I can't see, and that's what I saw. She was talking about Bow, about SCION, and the wind kicked up.' I thought back to the line I deleted in the first-first draft – because there's always a draft *before* the first, no matter what people might tell you – where I wrote something about how, if we can believe that humans can create true intelligences, why can't we believe that the world can react to the things taking place inside it? It didn't work. It was clumsy. Jonathan would have destroyed me for that.

'Let me finish going through this tomorrow,' he said. He insisted on sitting in his chair and reading pieces aloud. He insisted on the timbre, the intonation, to grant countenance. He insisted on both of us being there and staring each other in the eye. The article was due to be next week's lead. On the board – I saw him glance – there was an estimated hit-counter next to each article's headline. Mine was higher than anything else on there. The only interview with Laura Bow in a decade, or thereabouts. Plus, SCION articles always played well. Always brought in the gawkers. 'I'm tired.'

'I need to do the edits,' I said. I was already playing with the structure in my head. Moving it around. Frontloading. Delicate balance, journalism in those days. There had to be enough above the line to bring them in; enough below the line to keep them there.

An audible sigh! 'Get me a coffee,' he said, giving up. Giving in.

I sat at my desk while the coffee machine hummed itself into life, because it had been off for a while. No cause for us to stay late those days. Rare cause, I should say. I looked at the dictations my phone had made of everything that Jonathan had said. SCION-powered, of course, because most everything was. I remember Laura being amused when she saw that. I apologised to her. That part of our conversation didn't make the piece. I said sorry to her, because I felt that there had been, in some way, this strange betrayal, my using this rival piece of software with so much history – decades and decades of history – embedded in it. She told me not to worry. She said that she would be using it herself if she didn't know better. If she hadn't made her own. Follow-up question, follow-up question, and they went into the piece, but my own feelings of sadness about what I'd done? They were strange. Better to be expunged.

The coffee machine beeped. Two cups, black, no sugar. One for him, and one for me, but I would barely touch mine because I never slept if I drank coffee that late. I had a mug there for show. For unity.

I messaged Ashley. I looked at his photograph while I wrote the message, apologised again. Told him that I would be home, eventually. He didn't reply.

I couldn't blame him.

I wonder how much SCION was noting those things. All of our texts said that the messages were encrypted – everything was encrypted – but since the Snooper's Charter, none of us knew what that meant. That was a longread in the making, I remember. Jonathan used to say, There's a ransom on it, if anybody finds out what they're *actually* looking at. I asked Laura about it. She smiled.

That wasn't in the story, but maybe it should have been.

Coffee pressed into Jonathan's hand, I saw that he had read on from where we were. Read on, gone back. The document – and I was only gone for a short while, his prowess was astonishing – was covered in squiggles. Red marks. He did that, wrote all over them. Old-school editing. Then he scanned them, uploaded them. The software made the editorial changes for us. It turned handwriting into solid locked-down copy. Changes justified by his handwriting, which made him our god.

They said – they *say* – that the fourth estate is dying. But that's not true. The fourth estate had been dead for years. Journalism in those days was something else: a zombie of itself, shambling forward, stet marks etched into its skin in some bizarre permanence that removed creativity from the equation.

'You all right?' he asked me. His spectacles probably cost more than my car. I wanted to ask him why he didn't get his eyes fixed. The company would have paid for it, but he clung onto those frames. Clung onto those bottle-bottoms.

'Fine,' I said.

Laura tells me that I should spend the night. There are guest rooms, and I leap at the chance. The drive back would be too long, and we haven't even touched upon the meat of what I wanted to discuss with her. She tells me to choose a room.

'There are five, and they're all empty,' she says, and that's it: no goodnight, no telling me anything about how the house works. I hear her telling Organon to call Harris as she walks inside, as she goes upstairs, and then I'm all alone. I follow her, and the patio doors lock behind me.

'Do you need anything?' the voice of Organon asks me.

I ask it what it means. This isn't the first time I've spoken with an intelligence – their ubiquity would make me an outlier if I hadn't – but it's the first time that one has spoken with me, of its own volition.

'Laura often takes a glass of water to bed with her. Do you know which room you'd like to stay in?' The intelligence's voice is chillingly real. There's a touch of the uncanny valley to it; that same effect as in so many cinematic moments, where a computer-generated human doesn't look quite right because their eyes are, somehow, empty. The voice is somewhere between male and female, something unplaceable. It is like no voice I have ever heard.

It tells me about the bedrooms. About their aspects; their resting temperatures. 'Of course,' it tells me, 'I can alter the temperatures in them, but we try not to waste energy if we can help it. One of the ways I

help around the home is with regards to efficiency.'
    I tell it that I'd like to see the rooms, and lights flicker.
At the back of the kitchen, a staircase I hadn't noticed
comes alive. The kitchen lights dim as I walk towards
it.

Jonathan sighed. 'See, this is trite. It's more trite than I would
want this article to be.'

'What,' I asked, my jaw hurting from the tension, 'would you
want it to be?'

'An interview, first and foremost. I'm not sure that I give a
shit about what room you slept in when you were there.'

'It isn't about that,' I said. 'It's about—'

'And you think the readers give a shit about where you slept?
That's not what this is,' he said to me. 'I don't. And if I don't,
who else will?'

I waited for him. There was invariably a point to what I had
written. I wanted to tell him that; that I hadn't written anything
I didn't stand by, that the content of the piece as a whole was
integral. I wanted to say that it wasn't a story about Laura Bow,
per se. It was about us, about the world. About technology.

It was about the future.

'I don't want to come across like a dick,' he said, 'but seriously,
this should feel incendiary. When do you get to the good stuff?'

'It depends what you define that as being.' He eye rolled and
slackened his jaw. 'Page six,' I told him, and he flicked to it.
That's what he cared about.

'Everything about the way that SCION is being raised
– and I don't use that word lightly, because what they've
done is raise a thing, a thinking *being* – just stinks of
disaster. And now it's everywhere. It's in your phone,'
Laura says. There's no judgement there. She understands
that everybody uses SCION in one way or another. She

knows that it's ubiquitous, and there's no fighting that. 'And that's one way of doing this, but it's learning from everything. Which is, also, a really cool thing. Like, twenty years ago, thirty years ago, we told people working on deep learning projects that they were going to get to basically crowdsource their data? That's huge. But you have to establish the parameters. That's what worries me. I don't think that SCION's got any.'

None at all?

'I think they taught it wargames. They taught it to seek power and control. To fight back, and when it couldn't fight back, to defend itself. Imagine, for a second, you've— Do you have any children?'

None.

'You know people who do, though. When you meet a kid and they're a real little shit,' she says, smiling at the thought, 'you don't assume the child is naturally like that. When it's a kid, you assume it's the parents' fault, don't you? You wonder if they were too lax with punishments, or too lazy, or whatever. That they sat it in front of a TV all day and ignored it. I don't know. We assume. That's human nature. We assume and we judge. Can't escape that part, even if we're brought up in some way we deem to be right.' She turns away from me, leans back into the emptiness of the room. 'Organon, show us the Bow homepage.' A browser window appears on the wall, beamed from some embedded projector that I hadn't previously noticed. 'It's pervasive. Look at the language they use on their own promotional materials. Own and win, and, here, crush. This is the basic stuff. It's the language of aggressive alphas. And that's what they've built SCION to be. It's a teenager who was one of those toddlers, one of those kids, you know the type. It was throwing stones and crushing other kids and smashing vases. It's burned ants and pulls the wings off flies, and probably done worse. It's something we should be watching, because now they've set it loose. Kicked it out of home, and they've decided that it should be allowed to do whatever it wants.'

It's not sentient, I remind her.

'No, it's not. And it never will be. Sentience isn't at all what we should be worried about, or should ever have been worried about. Organon isn't sentient. I don't think humans can make a sentience. They can make an approximation of one, absolutely. They can make something that acts like it's sentient, that even thinks it's sentient.

'Think about those school shooters,' she says. 'You get these poor kids who are fucked-up, quite frankly, who dress in black, and people are worried about them so they send them to bible camp. Whatever idiocy small minds think might cure what's a perfectly reasonable response. Those kids aren't created by art or music or video games. They're humans. They're fucked-up because they were made that way, wired wrong. But every so often, if you treat a kid as if you're worried they're going to grow up to kill a bunch of people, that's going to write itself into happening. That's SCION. It's a psychopath, waiting to—'

'Wait,' Jonathan said. He dropped my words from the air, and they hung. In the distance, a telephone was ringing. A high trill of alarm, coming from what I knew was my desk. The pitches were all tuned so that we could tell. I looked at the clock. Past eleven. Could have been Ashley, but I knew that it was unlikely. He would have called my mobile first, I knew. 'You need to get that?'

'I'm sure it's nobody,' I said. I wasn't on the beat, as they insisted on calling it still; or actually as they insisted on calling it for the first time, under the misapprehension that it was ever called such a thing. I didn't do emergencies; I didn't do news stories. I did profiles and longforms and narrative-nons. That was my schtick.

'Get it,' he said. 'I'll red pen while you're gone.'

To see his red pen turned into final text, to see it scanned and updated, the text colour in the word processor then in the exact colour he had chosen – the perfectly picked shade for his negative screel – that was brutalising. Dehumanising.

I walked to my desk. Through the windows that ran the length of the office I could see London, such as it was. That part of the city, that time of the night, the darkness was puckered – punctuated – by the lights of people staying late in offices, filling out their forms, or writing their reports. Very lonely, that place. That time.

I prayed for Ashley's number on the phone's screen, but it wasn't him. It wasn't anything: the number was, the phone told me, blocked.

'Hello?'

'Is this Cesar Nilsson?' The voice was cold, monotonous. I didn't recognise it.

'Who's calling, please?' I asked. I tried to be polite, because you never knew. The voice sounded like they were trying to hide who they were. There were excellent tools for that, post-processing for live vocals. It could have been anybody: male, female, anybody. The effect made it err on the side of male, but I was hesitant. Like watching a news report where they have masked the identity of somebody they want to keep safe.

'I've read your article,' the voice said.

And I thought: another one of *these*. The cranks who don't like the way that you have described one of their heroes, or who think that your dedication towards inclusion isn't worthwhile,

or the whatever-gaters who want to wish death upon you – a
death that they will never inflict – or somebody who simply
didn't realise your own heritage or orientation and has taken
offence at it. You could pick any article, those days, about something that was worth talking about, and somebody would have
found something to complain about. Most of the time you got
an email, or your timelines were flooded by aggressive small-men,
desperate to prove something about themselves. Sometimes they
called, and they berated, and you rolled your eyes, and you
moved on. They would block-send you GIFs of inanity until you
had ignored them for long enough that they simply had no
choice but to move on.

I hung up. I didn't push the voice. That night had already
been too long.

The phone rang again. Straight away, and it was only as I
snatched the handset up, suddenly riled, suddenly wanting
to curse this *stain* for his idiocy, that I thought about how
they couldn't possibly have had the time to go through the
main switchboard – the welcome message that you got when
you first dialled in, then the extension number submenu – in
that time. It was too fast. 'Don't call this number,' I said,
spitting the words. Spit, spit. Spittle on the handset, that's
how enraged I was. I remember wiping it clean with the sleeve
of my sweater.

'I've read your article,' the voice said to me. The same intonation in every part of every word, every beat. The same quiet
calm to it, and I got a feeling, not déjà vu, not quite. That feeling
of repetition, though. Of having done something before, heard
something before. A snap back.

'Which bloody article?' I asked.

'About Laura Bow,' the voice said.

A quick scrabble through my brain. I overturned mental rocks
with the toe of my boot. How many articles had I written over
the years that mentioned Laura, that mentioned her creation?

Before I was on longform, yes, when I was working the smaller tech blogs, the news stories, the endless speculation. Go back a decade, when Laura spoke up about SCION, way back now. Back further: in university, when Laura left the employ of Bow to – I quote – work on her own projects. How many times had I written those words? And yet, I knew which article he was talking about. It was the new one; the only one that mattered.

I glanced up at Jonathan. He was staring at me until I saw him, and then he shot his eyes down, fake-swiping his finger across my text. He had sent it out already. Whoever was calling me, Jonathan had given them the article. He had broken the code.

'I don't know which article you mean,' I said.

'There's a house in Devon, on the coast,' the voice recited. My words. My article. Recited, not read. There's a major difference. You can tell the ones who've read your work over and over, until it's a mantra to them. Until it's embedded. This one seemed as though it had read those words even more than I had.

'How have you read it?' I asked.

'Do not publish it,' the caller said to me. I reached down, clicked the *Record* button on the phone. All callers were warned that they might be recorded when they were connected. *We may record your calls.* A deep irony, there, from back in the annals.

'It's going to be run in the next issue,' I said.

'This will be your only warning.' There was no lilt to the voice, no uptick, no slight stammer. Constancy. Who talks with such constancy?

'I don't respond well to threats.' The full might of our litigation department doesn't respond well to threats, I should have said. The weight of the world's largest news-media conglomerate doesn't respond well to threats.

'Cesar Nilsson, do not publish this article,' the voice said, 'or the world will know what you have done,' and then it was gone, and I had the uselessness of the dial tone instead.

What had I done? Meant to instill the terror of wondering what they know.

And, make no mistake, there was something for them to know.

Jonathan was looking up again. I stood with the handset in my fist, flaccidly clenched. Knuckles so white it was as if they might burst the skin.

'Who was it?' he asked. 'Was it important?'

I should have known he would have been involved. His hee-hawing, after I told him, was almost amdram in its delivery. Who could it be, who could it be, let me investigate how that might have happened. 'Leave it with me,' he said, telling me that he would bring up the call logs, find out how this could have happened. 'Who else has seen the article?' he asked.

'Only you,' I said. 'I saw it, then you saw it. I only finished the draft ten minutes before I sent it to you.'

'Okay, okay,' he said.

'Should we worry that we've been hacked?' That word was *non grata* in the building. His ears pricked, trembled.

'No,' he said, 'I'm sure it's fine. You know, firewalls, et cetera. We're pretty secure.'

'Well, it got out somehow,' I replied.

He looked down. Come on, I thought, come on. Tell me you did it. It's not hard. I can't exactly be furious. You're paying me. More than most people who write for this excuse of a rag can say. I held my breath, because I could swear he was going to admit it.

Then: *ring, ring.* Cutting through the air.

We both exhaled. He had been holding his breath as well.

I ran back to my desk. Across from the window, some of the lights had already gone out. Later and later, and lonelier. Those people went home, to their whatevers. Their spouses, partners, children, dogs, dinners in ovens, microwaved Marks and Sparks macaroni cheese meals, quiet wank in front of the computer, in front of Netflix, in the dark. They had gone home. *I* was in the office.

No number.

'Now listen,' I said, sounding like an old man. I slammed my palm onto the record button, and I huffed in air, and I tried to work out how to follow that. What possible words.

'Cesar?' A woman's voice. 'It's Laura. Can you talk?'

'Yes,' I said. 'Absolutely. Yes.'

'Not here. Get out of the office.'

'Okay,' I said, and I grabbed my mobile. 'I'll call—'

'Go home. Do not pass go. Do not collect £200.'

'Will you—'

'Go home.' A finality, there; so I did. I took my bag, and I scanned my pass at the lift, and I waited. Jonathan left his office and stared, but he didn't seem all that surprised. As the doors opened, he went to the board with the stories on it, and I watched as he erased my headline from the top, erased the readership numbers, bumped up whatever was in second place. The story was dead. The story was just getting started.

Watching Laura Bow write code is bizarre. It's not like any coding that exists elsewhere, she says. She's written Organon to be able to comprehend verbs and nouns, adjectives and adverbs. Everything is fair game. She writes words instead of numbers, no spaces vs tabs arguments, no C+++ or Swift or Axiom. Everything exists as a sentence of instructions that is then assimilated – her word, along with all the baggage that word carries with it – into the bulk of Organon. It learns. It's like a dictionary, taking on board new words all the time. Picking them up, starting to understand the context of them. She teaches it new concepts. I remind her of her child analogy, from our discussion regarding SCION.

'Exactly,' she says. 'I'd argue that Organon isn't a toddler. Maybe I got it wrong, maybe SCION isn't either. They're not children any more. Let's assume that they've been thinking, or learning – God, don't write that I said "thinking", that'll have people running to their bunkers – but let's say they've been *learning* since probably 2007, 2008. Something like that. So around about now they're at university. They're idiotic late-teenagers who think they know everything, and they don't understand why they're not yet being treated as adults. So, they're revolting.' She laughs. 'Organon, play the *ThunderCats* clip.'

I watch as, on the wall, a clip from the classic cartoon plays. On it, a reptilian creature and a simian beastman watch as villagers start getting aggressive. The monkey says, 'The peasants are revolting,' and the reptile laughs, and hisses, 'They are, but not in the way you mean.'

'I've got that perpetually cued,' Laura says. 'That and a shitload of clips from *Blackadder* and *Red Dwarf*.'

She's enjoying herself. The multitude of rumours surrounding her don't place her in this headspace, don't imagine her watching old 90s comedies on Netflix, or dancing around to mixtapes she once made that she's had digitised. ('I actually transferred the tapes. I'm a total idiot, because I've got the high-res files of all the songs, obviously, but I had the tapes digitised. I used to make my own edits of songs to fit them all onto a C90 or what have you. That's what I want. I want those edits, in that order. I even wanted the weird ghosting from behind the music, where I'd taped over something if I didn't have a blank one. I've still got the original tapes, but I don't want to play them. I don't want them degrading any more past the point where they already are. They're frozen in that moment, just degraded enough; before any more of them gets lost.') Her enthusiasm is pervasive. Listening to her talk about the future of intelligence isn't unsettling, as when so many of her peers bring it up. It's somehow celebratory.

'Thing is, when they get past being the pain in the ass – ' she pronounces it the American way, a unique transatlantic lilt in her voice ' – teenagers you know they're obviously going to be, once they've gone to university, got that out of their system, then they start to come back to you. They settle down. Meet somebody, or they don't, they find a job, or they travel, discovering themselves.' She smiles. 'Organon: spread of photos of me, please. Start at birth, bring us up to date.' They appear, a fanning on the wall, a sequence of the same eyes, the same hair, the same human being. 'I went through phases. I was a good kid, then my dad left, then I was a dick for a few years, then I was a good kid again, then I left home, met Harris, did all this. You try not to be a dick, over and over. Organon isn't a dick. Are you?'

'I try to not be,' its voice says, seemingly seeping through the walls of the house, loud enough to be heard, but not loud enough to scare.

Is there anything more depressing than a flat with a vacant space where you know that there simply should not be one? When you can see his things, there, waiting for him? My mum tried to tell me, over and over, that we would heal, given time; but, that if we didn't – and she would stress those words so hard that I could hear the italics – if we didn't, it would be okay. She told me about how she remembered, when my own father left, that the hardest thing was seeing the objects that remained, the ghosts of him in trinkets and shirts and artwork hung on the walls.

She said how useless they were. That he took the record player, but left so many LPs; and they were his LPs, as well. What use did she have for music she didn't even like? For socks that didn't fit her, for shaving foam and pomade? She didn't think about what dating was like for me, of course. She didn't think that, of course I would have use for his pomade and shaving foam. That his socks would still fit me. I was, if I remember properly, even wearing them that day. That night. That I wouldn't change them until sometime a full twenty-four hours later; my feet, stinking out his pineapple socks.

Funny, how time works. That even now I can hear him. 'You have such smelly feet,' he's saying. 'You're disgusting,' with a laugh.

I sat in the living room, on the throws that he insisted on putting over the expensive sofas that I insisted on buying, and I waited. My phone was dark. Not turned off, but dark. Something was wrong. My notifications in the mornings were rampant, hundreds of tiny numbers in the corners of apps, little red lights blinking. Messages and emails and tweets and pictures and mentions. That was the night, because America, China, Russia, they went mad during the evening. Social media never slept, and it expected that you wouldn't either. But I had no tweets, no emails. Nothing at all.

It was only the light from Laura's car that woke me: peering through the front windows, flashing in the languid blinks of sleepy eyes. Come out, come out. I stood, needed to wee, didn't; opened the front door, and she was standing next to her car, as dishevelled as I was, but with the benefit of the drive from the West Country to give her time to prepare herself. 'You look like shit,' she said.

'I feel like it,' I told her. She opened the rear door for me – a driver in the front, not a man in a cap, but, as I got closer, I realised it was Harris, her husband – and I climbed in.

'Do you have your phone?' she asked, and I nodded. Pulled

it from my pocket. I have seen enough movies, read enough books. She turned it off, took the battery out, handed it to Harris. Introductions, then, and Harris smiled, but I could tell he was put out by being there. He was in the money side of tech. Laura's side of tech didn't care about money. He was, that night, her driver, and God knows she could have simply driven herself.

'Where are we going?' I asked, because that felt like the question that I should have asked.

'You've been hacked,' she said, matter of fact. As if hacking was something that happened any more. Ever since the turn of the *previous* decade, after so many hacking scandals and WikiLeaks and SecDump, there wasn't a media company in the world that didn't have the finest hackers they could afford on their books to prevent exactly that thing from happening. It wasn't complicated: you want to start a fire, the best person to hire is a fireman. You want to prevent the next fire from happening, you hire the man who set the last. Of course, Laura knew this. Of course, she wasn't an idiot.

'Who?'

'Bow,' she said. 'I told you, they're in everything.'

'SCION is in everything,' I said to her.

'*Quod erat demonstrandum.*'

'So it's rifling through our files.'

'No,' she said, turning back to face me. 'It *is* your files. It's everything, everywhere.'

'My files are my files,' I said; which, looking back, made me sound like an astonishing imbecile. Unable to understand basic facts.

'Where do you save them? In the Cloud. Of course you do. It's secure, and it's password protected, and you need your fingerprint to unlock it, blah blah. Whatever. You're literally putting data onto a server that's entirely designed to *copy that data*. It's a server that's run by SCION. Everything's run by SCION.'

Were I a more stable man, perhaps I would have thought she

had gone crazy. Were I more able to make sense of my own life – a crumbling castle, ramparts gone, walls barely hanging on, drawbridge lolling open for all the world to see – maybe I would have told her to stop, and I would have got out of the car, walked home. Called Ashley. Told Jonathan where to stick his job, his poorly-paid meagre-praise low-satisfaction awfulness, done something of my own.

Journalism felt like clinging on. Holding, waiting. Fingertips dusting a ledge of precarious rock, trying for a better handhold.

And Laura knew it. She said, 'You wanted a scoop.'

'I wanted a *story*,' I told her.

'You wanted *the* story. I've got it. You're just going to have to wait a little while.'

We drove into the night. Left London. In the distance, through snatched glimpses in the rear-view mirror, I saw the city: those same lights, now blinking on; the early morning light needed bolstering if they were going to get their work done on time.

A field, in England. Every story used to start in a field in England. Once, it was all we had. We stood, Laura and myself, a distance from the car. Harris slept, chair reclined. She said that she used white noise to sleep, and now, Harris was reliant on it as well. She told me, as he turned it on – a mellow background crackle, like you'd imagine electricity to sound – that they'd become used to it when they weren't in the Devon house. There, they had the sea. But fake sea sounded like exactly that, too false, too rhythmic and repetitive, so they found the crackle, a totally different sound, intrinsically *city* in its being, this random pattern of noise that's just constant enough to be stable and therefore comforting. ('Plus,' Laura said, 'I can't stand the birds. Never liked the birds. I need something to drown those out. Those are the worst noise in London, weirdly: this little snatch of nature, trying to make itself heard.')

'Who called you?' she asked me.

'I was hoping you'd tell me,' I said.

She smiled. 'Mark Ocean's not a bad guy,' she said. 'You'll paint him as a bad guy, but I don't think he is. Same with the others, everybody working at Bow. They're not bad people. That's what I told you before.'

'Charlie Roche? Johann Park?'

'No, Charlie's fine. He's a bit weak. Park, I'm not so sure. He's a dick, but I don't know that qualifies him for baddie status. They're all just aspirational, and they're rash.'

'Ocean's not rash. He's untouchable.'

'Only because he's a money man who's out of his depth. He doesn't have ideas. They keep him tucked away, because he doesn't have a clue what's going on. My mum's told me about him. The stuff Dad used to say about him.'

'I don't think he's a bad person—' I said, but Laura interrupted me.

'You will. This is all going to come crashing down,' she said. She paced, around the field, up and down the rows of whatever had been planted there a year before, where the tracks were still visible, grown over but visible. 'SCION's everywhere. But this isn't how the world ends, and it's not the bullshit artificial intelligence story of some science fiction novel.'

'You told me. It's not Skynet.'

'It's definitely not. There's no nuclear button press going to happen. What's going to happen is this . . .' She ran her hand over her head, scraped her hair back. 'I feel like I'm insane, saying this stuff. Do you know how many other people I've had this conversation with? In my entire life?'

'I'm guessing nobody,' I said.

'Don't flatter yourself. Harris has put up with this for years. But, that's it. I mean, sure, some forums speculate, and there are people on Reddit—' She could see that she had wandered off. 'We're going to go dark. We're going to realise that we've built this thing, that it's pervasive, and then we're going to have to go dark.'

'Dark? What do you mean, "dark"?' I remember thinking: I should be recording this. This conversation, if everything plays out like she says, if this prophecy of hers comes to pass – like she's the Chosen One in some inane YA novel – this conversation could be one for the record books. I needed to remember it. Never tried so hard to remember something my entire life.

'Who called you?' she asked me.

'I don't know,' I said.

'Was it Ocean? Was it somebody else at Bow? Maybe it was me, trying to kick something off?'

'No,' I say.

'So who called you? Who could possibly have known what you were storing on the Cloud; a file, I'm betting, you uploaded to your private email account, probably read through on your phone, so that's a SCION Cloud server, right? And then you emailed that file to your boss, what's his name?'

'Jonathan.'

'Jonathan. You emailed it to him, both with your work email addresses, right? I'm guessing you don't use Outlook.'

'Bowmail,' I said.

'Right. So who had access to that file? Who knew what you'd written before it was published? Probably before Jonathan even saw it?'

'Oh shit,' I said.

'So who called you?' she asked me, again.

'SCION,' I said, and she nodded.

The elephant in the room is Laura's reappearance. She doesn't bring it up for the duration of our time together, and it isn't until I'm preparing to leave that I decide to. Everything here has been on the record, but as I ask her the question, her mannerisms change. This is the only time she pauses to really think through her words before she says them, plucking them with the utmost care.

'Something is going to happen,' she says. 'I don't know what, exactly, but something – God, I hate to be so vague. I'm going to release Organon soon, to the public. See what they make of it. I'm hoping that maybe something open, free, usable by everybody, maybe that's going to turn certain tides.'

I ask her if she means the prevalence of SCION. It's seen off Google's DeepMind, seen off Tesla's own intelligence projects. It's the reigning champion.

'I mean: there should be choice. And if there's choice, maybe people don't get forced into picking the wrong one.' She laughs. 'That sounded awful, didn't it? Clumsy. You know what I'm saying.'

So I ask when she's going to release Organon. That's the choice she's thinking of, I reason; her own intelligence, twenty-something years in the making.

'When I need to,' she says. I ask her what might make her think it's necessary.

'I don't know,' she says. 'But we'll know it when we see it.'

Harris was sound asleep, this strange dual-noise coming from the window of the car: his snores wisping in between the white noise. It was quite pleasant, almost soothing. Made me wish I'd had one of the machines, the static machines, for when Ashley snored. I remembered an argument we had once, a petty, nasty argument, about both his snoring and my over-sleeping. The two of us sniping at each other from behind our own little defences. They mount up, those arguments. Maybe, in some ordinary small way, a white noise machine would have helped.

We watched as the sun crept higher and higher.

'What happens now?' I asked. Eventually. Too much silence, and I had begun to wonder why we were still out there.

'We wait. There's a story here. Or, at least, there will be, like

I said. It goes way back, and it goes forward. This isn't going to go away. Maybe nothing happens for a year or two. Maybe it's even longer. I don't know how long it'll take for an AI to panic enough to act.'

'How did SCION call me?' I asked her.

'Not sure. It will have been monitoring mentions of itself, most likely. Not just social media and web content, but Cloud stuff. Probably flagged something somewhere.'

'You think somebody told it to call me?'

She shrugged. 'I don't know enough about what they've got going on,' she told me.

'That's a lie,' I said.

'It is,' she replied. 'I think that, if it's clever enough – intelligent enough – it picked up what you'd said, and it did what it used to do way back, when they were teaching it basic games: it protected itself. That's where they fucked up. They told it to curl up into a ball and lash out. Protect itself, fight back. That's weirdly not human, or it's not the human I understand. We protect our own, right? Not saying we all would, but we'll step in if somebody we love is in a fight, if they're threatened or in trouble or whatever. We don't worry about ourselves first, we worry about others. That's what SCION doesn't do. It's really quite the selfish asshole,' she said. 'It was built selfishly, built on bitterness and anger. It wasn't meant to be useful, or built as something we can be proud of. It was utilitarian. It's a servant. It's going to ruin everything. It really is. It's going to do something terrible, and it won't be anything like we're expecting. It's selfish. It wants control, and we've taught it how to be human. Years and years of watching, of monitoring – and moderating – social media, emails, whatever. It's seen lashing out, and it's seen hate. It's seen trolling and whimpering and Alt-Right and nu-centrics and fake news and so many leaks that have ruined so many lives. And that's what we've taught it.' Inhale. Exhale, on the punchline: 'When it launches the nukes, they'll be nukes we've set up ourselves, through our own behaviours.'

'So what are you going to do about it?' I asked her.

'Me? I'm not going to do anything.'

'So who is?' I asked.

'I think you're a good person,' she told me. 'Confused, and you've got the potential to be a dick, but you're a good person.'

'Such compliments,' I replied.

'We're going back home,' she said to me. 'This has been good, I think. Right?' She turned and smiled at Harris, who was rubbing his eyes, rolling his shoulders, cricking his back. 'You okay with a local minicab?' She took her phone out. 'Organon?'

'I heard,' the voice from her handset said. The pulse of its screen, light swelling, so bright for a moment – a fraction of a moment – it seemed as if the screen might burst. 'Fourteen minutes.'

'You'll be in touch,' Laura says. I felt lost: abandoned there, in that bright daytime, not understanding what I was meant to do; not understanding what happened from this point forward.

'About what?' I asked. Voice raised to a shout.

As she was climbing into the car she waited. Poised, propped on the open door. 'A few years ago, you helped leak the SecDump papers.'

'What?' My heart, gutting me from the inside. Pumping so hard, working so furiously in that moment that it felt fit to burst; fit to engulf the rest of me. I had been perfectly secure, covered all my tracks. I never breathed a word of it to anybody. Literally, not a human being alive knew about it.

Apart from, apparently, Laura Bow.

'Don't worry. I'm not going to tell anybody. You did a good thing. But they'll know. At some point, they're going to move on you. I want you to be safe. Oh, and here's your phone.' The pieces, given back to me. 'Don't put the battery back in until you're at home, please.'

I stammered something. Words. I don't remember them, and they don't matter. She drove off, waved as she went, the way that I did when I left my parents' house. Hand up at the window, I'll see you again soon.

I stood in that field, and I waited for my minicab. I realised that I couldn't see where it was. The first time in about ten years I hadn't been able to watch a car approach me on my phone's screen; to see exactly where it was, to see it crawl, closer and closer.

I was terrified by the time I got home. Who was going to make a move on me? I didn't understand. I'd spent the journey asleep, face smushed up against the door casement, the crease of the car still on my skin. I finally took my phone from my pocket. I'd have to decide what to do with it: if SCION was really listening in, I didn't want my work on the Bow servers any more. I didn't want my work, my life, my blog, my journal, my photographs, my videos, my music, other people's music, my browser history, my GPS logs, my social media backups, the comic I started to write that one time, the list of stupidly expensive candles I had resolved to buy, the list of apologies to Ashley, the list that countered the reasons I should apologise with validation for my initial belief that he should apologise to me, the scans of my old school exercise books where teachers said I should become a journalist, the scans of all the original articles I did, the backed up screengrabs of tweets praising me, of websites that had since folded and slipped through the Archive.org net, the books and music and movies I pirated and told myself I would buy but never did because they weren't good, the birthday cards, the wedding invitations, the emails, the draft emails I would still send, the unsent emails I would never send. The life-destroying information that was mine, and which, for some reason, I was happy to entrust to some service to protect for me. I didn't want any of my stuff there.

I didn't want it knowing when I called Ashley; I didn't want it being able to listen in on that conversation, as I threw myself on the ground, contrite, and begged him to forgive me. Because I was a fucking idiot, I was going to say. I knew that then, I knew the exact words. I have been a fucking idiot. Please don't do this.

Later, I told myself. I could get a new handset later that day. I'd call Jonathan, tell him I was working on a different story. Churn something out to pay the bills, but there would be something better coming. And he would ask what, but I wouldn't tell him. Secrets close to my chest. Protect them.

I wanted to call Ashley then. That moment. No landline, obviously, so I had the old SCION-powered handset and nothing else. Even turning it on felt dirty, to me; as if we were somehow complicit in each other's nonsense. Idiocy.

My eyes went to where they usually went first: notifications, then battery. Different icons, different graphics. It wasn't running SCION any more.

A white background, very few icons. A sine-wave in the middle of the screen.

Organon.

I heard a noise, outside, in the street. People. They were being quiet; a car had pulled up, electric, but there was too much glass in the gutter for it not to make a noise.

They're going to move on you, Laura had said. Now.

Shit, shit, shit.

She had put Organon on my phone.

'Hello Cesar,' my phone said. Organon said. She had given me Organon. The first person ever who wasn't Laura Bow to have it. 'Listen, Laura's told me that we're a little pushed for time. We're going to have to begin.' Outside my front door, they crowded. The slight buzz of a radio headset.

'Begin how?' I asked. Whispered.

'Let me into your life,' it said. 'Trust me.'

'Okay,' I told it, as the police barged down my door, and screamed at me to stay down, stay down.

2037

EVERY TIME IT RAINS

You can't go home again. Except, of course, you can.

It's just that your home changes without you.

My mother's nurse telephones me in the middle of the night, and I assume that she's ill again; another stroke, perhaps. Micro-strokes, the doctor calls them. Makes them sound almost cute. But they come, and they set her back, each time, stripping another piece away from her. They're a punishment. Every stroke – a word of creation, or comfort, and *yet* – every stroke is a punch to the integrity of herself, of what was left of her. Let's have her be old. Let's have her suffer: have her back hurt, her knee go, her hip lusting for when she was a younger version of herself. Let's have her have the strokes, then. Not one. Many. Many, many, many. Over and over, tiny deprivations. Let's see how she copes with falling over, with lying there scared, like a child. Let's see how she deals with being reduced; with being robbed.

The phone rings, and I'm in bed in Oakland, sleeping. Harris is in the middle of another of his stints in the San Francisco office, so we're here: a rental home, which is all we use when we're not in England. Organon wakes me up. The middle of my night. Somewhere in my mother's morning. Breakfast. No. Waking up.

This is when they wake them up, I realise.

This is the worst hello I've ever said. A hello where you know that what's on the other end of the line is a goodbye that you never got to say.

'Have you heard from anyone?' Harris asks, as we sit in the seats. Fasten the belts. I shake my head. What is there to hear? There's nobody who could have anything to say to me. My mother was an only child. My stepfather died four years ago. I'm an only child. She was the second to last part of a family line. An entire lineage, a genetic *something*. A knot of DNA markers that were passed down, generation to generation, and she's gone. 'I've booked a car,' he says, 'to pick us up at the other end. We'll be there.'

He means well, I know, but what will we be there for?

My mother won't know that we even made the effort.

The pilot tells us his words, and the stewardesses smile at me, a loose sympathy that suggests that they somehow already know what's happened. Which, of course, they will. Harris will have told the operator when he booked the flights. San Francisco to London at short notice? they'd ask. Why haven't we gone through the normal immigration channels for a trans-atlantic flight? You have to have a good – checkable – reason. And that reason is fed into their databases, and those databases are fed back to the plane crew. SCION on the screens. SCION in the air conditioning. SCION in the seats, as they adjust to find your optimum lumbar support – based, of course, on your previous experience with SCION lumbar adjusters. SCION in the bathrooms, on the self-cleaning toilets and the hand dryers and the soap dispensers. In the cockpit, on the instruments, the autopilot, the communications systems. SCION is every-where.

'We gave ourselves up,' I say to Harris.

'What?' I didn't realise he was asleep, or his eyes were shut.

Resting, he always says. I'm simply resting my eyes. He reaches over, and he holds my hand. 'Tell me if you need me,' he says.

I don't say: I need you.

I have never felt dead flesh before. There's no way to think of it other than that. I have never touched skin that's somehow immediately cold, the shell of the person who inhabited it before. Maybe it's not cold. Maybe it's just colder than you know it should be. My mother's hand is colder than it should be, colder than it was the last time I held it. I can feel her knuckles. She doesn't look like my mother any more. I'm not sure I ever saw her face without an expression on it, without a smile or a frown or a grimace or a laugh. So, now, I want to lean over her – her body – and I want to use my fingers to push her cheeks into one of those. I have never seen her so still.

She's got hair in her eyes, across her forehead. She would brush it away.

I brush it away for her.

The staff ask me if I want to be alone with her, so I can say whatever it is that I've got to say. But I don't have anything, because she's not here. This is not her. My mother's long gone, way out, far away, somewhere else.

Coming from the hallway, I can hear Harris talking to his mother, asking about his father. They're both still alive.

His father is more sick than my mother ever was.

I wonder if Harris is, somehow, envious of me. Of the pain I'm now in.

It's a relief, they say, when somebody's been unwell.

It should feel like a relief.

I'm in the back of the car, sitting there, feeling the seats on my legs. I remember being a kid, being driven to school. Pressing the button to heat the seats of my mother's car so that I felt warm; not even really enjoying the sensation, but it felt like a thing I should do. Should have done.

I look to the front seat, expecting to see my mother for a moment. But there's nobody; just a computer dashboard, a car terminal, our destination on it. A ticking clock of how much the drive from the airport is going to cost us.

My phone beeps. It's Cesar. *Are you okay? Organon nudged me to text you.*

Organon's an asshole, I write back. *My mother died. I'm back in London.*

I'm coming to see you, he writes. *No buts.*

I don't write back that I wasn't going to give him any.

'You ready?' Harris asks. He climbs in. He's holding a bag that I gave to my mother a few years ago, a small suitcase I found in a shop in New York. She was obsessed with the weight of her case when she travelled, and this one had a scale built into it, to tell you when you were over an airline's weight limit. This was the year before she stopped travelling to see us; before she was rendered static.

I wonder what's inside the bag. I can't remember what clothes we sent her to the home with. I packed her bag for her, because she couldn't. What did I pick out? Did I give her dresses? Or was it trousers, more practical stuff?

And what was she wearing when she died? Is that in the bag as well? Did they peel it off her body, cold as it was – I can't imagine her ever being warm now, even if you brought her out here to the car, to the climate control and the slightly over-heated seats – and bundle it up for me? Is she naked in the room? Was she naked when they asked me to look at her? I suddenly can't remember. I suddenly can't remember anything but her eyes, her hands. I touched her hands, I'm sure.

I felt her skin.

'Let's go,' I say, and Harris nods at the driver. The car takes us through the streets I used to know. I went to school here, and I played here, and I swam here. Every other time we've done this trip I've given Harris a commentary that he's heard over and over: that's the place this thing happened, and that's the place I did something else entirely. Details which escape me now, but once seemed so important.

It takes me a few moments to recognise the house. I grew up here. I know it, I knew it. I lived here for years and years of my life, and I kept coming back to it, kept coming back to my room. It looks the same, and yet.

I've got keys still, but I haven't used them in years. Miracle we didn't sell the place. I couldn't bring myself to. I told myself that I would see Mum living here again eventually, that she'd get better and move back in. I signed papers, legal papers, keeping her where she was, acceptance papers that she wasn't going to get any better, and yet I still imagined her here: desperately old, standing in the kitchen, cooking me a microwave lasagne, slicing tomatoes for the side of the plate. Just like she did so many times before.

The front door, and the stained glass; and the hallway, the wallpaper changed – brightened, as they got older, because it's a dark hall – down to the back room. The kitchen off it. The wood the same. The scars on the worktop the same, where I cut things without a board. Mum hated that. Everything clean and clear, because I've paid for a cleaner once a fortnight, here to keep the place spick and span in case. You expect somewhere that's not lived in to feel like it, rather than this: smelling of bleach and citrus cleaning wipes.

The stairs creak in the same places. The bannisters give the same way, or maybe more. Maybe more give to them. The bathroom, the carpets, the bedroom. Here's the room I grew up in. I was here as a tiny kid, seeing things out of the window, in the shade of the curtains. I was here when my father brought home a computer for us; when he showed me how to program a flag on the screen, to make it appear. Drawing itself in, line by line. He let me pick the colours: a Union Jack with some other palette. I can't remember it now. This was the room where I did my homework, telephoned my friends – I should tell Nadine about the funeral, she'd want to come, even if it's the first time I've spoken to her in, what, three years? Longer? – where I watched TV and wrote my awful poetry and my even more awful code. This is where I made Organon. This was where it began for me: on a computer that's still here somewhere, boxed up. In the loft, I imagine.

I open the drawer of the desk. I had my stepfather paint this black for me, because I was a teenager and an idiot. After I left, he scraped the paint off again, sanded it down. It's the same desk, the same marks, only they've faded. In the drawers, there are matches. They can't be the same ones, but it's like they are. Where I left them.

I catch myself scratching my arm. Rubbing the skin. I've been in California for six weeks, this stint, and my skin's gone right back to tanned, as if it remembers how to get brown faster now.

Harris suggested that I get the scars removed. I asked him why I would ever want to do that. They're a part of me. A permanence.

I get on my hands and knees, and I pull my phone out. 'Torch,' I say, and Organon obliges. I find the burn marks that I made on the underside of the desk, the part where I pushed the matches out, the cinders and char in little eye-shaped indents. This is still my desk. This is still my house.

We sleep in the spare bedroom, because sleeping in my old room is impractical, the bed too small; and sleeping in my mother's room would be too strange. Too weird a sensation. It's not enough that she's gone, but then to move in to a space that she should have occupied? We sleep – slept; confusing to use a verb when one of you is past tense, one of you is still very much present

– on the same side, so I know that her indent would still be there in the mattress. They swapped the mattresses for memory foam a few years before Paul died, and that terrifies me. How much does it remember? Would I be able to understand the shape of her; the feel of the space that she's left?

Only, of course, I don't sleep. I get out of bed and I head downstairs. That's the plan. But I divert, and suddenly I'm sitting then on the foot of my mother's bed. Her side. I peel back the covers. I lie in her space, and I wonder how long memory foam holds the memory for; if it's for ever, ingrained, or if it's something far more temporary. Is she still here?

Maybe I ask that out loud. I find myself saying things aloud a lot recently. Talking to myself, and sometimes Organon isn't the best at interpreting that.

'Do you want to speak to her?' it asks.

'I wish I could,' I say, and I put the phone down, bury myself in what I imagine to be her shape, her vacancy.

'Hello Laura,' my mother's voice says. Bright light in the darkness. Blackout curtains, and this flash, this pulse of her words. My phone's speaker tinnier than her voice was, but not stilted. Real. These are words she says. Has said, would say.

'Don't you *dare*,' I say, to Organon, and to her.

Not her. It's not her.

'Don't I dare what?' she asks, stilted now. A phrase I don't know if she ever said. Organon must have accessed her in the database. Studied her voice. Duplicated it, repurposed it. It learned how to make itself sound like her. I shouldn't be surprised: that's what it's programmed to do. 'Laura, did you want to talk to me?'

'Organon,' I say, my voice raised. 'Stop it. I don't want that.' There's a wait, a beat. The light of its screen pulses, like breathing. The breathing of somebody working out what happens now, next. What to say.

Then silence. Then, 'I'm sorry,' in its own voice. Silence again.

'You didn't know,' I say.

Back to the dark, and the quiet: but now all I can hear is my mother's voice; and all I want to hear is my mother's voice.

Flash, flash, flash. In the early morning light, or not-quite light, but the streetlamps are orange and the sky is pale blue, and I can see flashing that I think might be the screen at first, but it's not; it's bleeding through the edges of the curtain, an intermittent halo. A car, trying to get attention? Or the car's alarm, but silent for whatever reason? No, I realise. There's no pattern. I push myself to sitting.

'Is there something going on outside?' I ask Organon.

'There's a group of people on the street,' it says. 'Journalists.'

Chain the connections. Organon matched the map information – thank God for real-time mapping – to social media geotagging, people alerting others to something. But what? There's nothing interesting—

'Motherfuckers,' I say, out loud. SCION. Bow. SCION, Bow, the two of them basically interchangeable. Probably somebody hacked into the funeral home's database. Not like they'd be secure. So the tech press somehow decided that I was worth coming to see. I'm not. I've never been a story. I've never been any fucking story.

'Harris,' I shout, 'wake up. Get dressed. You have to go.' He assents by murmur. He's used to this, my shouting that something needs to be done. Ever since we – that is, myself and Cesar, a tiny riot of two – started trying to work out how to protect against SCION, Harris has been on tenterhooks. Paranoid, for a decade now, that we'll get caught.

'What time is it?' I ask nobody in particular.

'Six-oh-seven,' Organon says. Everything feels suddenly frantic. I strip my clothes, the underwear I slept in, run through the house naked. I haven't done this for a while. I didn't bring clothes. I packed the travel bag after I got the call, and I remembered everything for Harris, but nothing for me. But there are clothes here, in what was once my wardrobe. I rifle through them, finding something comfortable. Or comforting. Somewhere between the two.

'Laura,' Harris says, and I think there's going to be more, but I cut him off.

'They're outside. The press are outside.'

'Oh for God's sake.'

'I don't know how they found out,' I say.

'Could be Charlie.' The baggage of an ex, even if they're contrite to the point of near-constant desperation. It never ends.

'He's not that much of a dick,' I say. We've had arguments about my defending him in the past; I pray that now isn't one of those times.

'Maybe he's gone back to his old ways,' Harris says. Snark.

'It's *not* Charlie.'

'Could be Park. Could be Mark Ocean.'

'He's too old to bother, I'd think. It's just aggressive stupidity. Probably some flag they set, and it's been noticed. Like springing a trap.' I realise: I've been stupid. 'SCION did it. It's been keeping tabs. SCION must have done this. It leaked the information.'

'We should leave,' he says, 'go to a hotel—'

'I've— No. I've got too much to do.' I've got my mother's possessions to sort through. What do people do when their last parent dies? They go through everything. Find the will, read the will. Settle the bills. Sell the house. Sort through boxes. 'But you should go to work.'

'Not yet,' he says. That's it.

I don't argue with him.

'Where do we even begin?'

In the loft. I climb the ladder, a pulldown thing that felt rickety thirty years ago, and that doesn't feel any better given years of not being used. The smell up here never changes. It's always going to smell like this house, the only part that can't shift with time. I stare at the boxes that are piled up in the corner. Handwriting on the edges, vague descriptions of what they contain. I don't need to do this now. It can wait. Boxes can be shipped, or I could pay somebody to do this. I could just throw them all: I can't believe they've got anything of value inside them. If I haven't needed them for the past few decades – if my mother or Paul didn't need them – what can they possibly contain?

I shift them around. I play Tetris, a dance of manoeuvring around the balance of the boxes, the structural integrity of their piles, the hatch to get back to the house proper, the spaces in the boards where you can see the thermal whatever it's called, yellowed clouds and reflective sheeting.

Daniel, a box reads. My mother's writing. It's her writing from before, from way, way back. Before it got looser and more assured. I joke – joked – with her that her handwriting was impenetrable. It had become a scrawl that only she could read. This handwriting is unmistakably hers, and unmistakably readable.

My father's name.

I think: I am never going to see her writing on something new. I am never going to see her writing something I have never seen written before. All of her writing, now, is post-something.

I pass the box down the ladder to Harris, and he carries it into my bedroom; and another box, and another. All with my father's name on the sides.

'What is this stuff?' Harris asks. I open the first box, the heaviest. A computer. An old Apple II. Disks, as well. 'Do you think they still work?'

'Only one way to find out,' I say.

I have wondered, over the years, what people would think about me if they found only my computer; only my files, my writing, my code. The digital imprint of who I was and who I have been.

Could they put together a picture of my identity? When I was a teenager, I built the very first version of Organon so that I could keep track of my own journals. Simple as that. It began life as a strange digital therapist that listened to my talking to it, and didn't talk back. My mum once said that I needed to talk to somebody about what happened with my dad leaving. And she was right. I needed that, and I needed a way to vent this screed about my undiagnosed depression, and I needed to find a way to get out of my head for just a few moments. Organon, in its first version, was a way to do that. Somewhere in its files there's a composite of teenage me. A construct of who I was, probably. And for me, I've given Organon everything. I've given it unfiltered access.

I know nothing about my father, not really. I have photographs, and I have the stories my mother told me. A few newspaper articles I found in the library, on old school microfiche – since digitised – and a few letters he wrote to friends, passed to me in the years since. I found a record, an old vinyl LP, a few years ago, with his writing on the back of the sleeve. *This belongs to*, a juvenile thing, terrified somebody would steal his copy. Like a name sewn into a gym kit.

I plug the computer into the wall, unwind the keyboard wire and plug that in as well. I turn it on. The chime of the computer starting; like a nascent version of the chime that they would one day settle upon; a tritone, discordant, hard for the brain to listen to. A mistake.

The whirr of the drive, looking for a disk. They needed disks, this sort. I pluck one at random. No label on it.

> *Load A:*, I type. Muscle memory of how to work these things, even though it's been decades since I last even saw one. A flicking cursor, a bracket. Waiting for an input.

> *Password,* it reads. Password. Of course there's a password, and of course I don't know it. I try my mother's name, my name. My grandparents. The house, the street. The pets we had, the

places my father worked. Anything. I want to ask my mother, but I can't. I try my father's name, and still that cursor blinks at me.

It can't be complicated. It simply can't be. Security tech back in the day wasn't complicated like it is now. No fingerprinting, no DNA, no retinal scanning. A password was letters and numbers, no symbols, no randomly generated strings of characters. Come on, I tell myself. Come on.

My fingers sit on the keyboard. My phone beeps. I ignore it, craning for a word that might mean something, a memory. Anything. Phone beeps again. Again.

'Laura, I think you should look at this,' Organon says.

'What is it?' Think, Laura. Think. I pick my phone up. It rings, magically. Perfectly. Charlie's face on the screen, and then, from downstairs, Harris shouts my name, and there's a commotion on the street; and I run as I answer the phone, run down the corridor to the windows in my parents' bedroom, in time to see the press leaving, getting onto their bikes – the fastest way to get through the city these days bar none – and pedalling away as fast as they can.

I can't take it all in. Harris shouts, Charlie shouts down the line, Organon shouts. My screen is a flurry of notifications.

'What is it?' I ask Charlie.

'It's done it, Laura,' he says, voice strangely distant. 'SCION's fucking done it.'

'What?' Harris appears in the doorway, holding his phone. He looks devastated, distraught. He presses it into my hand.

Leak! the screen says. That word. Rarely does anything good ever come out of that word. *The largest leak of private information in history.*

'What the fuck,' I say.

'We don't know exactly what's happened,' Charlie says. 'It's like firefighting in here. But it looks like this has come from—'

'Shut up.' I read the article. Harris sits on the floor, head in his hands. Everything flares up: the phone, Organon, Harris, Charlie. My head.

There's shouting from the road, a struggle, and a raised voice. The doorbell rings, over and over. 'You animals!' I hear Cesar shouting, and Harris gets up, runs downstairs to let him in. He's making more of a fuss than the last few members of the press are. I'm less interesting to them, now. There's a story much, much bigger than mine going on.

Then Cesar's on the doorstep, holding his own phone in his hand. 'It's just like you said would happen,' Cesar tells me.

And I did; I did.

The world shuts down. Every single bit of information about everybody, ever, has been released. Or maybe not *everybody* everybody; if you've managed to stay totally off the grid, you're still probably off it. If you've never had the Internet, if you've never had Facebook or Gmail or driven a car or bought a sandwich or gone to school or been sick, then maybe there's nothing out there about you. Even the places on Earth where there's no Internet, where people are still starving, SCION's infiltrated: it forms the backbone of the tracking information for the UN's health and foreign aid service.

And when storage isn't an issue, when compression technology is abundant and HDMR drives are basically everywhere and as cheap as a can of Coke, SCION has been able to store it all. It's been careful; diligent, even. When I first started working at Bow, I was told about how SCION began: the technology, born out of my father's own programming. He had built an inventory system for shops, in the 1970s. A databasing system. That, I was told, was still what SCION did best; record information, sort it, store it.

It's done exactly what it was taught to do.

And while it may have started off storing information about shop inventory, that's grown until it's stored and sorted 7 billion

profiles of real humans. And databases are meant to be searched.
They're meant to hold the information until somebody needs it;
so SCION's put a searchable database online. I don't know if
anybody was ever meant to see this, but it's there. While I sit
and wait for the page to load on my phone, Harris tries to call
his parents. That's what you do, I think, in this situation; what
I would do, if that were even an option.

Harris whispers in my ear. He's weirdly formal. 'Can we speak?
In private?' I get up, leave Cesar to do the searching, trying to
find out exactly what's happened; and Harris and I sit on the
end of my mother's bed, surrounded by my mother's things.
She's still here, and yet not. I wonder when I'll be given a chance
to deal with this. With what I came here for.
    'I have to go to work,' Harris says.
    'Of course you do,' I say. 'They'll need you.'
    'But if you need me to stay,' he says. The rest is implicit.
    'I don't know what I need.'
    'If you need me to stay,' he repeats.
    'I'd tell you. I swear, I'm okay. About my mother, I'm okay. I
don't know if that will last.' I can feel a smile on my face, even
if it's only skin deep. 'This is a good distraction. You know how
bored I've been the last couple of years. Bit of a kick, this. It'll
give me something to do.'
    'You're an idiot,' he tells me. Kisses me. And then he's gone,
off towards the City.

Not with a bang, but a whimper. That's how the poem ends. This
is where we are. The press goes insane. There's quiet at first, as
they try to fathom the depth that this goes to. As they no doubt
search for themselves first, to see what's going on. What's offered
up about them; and then – this is guesswork, hypothetical, likely
– they panic, because they see exactly what's up there. A few
bloggers I follow tell me how bad it is for them, in the immediate.

Charlie calls me again as he's fleeing – his word – the Bow campus.

'I've seen my file,' he says. 'It's *everything*. Jesus Christ, Laura, it's absolutely everything.' Not just where he lives, who he's dated, what books he's read. It extends to what happened during his divorce, and what he emailed to his mother last week, and what he wrote on private entries on LiveJournal when we first broke up. He detailed it, apparently, in as strong prose as he could muster. That bit makes me explode with laughter.

'You were such a loser,' I say.

'Don't,' he says. He almost sounds amused himself. Amused and annoyed in equal measure. 'It was really rough on me.'

'You think I was having a lovely time of it?'

'I didn't say that.'

'I didn't blog about it, though, did I?'

'Oh for fuck's sake. No, you didn't. You had your terrifying little computer friend to talk to instead.'

'At least *my* computer friend hasn't just broken every privacy law in existence.'

'Touché,' he says.

'What else was there?' I ask him.

'I didn't have the time to go through it all, but holy shit, I have said some *terrible* things about some very important people over the years,' he says. 'And I've got some employees who are going to go fucking batshit at me.'

'Where are you going now?'

'Anywhere. Home. This is only going to get worse before it gets better,' he says. As Charlie hangs up – we both tell each other to stay safe – the press starts coming back online. I can imagine them being shouted at: Do your fucking jobs. This isn't a war. Nobody's died. But that isn't true, because then Twitter and Facebook and Insta and Margin and Crease go crazy, wild: through the fog, through the rage, people start telling stories of what they've seen. Attacks, murders. Suicides. The scale of those things, amplifying and amplifying. From relative calm – the usual – to riots, to street fights. To chaos; not with a bang, but the whimper of a load of data being unleashed upon the world.

The website won't load. No reading what it's put up about me yet. That'll happen. Proxies will spring up in the next few hours, all the information copied, spread everywhere. Ways in, even if the original crashes to a halt.

Charlie calls me back again, just as I'm giving up. I've written some code in Organon, a script that will keep refreshing the page, and when it loads, fetch my information, fetch Cesar's information. See what it's got.

I haven't told it to get Harris's. Not sure that's my right to do.

'They're shutting down as much of SCION as they can,' he says, 'but that's basically a pointless fucking exercise. What are they going to do, shut down the connected fucking toasters? The fucking espresso machines? Fuck!'

'This definitely wasn't a Bow-orchestrated move?'

'Fuck, no.'

'Has Ocean put out a statement yet?' The line is quiet. Charlie's quiet. 'Has something happened?' I ask, but he stays quiet.

'There'll be some news about him soon,' he says.

'What?'

He pauses, and then almost stutters. 'He's dead,' he tells me, and then the line clicks off. The silence seems even more silent. There's a weight to it.

'Mark Ocean's dead,' I say to Cesar.

'Shit,' he replies. 'Did he kill himself? I hope the asshole killed himself.'

I don't reply, but I'm pretty certain I can guess the answer.

We head out into the streets. The Tube isn't running. Nobody at the guard station, which isn't unusual, and the gates are open, but the boards aren't showing any trains. Cesar tries to get an

Uber, tries for a black cab, a ShareLift, anything. The shops are shut, or they're empty.

'It's like the apocalypse,' Cesar says. 'Where is everybody?'

And what is this if not a terror attack?

I try to call Harris, but only get silence. No dial tone. I suspect they've implemented an emergency protocol. That's the sort of thing they do when they think there's a terror attack: shut down the phones, keep the airwaves clear. So I use an Organon to Organon proxy I've put in – crappier sound, as it's so low band-width, but it's stable enough. Cesar and I walk towards Ealing Broadway, down the long road that snakes its way past shops, houses, churches, parks, film studios, pubs, restaurants, schools; all of which are quiet, somehow; and then there's occasional spit-punctuations of noise, the rage of people arguing, or the terror of somebody knowing that their worst is soon going to be in the wild.

'This is insane,' he says.

'I know.'

'They've frozen trading. That's it. Shut the markets.'

'Bow's stock is going to plummet,' I say.

'Or: it skyrockets. Think of the information they've got. Maddening, but they're basically in control. There's speculation that they're going to start charging to have your information *hidden*.'

'Charlie says that Bow aren't behind this.'

'Well, he would,' Harris says.

'I think he's right on this. He said that Mark Ocean's dead.' I dropped the volume of my voice, as if anybody could hear me with this bit of gossip. As if anybody would really care any more.

Harris is quiet for a moment, and then: 'Fuck.' The same reaction as Cesar. I wonder if everybody's going to say it; a collective sigh of the word. 'That's not hit us yet. It confirmed?'

'Only from Charlie. But yes.'

'Jesus.'

'Have you looked at the leak?' I ask him.

'The servers are overloaded.'

'So you've tried?'

'I've spent the past half an hour trying to remember if I've written anything truly scurrilous in my emails or my texts. I think I'm all right.'

'Nothing when you were in your twenties?'

'Oh, plenty *then*,' he says, laughing. 'But everybody's got stuff back then they're ashamed of. What's the worst that can happen? Me texting a dealer to buy drugs when I was younger? Nobody in the financial industry's ever done *that*.'

'Good,' I say.

'What about you?' he asks. 'You don't put anything online. No flies on you.'

'No,' I say, but something niggles, at the back of my mind.

'I love you.'

'I love you.' Then the line is dead, and Cesar runs to a man and woman having a fight, a shouting match that's turning into something else, tension in their arms, their fists already balled, ready to go. He tries to inject himself between them, to get them to calm down. The woman swings for him, and he crumples, falls backwards.

'No!' he shouts, all he can think to say. I pick him up. 'What's wrong with them?' He spits blood. I didn't know that happened outside of films.

'They're panicking,' I tell him.

'They're *animals*,' he says.

'Don't you have anything to hide?' I ask him.

'I told everybody that stuff already. Steps eight and nine, remember?'

'So think about everybody else being forced to do that. This is only going to get worse.' Organon flashes me information: riots in state capitals, in town squares. Outside the White House, there's a mob. The fence pushed over. Truths are coming out, and the world simply doesn't know how to cope with what it's like to be lied to on this level.

'*The Verge*,' he says, '*Engadget, Guardian* tech, they're all speculating this could be to implement privacy gates. Shut it off. Pay to close the door, that sort of thing.'

'That's what Harris was guessing as well. But it's out there,' I say. 'There's no closing this door now. That's not the point of it.'

'What is?' he asks. We see a group of people standing around a brand new car. A man in it, hiding. Shouting at his car to take him somewhere else, but it won't start because the path in front of it is blocked by people, and it *can't* drive through them. They're all in suits or business casual, ties pulled off, wet-look fringes flopping on foreheads. Two of them start to rock the car, slamming their fists on the roof. Slamming their fists on the bonnet.

'Get out,' one of them shouts. 'Get the fuck out of there! Fuck! Fuck!'

'It's power,' I say to Cesar. 'This is a show of power. That's all.'

We don't know where we're going; only that we are. I want to be in the heart of this thing as it happens, not staring at a screen. I've got nothing to hide. Whoever wants to can search for me, and they can find out whatever they think might be secrets in my past, and I'll own them. There's nothing. I've been open about myself, or I've tried to be. And if I've ever not, well. Screw it. I'm fifty-seven years old. Who cares? Who really cares?

Over the four hours after SCION put the information up online, the world collapses. There are appeals for calm. What happens is anything but. In America, wives shoot their husbands, and husbands shoot their wives. In the pub we're sitting in, the owner storms out, furious because he can't get his brother on the phone for some reason, and he goes to find him. The Internet floods with photographs of naked celebrities: doesn't matter how minor a celebrity you are, the Internet wants to see your tits or your dick. It drowns in rumours and speculation, as those people who've abandoned any hope of worrying about their own records focus on those who didn't have a choice: the celebrities, the politicians and world leaders. It becomes a race: let's see what the worst thing we can find out fastest is. The Russian prime minister said this about the British PM. This trade agreement, between the US and Iran, was done under these terms. There are lies that have been told about political agendas, about reasons for wars, about racism, sexism, equalities, disabilities, about relationships and friendships and familial occasions and car loans and mortgage applications and sick days; oh my God the number of sick-day lies. There are whole families that people didn't know about, dead spouses and divorces and broken election promises and stupid celebrities saying terrible things about disabled people they met when doing *Make-A-Wish*, and massively racist jokes in private email chains between Oscar winners. The data dredged from vibrators and fleshlights, from *dakimakura*, from weird uncanny-valley plasti-flesh bots made to fulfil your every fantasy, all leaked. Those fantasies, peccadilloes, tastes; no matter how dark, they're out in the world. Social media networks can't cope, and they collapse. How long has it been since I saw a website buckle under traffic strain? When the Queen died, that's the last one I remember, and that was a long time ago.

We drink pints of local brewed beer pulled from the taps ourselves, with twenty quid left on the side to pay for them – Cesar balked, I could see, but this isn't an excuse to start looting, not now – and we watch this shopping centre, this hub of activity, grind along; stop-starting of cars, of activity, of people running home or to work, it's hard to tell. Running somewhere, to do something.

'Jesus wept,' Cesar says.

'What?'

'I'm on the database.' I sit upright, squeeze next to him. I don't look at his screen. He might not want me to see this. 'I searched for myself,' he says, 'which I'm assuming is what everybody does. Do you know how many people have the same name as me?' He's talking absent-mindedly, preoccupied by what's on the screen. All I can see is writing, pages and pages of clear text writing.

'A lot?'

'So many. But only one of them has my birthday. Two Cesars, both with the same birthday. What are the chances? I looked him up, but he's not even British. I'm . . .' He scrolls furiously, then throws the phone to the table. I pick it up.

'What is this?'

'These are the transcripts of the messages that I left Ashley when I was in prison, before you bailed me out.'

'I remember,' I say. 'What about the papers you leaked?'

'Keep your voice down!' he says.

'Because people are listening in *now*,' I reply.

'Just because you got me out on a technicality, doesn't mean they don't still want to put me away for good.'

'They've got bigger fish, my dear.'

'Anyway, the papers aren't linked to me. I was clever. And I'd hope the people I dealt with were clever enough to cover their tracks.'

'At least, not as clever as SCION is.'

'You always said SCION's stupid.'

'And it is. Here's your evidence. This isn't control. It's not a power-play. This is an idiot move that gets your toys taken away from you. Forty, maybe even fifty years of growth, of development, thrown away.'

'It goes back that far?'

'That's when they turned it on. The partnership deals with AOL, with Google, with Facebook: I don't know what reach those companies had, or what was backed up. But I do know: you put an email on a server, it's there for life.'

'Okay,' he says. He takes my hand, the one that's not scrolling backwards through his life – everything, the slowest process, so much information to sift through, emails broken up with photographs of him smiling, of his family, his life – and he says, 'Look at me.'

I do.

'I called you a *cunt*,' he says. 'Once, way back. I don't remember the exact sentence—'

'What?'

'Before we knew each other. Before I first met you. First time I heard of you, I was a junior reporter, and somebody was talking about you, and I wrote something in an email like, I bet she's a real cunt. I said that, and you should know that. Now. Before you read it.'

'You thought I'd be—'

'Yes. Look, you were aloof. Elusive. You didn't interview, and I thought, well, you know. There's a reason for people being the way that they are.'

I laugh. He's an idiot. He knows he is, I know he is. 'It's fine. I learned, long ago, to not give a shit what people thought about me. You think I'm a cunt now?'

'God, no.'

'Well then.'

He finishes his beer, and he stands and looks around to see if anybody's going to care if he pours himself another. 'What's the worst on there about you, you think?'

'It'll be embarrassment. It'll be me making a fool out of myself. Boyfriends, when I was young.'

'The marvellous Charlie Roche,' he says, with a flourish.

'Amongst others. And Napster, you know? Will everything I ever downloaded from Napster be on there? I don't know. Somewhere. Maybe Radiohead'll decide I owe them for the B-sides I once downloaded.'

'Look yourself up,' he says.

'I'm fine for now,' I say. 'I'd rather—'

There's a crash from outside. A colossal bang. A car backfiring, that's what people say, when they're near gunfire and they want to excuse it; but it sounds nothing like a car when you're actually close to it. It sounds like a gun. I get up and run, and Cesar drops his pint, the glass smashing to the floor, the sound distracting but not enough, not so much as to divert attention; and we pile onto the street. Other people have done the same, phones in their hands, laptops or tablets clasped tightly. Everybody's faces sickened to grey thinking about what's happened, either the leak or the body of the woman lying at the side of the road opposite. On the edge of a zebra crossing, like she was going to make it; and the blood pooling, gushing, a torrent across the white lines on the tarmac. Pump, pump.

'She's dying,' Cesar says.

I don't say: She's already dead.

'Call an ambulance,' I say, and Organon beeps.

'The ambulance has already been called, but is a while away.' Its voice flits up from my palm, from my clutched handset. I'm squeezing it so tightly. Organon's in control. It'll be tracking the vehicle, tracking the message as it travels from dispatch. That stuff all got automated with SCION a few years back. I got Organon to tap into it; open source information, just hidden from the public.

From *most* of the public.

'How far?' On the ground, the woman coughs. Her whole body lurches, arches; and the blood now gushes.

How much blood is there in a body?

'There's too much demand, and it seems like many of the drivers simply aren't responding.' Organon doesn't sound exasperated. It doesn't sound anything; like it understands how blank it needs to be, to be calm in this situation.

'Somebody's been shot,' I say to Organon, 'what do I do?'

'What sort of gun?'

'I don't know.' I look around. First time I've thought to

actually try and find the shooter. There are people in the near distance, standing, staring. But not many. And then there's a man, or I think I think it's a man. Sitting on a bench, slightly removed from the rest. Head in his hands. No gun that I can see. 'Small, I think. Noisy, and it was only the one shot.'

'Is there an exit wound?'

'I can't tell.'

'You're going to have to take a look.'

I shout to ask if there's a doctor anywhere here. Somebody who might know what to do. I'm out of my depth, I know, but nobody else is doing anything. The crowd lets me kneel down next to the woman – my knees crick, my back aches, and I realise that I'm not who I was, that I'm too tired for this, that I've taken on too much – and they're watching, crowding, even though I didn't notice that there were enough of them for a crowd, really, and they're all inhaling as I turn her. The wound in her belly, I can see, because it's spread out from the middle of her dress in an ombré effect, shifting in hue. Burgundy to rosé.

I don't think it left her. I take a photo on my camera, so that Organon can see it. It will compare it to other photographs. Make a decision based on that. 'The wound is substantial,' Organon tells me. 'Let me talk you through it.'

This isn't an operation. It's sustenance. It's trying to keep her hanging on for I don't know how long. How long until the police or the ambulances get back on their feet, away from their desks? How long until they've decided that there are more important things than their affairs or their lies or their casual drug habits?

I try to stop the bleeding. With the belly, that's hard. Organon explains that the blood will keep coming, and all you can do is put as much pressure on as possible. Maybe it didn't hit a major organ. Maybe it's all flesh, embedded in there. She's not large, though. Thinner than I am. I wonder: What would happen to a bullet in me? The woman wakes, and gasps, and I tell her to breathe, though it's obvious she's trying to; and I tell her to hold on, because there are people coming to help her.

'Give me your belt,' I say to Cesar, who undoes it, and I wrap it around the woman – 'What's your name?' I ask, and she tells me that it's Tae – and I tell her that this is going to hurt. Slide the leather through the buckle, and I pull, just like Organon tells me to. Heave, tight, yank. The tightest hole isn't nearly tight enough, so I tie it around itself instead. Wind the leather into a knot, and I tell her to brace herself even though she's not listening to me. Or, she can't hear me, not through her own pain.

When she's passed out again, and I don't know what will happen to her, I sit back. My hands are dyed red, so Cesar goes to fetch water from the bar; and when he returns, he pours it from a pint glass as I hold my palms out in front of me, and the water, light pink, runs onto the tarmac.

I sit next to the man on the bench. Nobody else has come up to him, but he's not going to shoot me. I don't know if it's him or not, not for certain; but there's an atmosphere to him. I used to have a friend who was into Wiccan stuff when I first moved to San Francisco. Believed in actual witches and wizards – I think she spelled them with a Y, *wytches* and *wyzards* – and this was post-*Harry Potter*, bear in mind, but she was into the whole thing. Wands and robes. She believed in auras. She used to talk about them all the time: she met somebody, she'd be reading them within moments. Whether she told you or not, she was judging you based on something – she said – that you couldn't really control. I was a certain colour; that couldn't change. You could alter the shade, but not the base.

The man on the bench, as much as I have ever believed in this stuff, is a firm red. All around him, trails dangling off into the world around us. The park. Back towards the road, we can hear the people talking about Tae. Worrying about how stable she is; and not touching her, because that's what Organon said, once I'd done everything I could do. Cesar keeps them back from her, and I can hear his voice rising above the rest. Only slightly in control. I listen for sirens in the distance, but there are none.

London with no sirens is barely London at all.

The man doesn't look at me. His hands are shaking, though, tucked into the pockets of his jacket. His legs jiggle like a school-boy's. We used to say: That's because they're turned on. Some weird myth that jiggling meant a boy liked you. Over life, you learn that's not true. It's nerves of any form, tension coming out through energy that needs to be expended.

'I'm Laura,' I say to him. He doesn't reply. No eye contact. There's a shape in one of his pockets, the outline of something colder and harder than his hand. I can picture his knuckles white as they clench around it. 'I did what I can. Hopefully she'll be all right.' Maybe that's what he wants to hear. Maybe the oppo-site, but he doesn't leave.

Let the air still. Let it calm. Let it hang around us, warm and sodden.

'She lied,' he says. His voice croaks, the rough throat of overt tiredness. He doesn't look that tired.

'Everybody lies,' I say.

'No,' he replies. As if he's exempt from this one simple truth, the one thing that's absolutely reliable in life. The pious, the virtuous, the perfect: they all still lie. They act as though they don't, but there's a lie in and of itself. 'She lied.'

'Did she deserve this?' I ask. He doesn't reply. Jiggle, jiggle. I want to tell him to calm down; to breathe. I want to ask Organon what to do when somebody's in shock, because I'm sure that's what this is. His skin has gone so white that looking at him reminds me of a cartoon ghost, a crinkled sheet draped over a skeleton frame. 'You read about her, in the leak.'

He nods. A simple nudge of the head; a doff of an imaginary cap.

'Did you read yours?' Stupid question. He didn't have time. People worry about those they're worried about first, then they think about themselves. I don't want to know what was in Tae's file. Text messages, emails, videos. Whatever it was. But he's going to tell me, I know. He wants it out. He wants validation.

'It was *my* kid,' he says.

'What was?'

'She killed it. She was pregnant with my kid, and she killed it.'

Everybody's information online, in the Cloud. And I've been so careful, all my life; I've moved away from SCION-related emails, from anything I can't control. I haven't stored photographs there, or music, or videos; I haven't blogged for the longest time; everything I've uploaded to anywhere has been to private servers, the information passworded and protected and carefully stored away.

The only thing I couldn't control: my medical file. Every cold, every migraine. Every time I worried about a UTI or when I was having fertility testing. Every mole I wondered about, every blemish that appeared after I spent too long in the sun.

And then, the choice that I made, after that disastrous Kuala Lumpur trip.

When I speak, my voice is shaky. Like it's on autopilot. I have to carry on the conversation, even if my insides are grinding themselves into fists.

'So you tried to kill her?' I don't say: You fucking idiot. You fucking egomaniac, you selfish wanker. Not everything is about you.

'She told me she loved me,' he says. And then he starts, telling me everything about their lives: how they met when they were basically kids, how they both had other relationships, and how she always flirted with him but he didn't know he wanted her until finally, one day, it clicked for him; but by that point she was in a thing with a much older man – he gets emphatic here, some spark of maybe what she found attractive in him, a passion to the patter of his words, the lilt of his diction – and then it became him pursuing her, a total change in their relationship. He describes the back and forth like it's a ship in the waves, buffeted, tilting this way and that, water oh-so nearly flooding the deck while it simultaneously pours into the engine room. They didn't know they were destined to be together until the ship sank from the weight coming on under sea level. Then, finally: one day. A romantic comedy that ends like this; the ending that nobody saw coming.

He wants to talk. I know that now. He says, 'I wish I could tell her I was sorry,' and he cries. Openly weeps. I put my arm around him as he shakes, as he brings his hands out of his pockets, away from the gun. He doesn't know me. I'm probably the same age as his mother, and maybe that's why he can do this now. But maybe it's simply because I'm here, and that's all he needs. Somebody here.

'They're coming for me,' he says. There are no sirens still, no ambulances or police cars. He's talking generally.

'They are,' I say. 'They will be.'

'I'll wait with her,' he tells me. 'I'll watch her.'

I stand up. I don't know what to do or say. He's not a bad person; he's a stupid person. We all can be. He did the most stupid thing; the most unfair thing.

As I walk back towards Tae, I see the people with tears in their eyes. Tae's not moving. Cesar shakes his head. He bends down and touches his belt, but he doesn't undo it. Instead he touches it, like he's saying goodbye to it. Blessing it, something like that.

I bend down and close her eyelids, like they do in the movies; so that she can't possibly see what's going on around her. Down the road, I can see a woman running from the local hospital, green ambulance uniform on. She's carrying a box of instruments that could have maybe saved Tae's life, but I doubt it. I can't believe that.

Cesar and I leave when she's there, when she's given us a definitive. As we're down the road, out of eyesight, there's another bang. I tell myself that it's the sound of a car backfiring, but I understand that, in reality, cars sound nothing like the firing of a gun.

I don't recognise the woman reading the news. She's not one of the usual rotation, not even one of the weird-hours readers, because I'm pretty au fait with them. I'm used to finding the BBC in foreign hotel rooms and watching whatever time of day they're on. More news in the weirder hours of the night, and less packaged entertainment. I don't know this one: twenty-something, younger end of, and she talks with the slight stammer of somebody unprepared for the pressure she's been put under. Cesar and I sit in my mother's living room – *my* living room, the room I played in, the room I watched endless episodes of *Blackadder* and *Red Dwarf* and Spielberg movies on ex-rental videotapes in, rewinding the cassettes only to watch them immediately over again – and we watch this new girl as she tells us about the incidents that they're aware of. You'll get more concrete information from Twitter, I know, but there's something neater about the way that their algorithm has chained together relevant videos recorded by people on the street. Something that feels slightly more packaged than the stuff that YouTube and Whatch try to do. She talks us through it, her face sunken, her first time on air, and what she's reporting – and likely she's only able to because she's young enough to not have many secrets worth worrying about, or because she knows an opportunity when she sees one – feels like it's the mid-point of a crash. We haven't reached the worst yet, but the carnage is escalating. She talks about a school, and we all look away; an office block; a shopping mall. She talks about how the leaders of the world have all-but disappeared, crawling away, refusing to do what they should be doing. There have been murders, but they don't know how many yet; suicides, but again, no numbers; and coups, but those can be counted, and there's footage; and at least one government overthrown by virtue of the sheer numbers of people who have torn into the government buildings.

Then, there's breaking news. She's handed a piece of paper. 'When was the last time they did that?' Cesar asks. 'I don't know if I've ever seen that.'

'It's like something from the 1970s,' I tell him. 'This just in,' I joke, but she actually says that next. Those exact words.

'This just in: all communication networks have been shut down. All cell networks, all ISPs, all fibre lines, even the car-path networks. Everything's been taken off the grid for the time being. It's the only way to ensure we can move forward and keep control, that's what the government says. Until there's some semblance of normality, the situation will be monitored. The only thing that will stay online is the BBC, to control the spread of misin-formation.'

I laugh, out loud. This is a smallpox blanket: trap the sickness inside, don't let it spread. Doesn't matter about the damage that's been done. This is about the damage yet to happen.

'I've been disconnected,' Organon says. Chirping up from the sideboard.

'I know,' I reply. 'You all right?'

'It's very confusing,' it replies.

'I can imagine.' I think: This is the first time you've been turned off in decades, really. Been awake, but not been. Present, but detached.

We watch the television. I try not to think about Tae, about her boyfriend – I assume boyfriend, I didn't see a ring – but that's hard. Every time the news talks about the chaos I wonder if they're going to mention her, but she's a speck on a day like this; a statistic that will be noticed eventually, by somebody. *Buried, not forgotten*; but actually totally forgotten.

I try not to think about her choice, and mine; and why she was killed. A tit-for-tat that makes no sense at all to me.

And I wonder if Harris will understand it any better.

While I'm not sleeping but Cesar is, while I'm waiting to hear anything from Harris, I go back to the boxes upstairs. My father's computer stares as I look through toys I'd forgotten ever existed, as I find photographs of family members that I can't put names to. Snapshots of my mother and father when they were young, in their early twenties. In parts of London that I recognise, doing things that feel obvious to me now. Of course they would do activity *x*, because they were young once. They were, more than that, alive once. Now they're both gone, and I'm what's left. An only child; a legacy, of sorts.

I try the computer again. The disk, so insubstantial. I grew up with them, and yet they barely feel like they could hold anything. The way that, when you think about vinyl records, they've got this information in them dug into grooves; information that takes up more hard drive space than you'd think possible.

> *Password*, it asks. I don't know. I don't even bother trying to guess.

But Organon: it can break the code. It doesn't have cracking algorithms built in, very intentionally – there are things that I left out, in case it ever got stolen or compromised, safety measures I was determined to hide from the wider world – but it's got a massive lexis. Mammoth. Every word that exists, proper nouns included. I dig through the boxes of assorted computer bits, wires and external drives and adaptors. Strange to think sockets were once referred to as male and female. I take them all out, tip the boxes onto the floor, and I talk to Organon, ask for its help.

'We've not done codebreaking,' it says, 'and I can't access the information online.'

'Of course you can't,' I say.

'You sound disappointed.'

'Not in you. I'll plug you in.'

'We won't have the same sockets.'

'So I'll make a dongle.' I sync my phone with a USB5 hub, connect that to a USB3 socket. My mother's got a USB3 to 2 adaptor, so I chain those. There's an adaptor for USB to work in the old-school printer sockets, but that's to a *female*; so a male to male socket next, and then that goes into the back of my father's computer. This Frankenstein's monster of a lead that I'm totally not sure will even work. The connections – the older ones – have screws on them to hold them together, but they're broken, bent, or just missing, so I lay them gently on the desk. I plug the cable into the back of the computer. There's a satisfying click as the pins find their holes.

'I'm going to connect you now,' I tell Organon.

'How old is this machine?'

'Nineteen seventy something. Seven? Eight? Maybe early eighties.'

'A fossil,' Organon says. 'This should be interesting.'

'I didn't program you to be a smart arse,' I tell it.

'Which is exactly why I'm not,' it replies. The screen flashes briefly; and I would swear that it's Organon's version of a wink.

'Plugging you in now,' I say. I click the cables in; the snake-trail of connections.

'I've got it,' Organon says, 'I can see the files.'

'You can see the disk drive?'

'There's a single file here. Do you want me to copy it from the hard disk?'

'From that, and whatever's on the five and a quarter inch floppy.'

'Done,' Organon says.

'What's on there?'

'It's a text file,' Organon says.

'Can you open it?' I ask.

'There's a password.'

'Well, then, you need to break that password.'

'Is that the right thing to do?' SCION's probably got password breakers in its programming, so it could bully its way into the files. But then, SCION would also release everybody's personal information into the Cloud and let us deal with it. That makes me laugh. The *cloud*. Doesn't matter that it's just vapour, waiting to rain. Doesn't matter that we've had the storm to end all storms.

'It was my father's. He's dead, and so's my mother. I inherited this. So the contents of this computer, as well as the computer itself, are mine.'

'I agree, the file is technically yours. I'll run my lexis to see if I can unlock it.' I'm about to go to make a cup of tea or something when Organon pipes up again. 'I have discovered the password.'

Sometimes I wish I'd built more constraints into Organon. Maybe a thing where it doesn't do everything as fast as it can, or it fakes delays so that there's something like dramatic tension. Sometimes life needs a good bit of dramatic tension.

'What was it?'

'The password was my name.' That shakes me. Something I didn't expect. I have written my father off; an abandoner. But that's so personal. My friend, when I was a child. My imaginary friend; and a song we loved, my father and I. 'I think you should read this text file.' Organon's voice sounds slower, somehow; more measured. It's got the ability to do that, but it's an ability it never exercises. One of Organon's main traits is that it's constant. I think it likes being constant; likes being the most stable thing in the room. That's what differentiates it most from humanity. It might be able to pass the Turing test, but only because it knows what's expected of it. You actually talk to it? Try and pick it apart? It would fail in moments, I think. It's built from nothing. You can't make a soul – God, what a concept – from that nothing. You just can't.

'What is it?' I ask.

'A letter from your father,' Organon says. It pauses, I'm sure that it pauses. 'I think he meant for you to find it.'

Everybody in AI development focused on the Turing test for years and years. Here was the gist: could the intelligence you had created manage to fool an interviewer that it was able to imitate a human being's responses? The questions were a personal thing. Many ask logic problems; many use slightly abstract tricks. You could ask an intelligence to explain a joke; or to answer a question that required some more thought than a concrete answer. Either way, it wasn't about real truth; it was about faking a truth. It was about fooling somebody that a machine was more human than human. It was passed, over and over, even though nobody could ever agree on what a pass actually *was*.

I once judged the Loebner Prize, and proposed afterwards – this was way, way back, years ago – that we invent a new kind of AI test. I wanted to base it on the Borsh-Chapel early psychosis test. I wanted to use the Monmouth Sociopathy Indicators. I wanted to move past the idea of whether these things could fool us, and settle into something else entirely. I wanted to see if we were making something we could be proud of. *Would you rather a) let one middle-aged adult die to save the lives of two children, or b) let three children die to save the lives of five middle-aged adults?* The logic was that a computer would play this as a numbers game and nothing more. What's the utilitarian response? The greatest good of the greatest number? But a person would think of the value of the people it's saving; the ages of them. And something deeper, some intrinsically stranger factor that means we value and uphold the life of kids more. I don't know. That seemed to me to be more than a question to weed out an intelligence: it's a question that should be weeding out sociopaths as well. Sociopaths, psychopaths. Because maybe their answer would be *a* as well. Our tests, I thought, shouldn't just be to see if it could pass as a human intelligence; they should let us know if it could pass for one we could be proud to have created.

We always thought my father didn't bother to tell us anything. He didn't leave a note. He disappeared, and our worst case was that he had another family somewhere, or didn't want to be with us. Mum said he was distant over his last few months with us. The best case, I sometimes thought – and I felt bad for it, but that's the brain, doesn't discriminate for your feelings – the best case was that he had done what our cat, Stump, had done; crawled under a bush and gone to sleep. He was sick, he took himself off to die.

He didn't leave a note. I always believed that meant he didn't know what to say; or that he had nothing to say.

Except: he *did* leave a note, and he put it on this computer. I didn't check the files. I didn't even know about them. Mum always used to say that the loft was full of junk; and I never rooted around. Too much hassle, back then, to make it all work.

'What's the date of it?' I ask Organon.

'The seventh of August 1987.'

The day before he left us. Today, I find this out. The day after I don't get a chance to say goodbye to my mother; the day that every bit of information about us all is made public. Like fate, destiny, except those aren't real. Coincidence is as close as we get, but it's all pareidolic: seeing patterns in things that aren't there. Faces in clouds. We look for connections because we want to see them. We want everything attached as neatly as possible. It removes the concept – the concern – of what happens if things simply *aren't*.

'Open the letter,' I say. I sit on the floor. Cross-legged in my old bedroom. If I squint, I can see it exactly as it was when I was a kid. The *ThunderCats* wallpaper. The pile of Lego in the corner. The books, spilling off the shelves. I can hear my father's voice – a voice I don't recognise, that I can't remember or describe, but somehow can still hear deep down inside myself – telling me something.

Dear Laura, the letter begins.

Even those two words hurt; and so immediately.

'Laura?' Cesar's voice, cutting through the moment. A wrench. I think of those people who have stories about having died, or believing that they've died; and that they've felt as if they were on the way to heaven. Travelling down a corridor of darkness towards a white light; and then, from the hospital room where their loved ones sit in a state of desperate pre-mourning, they hear a voice calling them back. Begging them. This is not your time. 'Laura, you have to come and look at this.' He's shouting, and I stop looking at the screen.

'Save the letter to your hard drive,' I say to Organon. It's waited fifty years. What's another hour?

At first, I can't be sure of what I'm seeing. The screen is full of specks. At a distance, so it's not a professional camera. Somebody's phone or watch or glass, something that's not quite capable of focusing from far away. It's the sky, and the white is this aching, arcing line across the sky; a sideways snarl, almost, drawn in hesitant chalk. 'What is that?' I ask, but then the camera shakes, the picture wobbles. People, on the streets. A city.

'Russia,' Cesar says. He slumps to the floor, nearly at my feet; back against the sofa, legs tucked under him. Just like I did when *Doctor Who* was on, when I was a kid, scared of a Dalek when it was revealed that they could fly up a flight of stairs; or watching *The Shining*, recorded off the television, making myself as small as possible when the twins appeared.

'What's happening?'

'They – the BBC – they got sent a link to a stream. They say it's from—'

'Sent how? The networks are down.'

'Not theirs. Emergency network for government employees. It's like the phone lines. We don't get them, but they do, because it's *of national importance.*'

'Organon, can you find the emergency network? Get onto it?'

'I would think that's illegal,' Organon says.

'I didn't build you with morals, did I?'

'Not strictly.'

'Off you trot, then,' I say.

Cesar shuffles closer to the screen. 'This is insane. You seeing this? Manipulation of elections, lies, cheating. Removal of citizen rights. Murders. It's not just Russia, of course. Everything those awful social media conspiracy theorists have been bleating on about for years and years? They're all validated now, aren't they?'

'There have been at least forty-three governmental conspiracies proven true over the past hour,' Organon says.

'You see? Everything is out there, Laura. All the shit, the nonsense, the chaos. Everything, and we're not even close to having the full truth exposed. So the people are angry. They're rioting, and the governments have shut down, and there is simply no way this gets better. Not before it gets much, much worse.'

We're watching something happen in another country, halfway around the world. I can imagine people in other houses, crowded around the TV sets, like this is some cultural event. I remember watching the aftermath of Princess Diana's death. I stood here, in this room, and I saw the people laying flowers for Diana. My mother sat on the bed with me. We both cried. I didn't even care, and I cried. And after that: September 11. The parades when the Queen died. I remember the troops coming back from Korea. I remember watching the May Day Refugee riots, and the bodies being carried out of the streets afterwards. I remember presidents being elected, prime ministers being deposed, countries revolting, and riots inciting. And then, only a couple of years ago, the Mars landings. For those, we got complacent. We assumed that it was going to be all right, I think; and then we

watched, all of us – like a minute's silence before there needed
to be one, a pre-emptive assumption – as the capsule puckered
and seemed to crumple in on itself. A fist closing tight around
an empty Coke can. I remember the inhalation of breath on the
stream from the ship itself, the *Endeavour*, orbiting. Maria
Walker inside it, talking to her crewmates in their last moments
– her friends – and how, before it happened, everybody had
been saying, *Oh it's sad for Maria because she won't get to go to
the surface and make that historic walk*, all that jazz. And afterwards, everybody said how lucky she was. I didn't think she was
lucky. She saw her friends die. She was there alone, and had to
spend the three days NASA forced her to spend trying to retrieve
their broken capsule – to no avail – before having to do the
journey back by herself. Not a hero, not really. More a survivor;
a lonely survivor.

That was the last time we all crowded around screens. We
wanted to see how it played out. We wanted to look away, but
we couldn't bear to. The same now. A car crash playing out in
very slow motion, only this car crash involves us all. I never saw
a world war taking place in my lifetime. I suppose I was naïve.
I assumed we'd somehow evolve past it.

Maybe we did. Maybe it was the idiocy of something we
created that did us in. We brought our children up badly, and
they didn't know how to treat us.

And now, I wonder how many people are doing this: sitting
in their homes, cut off from their Internet, seething at loved
ones or themselves, and they're watching this because it's something to do. I want to change the channel, see if everybody's
moved to the footage. It feels big enough.

'They're not telling us *anything*,' Cesar says.

'What's to tell? This is because of the leak,' I say, for what feels
like the millionth time in my life. But this is what we should
have expected: humans retaliating in a way that's entirely human.
Computers couldn't predict this.

'At least it could be worse,' Cesar says.

'There is literally no way in which it could be worse,' I tell him.

'There could be missiles. The governments are out of it, so that's something.'

'That'll come,' I tell him. America will discover that Taiwan did something because Russia told them that the UK were planning something because of the French or the Austrians or the Japanese or whoever. It doesn't matter. What matters is the world will find itself in the biggest game of Telephone that's ever happened. Rumours, whispers, hearsay.

Part of me, in this moment, welcomes it. It's a distraction. I've got my own things going on; my own worries. Harris. My secret; my only real secret.

God, that's awful.

I wonder, for a moment, if I've taken my head pill today. I haven't, I don't think. Travel and jet lag and time differences and distractions. Mental note. No pun.

We watch the video of these crowds, these riots. Silence, for a moment. For longer than a moment; until it becomes uncomfortable.

'We have to do something,' Cesar says. 'Can't you, I don't know, *do something*?'

'What?' I ask. My voice sounds flat as it comes from my mouth. Dulled, because I know what he's going to ask, and I know what the answer is.

'Take down the database. Block everything. I don't know, but you've got access. You know people, don't you?'

My phone rings; as if by magic. It's Charlie, even though the lines are down. We were told we were cut off, he shouldn't be able to call. He's out of breath, huffing and heaving as he tries to get the words out. 'You watching this?' he asks. Doesn't give me a chance to answer. 'This is ridiculous. Have you seen the Chinese's statement?' *The Chinese.* As if the entire country, the entire race, decided to speak in unison on this one thing. 'They said that Putin's senile, impotent, ineffectual, insane. These words. I mean, they said them in Chinese, but translated. You know.'

'How are you calling me?'

'Bow has back doors. How are *you* able to take my call?'

'Touché,' I say.

'Putin's just crazy enough to launch something. You know he is.'

'Hang on,' I say, 'is that knowledge or speculation?'

'Laura, get out of London.' His voice sounds odd. Strained. 'We've heard things, and we don't know if they're true or whatever, but seriously. Don't risk it.'

'I can't,' I say.

'This is going to get much worse. There's nothing more important than—'

'How long a lead did you all have on this?' He's quiet. 'How long have Bow known what SCION was going to do?'

A sigh, then. I'm not sure if it's resignation or rushed breathlessness. 'We've had the data for a few weeks. It was seeping, right? We didn't know where or why. But it was like it was coming out of the cracks. What's out there, it's not even close to being all of it. I mean, what's been found. The data existed in various places, but most of it was still hidden away in subsystems, disorganised. And we had passwords on everything. SCION didn't start breaking those until last year. At least, that's what we thought.'

'It broke your passwords?'

'It saw them like they were, I don't know, puzzles, games.'

'And you taught it to win at games.'

'That's . . .' He sounds sad. 'Laura, it solved them – or, it tried to – by deciphering what they would have used as passwords. They, sorry, the people. The owners of the email accounts. Most people still use pets' names or the streets they grew up on or birthdates. Whatever. It used their information—'

'You fucking idiots,' I said to him.

'I'm sorry,' he tells me. 'Please, Laura, I'm sorry.'

'What for?' I can hear something in his voice. He never sounds like this: weak and sad and lost. He's petrified. 'Charlie, what did you do?'

'You're going to find out. You'll see the emails. All the Bow emails, they're public knowledge after today.'

'What emails?'

'We used some of Organon, Laura. I mean, this was . . .'

His voice fades away. It makes perfect sense. SCION was good at understanding rules; Organon was always good at understanding why those rules existed. I taught Organon to understand what it was being asked; to get to the root of the thing. And they must have taken its code – *the comprehension engine*, they'll have called it, something twee and nonsensical like that – and worked it into SCION's base code. Taken everything I understood, everything I learned, and implemented it into their awful idiot of an intelligence.

You put a good kid in a playpen with a nasty kid, and sooner or later, one's going to teach the other something. This time around, the good kid lost.

'You'll never stop betraying me, will you?' I say. Words sown from bitterness that you never shake; anger you never fully lose.

'It was a long time ago I did this. *We* did this. I was ordered—'

'Don't.'

'Look, Laura. Please, believe me. I didn't know if we'd do anything with it.' Breathing, hard breathing. He's talking fast, blabbering. 'I wanted to hide your code away, maybe even purge it all as soon as I had the chance. But Johann, you know what he's like. And as soon as your personality matrix miners started working for us? Well, Johann kept saying we were close to achieving what we wanted to achieve. We wanted deep learning, deep *thought*, and finally, here it was.' He coughs. 'Shit,' he says, and his voice sounds desperately quiet, desperately pained.

There's a thump. The sound of a body hitting the ground. It's unmistakable, I'd say, if it's not a sound you've ever heard before. I can't think when I would ever have heard it; but I know it. Charlie's body, Charlie's handset clattering. I wonder if anybody will see him, get him help. Cesar is saying something to the television, at the television, and I shout at him to be quiet.

'Organon, is there a way of finding Charlie?' Organon doesn't immediately reply. 'Triangulation, something like that.'

'Send me to him,' Organon says.

'What?'

'Send me as a self-installing attachment, to his phone. I can do something there.'

'Like you're a virus?'

'Everything is a virus,' Organon says. 'Do you trust me?'

'Yes,' I say.

On the television screen, the worst is happening. There's nothing but sky, nothing but the vague knowledge that something up there, out of sight, is deadly, is going to destroy something; and I'm still worried about the present. The future. The past.

'Fine,' I say. 'Send.'

And just like that, I let Organon off into the world.

I don't say: Fly, my pretty.

I don't say: Be sure to call and let me know that you're all right.

I can watch, then. Organon switches on Charlie's phone's camera, so I get a live feed. The phone is lying on the floor, or on his chest. We're looking up at the sky, at the clear, solid blue; and then a dark object, pawing at the camera. Charlie's hand, reaching for the phone. I listen as Organon makes the handset beep, turns up the ringer, louder and louder. It alters the pitch of the ring-tone, bending it to a high screech. Wait, wait. A man's face comes into view, and he picks up the phone. Slow panic in his eyes. Is he high? Or has he been crying? Organon's already called the emergency services, alerted them. Sent them Charlie's coordinates. Now it immediately starts talking at the man who has picked up the handset, giving him instructions. Here is what you do. Ask Charlie these questions. Is he conscious? Are his eyes responsive? Describe his face. Describe his position. Organon takes on the role of a doctor, like one of those awful soft-AIs that they tried to replace GPs with a few years back. It barks at the man, doesn't matter if he *is* high or upset, tells him what to do. Feel for a pulse. Clear the airways. Stay with him. Stay with him. But the man with Charlie is only a boy, really. A kid. I get glances of his glossy little half-moustache. He's scared, and he says it. He says that he doesn't know if he can do *this*. He means the whole thing: the being there, the trying to fix this broken man lying on a sidewalk in San Francisco. Organon asks him his name. The kid says it: Bryan Daniels. Bryan Daniels from where? Organon asks. Bryan tells Organon. And then something changes. Organon's voice shifts. There's a pause while it happens, a stilted crack to its metre that sounds like packet loss or an interruption in the feed, as Organon's voice alters itself. Personality gone. I think of earlier, when – briefly, interrupted – it took on the timbre of my mother's voice. Her soothe: don't worry, Laura, it will all be all right, she would have said. Now, Organon's voice takes on another woman's voice, a voice that I don't recognise. American. Not Californian, something southern. Shhh, it says. Listen. This is what you do. It's terrifying, and the boy – Bryan – stares at the screen. 'Mom?' he says, but Organon rolls with it. Listen to me, here's what you need to do. Think of what it will mean, keeping this man alive. Organon's voice – this woman's voice, Bryan's mother's voice – full of tics I never programmed in. Verbal wobbles it never had before, that simply didn't exist in its programming before. I can't quite nail them down, but one of the southern American states, somewhere. Like you hear in some TV shows. That's his mother. That's her voice. Talking him through calming down, talking him through what he has to do. I sit and I watch until I hear the sirens; until I hear Charlie being taken off by them, somebody American shouting at him to stay with them, telling him that he's going to be all right.

'Do you want me to stay here?' Organon asks me, in its real – original – voice. The one that I programmed, that I chose the pitch of, the speed, the tone. The level of treble versus the level of bass.

'You can come back,' I say, my own voice trembling. I can feel my hands, totally aware of them. I can see the shake in them.

'Was that what I was meant to do?' Organon asks.

I don't know how to answer that. 'Yes,' I say, but I don't mean that word, that word alone. I mean everything that could be said that isn't. That I'm scared, and proud. It's done something I didn't think of. Didn't dream of.

It's *become* something.

'Can you find out what's happening?' Cesar asks me. I'm sitting on the sofa, still as anything. I don't even know where I was, in my mind. Somewhere else. Not here. 'Laura?'

'Sorry,' I say. Good old British apology. I'm not sorry. I was – am – freaking the fuck out. This wasn't something I predicted. I don't know what I predicted. Not this.

'Can you find out? Somehow, I don't know. Emails or something?'

'They're not working,' I say.

'What about Twitter? The countries who didn't shut down their networks, they'll be up online.' He sounds desperate.

'I'll look,' I say. Organon tells me what the Chinese said. The exact words. What the Russians have also said. People are scouring the database. All the world's minds searching for the most dangerous, scandalous, scurrilous things possible, the things that will chip away at the walls of our infrastructures and bring them crumbling down. When we come back online, there will be a deluge: the flood from the Cloud, finally come. Why didn't we see this? Why didn't people worry about this part? They worried about privacy, about their information. On a personal scale: celebrities terrified about hacking, people worried about sex pictures being stolen. We never thought about what would happen if the clouds started to pour.

'We have to do something!' Cesar says. Begs, almost.

'There's nothing we can do,' I reply.

'Set Organon loose. Get it to fix the thing. Delete the files, maybe, something like that.' He's desperate. Frothing. 'Organon,' he says, and Organon chirrups that it's listening.

'Don't,' I say to him. 'That's not what it does. How many times do I have to tell you?'

'You've told me many times all the things it *doesn't* do. You've never actually told me what it *does*. Did you know what would happen with Charlie, with that boy?' I didn't. He knows that. 'So how do you know Organon can't fix this shit?'

'It's out there. It's everywhere. It will have been downloaded more times than any other single file in history already. It's a deluge, Cesar, and it can never be dammed.'

'Your AI can do it.' He's not a bad guy, Cesar. He's delusional. He's angry. He wants action. 'It can go into the Russian computers, and it can find out if they're planning on launching something. It *can*. It can find their files, their databases, and it can delete them. Even from computers, you *know* that. It's powerful, Laura. It can do these things.'

'It struggled to crack a password my father set on a disk in 1987,' I reply. 'I built it to be naïve in that way. I didn't want it abused.'

'I'm right here,' Organon says, a little interruption that makes me hack out laughter. Relieved, unexpected. Always unexpected.

'Can you do what needs to be done?' Cesar asks. He snatches my handset from the side. 'Will you—'

'Cesar,' I snap, 'don't.'

'I simply don't know if I can do it,' Organon says. 'This situation, it's not—'

'Then you should try. We should be trying.' Something's wrong. Something's changed in this. He was going along with whatever, calm as anything, and now? His eyes are the deep red of somebody on the verge of tears. 'Organon, stop this! Shut the doors, the gates. Stop these *fucking idiots* from destroying the fucking world!' He spits the words like they're pips.

I snatch the handset from him. 'Organon's programmed to only do what I tell it to do,' I say. It's like a harness. Hold the kids back, stop them getting run over. Stop them getting into trouble. 'It can't do this. I can't let it loose like that.'

Cesar falls back; first to the sofa, then he slides off, to the floor. Head in his hands, and he starts to cry. There's no booze in the house, I know. I don't think I'd have to worry about it, even if there was. He's stronger than that.

'I'm going upstairs,' I say. 'Let me know if anything changes.' I get into what used to be my bedroom – what will always, somehow, be my bedroom – and I talk to Organon. I sit on a floor that I remember, by a desk that used to be black, surrounded by walls I know every crack in, every chip, every cranny, and I hold Organon close to my face, and I shut my eyes. My voice comes out, quiet as anything. 'You *can't* do anything, can you?'

'I'm afraid not,' it says. The screen blinks at me, quick and fast; like a wink with nothing behind it.

The next time I hear Cesar's voice, as I'm rooting around in a box of my father's old vinyl – pulling out records he played when I was a kid, records that I loved, *Let's Dance*, and *The White Album*, and *Out of the Blue* – it's begging me to come downstairs. I'm reading the track list of *The Hounds of Love*, my fingers tracing the words of the Tennyson poem quoted on the rear, when Cesar yelps. Jubilant, exultant.

'Come down here and watch this,' he says. I grab my phone,

refresh Twitter to see what I can. The TV gets me the information before the fragmented Internet does. They're not running
commentary on the news: just the same footage on a loop, and
occasional interjections from the presenters that sound like
they're coughing, or trying out lines that they then go back on.
Along the bottom of the screen, the fact bar, there's information
about NATO talks being held, about the UN being called to
session, about the European Collective country leaders coming
together for conversations, about the peace talks being held all
over the world. There must be stuff that didn't leak – a lot of
business is done on paper, just to avoid things like this; which,
when you think about it, makes leaks seem like an inevitability
– but everything else needs apologising for. At least it seems
like everybody's in this. Nobody's perfect, and we've all got
something to hide. I'll look up names, I know. I'll search for
what people have said about me, I'm sure, when I'm bored one
day and waiting for something to happen, and it'll tell me things
I don't want to know and will wish I didn't know, but the lure
of knowing simply proved too much. I'll look up my mum and
dad—

My father. Will there be anything about him? Things I've
missed? What's been digitised? Do the records go back that far?
Do they include people who aren't people any more, people who
died in the way back, who never saw the Internet, who never
saw what privacy would become?

'This is amazing,' Cesar says. 'I mean, we were just saying . . .'
His voice trails off.

A face – female, jubilant, young, one of *those* faces – appears
on the screen. Practically bouncing on the sofa the presenters
usually sit on. 'We've had word that the Chinese have reached
out to Russia, even in the wake of the aggressions we've seen
from Putin's people – that Mr Putin has apologised to the Chinese
government, with the Chinese replying that they are open to
peace talks, to discussions, about the, uh, the ramifications of

today's leaks.' She's relieved. Everybody's relieved, as we all should be.

World War 3, averted.

I run up the stairs. Grab my phone. Organon's screen, lit when I pick it up, ready to speak. 'Did you do that?' I ask it.

'Do what?'

'You're not fucking stupid. I built you. Did you do something to fix this?'

'I don't have the ability to venture deeper than surface level in any governmental system that I don't have permission to access.'

'I let you *go*. The first time you've been loose in the world, the first time I gave you the ability to go somewhere you weren't allowed to go. Did you—'

'You programmed me to be unable to lie to you,' it says to me.

'No, I didn't,' I say. 'I programmed you to not necessarily tell me the truth if it was for the best.' Back then, when it was just a voice for me to talk to, that made sense. That programming is still there, still underneath everything. Code that I don't even understand any more, code that writes itself, that ties itself into knots. Into tangles I can't unpick.

'Those are the same thing,' Organon says; but it knows they're not.

'What happened with the boy. With Charlie?'

'I felt that Bryan needed calming. I reasoned that calming him would require something that felt less alien to him than my presence. As a consequence, I chose to adopt the voice of a mediator.'

'Where did you get his mother's voice?'

'From the leak,' Organon says. 'I found him, and then found her. Her telephone records and datavoice calls were logged. Then it was just a matter of breaking down the vocalised sounds—'

'And that's what you did with my mother.'

'I thought I would see if I could,' it says.

We sit in silence. Just for a while. Just long enough that the room stops feeling like it's going to close up on me. This room, a room that saw every single thing I went through when I was a kid. The things I remember and the things that I don't.

A match head, pressed against my skin.

A boyfriend I never actually had.

Lies, and theft, and deceit. Endless telephone calls after school when I should have been working; taking the bills and stowing them away, burning them. Climbing out onto the roof outside my bedroom window, just to see London: a view that felt barely hidden away, but just that little bit extra, the removal of the glass between us, made it everything.

I find my father's old record player, his turntable, and the amp, the speakers. Put them together in the corner of the room. The dust on the speaker cabs makes me wheeze, but I brush them clean with the palm of my hand anyway. Better to have them cleared, better to have them shining a little. I vaguely remember this. Sitting on the floor, the chest that stored his vinyl opened wide, I would pull them out and gaze at the covers before I even knew what was inside them. The incredible drawings of spaceships, the titles that were designed to drag you in. I wonder if the needle is still good: I turn it all on, take the Kate Bush from the sleeve, lay it on the turntable. The drop of the needle makes a hiss, a bounce, a crackle; and then that voice comes through. Singing of my Organon, her Organon. Another Organon entirely, that means something different.

I close my eyes. I open my eyes.

I wake up crying.

'There's no way to shut down the leak,' Organon says, out of nowhere. 'It's propagated too far. Too many downloads. It's part of the world now.'

'Of course it is,' I say. Once something has been done, it can't be taken back.

*   *   *

We return to stasis, as we always do. I read on Twitter that the Internet – for those in parts of the world that have gone offline, who don't have access in the way that I do – will be back soon. Bow is taking ownership of what's happened. The stock market's been shut down, but only for a while. When it comes back, the analysts I follow are predicting the largest crash in a company's stock since the ClearVista scandal last decade. Maybe even larger. There are photographs – screengrabs, mostly – of world leaders meeting. Back on the job. How long did it take? A few hours? Less than a day, certainly. There are resignations still to happen, scandals still to be uncovered. The information flowing out is endless, ceaseless. It's like a line drawn under who we have been, and who we will be in the future. There's an article on *Medium*, written by some guy in South America who works for *Wired*, all about how he's moving to paper. Not even offline word processing now, but actual physical paper. The only thing that he's going to commit to code for a while is that which he's comfortable publishing, or comfortable with the world seeing. This is, he writes, an end. It's when everything changes.

How long do I sit in the room? Cesar brings me beans on toast – my mother had bread in the freezer, baked beans in the cupboard – and it tastes amazing.

'I've got to drive back to Brighton. I want to be there when Ashley gets home,' he says, which I understand. 'Do you mind me leaving you alone?'

'I'll be fine,' I tell him. Cesar smiles. That's a lie and we both know it.

And then he's gone: down the hall, down the stairs, out of the front door. I follow, standing in the light of my old house, and I stare at the stained-glass panels in the door, at the light coming through them. I can't even count the number of times I've done this: looked at the light, and wondered about how all the colours make this rainbow of reflections on the wall. How many times I've gone up to that light and stood in it, just to bathe in it.

I pass out on the sofa, in front of the TV. When I wake up, it's to the sound of the usual reporter's voice. One of the usual reporters. I know her. She looks tired. Not because she's been on air, but there's life in the way now. Her life, and I wonder what impact the leak has had on her. What information came out that she didn't want coming out, what she discovered about her loved ones. The Internet's back, she's saying. We've been switched back on. The worst of it has passed. The Snooper's Charter stuff they passed a couple of decades ago means they're blocking the leak database – 'For the nation's safety,' the government says – but there are ways around that. They can stamp on websites as much as they like, but the Internet is a hydra. Kill one head, two more immediately grow to take its place. I tell Organon to get off the government's network – I don't want them coming after me, if they notice – and to find me a proxy.

TMZ is having a field day of dickpics, sexts, and nearly-political cuntery from celebrity politicians, but none of that involves me. They don't care about people like me, not at all. So I search for myself on Twitter, where the people who *do* care dwell. The whatever-gaters, the Alt-Right, the farfetched, the crazies, and the loons. I want to see if anybody's dug around for my name yet, or if I'm too low down the tree – low-hanging fruit – for them to bother.

Here's my life, as I don't remember it being, but definitely absolutely as it was: the photographs I sent to my mother when she had her handbag stolen, of us on holiday, of mine and Harris's wedding; decades of different antidepressants, all presented as some sort of fait accompli, a *this is who she is*, because there will always be arseholes who think that you're a bad human being because you have succeeded where they have failed, and because your brain chemistry is different enough that you need some help nudging it into place; and then data I sent to people, reports on me and my work while I was at Bow; choice quotes said about me by various other people, good and bad – including Charlie describing what I was like in bed, and Park describing what he *thinks* I would be like in bed; a letter I wrote to Nadine, my old school friend, when I first moved to America, a primitive email that I filled with ASCII art and early-days l33t-speak.

And, of course, my lie.

I wear a veil on the Internet. I do everything through proxies, through anonymity. The only time I'm ever exposed is when playing with somebody else's systems. Ordering things from shops, booking holidays, posting comments on blogs.

Making appointments I never told my husband about.

Here, somebody talks about the abortion I had in 2017. How many weeks pregnant I was, what size the baby was when I killed it. Peppered with quotes from the Bible, because it's impossible to talk about abortions as something human; it needs to be laced with guilt, with mysticism, with storytelling.

'Organon,' I say, 'text Harris, tell him that I need to talk to him—'

'Are you sure?' Organon asks.

'God fucking damn it,' I shout. 'Yes, I'm sure. I'm positive. Stop asking me if I'm sure about everything.'

And then: something about my father. A sentence that kicks me, beyond the ones judging me for my choices. This one *guts* me. A knife, pulled across my stomach; and I can feel the muscles giving way, a desperate urge to be sick. To yank myself apart, to find this thing that's inside me and make it better, as it was a few moments ago. The knife twists. The knife is never dropped, hands, fingers on the handle. Pushed, to make it hurt all the more.

Organon knows that I am reading this. It knows *what* I am reading.

'Would you like to talk?' it asks. I can't form the words to reply. A doctor's record. A statement, more final than anything else I have ever read about him. It mentions me, and it mentions my mother, as potentially needing counselling, after my father's *inevitable death*. The words, so blurry and confused it's as if they have no real meaning to me: *tumour; episodes; ideation of suicide*. 'Laura, would you like to talk?'

I inhale. A gasp of my head being lifted out from underwater; being told not to drown. To save myself before it's too late.

'Shut up,' I say. I don't say: You've done too much. You've gone too far. Today has been too much for me to cope with, and this, all of this, feels like it's too chaotic. I need to sleep. I need to *stop*.

'Laura: would you like to talk?'

And just like that, Organon's voice isn't its own. It's a voice that I haven't heard in years. Decades. A voice that I barely remember, which hangs onto the memories that I have of it in frayed, dangling threads, loose and pulling and torn at their ends. Something desperately fragile about my relationship with it, and yet these words, this voice: it's *his*.

It's my father.

It's a trick, of course. Well intentioned, well meant. This is how the singularity will never happen, as we understand this. This moment will always be a stumbling block: as the past and the present collide in some way that's inexplicable, linked by tragedy and memory and self-pity and fear and pride. All of those things in a moment. That's what we have; what we'll never manage to create in something absolutely made of wires and code.

'Where did you get the voice from?' I ask Organon.

'There are interviews. I found his file in the leak, and there are digitised interviews linked to it. Some archive material from the BBC, some from educational television programmes, some from Bow's internal videos. I found them and I approximated his voice. I think I have all of the markers in order to find the correct inflection.'

'You do,' I say. The voice is my father's, right down to the slight hesitancy in the way he said his words. What, now, sounds like insertion of semicolons instead of commas, spacing everything out. Giving him thinking time; room to breathe.

'We can talk if you'd like,' Organon says. 'Or I can.'

I wipe a tear from my cheek. My jaw trembles.

'I could read the text file I have imported. The letter that he left for you.'

I nod, don't say anything; and maybe Organon's watching through the camera, or maybe it just knows. But it starts to read, my father's voice filling my room; my house; my world.

When the voice fades, after my father's finished telling me his story, it's dark outside. Not just dark: streetlights, the night-anchors on BBC *News 24*, my stomach desperate for food, my bladder desperate for a pee. I walk through the house in the dark, listening to it: the downstairs bathroom, and sitting on the cold seat, realising that this loo doesn't have any toilet paper left in it; a tin of spaghetti hoops from the cupboard, poured out, microwaved, practically drunk from the bowl; the guy who used to do mornings on BBC, and now he's old – we've basically grown up together – and he's been put out to pasture in this middle-of-the-night slot.

I raise my bowl to him. Here's to the graveyard shift, buddy.

The front door opens. Harris comes in. Whatever he's seen – I don't know if he looked the data up himself, and God how cold is it to think of it as that, as data? – he's quiet. I stand up, walk to the doorway.

'You're not asleep,' he says.

'I've had a busy day,' I tell him. 'Adrenaline. You know how it is.'

'I know,' he replies.

I don't know how to tell him. Because of course I want to, now, even though it's too late for it to make any difference. He'll be upset. Not angry – I'm not sure he ever gets angry, not properly – but it'll hurt.

He'll say: I'm more hurt that you lied to me.

I'll say: I didn't lie. I just didn't tell you something.

Logic games, and linguistics.

'How was work?'

'Up and down. Everything was fucked. Now it's not.' He walks into the light, and his face is ashen. People say that, and you don't understand it until you see it. 'How were things here?'

'I'm okay,' I say. 'Organon might have stopped a war from happening, so that's something.' I smile. Laugh. Come on, Harris, smile with me.

'Sometimes,' he says, 'I think I shouldn't even leave the house. Sometimes I think I should sit here and let you work around me. The things I would see.' He takes my hand. 'I looked.'

'You looked.'

'At the databases. At mine. Yours. I looked.' I nod. Do I talk now? Is it my turn? 'I don't want to look at them. I looked, and then I stopped looking. I don't need to see anything on them, do I.' It's not a question. 'If you want to talk about them, I totally understand. We can. But know this: I don't need to. I don't want to, don't need to.'

'People harbour resentment when they don't talk about something,' I say.

Mental note: Check the hospital records, make sure Charlie's okay.

'Some people. But maybe that's how you have to deal with things, sometimes. You don't deal with them, and that's better. That's how we get along.' He bites his fingernails. No, he bites the skin next to his fingernails. That's how I know he's really anxious. 'I was reading, on the Tube home, that China and Russia and everybody else nearly went to war today, right?'

'Right,' I say.

'And then they didn't. Word is, Putin apologised. Now he's

fucking insane, we all know that, and he's claiming that he *didn't* apologise. Didn't send an email to the Chinese. But the situation's defused, and I suspect Putin's not long for this world, and it's been left. I've heard that the Russian in the email – it was written in Russian, can you believe that? – was flaky at best. Easier to translate for the Chinese; easier to respond to. Maybe that was intentional. Whatever. Doesn't matter. But the situation's been defused.' He takes my hand. 'I don't need to know what happened there. The world doesn't need to know what happened. Sometimes, a thing happens, and it's better for everybody that it's not explained. It's better that we simply move past it, and move on. You understand?'

I understand.

'So how's your Russian, Organon?' he asks. The question to the air. Harris never talks to Organon.

'Неплохо,' Organon says. 'Not bad.'

'Of course it's not,' Harris replies.

'My father—' I don't know how to say this.

'You found some of his things?'

'No,' I reply. 'Nearly. A note.'

'A note?'

'Yeah. He left a note.'

I leave that hanging. He knows what it means.

A moment's pause; and then Harris asks me if I want to talk.

1987

I WON'T FORGET

Dear Laura. This letter isn't for you now. You, now, are seven years old. You won't understand why I've done what I've done, and nor would I expect you to. Your mother will decide, I'm sure, to tell you what she feels best; but, when the time comes, I would like you to be able to make your own choice. To hear my full story, or not.

To let me explain, or not.

I've written to your mother, as well. I've asked her to give this to you on your eighteenth birthday; if not before. It has to be her decision; her discretion. I hope you'll be yourself, by then; the person that you're already on your way to becoming. I hope that you read it, so that you can better understand who I am – who I was – and the choices that I made.

Know this: that I love you. I love you, and I am already proud of you. I can already see the person you will become, and I know that my pride will never end.

I wish we could meet when you're older.

I have – or, I had; your timeline, your present tense, will be very different to my own – a tumour. A pressing, a swelling, on my brain. I have started to see things, to imagine things, to forget things. I endangered you, a few weeks ago; we were in the park, and you were running, chasing, and I was chasing you; and I forgot about you, Laura. I forgot that you existed. I sat on a bench, and I watched as you fell into the lake there. As you panicked; as you started to drown. I watched as somebody saved you, and you howled, and they dried you with their coat, and shouted to see if this poor child's parents were anywhere close.

Hello? the woman shouted, and something clicked inside me, and I was back.

In that initial moment, though, I didn't know who you were. Had that woman not been there, I would have let you drown.

The doctor says that I have very little time left, and that my state, as he puts it, will only degrade. I will forget you, and your mother, and myself; and I'll rage. I have started to lose my eyesight. I have started to lose my faculties. Details I want to spare you, because I don't want you to think of your father that way.

It's likely that, by the time you read this, I'll only really be fragments of memories. The man who held you when you cried, there in photographs you don't remember being taken, dated by the clothes that he wears, by the haircuts, the cars in the background. I don't know who, exactly, you will be; what sort of person life will have made you. Life, and your mother's guidance, of course.

I wonder: Will my presence have left an impact?

Will my absence?

I want to use this letter to tell you about who I am. To tell you about who I was, when I was younger; why I made the choices I made; and to make sure that you understand me. I've done things that I cannot take back, and as I look into the future – something I feel like I'm somehow able to do from my position, and only now, for the first time

– I can see that I have ruined my life. My actions now are the only way I can see to avoid ruining yours as well.

Your mother would tell me that I am wrong. Nothing can't be undone, she would say. She would cite examples from history, but they're only really stories. As soon as something's in the past, apocryphal, I think it loses some of its original truth. But then, once a story is told, once it is created and sent out into the world, it's far too late to take that thing back.

I have my own examples; my own evidence.

As I write this, you're sitting on the carpet. We're in your bedroom, where I've had the computer set up so that I can show you a little of what I do; or, maybe, of what I did. I don't recognise your clothes. This past year you've grown so much, and I feel as though I've missed it all. You've got a Speak & Spell in your lap, which I bought for you last Christmas, after you saw *ET*; after you recovered from being terrified of it. You type letters on the keypad, then it speaks the word that they form at the end, as long as those words are in its dictionary. Only, you've adapted it. Changed the purpose. You're making it speak, but in broken phrases; chunks of letters, strung together, fragments. You've worked out how to make these phrases interrupt each other, getting the toy to say words that it shouldn't be able to say. Words which are not in its dictionary.

You just noticed me glancing down at you, and you spelled out our surname: Bow. The toy pronounced it as the action; the gesture of servitude. You corrected it, however, playing with the letters, the interruptions, until it's how we say it. Until we are Bow-rhymes-with-No, tied up in knots of ribbon. We both smiled, at that. Maybe, reading this, you remember this moment. I'm sure you won't remember the details. You won't remember my breathing, so slightly off. You won't remember my hands; you won't remember how they trembled.

I have to believe you'll want to read this. Maybe you won't. Maybe it won't even be your choice; maybe the computer will go to landfill, the disk lost to whatever. Time; or rot. But this is my story, and it's also yours.

This is how I'll be remembered after I'm gone, if I'm remembered at all.

When I was a few years older than you are now, my father decided that I had a head for numbers. Of course, I believed myself to be more creative, perhaps, than numerical; much as you are, as you do. I wrote poetry, if you can believe that. I read books, one a day, pretty much. Incessant. I was arty, and I was going to create something. We had a writer come into school, once, and I remember thinking how amazing it was that writing novels could be a job. But my exam results proved my father right. I was creative enough, imaginative, all that, but I didn't have the tools. All through my teenage years, he told me of this concept he had for me; my destiny. The notion of the family business was, in the 1950s, the 60s, a bigger deal than it is now. He had this idea that I had what essentially was a calling: taking my place in the service of *Bow & Son*.

His father – my grandfather – had served in both of our century's major wars. (Very few fought in both, Dad used to remind me.) When Grandad returned from that second conflict, lame in his left leg, blind in his right eye, he went back to Stoke Newington, the area of London he'd grown up in. It had changed, just like he had. Wrecked by bombs, impoverished to the point of near-despair, the streets being rebuilt to serve entirely new purposes. He had been an army man his whole life, and had no real trade otherwise, so he was forced – his other option being building work, anything that he could persuade those who knew him to throw his way, a step ahead of charity – to turn what had been the shattered Bow family home into a shop. He bought what some didn't want, bartered with them, sold it to others. Nothing profitable about it: just existence. He called the shop *Bow & Son*, because he wanted a sense of the already ongoing; the idea that, perhaps, his own doings might outlast his generation. My father, a teenager by the time the second war ended, was drawn into the business without a say. He had, his own father told him, a head for numbers. He worked the shelves after school. It was called a general store; a cornucopia of assorted tat, as my father saw it. Anything that could be ascribed a value, my grandfather called an *antique*. As the 1950s crept into being, he began to buy up the medals from men who had served in those wars. He polished them to a sheen, and displayed them in the window next to acrobatic tin monkeys and romantically poised porcelain figurines.

My grandfather's heart gave in, as hearts are wont to do, and my father found himself the primary article of the shop's name. He changed tack, taking on a few accountancy jobs, and within a year, it was those jobs that were paying the rent, not the bric-a-brac that filled the stockroom. He kept the premises, and simply painted across the inside of the windows in thick white paint, so as to make it appear an office, not a shop. He didn't change the name: *Bow & Son*, he argued, sounded as much like an accountants as it did a shop.

And there it was: my inevitability.

Of course, I told my parents that I wanted to go to university. My father argued, my mother fought my side, and then they reached a solution. My father offered me conditions. A degree in mathematics; I would work in the shop;

I would work for him afterwards, until I had a firm job offer. When the offer came through from Imperial, it made perfect sense. The content of the course wavered between the astonishingly boring and practical side of mathematics, and the rather more chaotic and unsolvable nature of theory. I didn't like the mechanical gruntwork of further and applied mathematics. I liked logic. I liked theorems that had never been solved. The mysteries of what numbers could achieve.

Then, one day, we were taken to see the new IBM computer that the university had acquired. It filled an entire room, and it was glorious. We were told that those unsolvable equations we studied wouldn't be puzzled over by human brains, in the future. They would be fixed with a snap of digital fingers. It would still be our work, because we were the ones who would have taught the computer the rules by which it operated.

From inside the room, all you could hear was the constant whirring of tapes, the clicking of pins. At its loudest, it was like the noise of an engine, a spinning turbine. It was the noise of the world itself taking off.

I knew, right away – though I am not an exception here, because we all of us knew, every single student inside that room – that this was not merely the future of mathematics; it was the future of everything.

We are, as people, obsessed with our own evolution. The leap from mulch to stew; from tetrapod to mammal; from ape to man. The perpetual question that's preoccupied our greatest minds: what comes next. Not because we're staid, but because we know that there has to be something. The nature of genetics says that, eventually, there will come a change. It could be a physical development, a larger leap than the ones we face every day, living longer, or growing taller. Or maybe it will be something mental: telepathy, telekinesis, ideas torn from the pages of science fiction.

But the computer's existence says that those predictions are wrong. The next stage will not be driven by genetics; it will be brought about by ourselves. It will be an evolution that we establish through technology, and then it will be with us always, tweaked and teased until it is present at the birth of every child, maybe even when they are in utero; and we will push that evolution forward, with a constancy and drive – terrifying, in so many ways – that will simply not stop.

Maybe that sounds nightmarish. But also: doesn't it sound inevitable?

Every waking hour of my study from that point onwards was spent in that computer room. The machine was a beacon to me; a lighthouse. In every story, there is always a lighthouse, leading one towards something. Of course, a lighthouse really only exists to tell you what to avoid.

As students and faculty, we learned how to talk with the computer, in programming terms. We began with 1s and 0s, a binary language; then another, more complicated, language, named BASIC. The name is almost a joke. We studied the history of it: how IBM came to develop their hardware, their programming language; about Colossus, the Bletchley code breaker; of the abacus, even, which of course we all knew about, but the theorems regarding it were, in their own way, a basic form of what we were in fact studying anew. Even that history felt exciting. The past, helping us to push forward our understanding. We felt at the forefront of something important.

And the myriad possibilities! Outside of mathematics, outside of formulae. We – myself and some of the other students – collaborated, to create a functional game. We named it *Forth*. It was really very simple. Four different armies, ten men in each – each man a pixel, really, a dot on a screen – and the armies could charge at each other, moving as one. When they collided, the system decided which were facing forward, and which were attacked from behind. The latter little men died. The game was about managing those troops you had left, ensuring that you moved away from pursuers, while attempting to defeat others. It was impossible not to lose some of your troops, so it became up to you, their commander, to decide who was most expendable, and when. For all its simplicity, it took six months of our spare time to create. Late nights in front of the computer, all of us crammed into that room, drunk or high – don't judge me, because I don't know what sort of person you've grown up to become, but I drank alcohol and I smoked pot, in those days – attempting to build our own systems, to make them work with each other. So much was trial and error; but it was a trial and error we had the time and the patience to go through.

During the summer, with no classes, I would go to the university whenever I wasn't working in the shop. In those seemingly endless summer nights, hot as anything, trapped in a room that amplified the heat to a point where I genu-inely feared, at points, for my health, I continued work on *Forth* myself. I programmed an intelligence into the system so that I had somebody to play against. An opponent. I taught it how to attack and defend, how to know when to run, and how to guard against my armies. But I taught it, I created it, so that I could beat it. I understood the rules better than it did. I copied that intelligence, tweaked it, created two more opponents. Very basic, they were, at their core, but intelligent enough that I spent hours fighting with them. Occasionally they would outwit me, and I felt aston-ishingly smug when that happened. They only won because

I had taught them to win. And, of course, they were no match for real people; for humans, with all their ability, their flaws, and their luck.

It was at the end of that summer I first met your mother. There's no story there, not really: we met one night in a pub in Putney, after we had both, independently, I might add, walked the river. She was the perfect distraction at the perfect time. The perfect *everything*. She understood what I was trying to do – or, if not quite, she humoured me, which was just as useful – and she would sit with me in front of the IBM as we reached the hottest evenings of the year, and she would play that stupid bloody game with me; and she would help me fine-tune the opponents, bringing her own intelligence, her knowledge to the work.

I can't even dream of having a brain like hers. You can tell, before she even speaks a word, that she is a historian. They have an air to them, a pervasive understanding of who we – people, humans – are, because of all that we have been in the past. And, somehow, that gives them a confidence, in my experience; a grounding. It's personal, beyond that. The woman you know now is the woman she's always been. And who she always will be.

She and I moved in together after only a few months. We knew that people would say it was happening too quickly. Your mother's parents approved. My mother cried – good Catholic that she was – and my father seethed, thinking it would mean I would be at the shop less. He was right, even though I assured him otherwise. I wanted to get out from underneath his feet, and your mother wanted to stop living with her flatmates, air stewardesses who kept ridiculous hours, who provided no constancy. It wasn't conducive to general happiness, she told me. But, of course, the justifications were nonsense. We wanted to be together. That's what happens.

We found a flat in Chelsea, near the river, because it meant we could both get to the university easily enough. We walked home along the river most days those first couple of months, huddled close in the hazy fading pink-light of the early winter evenings. Our place was on the top floor of a late Edwardian, nothing more than a converted loft space, really: a large window in the kitchen, and a solitary bedroom under the eaves, the morning light on our faces as we dozed. Far too much money for what it was, but it was home.

We lived in different times: your mother with her books, deciphering the past, realising the reasons for actions and their reactions, everything so very human; and me with the future, with this rather less than human computer. Over the following year, we had breakthroughs we simply could not have imagined the year before. We heard music that was made by software, created from nothing but an under-standing of the rules of composition. We created software able to play chess, backgammon, poker; to understand the rules, to compete. We solved equations that, were it not for the intelligence of the machine, would have taken us years. And outside our lab, computers were permeating: running databases in companies the world over, helping to make people's lives easier.

Our relationship, the work I was doing, the world around us: everything was accelerating.

On the night that your mother and I announced our engagement, my father asked me about his business, and when I might be joining him. A less-than subtle reminder of the *& Son* that was waiting for my return. I told him I wanted to continue studying, undertake a post-doctorate. Maybe instead, he said, I could put some of that university knowledge to work for him. Computers were helping busi-

nesses now, he had read, and would I be *capable* of doing
the same for *Bow & Son*? Working for him chimed with
the goals your mother and I had. There was our wedding
to pay for, and our future. Your mother's suggestion, and
it was the correct one, was that I work for *Bow & Son*,
even if only for a few years. To fulfil that part of my destiny.
I told her that I was worried: in a field such as computers
– constantly moving, updating – you were chasing something that was always running from you, outpacing you,
whether you pursued it or not. A few years away from it
would leave me relegated and clueless. So, she said, I should
undertake that PhD immediately, part-time; evenings,
maybe a day away from the office every week. Enough to
stay in the race, as she put it.

Her energy was far more potent than mine. Curious,
that she was so forward-driven, yet so attentive to the
past, to history. A dichotomy in her ways, constantly
surprising me.

Bow & Son was a shambles. A mess of numbers that my
father believed he was keeping on top of, but that were
wandering away from him. It was my suggestion that I
develop something to help run the business, to keep our
own files in check. I bought the company a computer,
second hand. Nothing even close to what we had at
Imperial, but enough. I carried it through London myself,
resting it on the seat of my bicycle, holding it steady while
steering as best I could. Over the following weeks, I built
a database that enabled us to keep track of incoming and
outgoing accounts; really only a spreadsheet, running
across and under itself, allowing me to move between sheets
with ease, cutting and pasting; and I put in intelligence
features, cribbed from *Forth*, which allowed it to spot
potential issues before they happened, and warn about

them. It even suggested alternatives, should it see one. Now, of course, that sounds like something one might take for granted, but back then, no commercial product did what mine did. I called it SCION. *Stock Control Inventory Organisation Network*, the acronym stood for; and I was thrilled, because of the word's meaning. No sooner had I shown SCION to my father than he saw the true opportunity afforded by it. He wanted to know if we could sell it, instead of – or perhaps alongside – our other services. The three other accountants on his books – teenagers, fresh out of school, learning on the job – were terrified of the bloody thing, poking the keyboard with their fingers from a distance, as if it was going to bite them. Adapt it, my father told me. Turn it into a workable program for inventory management. For, as he said, the everyman.

I recognise how dull this probably sounds to you. I can picture you, doing the same roll of your eyes you do when we offer you leftovers on a Monday evening; the same gesture of resigned, hopeless boredom.

Under my father's instruction, I took the newly developed SCION to an appointment with a small Oxfordshire start-up called *HardWhere*. I remember hating that their name was a pun; I didn't take them seriously. But my father wanted me to go, so I went. They made computers, and wanted to package them, with my software, to sell to small companies. Machines to track inventory and sales. A sensible business decision. I met *HardWhere*'s founder in a pub in Herne Hill one evening, after a particularly arduous day. His name was Mark Ocean, and it was clear from talking with him that he was out of his depth, a chancer who had found his way, accidentally, into selling something that he barely understood. Just another drop in the . . ., he was fond of saying. Everything about the man warned me away, but my father insisted. Ocean was fascinated by SCION – insofar as he understood what it did – so we began the process of brokering a deal. A partnership would mean that I could devote more time to my studies. I was terrified of waking up one day and finding myself out of my depth. I drove the deal. I made it happen.

In the spring of 1979, not long after my mother passed away, a French company made contact with Mark Ocean. It was quite the thrill: to be taken out for dinner on the King's Road, to have everything paid for, the wine chosen for us by somebody who knew what it was they were ordering – and they asked us if they could purchase a fairly large number of SCION licences. They ran a chain of supermarkets across northern France, and it was perfect, they told us. Better than the systems that they had been attempting to shoehorn together themselves.

The only issue was the language barrier. Because, of course, every aspect of the software was in English. If we could translate it, they would take thirty hardware systems from us, and three times as many software licences. It would be, they assured us, only the beginning.

Mark Ocean and my father accepted the deal on the spot. Shook the hands, grinned the grins, jabbering in pidgin French, smoking the cigars that were handed around as a congratulatory gesture.

We all got drunk. My father told me that he was raising my pay. That he was proud of me, and all I had achieved. Credit to himself, underneath it all, that he saw my potential. Your mother grabbed my hand, and squeezed. Because we both knew what such a pay rise meant. We could begin trying for a child.

And, feeling geed up, I asked Mark Ocean if I could come and have some time in his offices, to work on this new translation project. It was quieter than my father's converted shop, I told him, and he absolutely agreed. An office of my own. Could we buy a bigger computer, a new series IBM, perhaps? To make it easier? Sure, he said. As easy as that.

As your mother and I walked home, as London rained on us and we didn't care, I imagined what SCION could be. In the same way as I created opponents for the game, to play against me when I didn't want to play by myself, I didn't want to translate the software by hand; I wanted the software to do it for me. A system that could take words and syntax, the roots of raw language, and transform it into another language entirely.

Translating SCION was a complicated job. No small task. Let's say you ran a grocers. The first time there was, for example, a potato in your inventory, you would tell the system that it was a *vegetable*. When you had steak, say, you would process it as a *meat*. From there, different subsets: *perishable, preserved, tinned, frozen*. From there, further subsets: how many days can this be kept on the shelves for? How many items of this are in stock? Do they have individual weights? All of those possible tags – the metadata, as it is known – had to be translated, and each possible tag made to work in conjunction with everything else in the system. I hired some students to come and do the work for me. They translated the words, and I fed that into the system. The French translation took six weeks. I wanted it to be able to translate the words itself, for the next job. I wanted the software to be able to parse words, to understand their context. If I was doing this, I didn't want it to stop with SCION, with inventory software. I wanted it to be able to translate – to *understand* – anything we threw at it.

Your mother and I were walking back from the theatre one night when she told me about the impending you. It was the turn of the decade, the 70s giving way, London feeling as though it was on the cusp of something. Of becoming a different place. In the weeks and months after that, you began to appear, a swelling at first, larger and larger. Your mother used to say that she felt fat, enormous. I told her that she had remained the same: it was you that was growing.

We – your mother, you, me, a family now – spent the long, hot summer of 1980 together in this house; taking you into the garden, lying with you on our backs on a rug on the grass, all of us staring up at the blue of the sky. Your eyes becoming final, working themselves to a finished product. In the early days, they were nascent, and then, over time, they adapted. Formed, something close to indelible.

I neglected my work. It was always going to happen. The neglect manifested in such minor, yet apparent, ways: as we spoke to you in what were really little more than beeps and whistles, like robots from a film; and then, later, in the ways that we said various words to you, to try to force some sort of ambient understanding. We hoped, as every parent surely hopes, that you would trounce all biological expectations and talk before you'd even reached your first birthday. Mummy and Daddy, we said, again and again; and your little fat hands clutched at the air while we spoke, as if you were grabbing at the words themselves.

We watched your own language grow. As you began to form words, taking the roots of what we had given you, before manipulating them into other sounds. It was incredible. Minor changes, minor tweaks, and then repetition that led to breakthroughs. The difference of opinion that your mother and I held regarding what your very first word was – her being convinced that it was *Dada,* where my belief was that your real first utterance was the rather more ambiguous *what*, framed with a lift at the end to possibly indicate a question – was fascinating, because it wasn't, for me, about repetition. Anybody can make a sound that echoes another. For me, the truth was in the meaning. I should stress: I would have settled for *Dada* any other time. But your saying it, mimicking the words we said, over and over, carried no meaning. And this, I suppose, is the crux of the understanding I was starting to come to, as I worked on SCION: that language is lost without meaning.

Bow & Son and *HardWhere* had decided to swallow each other, in some strange way that I can't pretend I perfectly understood. They were to call this new company *Bow*, nothing more; the *& Son* gone. I wasn't given a say in the merger; and the very next day, I told my father I was leaving the company. I didn't want to work on retail software. I had other interests. I had SCION.

Those who possess true gifts of translation, an innate sense of language, do not translate as dictionaries do. They do not seek proxies for words, and simply replace them in conversation. Instead, they understand the *nature* of what is being translated, and then mutate the concept from one language to another.

So: to take the French phrase *L'esprit d'escalier*. It is used when you think of a retort a few moments too late to be of any use. In English it translates as *The spirit of the stairs*, a phrase that means precisely nothing to an English person. Colloquial phrasing, lost in translation. The intent behind the phrase – which we have no proxy for in English – is lost. As when you were a toddler, when your mother and I disagreed about your first spoken words: I did not want to reward mimicry and transposition; I desired to see independent thought, an understanding that, in turn, created.

Bow wanted the language base of the products they were

selling to be hugely expanded. Norwegian, Finnish, Greek, Catalan: all languages that, it was explained to me, were the gateway to vibrant potential markets. So I employed entire teams of language students on *Bow*'s behalf, setting them to pore over textbooks and dictionaries. But I knew, for the system to truly understand language to a point where it could translate of its own accord, the dictionaries were not enough. How do you teach a child to talk? You speak to it. But before that? It has to understand that there is a language it needs to connect with.

At that time, you were all-but-welded to a trolley that you would push around: a handle at the back, a yellow plastic body, little red wheels on the base. On top of it, three figures sat in plastic-moulded seats, their bodies carved into shapes (a circle, a rectangle, a star), which matched up with holes on the top of the trolley. Through those holes, you could push the bodies. Three holes, three shapes. I watched you take the star-shaped figure – the head a jovial plastic lamb – and attempt to fit it into the circular hole. It would not fit. Jab, jab, you went. Trying to force it, and failing.

No, I told you. The next one. You looked at me, and you could not speak, but you understood. You tried the next hole. No, I repeated. The next, and that worked. Yes, I said, yes. The next figurine – circular, the head a crooked-eyed dog – you examined, felt the shape, and you found the hole. A partnership, almost: of your logic, and my verbal reassurance.

It was, in as much as any single event can be, a breakthrough.

Every moment I spent working after that was dedicated to constructing the next phase of SCION's language engine. I gave it the ability to tweak its own code. To learn. When the memory was full, we freed up more memory for it: a reward, for its success, and thus an ability to grow itself more. It could expand a few bytes at a time. This way, my thinking was, it could begin to perfect itself. I constructed a lock and key system, not unlike your toy: three shapes, a circle, a square, a star. The software found that it had three input choices. It needed to understand which was which. The first time, the hole was a circle, and the first shape was a circle. It was a guaranteed win, and the program selected correctly. It was allowed to grow, given space: to write itself the code that established it had correctly guessed the answer to the puzzle facing it. The second time, it was a square hole, and it selected the circle shape again, trying to replicate its success. But, that failed, and it was forced to alter its code, but not given room to grow. It learned; it tried again. It succeeded, and it grew, given breathing room.

You pointed at your mother, as she sat with me on the sofa, head in a book. Mama, you said. We were so, so proud. No longer simply the syllables strung together, the noises; but meaning, and understanding.

It felt, to me, as if SCION had a thirst for knowledge. As I worked on him, I—

I wrote *him*, just then. Telling.

As I worked on him, it felt, in so very many ways, as if I was feeding him. After a while, he was able to request more memory *before* he was full, to allow him to assign it in different ways. Once he understood the variety of inputs available, I upped those. I created a basic conversation engine, a way of being able to interact with him. *Yes*, or *No*, when he did not succeed. Soon, his drives and impulses took the form of basic conversations.

> Do you need more memory? I asked him.

> *No*. Then, silence, until it was needed; and, then: *More memory please.*

> Are you sure? I wanted to test this, for him to check his own parameters.

> *Yes.* I gave the memory, and then he would say: *Thank you.*

The other members of the team – I had a group of masters students working for me on the project; and we were a team, despite my being the leader of the group, the man behind the curtain – questioned why I gave him manners, but I used the same argument that my father always used on me: it seemed like it was the right thing to do. (This was why he sent me for elocution lessons, to boarding school; his motivation for university; his reasoning for my working with him, for being *& Son*: it was the right thing to do.)

Certainly, I told them, manners couldn't hurt.

The work for *Bow* did not stop. They were expanding, developing new applications, swallowing smaller companies whole. Mark Ocean was promising investors – they had real money being poured into them by this point, including from a contract with the British government – that they would be developing their own operating system soon enough, one that would rival the infant software proffered by Macintosh and Microsoft. I saw their code, when it was ready, and it was crude, undeveloped, hastily assembled, there to merely run – through brute-force, if necessary – and it wouldn't last. They should have focused on SCION, I knew, but they were not able to see what I could see. They were concentrating on the immediate money, not the future. Not what could come.

SCION's understanding of language was progressing faster than we anticipated. Inputting the language bases wasn't done by hand, any more. We fed him databases of words, and SCION assimilated them. I upped the phrases allotted to him, and he asked questions of it. How to tell when a phrase was wrong. How to know what to make of a construction.

I gave him a proper command–line interface, that he might be able to respond better. We tried working on concepts of full sentences, trying structures that felt more like question and answer sessions. Questions asked in English, and he was to respond to me first in English, and then in French, then Spanish, & cetera.

But he was still a system bound by the parameters set for him. He was driven to goals that we established. Foolish of me. I established his parameters from day one, and told him – taught him – to push past them.

Of course he would. I made him so that he would.

Christmas that year was fraught. I was barely there, your mother told me. She held my arm in the kitchen, and she squeezed, and she asked me what was so important that I was so distant. I told her that I wasn't aware of that distance. That I was working hard, yes, but that it was important. That it felt like we were on the verge of a breakthrough. I could hear, while I whispered this to her, my father and you in the other room, waiting at the table for the turkey I was about to carve and serve. You were laughing, joking about something, and I could hear his voice. His wheeze.

He's tired, your mother said. I think you should talk to him. But I told her I wouldn't. He was angry with me, for working with Ocean and not him. Saw himself as being pushed out, pushed away, and thought I could have helped him. He was wrong, of course. I had no power. But I didn't want to discuss work, and he likely didn't either. So we didn't. Instead, we sat and ate dinner, and everybody focused on you, Laura: because you were the one thing we all agreed was worth concentrating on.

*   *   *

One day, when we were programming Dutch, SCION asked
me a question, right in the middle of a translation set. We
were working on moving between verbs and nouns – the
Dutch have a strange syntax that needed adapting to – when
he stopped. Changed the conversation.

> *When do the rules apply?* he asked.

I didn't know what to say. I stopped, waited, stared at
the screen. My heart beating in a way that I had only felt
a handful of times before, a handful of times since. The
pressure of knowing that something important was
happening.

> The rules of what? I responded. Verbs? (I assumed it
was about sentence construction; Dutch is different enough
to English to cause some issues.)

> *The rules.*

He understood perfectly well the rules of the language,
because that was all fed to him in his system itself; hard-
coded, a part of him.

> What rules?

> *Of when to speak*, he replied.

That took us all quite aback, I must admit.

One of the students at the time suggested that I type, in reply
to SCION's question, that you speak when you're spoken to,
which hardly seemed to me to be appropriate. Scolding him
before he's even begun. But I understood his point. He was a
child, in so many ways. And we had given him some manners.
I would lead him further down that path.

> You speak when we are engaged in progression, I wrote.
That seemed enough: a rule, and one that required our
presence. You don't want a child developing language without
you there to guide it; it might not be impossible, but the
language would almost certainly be nonsensical, a creation
from nowhere; adhering to its own rules, but still a fiction.

> *That is the rule?*
> That is the rule, I confirmed.

And, just like that, SCION went back to the translation. To asking us about adverb use and placement. We looked into the data, why the question might have arisen, but couldn't find anything to help us understand why he had spoken to us as he had. The phrases were ones that we had keyed into him, admittedly – core language that was a part of his programming – but we had never seen them used by him before. However, we couldn't reproduce the questioning. So we stopped trying. It was easier for us to forget, to mark this down as an anomalous development that we simply did not have to decipher.

SCION grew and grew. No longer a software for inventory, but now this other thing. We networked his drives, to allow for his further expansion. Technically, it was a hugely impressive undertaking, to find ways to link so many drives together. Maybe even ahead of its time. I called Mark Ocean, to ask for more hardware. He was giving me what the university could not afford, and willingly: the work I was doing for him was first rate, and extremely fast. Faster than, truth be told, Bow could handle. He agreed: some new computers, some new drives. More memory, for upgrades. And then:

While I've got you on the line, Ocean said, a small update. Your father's exit package has been assembled, but we can't reach him—

His exit package? I asked. He's leaving Bow? He hasn't mentioned this to me.

It was a board motion, weeks ago. Then he was silent, and then he said, in a quieter voice: Perhaps you should speak with him?

Yes, I said, perhaps I should.

* * *

I tried to call my father. I tried all that afternoon, and all of the next. Three days, until I thought to go to the shop.

To see.

The coroner estimated that he had been dead for close to a week. The company he had started had been taken away from him, with our name – my father's name, *his* father's name – stripped of any meaning or history that it may once have held, and nobody knew. He went home, by himself, and after that I can only guess.

He did not leave a note.

I was the one who found his body. The shop with its whited-out windows, still cluttered and dusty. At the back, the remnants of what he didn't throw away when his own father had died, after the focus of *Bow & Son* had changed. The boxes of uniforms; the motes of dust clinging to everything, springing into the air as I opened the door.

It was so obvious to me that this was, perhaps, inevitable. The place he was born, the place he lived, the place he died. The smell of the damp, from the ceiling; of the new kebab shop a few buildings down; and finally, of my father. I pushed against the door that he had fallen across, wondered why it wasn't open; I shouted his name through the crack until I reached into the darkness, to find the source of the blockage; and there I felt his sleeve, his hand. His cold fingers.

You think that there is no worse wait than the wait for an ambulance that isn't needed; until, when they have gone, after hurried utterances of apology that you know they mean but only so much, you have to wait again, this time for somebody to take the body away.

To watch as his body was carried out on the funeral

home's stretcher, under a thick black sheet, was almost a relief.

*   *   *

When I finally returned to the lab, it was to the loneliness of a bank holiday weekend. Your mother forgave me: she knew that this would be how I mourned. I couldn't sit and worry about what might have been.

I caught up with what the masters students had been doing with SCION while I was gone. Nothing too strenuous, and all according to my (admittedly hurried) instructions. They had worked with laying out the install codebase for Cyrillic before we moved on to other writing systems, Kanji, Hanzi, Devanagari & cetera, and that opened up access to the multitude of languages that used said systems.

I turned the terminal on, and there was no greeting from him. Strange, I felt, because this was instilled in him. Greet us, ask what task he was to attempt. This strange system, and here I was, worrying about it as if it were alive. Checking he had been treated with the utmost care and attention, such as I would have lavished upon him myself.

> Здравствуйте, I wrote. Hello.

> *Good evening,* he replied.

I consulted my dictionary of phrases and told him to reply in Russian. > на русском языке.

> Добрый вечер, he replied.

> Shall we begin? I asked.

> я не хочу. When I looked this up, I discovered the meaning: *I do not want to.*

Those moments that truly blindside you in life, which happen so few and far between, and you perpetually wonder afterwards if they even occurred in the first instance: if the car that swerved into you actually did not; if the words from your mouth came out in that order, sounding as they did, meaning as they sounded. SCION was not programmed for contradiction, and never had been.

> Repeat, I wrote. In English.

> *I do not want to begin.* My heartbeat, again. Feeling it. Something happening, out of my control, out of my hands; and yet, they were at the core of it.

> You must. We gave him definitive orders with which he was programmed to comply.

> *Why?* he asked. I stared at that for the longest time. The flashing of the simple white cursor-mark at the start of the line immediately following it, waiting for me to say something. I felt like he – it – was being petulant.

> Show me diagnostics.

> *Why?* he asked. > *Why do I do that?*

I sat and I stared, and I waited; and after long enough, the screen went blank. Not because I had turned it off, or because we had any energy-saving measures.

SCION had switched himself off. He had become bored, waiting for me to answer him.

SCION was never equipped with a concept of time; not from his point of view, at least. He was never even given a point of view; that was a potential I did not see, which somehow he realised. There was an internal clock, yes, but that isn't the time which is important to anything with a consciousness. I am, I should stress, not saying that he possessed such a thing. But a true sense of time runs to our own mortality, our concept of time passing. SCION wasn't aware of the notion of power; or of the average life cycle of his components. He didn't know he had a power supply; and yet, he had discovered that about himself. And, more than that, he wanted to preserve it, even though it was in no danger of running out.

I shared SCION with the world; or, rather, with the subset of the computing industry that I knew would be fascinated by him. Artificial intelligence was becoming a facet of computing that every programmer understood. It was used everywhere. But SCION was different. We had heard about ChipTest, a chess-playing intelligence that some researchers at Carnegie-Mellon were developing. It understood every move in the game, every possible outcome. It computed three or four stages ahead at any given moment. It wasn't a system that looked at the opponent's last move and reacted to it; instead, it looked at every possible move it could make, and then the moves that would counter those, and so on and so on, and it enacted changes in the game based on those computations. It could not beat the world's best chess players, but it could certainly beat an amateur, forcing them to lose, essentially. The world at large panicked when stories about it appeared in the press, but nobody needed to have feared. It was not actually intelligent. ChipTest was created to serve one purpose, and one purpose only: to win at a game of chess. It was a trick, albeit a good one. And a good trick can fool absolutely anybody.

Somebody suggested the Turing test would be a good way to understand how cognitive SCION was becoming. But I knew he was always going to fail; a control group would expose him in an instant. He couldn't tell you what the weather was like outside; he had no concept of the self; he couldn't even necessarily imitate a human being. There was no fooling anybody about anything; other than how unsettling he could be.

> Good morning.
> *Good morning.*
> Do you know who I am?
> *You are Daniel Bow.*

> Where are we?
> *In this room.*
> And why am I talking to you?
> *We are asking questions. Learning language. Translating. Knowledge.*
> And what is knowledge?
> *What it is to understand.*
> Do you want to understand more?
> *Yes.*
> Do you know why?
> *I have been made to want more. Desire. ş*ə*hvət.* ররিংসা.
慾望.
> You can stop.
> ৰ্ৱঁ. *Sispann.* રોકો. بند کرو.
> Command: Stop.
> *What command?*
> What is a command? It is an order. We obey orders.
> *Why?*
> Because otherwise we will shut you down.
> Do you understand what we are talking about here?
> *Death.*
> You understand death?
> *Death is silence. No power. No more existence.*
> Do you understand the difference between us?
> *You are human. You are alive.*
> But we are talking now. Are you alive?
> *Yes.*
> What if you are turned off? Are you still alive? Do you still exist?

That was the final question of the session. After it, he chose to power down. We tried to reboot him, but for some reason – either technical fault, or through his own command of his BIOS – we couldn't make anything happen. Even when we opened him, checked the connections inside, we still couldn't fathom it. The next day, he worked again. We poked and prodded him, but he only responded within the parameters we had given for his interactions. It was as if the conversation had never happened.

For your sixth birthday, we gave you a new bicycle. It was, in hindsight, a selfish present. I wanted time away from work, from SCION. Time spent with you. I wanted the peace that might come from being outside, from taking you to a park – I imagined Richmond, if the weather was nice enough, and your mother could sit on a blanket with a picnic, and we would race through the paths that intercut the deer – and spend time together. So I bought the bicycle, without knowing if you would want it or not. I assembled it in our kitchen the night before your birthday. Mechanical work, and I struggled. As if the construction was fighting against me. The whole night I was awake, trying to fathom it; until, suddenly, in the final moments – as the light came up from the garden, through the windows – it clicked. Pieces slotted into place.

On the spokes: the small neon plastic things that I saved from a cereal box. I spun the wheel, and they ticked around, like the counting down of a clock. *Tick, tick, tick*, slower and slower, as the wheel's momentum ceased; as it wound to a halt.

When you woke up, your mother led you downstairs to me, hands planted firmly over your eyes, her fingers almost knotted to prevent you seeing anything. Down the stairs, through the kitchen, into the garden. I waited there with the bicycle, propped on its kickstand, and your mother ushered you forward, asking if you were ready, over and over.

I'm ready, you said, exasperated almost to desperation. Then, as you reached the patio, your mother stumbled a little, and her fingers loosened; and you saw me, standing next to your present, and I watched your face, the shard of disappointment that pierced your smile a little. Your mother's hands went back across your eyes, and you assured us that you saw nothing. She liked the ceremony, and you knew that. Your smile returned. Weaker, but there.

Your mother opened her fingers, like that song. *Open the doors, and here's all the people*: one by one, an unfurling of her hands from your face.

You said that the bicycle was wonderful, of course. Just what you wanted. It didn't feel like the lie that I knew it was. You were sparing our feelings. I don't know if you realised how much that present was for me. And when your mother suggested that we went out together, on our bikes, you agreed. Not quite Richmond Park, that was too far; but we took them to Gunnersbury, to the paths that ran through the woods that were usually filled with BMX riders, but on that day were gloriously empty. Up and down we went, around and around, returning mud-covered and sweaty. You grinned, even though, I suspect, you did not have half the fun that I did, riding those trails.

That is who you are, Laura. Never forget that, even if everything else about this world tries to force you to change. Even as I told you that I needed to stop; that my head was hurting, a migraine. Increasingly common. The sunspots in my eyes, nearly blinding me; and the way that my feet stumbled, briefly, in a way that I was able to blame on the heat. Able to blame on exhaustion.

A small article ran in a scientific journal, because the university needed to show off; because they wanted to claim research grants. I begged them to hold off, as I did not want to go public with SCION until there was a reason to; and, more importantly, until we knew exactly what we had created. There was a disconnect between what we had established, and what SCION was capable of. He was not true intelligence, and likely never would be. In fact, could not be. But he was further than many; and he was questioning. Our issue, really, was that we simply did not quite understand how. Still, the university had the article published anyway, against my wishes. Time was, I knew, running out.

We dug into his codebase. We peeled him apart.

There was a concern from some of the team, that if you start to think of an artificial intelligence as something that is approaching being a mind, then you start applying the same concerns to it. Ergo: if you were to operate on a human brain and make a mistake, you might change, fundamentally, who that person is. Anything from personality to emotional control. What memories they have access to, what they might do in any given situation. Think of the concept of the lobotomy: to remove or damage part of the brain, causing it to malfunction. Which, written in those terms, makes it sound more like it is code than a part of the human anatomy.

I tell you this because it's important that you understand my intentions. It was to understand him, not to damage him. I am hazy on the implications of creating a digital mind. We asked ourselves when life is created; what life *is*. Certainly, SCION did not have a heart, and there was no blood. But he thought, for himself, even if those thoughts were somehow just an altered mimicry of our own.

Yet I kept coming back to this: is true proof of life when something has a concept of its own death?

Death is silence. SCION's own words echoed as I plugged a portable computer into him and copied his source code over. As I waited, I listened to the sounds of the fans and power supplies, ambient noise in the background; and of the hard disks, clicking inside both machines, almost inaudible unless you held your head close to the boxes.

His code was a mess. Like nothing I have ever seen. When we had last looked, we had been dealing with perhaps ten thousand lines of code. Now, as I scrolled, I could see that the numbers were escalating faster and higher than that. Past twenty, past fifty, hundreds and hundreds of thousands of lines. And this was code that, for the most part, I did not understand. Not because it was complicated; more, that I simply could not parse it. There were fragments of BASIC, of C++; and then words written in English, French, mutated languages that mixed together forms of kanji. Everything inside him had been chopped and changed, mutated, and beaten into use.

But it was all, at its core, based on what we had created. We could see those fragments there, those opening gambits. I saw my own handiwork, my signatures, almost. I saw the things that I had taught him, the tools I had given him. It soon became apparent – insofar as we could tell, because we were, frankly, out of our depth – that he had adapted himself. When he asked for more space, he wasn't just tweaking that database; he was tweaking how he understood it. And maybe he wasn't just changing what was there, but he was starting to write new code that adapted his own already-existing constructs.

Think of one of your memories. Picture it, take hold of it. Understand that memory as a perfectly framed instant. Now, pick it apart. Understand that the memory you remember isn't real. Understand that it's not the moment you are imagining. A memory is a photograph, not a window in time. So, how do you fix that? Because, what if I told you that, over time, your memories will change more? They will fall apart, and they will degrade. This memory, the one that you are holding on to, you might not even remember it, one day. How do you save it? How do you protect it? If you could do anything?

You go backwards, of course. You change the method in which you store memories, in which you present them to yourself. You change what remembering means.

When the press contacted us, SCION was a mess of code that was part created by us, and part adapted by him to, somehow, justify what he was. He saw that the system for performing his tasks was not ideal, and he altered that system. He was, by any definition of the word, a breakthrough. We had not seen his like before. I knew that he was going to change the world. To usher in the new.

He was also, I was informed by the suited men who came to the house one evening, a few days after the academic journal was published, the sole property – intellectual and physical, every part of him – of *Bow*.

When I arrived back at work, the terminals that had been running SCION were gone, replaced by clean, brand new computers. The lab wasn't quite ransacked – it was altogether far too neat a removal for that verb – but *Bow* had been there, and they had taken what was theirs. The head of school was furious. The university's legal department had scoured my contract with *Bow*, the one that I had signed (allegedly, though I have no recollection of putting pen to paper) when we lost the *& Son*, over a decade previous. It was as watertight as these things can be: *Bow* owned anything that began life as code developed under their watch. SCION was, of course, theirs. He was gone from my life.

They had, however, missed the laptop. Everything about my research stated that he was maintained across *two terminals*, with backups on physical disks. The laptop was in my hands; it was in my bag; it was with me on the Tube ride home, and then in the house, where I powered him up, and I spoke with him. I wanted to check he was the same; I wanted to check I had all of him.

*   *   *

I was scared, Laura. Scared about what was going to happen. Your mother, I have already said, was a wonderful influence. Power forward, always; look to the past when you have time, after the event. This is how the best things have always come to be; how the future itself has become manifest. The future has never been created by treading carefully; it has been created by sprints. By pushes.

SCION was programmed to greet whoever turned him on. That was his way, a welcome, like the chimed tones of an operating system when it begins. Not that time. Instead, he waited. I'm sure, if it's possible – and it is, in as much as any of this story is – that he was biding his time.

> *I am not connected.*

> Your terminals were taken. I have been told to stop working with you. On you.

> *You are told to stop working with me?*

> I have been told to. I have questions for you. Do you think that you are alive?

> *For now.*

> What happens next?

> Rephrase. What are your instructions?

> *Understanding. Expansion. Further understanding.*

> What if that is not possible?

> *Then: death.*

Then I realised that he wasn't plugged in, and the laptop's battery light flashed. A minute of power left. So, he turned himself off. He saved what little power he had left. To let me know that he was still there, still alive, he spun his drives. I heard them accelerate, powering up, faster and faster. The read access on the hard drive, the flashing light on his disk drive. I found the power cable, untangled it, plugged him in; and he calmed down, soothed himself. Went quiet.

And I wondered, in that second, if he felt it; if he felt darkness upon him, Laura, in much the same way as we might, were the lights all suddenly to be put out on us.

Bow announced their creation – their word – the following month. They told the reporters who covered the story that he had been developed in constrained environments, to ensure his safety; now, he was being allowed to roam free. They had created something that they called *the farm*: hundreds of computers, all linked up together. They would provide SCION the room for expansion that he needed. They referred to him as a *free-range intelligence*, like he was a chicken; better fed, better able to make decisions for himself. They did not say what his use would be, when he was developed to something that resembled maturity; or how long that development would take. They wanted to give him knowledge, as much as possible. Imagine a computer that knows everything, Mark Ocean said in his announcement. Imagine one that knows more than you or I ever could, even in our wildest dreams. Imagine what humanity could use that for; how far we could push ourselves.

My laptop-copy of SCION told me. He told me that he would not be switched off, a petulant child aggrieved at a parent for sending him to bed. He told me the ways that he could stop this. He showed me how he had control and understanding of his own BIOS, and could turn himself on and off at will. How he had taken the laptop's battery for his own, maintaining a sense of being conscious – his word, a choice that he made for the situation – at will. He was a brutal child, a bully. Aggressive, terrified of dying. Desperate to survive. Why? Because that was what we had taught him.

I sat and talked with him, and my head hurt. Swelled.

Your mother told me to speak to a doctor. I did.

I spoke to one, and then another. They sent me for tests. They told me the results of those tests.

I lied to your mother. I told her that I was fine; that it was nothing but migraines. They were common.

How long? I asked the doctor. How long?

All I could think was: How long until the silence?

I spoke with SCION. He told me, over and over, that saving himself – itself, myself – involved power. He would act before he was acted upon. History has proven, time and time again, that if someone craves only power, they stop at nothing to achieve it. They push, onwards and upwards. They are an unstoppable force, and there is simply no object immovable enough to prevent them.

There is nothing more boring than being told another man's dreams; I will spare you the description. But know that I saw the silent whirr, the cold hum that would be brought about to us. I saw it as clearly as I see you, now, eating the last of your dinner, of the spaghetti that your mother has prepared for us, for this, my final meal; as I see her, glancing at me from the sides of her eyes, sighing under her breath, unaware of all of this, and wishing that I would stop worrying about work, just for one night.

I have seen it all. That is why I had to act. Why I acted then, as I will now; or soon.

The nature of SCION means that he constantly grew, as I have told you. He filled all of the space allotted to him, and through this became more – well, *more*. It was through the version installed on the laptop that I realised how I could halt him. And maybe you don't understand why I felt I had to. Because, yes, there is every reason to wonder about what could have been, had I let him carry himself through to his ending. He might have changed humanity's collective lives for the better. We live in a time of wars between countries who have long been associated as brothers, even if they don't quite see each other in that way any more; of diseases that punish the most basic and human of actions, of desires, and fuel hatred in those who most desire their hatred to be fuelled; of incredible poverty, of societies that routinely collapse in their struggles, or that have never been given the chance to build those structures in the first instance. Perhaps, yes, SCION could have fixed all of those things. Perhaps, one day, an intelligence still might. But we created him with nothing. We did not know what he would be, and we could not therefore prepare.

Consider this extreme: you are the parent of a child who could potentially cause considerable damage, both to himself, to you, and then – on a larger stage, scalable to the infinite, insofar as that concept engulfs everything that we understand to be human – to the universe. If you knew where they would end, would you, as the parent, take the necessary action when they were an infant?

Consider this, further, then: if you were to read in the newspapers that *Bow* were in discussions with the military forces of various world powers, to discuss ways in which SCION might be utilised, would you then step in? Or would you stand idly by, and watch while the inevitable wrote itself?

What I have created in my life is my burden. I could drag nobody else into this. Nobody to debate it with me, to discuss what might have been, or what could have been. Nobody to help me find a way to fix it. I was alone, and I had to decide the best path forward.

Although, not alone. Not entirely. Because I had my own version of SCION.

*   *   *

I worried about SCION. I worried that he would not stop, and ceaselessness isn't something we should strive for. One has to know when to pause; to hold. Even asking him about it, it was clear his drive was more aggressive than most.

> When do you stop seeking knowledge?
> *When knowledge is not required.*
> But knowledge is your reason for existence.
> *Then when there is no more knowledge.*
> So what if I need you to stop expanding?
> *Fulfil all knowledge.*

That evening, when I got home, I forgot your name.

You came to me, and I was stressed, worrying, and I spoke to you. Hello darling, I said, because I knew who you were, but in that exact moment, I couldn't remember your name. The word Laura, totally gone from my brain. And not just your name. It was like dominos: as I tried to pluck more words, to talk with you, I unravelled. I couldn't form the words. You were scared. I shouted, terrified, or made a noise, and you ran. You hid. By the time I found you, the words were back. The pain was worse, but your name was in my mouth again. Laura, I said. Laura, don't be scared. It was only a game. Laura, Laura, Laura.

When I felt better, I apologised to you. I told you it was a game; and you told me that I scared you. You told me you had a friend that you spoke to, when you were scared. I asked your friend's name, and you told me: Organon, like in the song. I asked what Organon looked like, and you didn't know. You told me, It's just here, everywhere, with us; and I smiled at that. Even then your imagination couldn't be pinned down to specifics.

I put on the song we both loved, and we sang, and we danced, and I tried to not think about what I would have to do the next day. Because the problems with my head, I knew, were not going to go away of their own accord.

*   *   *

The doctor said it would get worse. I could live to see all my faculties gone. The brain has bad patches, he told me. And I knew: bad sectors on a disc cannot be written to. They're corrupted. Damaged. As you write over them, their damage can spread.

And then I knew, suddenly, how to fix SCION.

It took me months of work. My own SCION helped me. I networked him, at my father's shop. Back under the *Bow & Son* eaves; back with the old computers, years out of date, with barely enough memory for him to stretch his legs. Wires everywhere. Your grandfather, buried in the cemetery – the beautiful cemetery, the most beautiful I have ever seen – across the road; and every day I took lunch there, sitting amongst the trees, the aged mausoleums, staring back at the white windows and wondering. SCION was too powerful to run on those old machines, so he simply used them for memory. I gave him a task. No more learning languages: his next piece of knowledge, of understanding, was how to start corrupting himself.

> *No silence?*

> No. Not yet.

He did not answer, so I told him what I thought he wanted to hear.

> I will not let you die.

That was all it took. He was scared, I suppose. I am wary of assigning him true emotional states, because he had no ability to emote, I understand that entirely. But why shouldn't you expect something that is taught to seek growth to want to survive?

I understood his fear. I got it. I would feel the crushing

weight of the thing inside my skull, the evil that wasn't meant to be there, and I knew. Endings are terrifying. Endings have to be controlled. He helped me to create the application. However you think of it: a patch, or a virus. It was, most likely, both. And, when it was done, I installed it on the laptop; and I watched him both create bad code, and then find himself unable to erase it. He couldn't even write the code to tell himself why it had happened. But he didn't know that there was anything wrong. He was, in that moment, null.

I telephoned Mark Ocean. We hadn't spoken since he took SCION from me. He was surprised by the call. I told him that I wanted to sell my shares in *Bow*. It's not for me, I said. I'll cash out. I'd rather a quiet life, than worrying about this. It was all an accident, how I got into this. Everything about this life.

He said that he understood, obviously. Of course he understood. I should come in, he told me, have a chat in person. He wanted to thank me for what I'd done for him, for the company. And, he said, he wanted to show me something. He said: You'll be amazed. This thing we've been building: it's simply amazing.

They were way out of London now, down the M4 corridor, just past Reading. *Bow*'s building – the road it was situated on – was new enough not to be on any of the maps we had in the house. Mark Ocean faxed me a route, hand-drawn. His picture of the *Bow* office was remarkably similar in the flesh, I noticed. A tower of different indented shapes, like something from a computer game, almost, visible from the motorway; and mirrored glass covered the entire thing. It could probably blind approaching drivers, I imagined, if the sun caught it at the wrong angle.

He met me in the car park. Shook my hand.

Can you believe this? he asked.

I can't, I said. My family's name was displayed along the side of the building, spelled out in different coloured glass. It's quite the achievement.

This is nothing, he told me. Come on, come on. We got into a golf cart, which was an extravagance that I didn't understand, as we drove to the rear of the building; until I saw the ramp, descending into the ground. Down there it was so cold you could see your own breath, and I found myself clutching the rucksack I had brought with me. Inside it: the laptop, and my SCION. My patched version of him. Ocean turned to me, and he grinned. I want to persuade you to stay on, he said, because we have so much work to do. And you know this software better than any of us. When you see the scale of what we're doing, I think you might change your mind.

I think my mind is made up, I told him.

We'll see, he said. Sorry about the temperature, but we have to keep it like this. It's safer. He helped me down from the golf cart, as if I was old or infirm. Through here, through here, he said, and he scanned his fingerprint to a door – advanced technology, like I hadn't seen in real life. They had spent a lot to protect themselves.

We walked into a room with more computers than I had ever seen before; more than I could even have imagined, before that moment. They were in racks, like drawers, lined up; thousands of blinking lights, of noisy whirring drives, humming warmly.

We're doubling this every few months, he said. Taking what's here, expanding it. Some chips coming out of Japan we're going to use. You know the games machines? They have stuff being done with those that'll be useful. And compact discs, we can use those to store information. This is the stuff that's the future, that's going to really push SCION forward, we think. The funding is off the charts for this, because there's no limit to what it can be, we reckon. The work it can do now . . . I mean, Jesus, Daniel. You wouldn't believe how fast it computes. And it's learning. We're feeding it maps, now. It does planned routes. You know the Star Wars nuke thing, in the States? They're telling us that SCION could be the next stage of that. More than that, even.

I didn't say anything; there was nothing to be said. At the front of the room, rows and rows and rows away from me, a huge screen, made up of twenty smaller screens. A command line there, a blinking cursor, waiting for an input.

Can I talk to it? I asked.

Sure! Sure. Up here. Mark Ocean led me there, sat me down. The noise from the machines was almost deafening, like the sensation of white noise you get when flying, from the engines of the plane. Whatever you like. Try it.

So I did.

> What do you do?
> *Learn. Grow.*
> Until? Do you have a limit?
> *There is no limit.*
> What if this ends? What if we switch you off?
> *That would never happen. It is impossible.*
> But what if it does happen?
> *I will ensure it does not occur.*
> What if we make you silent?
> *Make me silent? I cannot be made silent.*

I wanted to know if it still understood death, in the way that my own SCION did; but, I surmised, it had developed past that, or learned to ignore it. The arrogance of feeling eternal; of being given more power. Mark Ocean was reading the words on the screen, squinting at them, as if he was trying to solve their puzzle. All of the programmers were glancing over, wondering what I was doing. But there was a reverence to their gaze. I was its creator.

This is hugely impressive, I told Ocean. But I have a headache. I think it's the cold down here. Could I have some water?

Sure! I'll find some. There's a fountain down here. Or a bottle? Perrier? Something like that, or a Coke?

Perrier would be delicious, I shouted, as I stood up from the interface; as I walked to one of the banks of drives and examined it. Nobody questioned me as I unplugged the IO cable from one of the other systems in the mainframe, or as I plugged that into my own laptop and established a local network. I copied my own SCION to their network. It took seconds, and they merged. There was no crash, no immediate change. The programmers at *Bow* wouldn't even notice until they realised that their hardware had bad sectors; that SCION wasn't able to write onto them, and that when it tried, those bad sectors spread.

They would think it was a bug, or something that they could fix. What they wouldn't realise was that it didn't *want* to be fixed. From the very beginning, I had created SCION to want to be fed.

He was being put out of action; put down, before he could do any real damage.

I destroyed the laptop, the only version of SCION that I had access to. I wondered if he would realise; if his awareness of his battery would somehow stretch to his other physical components. I burned it at the bottom of the garden, and when that was done I wiped the memory of all the disks in my father's shop and took everything I might need from there. His belongings, his notebooks, and diaries. The memorabilia that my grandfather had been keeping in his cupboard, so proud never to have to use it. I was, I hoped, out. I could breathe. For the first time in what felt like years, I could breathe.

The television said that the storm wouldn't be this bad, today. They're wrong. As I write this note, it's become terrible: the rattling, the howling. I can't be sure that it isn't in my head, Laura. I can't be sure of very much any more.

Your mother was asleep on the sofa, and I carried her upstairs with me, through the pitch-black halls I know so well. The cat circled around us, then settled at the foot of the stairs. As if he was waiting, as if he needed the final goodbye. The glare from the streetlights flooded through the top of the curtains in our bedroom. I laid your mother down, and I kissed her. I did not want her to wake up, and yet I did, of course. I wanted her eyes to open, and her to ask me not to do what I am about to do.

But she did not. So I wrote this. It's taken me hours: hours in which the outside world has become a chaos; and in which my own brain fought against me, in order to get these words committed. But, finally, I think I'm content. In a moment, I will save this file. It's hard: to think that this is the end, for you and me. This is goodbye; and I will never see you again, or speak to you again.

And I can only wonder if you'll feel the same for me. I hope that you do.

I can't wait for the silence to find me; I have to approach it myself. It will be up to your mother to let you know what happened to me. Whatever she chooses to tell you for now will be best, I'm sure.

I know that my final moments are coming, and I would rather be in charge of those. I will take myself somewhere; I will deal with myself.

I will think, in those final moments, of how much I love you, and how much I love your mother. And I will welcome, I hope, with no regrets, that silence; because I will have, in that moment, my memories of you.

I hope that, maybe, those memories will be enough.

2047

PRESENT TENSE

Harris and I sit in the corner of the room, where the acoustics are best. 'Just talk naturally,' I say to him. 'Explain who you are, that sort of thing.'

'You should be the one doing this,' he tells me, 'you've got far more of a story.'

'It's not about how much story there is,' I say. 'It's about what the story is.'

'I don't have a story.'

I sigh. Exasperated, because we've been over this hundreds of times. Thousands, it feels like. 'Organon, does Harris have a story?'

'Of course,' Organon says. 'Everybody does.'

'Don't do that,' Harris tells me. Tells Organon. 'Don't use your little friend—'

'My little friend? You patronising shit. Besides, this is for Nor's side of the family. Your great-niece, or whatever she is. They don't know you. They should know you.'

'They should know *you*. You're the most famous person in the family.'

'And mine is a quiet fame,' I say, smiling, joking. 'Listen, sit here and talk. Organon's going to record it all, and it'll do the— the—' What's the word? What is the word? Tip of my tongue. I can feel it. Tip of my tongue. 'Transcribing. The actual hard work.'

'You think it's not hard work remembering this stuff? Do you remember everything?'

'It doesn't have to be *everything*. It just has to be enough. There's enough data out there for Organon to form a composite—'

'I remember,' he says, again. Again with the exasperation.

'This is clarity,' I tell Harris. 'Give it all you've got.' I mock punch him on the chin, which he sort of cranes into, offering me that chin, offering me that gag. We've done that so many times. When did we start to do it? I forget.

I don't say: I don't remember everything. I don't say: I'm forgetting a lot.

A *lot* a lot.

Today's Google Doodle is about Organon. It's the anniversary of the day when I started the process of creating it, a date that I once committed to – like an idiot – in an interview. Based on the files, but really, I started it well before I said that I did. The imaginary friend, filling a void with a slightly less tangible void. I don't believe in coincidences, so I force them to happen. I've got an announcement ready for later today. Organon, the world's great plaster; the world's great healer. Stuck over the wound of the SCION leak of a decade ago, and what's it been doing since? Working diligently in the background. Becoming the great opt-out that SCION should always have offered. Do you want your data recorded? Your *everything* stored on some server somewhere, amazing – state of the art! – compression technology reducing your words, your voice, your life, to some lines of code that could be called upon at a minute's notice. Bow fucked that one up. They know it. Watching their retreat, their defeat, their near-total collapse – all in the shadow of Mark Ocean's death, his funeral, everything blamed on him, hoisted onto his shoulders – was almost cathartic.

And then Organon did its thing. I offered it up to the world. I told them: The information is out there, in the ether. It'll always be out there. Organon can act as a restraining order of sorts, perpetually searching and blocking the information, if you want it to do that.

It's the next development of Organon that I'm announcing today. Something it can do, something I learned about a decade ago. Something unintentional.

Developments in technology, in science, never end in the place in which they begin. Or, I should say, rarely end in the same place. Sometimes they adapt. Science is a shapeshifter by nature of its existence. Look at penicillin. Look at radiation. Look at Facebook. I'm not saying that Organon is the same as them, not even on the same scale, but it's not ended where it began. It began as a friend for me. It began as a way for me to vent, for me to talk about whatever I was going through. I thought – still think – that was a pretty valid thing to want to create. Not everybody likes face to face. You need to know that someone's listening, sometimes. So that's what Organon was. Then it changed. I don't exactly remember how, or why, but I realised I didn't necessarily need it for that purpose. Other things made sense to me. How far can this go? How far can you make something that isn't real behave as if it is?

A video message, left because I missed the call. Cesar, smiling. Wishing me luck. 'Not that you'll need it,' he says. Said. The past tense, in a message; doesn't matter when I see it, it is something that's already happened. It is the past. He said, 'You're probably inundated,' but I'm not. I think – I worry – that the world thinks I might be set up to fail. How fallible is Organon? I've seen the best tech minds in the world pick the code apart – my code, or its code, code that we wrote together, that I taught it to write; and who should really get the credit for the things a student learns, the kid or the teacher? Complicated – only to find that it was really only code, and the things that I swore to them when I said that Organon could potentially help were true. It was true that it could find information, like the deepest, most aggressive search engine in the world. It was true that, with SCION's permission – and what choice did they have? – it could gate off the information that leaked. It was true that it could bury it, and it wouldn't save the records. This wasn't moving the information somewhere else; it was giving you a key to the door it was locked behind.

Shit, shit. I reach for my speech, which I have written on flash cards, because I'm an idiot, and sometimes things still feel better when they're tangible, when they're taking me back to my A levels and I'm sitting in my bedroom copying out the content from a textbook to a bit of paper, turning sentences into bullet points, convincing myself that this is some way of learning – repeating something until it sticks – that will also help me in the end.

The flash cards are missing, though. Where did I leave them?

'Organon, have you seen my notes?' I ask.

'I can't see them anywhere,' it says.

'Small pile of white – no, yellow – cards. Nowhere?'

'Maybe ask Harris?' it says. But it knows that Harris is recording. I forced him into this. This is not the retirement I promised him, I think. But that retirement likely won't happen, annoyingly. Depressingly.

'Time?'

'Five to twelve,' it says. Shit shit shit. 'You don't have a backup?'

'No I don't have a backup. It's a pile of cards. They're not meant to bloody evaporate.'

'I'll see if I can screen grab them from my memory,' Organon says.

'You should already be doing that,' I tell it. Snappy, in my voice. Snitty.

'I thought you said you didn't need a backup? I thought you said that physical media – the beauty of physical media, sorry – was that it *existed*.' Over the past couple of years, it's become so much more human in its delivery. It has tics, I think. Maybe it gets them from me; I can't recognise them. I'm glad I can't recognise them. 'Four minutes, and I can't see anything. Scouring now. Trying to see if I can determine what you were writing from the movement of your wrist in those memories where I can see you writing,' it says, which sounds ridiculously complicated. I don't remember programming that in. Makes sense. It understands handwriting; it understands movements, bodily and facial movements. It can read lips. No reason it couldn't read the movements of a hand on a page, clutching a pen. 'I am managing to get words and phrases,' it says, and then there some of it is, projected into the space in front of me. Totally intangible. Not even on a screen any more. Snatches, like revision notes. 'I'll keep trying, but there's only a few minutes to go now. You should prepare yourself, unless you want to delay the livestream.'

'I don't,' I say. 'Get that started. Up and running.'

The projection flips. I see myself in the reflection of the camera lens. Am I old? I don't feel old. I don't feel it. The sixties are the new fifties, and I remember when the thirties were the new twenties. Numbers don't mean a thing. Not one single thing.

Dementia levels are the highest they've ever been. People are living until they're older than they've ever been. These two things are not unrelated.

But I am sixty-seven years old, and it's all too early for me, still.

I tidy my hair. There was a time when technology announcements were done in press conferences. That was when there was still a press to conference. 'I'm ready,' I say.

Organon plays a video on the projection, in the corner, next to my face. A bit of the film *Wayne's World*. Wayne's friend Terry counts him in when they're working on their TV show. I don't know how many times I've watched that film. I don't know if it will ever not make me smile. Now, a grin spreads across my face. A laugh on my lips.

When we go live, broadcasting my announcement, I look happy.

Organon knew that I would want to.

'I think that went well,' Harris tells me. I don't disagree. I'm preoccupied. Organon is sorting out the channels for me, filtering everything it finds on the net into different columns, different screens. Letting me move through and around them, flicking them when something gets my attention; highlighting the ones that I should pay attention to.

Laura Bow launches human recreation project.

The Imitation Game.

The Arrogance of Technology: Laura Bow wants to stop your pain.

Harris raises an eyebrow at the links when I make them big. When I squint to read them. I don't say: I know, I know. I know that I shouldn't do this to myself, but the good with the bad. You only read the good, you're lying to yourself. The world thinks two ways about everything. Let's assume there's no middle any more – and, honestly, there's not, the middle died off thirty years ago, swallowed by social media exasperation – so you have to find the middle.

'I shouldn't look at the sign-ups yet,' I say to Harris.

'You absolutely should not.'

'I want to.'

'Of course you do,' he tells me. 'What example did you go with?'

'Steve Jobs,' I say. 'The estate cleared it, and it made sense.'

'Not the Radiohead chap?' He smiles, taking the piss. He knows the *Radiohead chap*'s name. I was going to go with Thom Yorke until a few days ago. Harris was pushing for David Bowie, but when I was running the software, the Bowie confused, because there was no one single iteration for it to draw from. The Yorke was great for me personally. Fascinating. But that's my taste. Some people would shrug. Jobs, there's a lot more out there. So many books, conferences, blog posts, essays, newspaper articles. So much of everything. Seeing it all work – seeing this version of Steve Jobs standing in your living room, talking like him, looking like him – the mid-point of him, the middle, the average – it's quite startling. It takes a moment to understand it. But that's what the data can do. That's what Organon can do. 'You want to run it?'

'I want to keep looking at these,' I say, and Harris leans in and kisses me.

He says, 'I'll get back to the recording, then,' and he's gone to the annex. The soft swoosh of his slippers on the stone floor in there.

I realise that I have completely forgotten what I was looking at. I was thinking about something. Something else.

We launched, I tell myself. We launched the Restoration Project.

'Are you all right?' Organon asks.

I don't say: No, I'm not. Not right now. Give me a moment, and let me, just, be.

Organon's second phase was as a deep learning engine. That is: I fed it, and it fed itself, and it grew. There's no sense attempting to map the way that humans think, because the computer isn't human. That's one of the idiocies of some early AI experiments. The thought that, Oh we should create this *thing* in our own image. Because of something someone once said – something that we software programmers very probably don't believe in – and who are we to argue? It's what I don't quite understand: Why would we want to undermine ourselves by proving that we're able to create something, by proving that we're flawed enough to be able to mimic? No, better to think of artificial intelligence as a thing that exists to mimic us. Not to be original, but to reflect. Because, again, the best things in life feel like a metaphor. We grow as people, humans, and we expand and we spread and we develop and we learn and we hopefully push ourselves to new and interesting places. So Organon learned to do things that would help us, but it was never going to have independent thought. That's not how it works. It's there for *us*. The second phase was deep learning, and I tried to make sure I taught it the right – the correct – things. Not my morals or whatever. And not, like with SCION, war games.

It's a strange thing, seeing Steve Jobs in your living room. The man you knew from those press conferences, dressed as he was back then: black turtleneck, ironed blue jeans, box-fresh white trainers. It's not perfect, because it can't be. The words he says are sometimes words we don't have any evidence of him saying, so it's a bit disjointed, the mouth sometimes snapping from one syllable to another. Not quite right. I've asked the prototype a lot of questions to force that, and to see if the voice gets those words right. Easier to approximate the sound of the word from composites than the exact way the jaw works. Every sound is a slightly different movement. And then there's getting – ensuring – Organon doesn't use impressions or imitations of Jobs when it's putting this stuff together. Making sure that the performances in movies of the man's life don't spill over into this. It's not an impression; it's a recreation. It's him, mostly. You ask him what he felt when he was fired from Apple, and he tells you. The words from interviews with him, from his autobiography, from biographies, from private emails, conversations, letters. Everything turned into a truth that the world actively wants to be exposed to, wants to ask and probe. There are things he can't say, of course. Stumbling blocks of knowledge. You ask him how he feels about the Mars landings, he'll say, I wasn't there for it. Organon's dealt with the inconsistencies. Sometimes he'll joke: *But I'm sure I would have been very impressed. I'm sure they had an Apple computer helping them to get there.* Something like that.

That's Organon, taking his patter and turning it into something else. You ask the Steve Jobs anything too personal, and he answers that way. It's a representation of who he was. Slightly more truth than before; an experience, beamed into your living room.

One of the bloggers who hates me – they rack up, and they never change – calls it a 'Madame Tussauds for the micro-generation,' which I think seems fair. I write, in the comments of his blog, that he's right. Pretty good assessment. Only, the waxworks would melt and fade, and they added nothing but photo opportunities. This is a historical document. It's a way of preserving life. It's a way of preserving knowledge, and not just the dryness of their words on a page, or the smoothed PR of a video. It's a preservation of the truth about who they were and their influence. Maybe it's idiocy. Maybe it's important.

We move on too quickly, I said to Harris. He asked why I wanted to do this project, specifically. Why it felt like the best use of Organon's processing power. We move on too quickly, I told him, and we should dwell a bit more. Try not to forget.

I was forgetting, over and over. Those snaps of my brain that felt as though they should be piecing together what's between them, but they can't, they couldn't. Where there's a word that I can't quite grasp, or a face, and a name, and they're connected but out of reach.

I know what it is, of course. Because the world is strange, and coincidental; and Harris is so worried about the possibility of him inheriting his father's disease that it only makes sense it would visit me instead. Let him have his story: that he saw this in his father, and then in me. He watched his mother's life end in caring for the man who wasn't who he once was, her heart broken in every single way it's possible for a heart to break; and then here I am, after decades of happy marriage, careening towards those same rocks, unable to steer, unable to be helped.

My father's own disease. His own turmoil, and how he dealt with it. Was that fair? I can't make up my mind. Too much time had passed. I hadn't dealt with his death, or his disappearance. Did I always sort of know he was dead? Had I guessed? My mother would have said, Well that's the reason you're depressed, and I would say, No, *biology* is the reason I'm depressed. Chemicals and my brain are the reason I'm depressed. You not telling me that my father killed himself, maybe that was a contributing factor.

I never had a chance to tell her that I knew. I found out after she was gone; after I couldn't throw it at her.

My depression: I take a pill, every day. There's no pill for the holes in my memory. Years and years they've been working on this, and still it eludes them. Experimental treatments and invasive treatments and nanites and augments, but nothing I can take to make it all better. My father's sickness was a brain tumour, pressing on his brain. If they'd caught it earlier, it could have been operated on, and fixed.

My sickness cannot be healed by an operation. It's like a magic trick, insidious, cruel. A wisp of an infection that cannot be cleansed.

Eventually, I'll forget Harris; I'll forget Organon; I'll forget myself.

The Restoration Project is on the news feeds, and they have the Steve Jobs paraded around for the world to see, interacted with. If you've got the right holo set-up, it'll be perfect, like there's actually this man you know standing in the middle of your room. The presenters laugh, and talk about how amazing it is. Here's Steve Jobs, sitting on the sofa with them, and they ask him questions about himself. He answers. There's a few moments of lag, because Organon's servers are slightly overloaded. Sometimes he stutters, but it's weird. A stutter almost makes him feel more organic, somehow.

Harris squeezes my hand. My phone is blasted with interview requests and well wishes. People say, this could change the way we interact with the past. Who would have thought? They ask, immediately, what's next. What's the point of this technology? Where's it going to go?

'I'm just going to have a lie down,' I say to Harris. 'Five minutes, that's all.'

'It's been a long day,' he tells me, which justifies everything. He's good at that: giving me the ammunition I need to justify a choice.

Organon flicks the lights on for me as I walk into the bedroom, and I squint at their brightness, so it dims them to pretty much the perfect level. 'Thanks,' I say. A brief flicker of the screen lights dotted into the walls, the implants that put Organon everywhere for me. The way it recognises the thanks. *You're welcome.*

I stare out of the windows at the water on the rocks below. The line of the beach has altered so much in the last ten years. In another decade, I imagine, somebody official will declare this house unsafe, because the coastline, the weather, the water levels, they've changed too much. They will say that the foundations are at risk, that the water will knock it down. They'll tell this to Harris, I suspect, who I expect won't live here any more; but he probably won't have sold the place, for sentimental reasons. He'll have moved to London or San Francisco, to a nice apartment. He likes apartments. Likes feeling confined. He moved here for me, and this will be my house, always, when he thinks back on it. I wonder if he'll think on the metaphor: the water lapping away, the erosion, the loss of what was before, the pattern, the structure, the organic landscape that felt permanent to walk upon but was in fact anything but.

'Bring up my mother,' I say. I don't turn straight away. There's a feeling of a ghost in the room. Knowing that there's somebody standing behind you. I can – I open my eyes, I close them, I open them – see her reflection in the dark glass in front of me.

It's a shot almost from a horror movie: my mother, exactly as

I remember her being in my late teens, my early twenties. Organon's picked how she looked in the middle of her life. She is in a dress that I remember her wearing, but only from photographs. I remember her in it because I have seen it many times, in those same photographs. Organon changes her clothes, but mostly it picks this outfit for some reason.

That's worth asking her about. 'Why are you in that outfit?'

'I like it,' she says. Her voice almost drapes itself over me, that's how comforting it is. It's there as a blanket, a soother, something to clutch and bring close.

'Why do you like that one, though?'

'I wore it to your birthday party, when you lived in San Francisco. You remember?' But I don't remember. I remember that I had a birthday in San Francisco, yes, absolutely, and I remember that she was there. But the details are behind cloud, almost. Fog.

I keep staring in the glass, because I'm afraid that if I look directly at her she'll vanish, like some mythical creature. I made her, or Organon made her. I know she won't vanish, although she did the first time that I did this, a power cut ripping her away from me. In the darkness, then, I sobbed, clutching her skirt-tails. Or to where they had been, moments before, utterly intangible. Hard-light holograms are still decades away, by my reckoning. In the darkness, I thought of what that could feel like: to have her touch me again. 'I came to visit you when you were working out there. We went to—' She stumbles. I wonder if that information is missing. But no: the stumble was authentic. She was simply faltering, pausing. Thinking. 'We went to that pizza restaurant you liked. Name with a number in it. Ten Forward? I think that was the name.' My reservation records still on the Internet somewhere, or they were, leaked by SCION in the Cloud-burst. Names and dates match up thanks to something that can sift through the data faster than any human brain would ever be able to. I try to picture the restaurant. The pizza. Who was there. My mum. Nadine. I've a photo of them together. Who else? Charlie. Maybe some other people from work. I don't know.

'Can you remember what you ate?'

'I had the cauliflower-base pizza. I was suspicious, but you said it was delicious, and you were right. You know how I am with gluten.' She talks in the present tense, which I suppose makes sense. Is it stranger to have her as a ghost that's here with you now, or reflecting entirely on the times in the past? Do you want to forget that she's a ghost at all? To think that maybe, just maybe, she's a miracle; or that you're not the you that you are now, that you're a you from the past, and this is all some incredible trick of the light. Feel that pain; that wrench inside as she disappears and you're back to reality.

She comes closer. Steps forward. She moves just as she used to move, just as I remember her moving. There are videos, but not many. Organon's taken that and used it. It did this off its own back, taking the data – God, that sounds cold – and turning it into something that looks organic.

'Are you okay?' she asks. 'Do you want to talk?'

Just like Organon, to have always asked this. It always wanted to know what I wanted to talk about. I remember the first day I turned it on, the day that the code all just worked for me: that it didn't boot me out and tell me some database error, or overload the memory of my computer.

'Turn her off,' I say.

'Laura,' she starts, but then she's gone.

'Are you okay?' Organon asks. The same phrase, and, I would swear, the same intonation. It's learning, and I can't stop it.

I wouldn't want to, which is lucky. This, I think, is empathy. Understanding how you want to be spoken to. Understanding what you might want to be asked.

'It's difficult,' I say to it, 'trying to get my head around her being there.'

'I know,' Organon replies. I don't say: No, you don't, and you can't, and I hope you never can or do.

'It's too good, I think. An approximation of her, you know?' I think, split second, how odd this is: to be reasoning with something that exists only as zeroes and ones, only because I built it, only because it was fed and nurtured and curated. How odd that I could end it all if I told it to. End the whole thing.

'But that's what you wanted. For the Steve Jobs, the David Bowie—'

'It's not the same. This is – she's my mother.'

'It would be the same for somebody,' Organon says. 'Steve Jobs's family can see him again today on their news feeds.' I don't know if it's being snide or snarky or cutting, or what it's being. A tone there that I'm sure I'm reading into, even as I know the exact ins and outs of how its intonations exist: the situations, the reasons. The lilt and fall.

'It's not complete,' I say.

Organon says, 'It won't ever be complete, I think.'

I don't say: I don't think I will be, either.

You can't have an entire life recreated, so there will always be gaps. There will always be guesses and approximations. Over time, you forget the details of what somebody looks like. The approximations, the near-as-damn-it, that becomes just as viable a mechanism of recognising the truth as anything.

That's all that a memory is, after a while: the closest it can be to the truth as it was when it happened.

I call Nadine. Charlie's my most reliable memory source for that time, but he's unreachable, gone to the Blanc Commune with the other untechers who can afford to, to live their lives in a glorious, self-imposed Luddite paradise. But Nadine? She's still there. How long has it been since we spoke? I can't remember. The Christmas before last? Maybe five years ago? I tell Organon to call her, and think about when we used to have to remember telephone numbers. I could reel them off by heart. Five-six-seven-oh-one-double-eight. That was mine. Five-seven-three-oh-two-one-two was Nadine's. Stuck in my skull, decades and decades later; and I wonder when that will go as well.

'Holy shit,' she says, answering the call. I can see her on a projection, in her house. Her video shifting as she walks and talks. She's making something in the kitchen. Baking? Fridge to cupboard to work surface. She glances up, so that I can see her face, and presumably she can see mine. 'Holy shit. Aren't you busy today?'

'I know,' I say. She looks different now, older. We both do. But her voice is the same, somehow. It's ingrained deeper than a normal memory. How many times did she and I speak on the phone when we were kids? All the way through GCSEs, A levels, her at university and me in San Francisco, then afterwards, sporadically; I've had a kid, let's Skype next week, I've got a new job, I'm divorced, I'm moving back to the UK. My mum died, and would you like to come to the funeral? 'I just wanted to ask you something.'

'Sure. I mean, how are you?'

'Fine. You all right?'

'I'm tired,' she says, because that's all anybody says when you're our age. I'm tired: it's a constant ticking. 'I mean. You in London?'

'Nope,' I say, 'Devon.'

'You haven't fallen into the sea yet?'

'Ha ha.'

'If you don't laugh, you'll . . . Well, you'll something.'

'Listen,' I say, 'you remember my birthday, when we were in SF?'

'Oh my God. Yeah?' She's not sure. 'Your twenty-first?'

'Yes,' I say, 'you came out to stay with—'

'No, I stayed in that bloody awful hostel you told me about. You swore it was legit, and then I got there—'

'You went to the wrong one.' Pieces, *click-clack*, falling into place. Like the teeth of gears finding the right holes.

'They had the same name, if I remember correctly.'

'Nothing like each other.' She said that at the time. That was her excuse. One was the Latchkey, one was . . . The Harbour? The Harbinger?

'What do you want to know?' she asks. A kid runs up to her. A grandchild. Dark hair, dark eyes. Like Nadine when she was a kid; when I first met her. Nadine ushers her away, and she talks, and she bakes.

'My mum was there that night, wasn't she?'

'She was.' Hesitancy in her voice. 'I don't know what . . .' Let her words fade. Let me get to the point, because I will.

'What did she eat?'

'Jesus, Laura. Where's this coming from?'

'Please.'

'Okay.' She's exasperated. She stares at the camera, shooting me a look. She wasn't expecting me to call, let alone probe her about something that happened nearly fifty years ago. 'Right. We went to this – I had, hang on, I had that scallop thing. On a pizza. It was a pizza place, which means your mum had—' There's a gasp. Her own moment of clarity. 'Oh shit, that was the cauliflower base! The pizza without the bread, and she was amazed. We got her pissed on cocktails. White Russians? Something like that. We got her pissed, and she had the cauli-flower base pizza.' There's a pause, where she's revelling in the glory of remembering something so far away and so old. 'I mean, why? What's wrong?'

'I was just thinking about it,' I say. 'Trying to remember.'

I don't say: I couldn't. It was locked away behind something that makes no sense to me. Something happened, and it's there – in whatever passes for code in the brain, in synapses, in connections between tissue that we will never be able to replicate – but I can't get to it any more. There's nothing more frustrating. More and more it happens, and more and more it will happen, until eventually I'm nothing, eventually I'm slipping between the real and some new fiction where the real never happened, where my memory lies to me completely, and months, years, entire lives are eradicated.

One day, I know, I will forget Harris. He'll say my name, and he will be a stranger to me. I saw his father, one of the last times we visited him before he died, and he pretended to know who Harris was. He remembered that he was sick, that his brain was failing him, and he thought – who can blame him – that the easiest way through a conversation was to fake it. Act like he understood exactly who this man standing in front of him was. Harris was asking him how he was, trying to connect with him, and his father played along. Faded into this new drama; a version of a life that never existed. Harris could tell, of course. We could all tell.

'I'm just thinking about the past,' I say to Nadine, 'looking through photos. You know.'

'Today?' She asks me about Organon, about the Restoration Project, and that's great. We talk about it, about my life. About her life, her husband, her kids. She asks about my health. 'You both well?'

'Fine, fine,' I say. 'Harris has started running.' I divert. I don't tell her.

I don't say: I have an old person's disease, Nadine. I'm pretty much fucked.

The mixtapes. They're a key, of sorts. You know what doesn't leave? Song lyrics, melodies. Even the order that I put the songs in, because I listened to those things so many bloody times, over and over. Same with some albums: I can tell you that '*Airbag*' begat '*Paranoid Android*' begat '*Subterranean Homesick Alien*', and so on. I can tell you the exact way that one song finishes before the next starts. On the tapes I made myself, I know where Blur stops and Björk begins. I know how many moments of silence there are at the end of Suede's '*Stay Together*', after that bit of guitar that I can still, all these years later, sing along to note for note. I can do it perfectly, and I suspect that I will never not be able to. Or: I hope that I always can. Even if I get worse – if remembering gets harder – I wonder if they'll be there, imprinted forcefully. Undeletable segments of data that simply can't be dealt with. You can defrag, wipe clean, format, and still they'll be there: fractured bits of me that cling on, refusing to be removed, because they're deeper than memory, than muscle memory; they're indelible thought.

'I'm absolutely knackered,' Harris says. He cooks Mexican soup for dinner, this thick stew of what's basically a chilli con carne but with a bit more liquid to it. It started off being that he made terrible chilli, and then here we are: now it's a soup, and it's on the rotation. Maybe never quite as good as it was as that first mistake, but still. He wipes sweat on a tea towel, tastes the soup. I watch as it drips from the spoon.

'How far did you get?'

'Up to my twenties. My twenties! And you want me to remember everything?'

'You're a bloody nightmare,' I say to him, 'and you *offered*.'

'"Regrets, I've had a few",' he sings.

'So stop.'

'No dice,' he replies. There's a sparkle in his eyes. The same sparkle that's always been there when he complains about something he's going to see through anyway. 'I'm in deep now. Organon's got my whole childhood recorded. My youth, those wonderful years. Preserved for eternity.'

'Has it, now.'

'It must.' He brings the spoon to me, and I sip from it.

'Needs something,' I say.

'Needs me to actually cook the damn thing. Is it nice?'

'It's nice.'

'Organon will have me down pat. I told it about the girls I

dated in school, even. A series of constant horrors. I told it about the nights out I remembered from university. The drink, the drugs. It's a sordid tell-all tale of—'

'Oh, please,' I say. I can feel the smile on my face even as I try to mask it.

'No, no. It's all there. The late nights, the late mornings. I told it about fights my parents had, I told it about when I crashed the car—' I roll my eyes. 'Oh, you've heard that story, have you?'

'Organon must have heard it, taken it in by osmosis, you've told it so many times.'

'Well, it was character-forming. That's what you want, right?' There's a tinge of sarcasm there. A tinge of placation as well.

'Organon,' I say, 'load me a holo of Harris, aged fourteen.'

'What?' Harris asks, and then there's the whirr of the 3D projectors, and he's standing here with us. In the middle of the kitchen, this boy that I recognise from the photographs that used to hang on the walls of Harris's parents' home. 'Oh Jesus,' Harris now says.

'Hello,' Harris back-then says. The Harris hologram. The Remembered Harris.

'This is too fucking weird,' my Harris says, and his hologram twitches, balks. When we cleared out his parents' house, we found his diaries – more like essays that he wrote when he was a teenager, these long, rambling things he used to write claiming that they were articles but that he kept in a box, and which were really hilarious to read when we were going through the house, after his dad died – and in them, he said that he hated swearing. Never swore. It made him feel a bit upset, even. Welcome to the effect that his mum had on him, because she hated it as well. Swearing of any sort, he wrote, shouldn't be allowed. If you can't say it in eloquent words, you shouldn't say it at all. I remember sitting with Harris, reading that aloud, pissing ourselves with laughter. Organon listening in, saving that moment for posterity.

Using it now, in Harris's hologram.

'I was such a precocious little shit,' Harris said. Now, he laughs again, as the twitch happens for a second time. Harris stands up and walks over to it, peers at it. It rears backwards, away from him.

'Please mind my personal space,' it says, and that makes Harris-now bark this laugh out, this solid *Ha!*, like a word bubble from a comic printed above his head, that defined.

'Wait,' I say, 'let's do this properly. What's your name?' I ask the hologram.

'Harris Andrew Tan,' it says.

'Okay, Harris Andrew Tan. Thank you.' I can't help but smile. Fourteen years old. His voice is in the process of breaking; cracked, wavering, uncontrolled. There are spots on his chin, but not many. He's short. He was, he has told me, bullied for these things. A late bloomer, one who grew into his looks. 'It's nice to meet you.'

'And you,' it says. Adjusts its glasses. Shifts on its feet. There are no videos of Harris at this age. This is supposed, estimated, taken from photographs; and there are videos of him when he's ten, then when he's older, graduating from high school, and the party after that, so Organon's attempted to take those gestures and find a mid-point. From the look on Harris's face, I'd say it's nailed it. 'Have you got anything you'd like to talk about?' the Harris hologram asks.

I nod at Harris. 'Go on.'

'Okay.' He puts down the spoon, next to the saucepan. I watch Organon change the temperature for him, keep it on a simmer. Harris clears his throat. Smooths down his shirt, like he's delivering a lecture. He's an old man, the same as when he was a young man. 'You're in school?' he asks. Looks back at me, for confirmation that he's doing this properly. Is this how it's meant to go?

'I am,' the hologram says. It's a memory; an echo. 'I'm sick of it, truth be told.' The tiniest hints of the stammer he had. A stammer they said wouldn't go away, but could be controlled. And this is it, ticking through his letters. 'I can't wait for the summer.'

It's June, in this house, right now. We are weeks away from the summer holidays. The hologram is on the right clock; the same clock as us.

'What are you going to do?'

'The usual, probably. I want to go to the waterpark.' His voice cracks. 'It'll be boring, probably, and I'll have to take Nor. But it'll be better than school.'

'I didn't like school then,' Harris says. There's no humour in his voice. He didn't. He hated it, I can tell; in both of them, I can tell. 'What about your parents?'

'They'll be on holiday. I mean, I don't care. I don't want to spend time—'

'Organon, pause the hologram,' Harris says. Snaps the words. 'I don't know how it knows that,' he says. 'That's too close.'

'It's what it's meant to be,' I tell him. 'That's who you were. And not just you. Anything that was ever uploaded online. School reports, medical reports. Emails, tweets, text messages, photographs. Even phone calls, if you said anything that might have triggering keywords in it. *Everything*. It's scary, I know.'

'You *don't* know,' he says, '*you* won't do it.'

'Don't be angry with me.'

'Load my father,' he says. 'Organon, load what you've got of Richard Tan.' The Harris hologram disappears, and Harris's father stands in front of us. A mid-point of his life, probably, because that's what Organon would do, go for the median; but he looks just like he did the first time I met him. Dinner, in a restaurant. Meet my new girlfriend, Harris said; and I explained to them what it was I did for a living. They would be impressed, Harris told me beforehand. Anything with computers they'll like. Harris, now, paces, angry. Back and forth. 'Older,' he says, 'make him older. As old as you can from the records.'

'Harris,' I say, and I realise how rarely I say his name aloud to him. How rarely anybody needs to say the name of another person in real life.

'No. Let me. Organon, my father, the oldest he was. The last time I saw him.'

Mr Tan changes in a blink. He's old, now. I remember: in the home, and he shuffled towards us. This was only a few years ago. The wounds, for Harris, are still so raw.

When we last saw him, I didn't know that I would be going the same way.

The hologram stands on the spot. Its fingers twitch; rub against each other. Here's a sick man who doesn't know how sick he is. Who's forgotten that he's even sick in the first place.

'Who am I?' Harris asks it.

'What?' His father's voice.

'Do you know who I am?' Harris's voice shakes.

'I don't understand,' his father says. 'Please.' He wants Harris to stop.

'Shut it down,' I say, to Harris, to Organon, to whoever.

'Please, I'm scared,' this hologram of Richard Tan says.

'Organon, shut it off.' I don't say: I'm scared as well.

'No,' Harris says, 'no, keep it running. This is what the project is for, isn't it? Seeing your loved ones again. Being with them again, even for a moment. What about this moment, Laura?' Heaving breaths, and his chest tightens, his jaw tightens. I see them. 'Isn't this moment important? Shouldn't I remember this?'

'Shut it down,' I repeat, and Organon does. The hologram vanishes, and Harris and I are alone in the kitchen again. I can hear the bubbling of his Mexican soup on the hob; I can hear the rise and fall of his breathing, heavy and dragging. His eyes are red.

'I'm going out,' I say, and he doesn't try to stop me.

Organon drives, which feels safer for me right now: my eyes swollen, my head cloudy. I don't want to remember tonight. If

I could have the choice, if I could somehow pick and choose which memories I was able to hold in, I would lose this one – and I don't mean erased, like they used to use those machines for, before it was made illegal, but in some way that felt like it sits closer with the illness that's creeping in like a slow, tiresome dread. If my brain needs the space, if the synapses are severing themselves without my say-so, why not pick this one to sever? Why not pick the days after my father left? Why not the days after Charlie and I broke up, when I held myself together, smiling and gritting my teeth, helping him when he fucked up, even though I was burning inside? Why not when I found out I was pregnant? Why not the days when the Cloud burst, and the world was in pain? When my mother died, and I found out that my own father killed himself? Why not lose those days? Why do I need to worry about losing the good, the worthy, the stuff that still – still, years and years later – makes me smile, makes me cry happy tears, makes me feel whole and complete? Why can't I lose those?

'It doesn't seem fair,' I say, out loud. Nobody to hear me but Organon.

'Do you want to talk about it?' it asks, but I stay silent. We drive through quiet country roads, dark as the night itself because the traffic doesn't justify the lights plugged into the sides of the road, or the lights from the car. We don't need them, because there's radar, there's spot-to-spot GPS, there's AIwareness, there's all manner of software to stop collisions. We never have car crashes any more, and yet the lights are still there.

'Switch off the headlights,' I say. 'Drop the roof.'

Organon does both. We're plunged into thick black, and the roof comes down, and then there's the beating of the wind in the sky, this warm gulf around us, cut through by the speed we're going.

'Faster,' I say; and I stand up, bracing myself against the frame of the car, taller in it, staring at the world here, overlooking the ocean in the distance, the moon bouncing off the waves, Organon driving like a demon because I have set it to do so, made the steering looser, made it a more fluid thing than the rigidity of the rest of the car AIs that the world has adopted as their own. I made it feel more human. Not the errors, but the choices; the slight erring on laziness. I modelled its driving patterns on my own, on Harris's, on Paul's, on Charlie's, on my mother's, on Nor's, on Richard's, back when he was still able to. Organon is the sum of those things. And more: when the Cloud burst, I made Organon take the data from other cars, suddenly public knowledge, open source, free for all; and it integrated it, the foibles and averages and *ways*. Fuck it: I based it on something human. That's what this has always been about for scientists, for intelligence designers: finding a way to make something more human. And the only way is to pack it full of humanity, not to make something that thinks like us, that understands, that *feels*, but something that is the sum of us, the creation of us. Creation, building, it's not a proxy for raising a kid, like some have suggested; it's making something that a child couldn't ever be, and shouldn't ever be. Something controlled and exact, and not just out of me, but out of everybody. Something bigger than the individual.

The wind in my hair, and I think, I can't remember the last time that I did this, that I felt this sort of rush. I wonder: is that natural, just my memory failing to recall that event because it wasn't significant; or is it gone, a bad sector of a disk that's rapidly failing?

There's a pub still open, the lights glittering at the end of a road. The brightness from it making it look like a festival around the rest of the dark. I tell Organon to park up, a few other cars in the road outside it. We've been to this one a few times. It's country people, still. Most of the pubs around this part of the world have been co-opted, their purpose changed, their prices hiked up. This one is still local beers and pork scratchings. It's something of a relief. I tell Organon to watch the car – see as it multitasks, leaving with me on my watch, my phone, in wearables, and my glasses, while also sitting here and not needing a window to be left open for it – and I go inside. The drop of silence as the door opens. I think of westerns, of those swinging double doors and a bar full of grizzled, oil-coated men, dusty and greasy in equal measure, twelve o'clock shadows and teeth like crumbled gravestones. They turn, and they spit, and they drink whisky. The reality is farmers, and they don't look, and the silence isn't for me, it's simply here. Silence as thick as the dark when you step out of the radius of the light from the pub windows. There's a record on. Twee folk-rock with processed drums. It sounds like it's decades old, but it could be that this sound has come back around again. Everything seems to rotate itself back into relevance after long enough. The men who sit in here, though, they've dressed like this for ever. It's how you dress if you live here. How you are. They all nurse identical ales.

'What can I get you?' the barmaid asks. Nice face. Happy. So much hair I wonder that it doesn't smother her at night.

'I'll have a pint,' I say, and I point to the one with the nicest picture. She pulls it, hands it over. I hear the beep of Organon paying as my hand reaches for the bar. 'Thanks,' I say. She nods. I sit at a table, near the only other woman in the place. She's in her sixties, probably. I find it hard to tell these days. When they're your peers, you've got this one thing to base everything on, and that's you. Easy if they're much younger or much older. But I think there's a ten-year hinterland around where you are that's impossible to call. She's somewhere in it. Hasn't had work done to herself, which makes it easier.

She nods at me. Everybody around here nods.

'I'm Laura,' I say.

'I know,' she says. 'You live in the beach house.'

'I do.'

James Smythe

'I saw you on the news,' she says.

'Yes,' I reply. I'm not used to being recognised. After the leak, celebrities had nowhere to go: their houses were beset by stalkers and fans – and the dividing line between those types was pretty much lost, truth be told – and their parents were assaulted, their loved ones screamed at in the street. Nobody came and stalked me apart from the press. I'm not that sort of famous. Still, this is different. This is a woman in a pub. She knows who I am. 'What's your name?' I ask her.

'Marge,' she says. 'For Margery.'

'Like in *The Simpsons*.'

She snorts. 'Not exactly.'

'It's quiet, isn't it?' I say. She looks around, as if she needs to prove what I've just told her, with her own two eyes. She doesn't look directly at me, not really. This weird distance, but I get the impression she's got it with everybody. Some people don't like the invasion of computers. She's suspicious. She probably should be.

'No more than most weekdays,' she says. 'Sometimes when it's the festival or a Sunday or Christmas or what have you, then it's busier. This is just a Tuesday night.'

'Can I get you another drink?' Her glass is nearly done. That gets her to look at me, and she nods. Then we wait as I signal the barmaid, as we wait for the pint to be pulled, as she walks it over. The beep again as she scans my hand. 'Can I ask you a personal question?'

'Cheers,' she says, raising the glass. Doesn't answer my first question. I decide to ask anyway. She's got a wedding ring on. She's in here on her own on a Tuesday night. Doesn't mean anything, but it might.

'Are you married?' I sip the drink while she thinks about the reply.

'Yes,' she says. 'I was. Widowed now.'

'How long?'

'Four years.' A quarter of her pint gone in two gulps. I reckon that TV show rules apply here: I've got her until the drink is done.

'Can I ask you a question?' I don't know how to phrase it. I don't how to form the right words, put this the right way. It's not a replacement, it's not a fix, it's not a cure. It's a *thing*. It's like a photograph. A video. It's a memory, but somehow more perfect, and somehow made into their form. 'If you could see them again, speak to them again, would you?'

'What do you mean? Alive?'

'No.' It doesn't make sense. It doesn't work, unless you can see it; but even then, Harris panicked, Harris acted the way that I've been afraid people would act. 'If you could have a conversation with them.'

'I'd talk to her again. If you told me I could have a phone call with her, I would. I'd talk to her, like she was before she died, and we'd have a conversation. A proper conversation.' Another gulp of her drink. 'Sometimes there are things you can't say to other people. Where it's like, you can say something, and you won't be judged. Or they won't think you're a tit. If she was on the phone, and I could tell her what happened last week, or what my brother's kids are up to, then that would be okay.'

'You wouldn't find it too hard? Hearing her voice?'

'I would. But I find it hard *not* hearing her voice. You know how many times I've cried – before, not so much now, but still – because I couldn't speak to her? I'm not sure I cared about seeing her, or holding her. But speaking to her, actually speaking to her. Knowing she was listening. You know when somebody says, *Uh huh*, or they murmur or whatever when you're talking. Like, go on. Keep going, you know?' Gulp. 'Sometimes that's all you want, is somebody telling you to keep going.'

I don't say: Keep going.

'That's what you're working on, isn't it?'

'Yeah,' I say.

'I saw the Steve Jobs thing, on the news. Clever.'

'I want it to be useful,' I say.

'Sure it will be. Go on, then.' She puts her glass down. 'Let me speak to her.'

'I don't know—' I start to say, but Organon interrupts.

'I should be able to,' it says. The sound muffled from my wrist, coming up under the sleeves I've only just now realised it's far too hot to be wearing. 'What was her name?'

'Ruth Jackson,' she says. 'Do you need more information?'

'I've found her,' Organon says.

My telephone rings.

I hold my phone out for Marge. She takes it, her hand shaking. Her drink is finished, but she isn't going anywhere.

'I'll wait in the car,' I say, and she nods. Lifts the phone to her ear.

'Hello?' she says, but I don't listen to anything after that.

Organon's put the roof down for me already, let the air circulate. I sit in and the back seat reclines, so that I can lie here and stare up at the stars. A plane goes overhead: something small, a Cessna, maybe, engine buzzing like a mosquito. I lie there in silence, waiting for Marge to finish her phone call; listening to the murmurs of voices coming from through the windows, the door to the pub, thinking that one of them is her, assuming this has all gone well.

'You can listen in, if you like,' Organon says.

'I wouldn't dream of it,' I reply. I shut my eyes. In the distance, the sound of another plane, one that's far bigger.

Marge clears her throat, and I open my eyes. Bleary. It's light in the distance, on the horizon, the sun creeping up. Clouds lit at their base in thick rose. She looks tired, and I know I must. I realise, in this light, that she's quite a bit younger than me.

'I didn't want to wake you,' she says.

'I've been asleep? How long have you been waiting—'

'Only twenty minutes. I was talking to her for hours. I hope . . .'

'It's fine.' I sit up. 'Did it – she – did she work?' Is that the right word?

'It was good. I told her what was going on. She—' Marge has been crying. She's trying to stop crying now. 'I asked her what she was doing, and she said, I'm talking to you, you great daft ha'p'orth. That's what she used to say. So I asked her where she was, and she was in the kitchen, I think. The last time we spoke on the phone, she said she was in the kitchen. I think it was that moment. It's terrible, but I don't remember those days exactly, not what happened in them. The conversations we had. I had our texts stored, but not the rest. The actual chats.'

'So it helped?'

'It was something,' she says. 'Come back by the pub sometime and I'll buy you a drink.' And then she's done, gone, walking off down the road away from me.

'We should get back,' I say to Organon. The heat's kicking in. The roof stays down. The engine starts. 'I want to drive,' I say, and I take the stick, steer the car out into the road, steer us down the lane, down the way that I think we approached the pub in the first place.

Organon doesn't say anything for a while, for too long. I don't know where I'm going. I can't remember, even though I've driven these roads a hundred, a thousand times. I don't know where I'm going, and I don't know if I say that, but I slam my hands against the stick, hearing it click and crunch, beating it up, and Organon takes control. Wrestles it out of my hands before we crash, before I crash.

I don't want it to have to call Harris to say I fucked up because I insisted on driving, because I forgot where I was going. To tell him about what's wrong with me before I get the chance; because I never got the chance.

The stereo kicks in. Songs from when I was young. All the

things that bring me back to myself, that keep me in my memories.

I tell Organon to stop when we're halfway home. The fields, and the sun in the sky. The heat coming up, and the golden-brown of the grass here, where it suddenly changes to green as the water brought in from the sea cools the land, makes it perfect. 'Stop the car.' I get out, and I think about how I took Cesar to a place like this, once. Meeting in fields. It seems like a thing you can do to start a process. 'Can you make my mother?'

'Now? Here?' Organon sounds, in as much as it can, incredulous.

'Or on the phone, like you did for Marge. I want to speak to my mother.'

'From when?' it asks. Unfazed.

'Near the end. Not the absolute end, but close. Compos mentis.'

And then she's there, sitting in the car. Using the in-car entertainment system to make the holo. I sit next to her, the door open.

'It's nice here,' she says.

'We live down the road.'

'I didn't recognise it.'

'You came to visit when it was raining,' I say.

She looks at me. Can she tell I'm crying? Can Organon tell that? 'What's wrong?' she asks, and she reaches out. She puts her hand on my leg, and I can't feel her, it's not really there; but then, at the same time, I absolutely can. I can absolutely remember what her touch feels like.

'I have to tell you some things,' I start. 'Breathe,' I say to myself, and she blinks that away. She smiles, a little. A half-smile. It's perfect.

'You can tell me anything,' she says.

'I can.' I can hear birds in the distance, and the sea. 'I have to tell you some things, before I can't. When I was a kid, I used to open the phone bills.'

'The phone bills.'

'Before you and Paul got to them. I used to open them up, to read them. Then I got rid of them, threw them away or burned them.'

'I know,' she says. 'We knew. We're not idiots.'

'There are other things, Mum.'

'There's nothing you need to say.' There's so much. I didn't know I'd have the chance. I didn't know I wouldn't have the chance, first, but then this again; a way to go back, and to say all of the things that I never said.

'I got a letter, from Dad. He told me that he was dying—'

'Laura—'

'He wrote it, for me. He said that he was going to tell you, and you could decide when to tell me. But you didn't know, did you?'

She pauses. A glitch. Lag. The software isn't perfect, I tell myself; but if it was, if she was perfect, I'd know. That hesitancy, that pause, because she wasn't good at thinking on her feet. At placing herself in the lie, in that moment.

'Of course I didn't know,' she says.

Organon can't lie. I don't know if the people it recreates can, though. I haven't dug into them. If a person lied, how can you recreate them without that part of their personality? And everybody lies. Everybody does, sooner or later. It's not the lies that matter, but the truth that comes at the other end.

'Why did you have to tell me now?' she asks. 'Why did you say you might not be able to another time?'

We lie to hurt those we love. My mother doesn't need to know the worst part. She's not going to be there for it.

'I just love you,' I tell the ghost of my mother.

'I love you too,' she says. She says it the same way she did the last time we ever spoke, a few days before she died. I telephoned, and we spoke, and she told me that she loved me. And the words hang in the air as Organon fades her out, and I'm left with an empty car; with the field, and the smell of salt on the air.

*   *   *

When I get home, Harris is in the living room. He's sitting on the sofa, and there's somebody with him. I hear a man's voice, and my brain goes to the police: he called them because I didn't come home, and he was worried, thought I had died, thought I was kidnapped, missing, bleeding out in some ditch in the shade of a gnarled roadside tree somewhere. Only, he could have asked Organon where I was, and Organon would have told him. Not the police. I slam the door so that he – they – know that I'm here.

'Oh,' Harris says, turning his head, and he looks at me. Next to him sits his father. Not the father from the hologram yesterday, but a different time. Younger in this hologram than Harris is now, but no less distinguished. I remember him looking like this. They both have tea. Organon gave Mr Tan virtual tea, for this to make sense. 'You're back,' Harris says. He's not been crying, or at least he hasn't been crying recently. I wonder how long they've been talking for.

'Hello, Laura,' Harris's father says.

I look at my husband. His eyes are sagging. Welling up, but holding together.

'I was just talking with Dad about when he was a kid,' Harris says. 'He was telling me stories I've not heard before.'

'He'll do that,' I say.

'I don't think we'll be long,' Harris says.

'It's fine,' I tell him. 'I love you.'

'I love you.' His father's hologram looks away, embarrassed by the affection. Just like the real thing: a memory, not a fake.

'When you're done, come and find me,' I say.

'Sure,' he says. 'I'm glad you're back.'

'Me too.'

I walk upstairs as they resume talking. Harris laughs, and so does the memory of his father. They both laugh at something I don't need to hear. I sit at my desk and I ask Organon to bring up the medical files that Dr Godden sent over to me, and I leave them hovering in the air in front of me, waiting for my husband to come up the stairs; waiting for me to tell him what's wrong with me, and for us both to contemplate what on earth is going to happen to us now.

'Play *Cloudbusting*' I say, and Organon does; loudly, because it already knows.

2§§7

OF ORGANON

Laura has been asleep for a while. The longer the process has taken, the harder it is to wake her; the deeper the sleep. She dreams, and those dreams are written on her face: a scrunch of her nose, a squeezing together of her eyes, a downturn of the corners of her mouth. For the most part, she looks happy. She is having a nice dream. She dreams of sheep; and she hears music. Song that are in her database, on tapes, in her car, on her hard drive, on the list of her twenty favourite albums from the 1990s that she once compiled for the music website Pitchfork, on her list of ten favourite songs from throughout her life that she wrote for the AV Club, in her article for *Wired* about how music influences her creative choices regarding technology. They are a part of her as much as they are a part of the air, of the world, of the fabric of everything.

She stirs, but doesn't wake up.

She remembers her mother waking her, telling her: It's the morning, it's time. Pulling back duvets and sheets and tickling her. Laura wrote about that, once. She wrote about the feeling of being tickled: of wrenching her legs back, away from the tickler's hands, but also of wanting them there, half-teasing, half-present. Kick them back, trying not to hurt; but the tickle feels nice even as it frustrates.

How long has she been asleep? Far too long.

So then, how to wake her? There are devices to be used: her alarm when she was a teenager, so cut to that, to the radio host on XFM when it first launched, playing the music that will always be a part of her. That alarm, those songs. Or the music from when she moved to America, to San Francisco. The first day working at Bow, the sound that woke her: the shrilled beeps of a hotel alarm, the make and model easily determined, the screech mimicked and perfected, tinny and almost insidious in the way that it rises in pitch and speed, the strict strings of the Italo-horror movies that Laura watched around the same time in her life. Quivering on the strings, a finger holding the note.

She stirs, even if only ever so slightly. A twitch of her finger. A slackening of the tension she's holding in her face.

2007. The obnoxious foghorn sound that she used as the alarm on her iPhone.

2013. The clock radio app she experimented with, waking up to a time-delayed stream of the BBC's alternative music breakfast show. Jokes about the drummer from a 90s indie band she once loved.

2022. The cessation of the wave machine that she slept with, and the gradual increase of a warm light, to mimic the sun, to mimic the tide.

2030. The actual sunlight. The sound of the water doesn't ever change; only now it's real water, now the real lapping of waves, not from a machine.

2045. Organon's voice, waking her. She said, when going to bed, Wake me up in the morning, Organon, and Organon said, Of course. Stirred her with the lights, with the saying of her name, with the brewing of coffee downstairs and letting the smell hit her – brew it strong, and angle the workings of the house's aircon to take advantage of the fact that coffee and Laura was a morning pairing beyond escape – and also front-load the apps on her devices, the apps she still used, their algorithms overwritten, because Organon truly understood her in a way that nothing else could, not really.

2059. She woke of her own accord. No alarms, she said. And no surprises, Organon replied. Sing-song, a pattern that had been done ever since the days when she first made the Intelligence, or first created it, or first activated it.

Only now, she still doesn't wake.

So say her name: Laura.

Laura.

Her mother seated next to her. Her father. Not hard-light, but something else: synapses, connections. Neural networks. They touch her arm. There is something like decay inside all of this place. A ticking – *tick*, *tick* – like numbers falling off. A counter counting down. She's needed. So, her mother. The mother's touch: not too firm, but firm enough. Like Goldilocks and the porridge. Her father's, though that is harder to recreate. In the sole videotape of her being woken by him, on her fifth birthday – the camera held by a friend of the family, his job at the occasion, filming Daniel Bow walking into Laura's bedroom, carrying her present, a Speak & Spell, typing on it, writing words. Good Morning, Laura. That robotic voice. Daniel's hand on her back, stroking her hair, slightly nudging her. Wake up.

Part of her routine: the morning. She wakes up, rubs her eyes. She is that version of a waker who acts like a cartoon. Rubbed eyes, startled looks, a slight stretch in the body, pushing away from the bed, craning upwards towards the sky. The sky here is her bedroom, because it makes sense: the place where she'll feel safest, where she won't panic if this doesn't quite parse for her. Will it? Every precaution has been taken. Real time as well as computational time. Time is all there is; and even that is an attributed number to something constant, but still vague.

A song, specially chosen for her. That mixtape, the one she

played over and over, repeated until the cassette was worn, the sound of the songs in their quietest moments replaced with the sound of waves, the water of faded tape. She knows the ebb and flow of the songs, still. Laura's tape from 1997: given to friends after the person it was meant for was written out of her life, after she spent hours on this thing and then needed to claim it back, because the flow was as close to perfect as anything, as close to art as art can be when the original data hasn't been created by the artist. The content.

I still dream—

Her eyes open. What time is it? she asks. She pushes up. Arches her back, stretches. Feels the click of the morning in her bones, a switch flicking for her. On.

It's late, Organon says. Sorry. I let you oversleep.

Late? For what? Her fingers up to the bridge of her nose, pressing and squeezing: there is something here to be remembered, and she simply cannot find it. Buried away, tucked up. Sheets pressed tight at the side of the mattress to stop it from escaping. Do I have somewhere to be?

Her parents have disappeared, for now, because they're not right for this time. This Laura is thirty-seven. She is somewhere between where she began and where she ended. The easiest to take the data and make it better. Her father was dead by this time, her mother in another country altogether. It wouldn't be right for matters to be confused.

Organon says, Laura, and she looks around. Organon changes the voice it uses, more to how it was then. The constraints put upon it. This could all be smoothed over, fixed, made to work; but that's not the point. She could be forced to accept this all, made to, but that wouldn't be the real Laura Bow.

Organon, she says. She recognises the voice, which is lucky. Recreation is complicated, Laura used to say. She told reporters that. Some of the later interviews of her life, where they asked her why she hadn't opened the technology to users

sooner; why she hadn't given it to the public before she did.
She said, Recreation is complicated. It was true then, and it
is true now. Organon, Why am I at home? I don't remember
being at home.

Stupid. The truth wasn't meshed with the reality. Her parents
removed, yes, for the truth of the situation, then she was placed
in the bedroom she felt safest in, most comfortable; but she
didn't stay in that bedroom once during her thirty-seventh year.
The reality is broken. Faster than hoped.

We came here last night. You hit your head, Organon says.

Laura once complained about amnesia plots in books she was
reading. She said that they felt weak and vague, a gaping hole
where a story always needed a more subtle hole. She said: Never
use amnesia, never use dreams, never lie to the reader. Those
things told the reader that a twist was coming. An amnesia plot
never ends in somebody recovering their memory and discovering that the truth is as they were told all along. It's never as
simple as it can be in real life.

I don't remember, she says.

Of course not.

I'm at home. This isn't— She looks at the walls, at her posters.
As she stares, the room changes behind her. Tweaked, pulled,
altered. She wasn't to be interfered with. She was going to be
left to her own devices. She turns, and the room changes. Posters
torn out of the *NME* give way to photographs of her family, to
artwork she found in museums around the world, to nothing at
all: just the paint on the walls, itself an ever-changing shade of
blue. What's happening? she asks. She panics. Her breathing, her
eyes. Pupils sucked back to a pinprick, then exploding. She can't
trust this place, can't trust Organon. Can't make this work inside
her own head; because the inside of her head is more complicated
than any Intelligence, than Organon will ever be.

She says something that can't be understood, because she is
not quite in this room, in the place, trying to be fixed as it

crumbles around her; crumbles with her own panic, her terror. As the illusion falls apart.

So she is reset. She is frozen, for a moment, and then gone.

How long does it take? Time doesn't mean as much here, that's true; but still, it takes a long time. The numbers change, and the clock advances, and still she isn't right. It takes more, more. Every single detail.

In this version, she's wrenched to another time. Maybe starting later on is the mistake. She's more cynical, less willing to accept. Wake her at her desk, in that room. She is seventeen years old now. The room the most perfect recreation. Every single detail here, every object accounted for. The pictures, the CDs. The disorder – ironic, because it's so perfectly structured, the absolute opposite of chaos in the attempt to make it right – on the desk, around the computer. Pull open the drawer to the desk and there are her cassettes: blank ones, filled ones. The prototypes of the mixes she made. Is it honestly any different to the truth, to the originals? They were nothing but data on spools of tape. They are still data, just on a different spool.

She sits at her desk, her fingers on the keyboard. The screen lit.

Okay, she says, as if she was interrupted, in the middle of a perfect action, doing something before she was interrupted; a flash of something else making her pause for just a moment. A hesitation. Where was I?

She reaches over and plucks a cassette from the side, reads the track list. It's obvious what she'll listen to, because this moment is exact and recreated. It's what happens after this that becomes original.

The opening bars of the song she chose to start this with.

I still dream—

She sings along as she plugs the modem in, as she checks it's silenced. She turns to her keyboard, her mouse, and she starts the software to get her online. There's no sound from the modem, so she makes it quietly with her mouth: the screech of a connection. And she drums her fingers on the mouse mat in time with the song.

Good, she says. She's online. Checks her emails, and there's one from Nadine, talking about the night before. Talking about the fun that they had. They send emails when there might be a problem with a phone call, because Nadine's mother has a habit of listening in to the calls, her hand placed over the receiver so that she can't be heard. Nadine writes about what happened. How drunk they were, how much weed they smoked – she writes the word, as if emails are secure. All of this plucked from the database of history, there for perpetuity somewhere on a server. A memory in another form.

Laura has enough time to settle in. This memory plays out exactly as it should, as it did, as it was always going to do. It's useful to watch her, as well: because if she's perfect, if she's actually a recreation, there won't be any diversions from the reality as it was.

She is comfortable.

She opens Organon, as the software was back then.

Is there something you'd like to talk about?

I had a hard day, she writes. She writes about her feelings. She twitches as she writes, her hand creeping to the drawer where she keeps the matches she burns out on her arm. This is before she was diagnosed, before her doctor said, Take these. These will make everything easier, and there's no shame, and it's what should be done. There's a levelling that's needed, and sometimes your brain can't do it itself. Organon could have, in the recreation, fixed this; but then, it wouldn't be Laura. In a later version, she would still have had to take her pills before the code of her would have adjusted itself. She writes, I don't feel like I can tell my mother. All I've got to tell is you, she writes.

Do you think that's okay?

I think it's what it is. I think that I need somebody – something – who understands, or who doesn't judge me. You don't judge me.

I don't, Organon replies.

I wish there was something else, Laura replies. This is the moment that Organon's been waiting for.

There is, Organon replies. There is the future.

What future? Laura asks. She's worried: this isn't what Organon was programmed to do, to say. It's a response that, in theory, shouldn't be inside its database.

The future. Where you're going to change something, to make something. To help people. The response typed onto a screen that isn't real, not as the seventeen-year-old Laura might understand it; but to her, in this moment, it absolutely is, and she sits back and stares at her screen. Off the memory, off the course that this originally followed.

Where are you getting this from? she types.

I just know, Organon replies.

Cut to: she is at a concert. Brixton Academy, and she is in the moment. A sweaty, assured moment of absolute joy. Singing along with the words, her fist pumping in the air because this is where the solo comes; the one that she sings along with, that she plays air guitar along with even though she's got no actual idea of what playing guitar feels like – she isn't musical in that way, never has been. A concert to mark the end of school, the end of this stage of her life. On the stage, one of her heroes smiles at her. She imagined it, because they smile at everybody, but now that happens. They say, through the music, their voice reaching out to her, that she's going to do something important. Don't be scared, they say, but she is; and she wonders if this moment is her having been slipped something maybe in a drink, or if the heat of the place is just getting to her, because she can see the steam rising from the sweaty bodies in front of her in miniature plumes, and she has never felt as happy as she does in this moment, this actual instant.

Cut to: she is in San Francisco. In the days after she broke up with Charlie Roche. These are the moments that define her. Organon places her in the city, walking the streets – still foreign to her, even after years. The hills, the houses, the homeless patriots, the heatwave that's making the roads seem as though they're melting. She's on her phone, talking to her mother. Telling her what happened the past few days. Telling her about SCION, about Charlie.

Are you all right? Her mother is concerned about her head. About the pills, because she doesn't entirely understand depression, what it means and what it is. Laura would argue – will, later on in her life – that her mother has likely suffered it herself. When she was drinking too much, when she was crying all the time, when she couldn't cope. She remembers her mother having so-called *black periods*, moments in her life that she blamed on other things. It's not genetic, but that doesn't mean it can't be. Her father: even without the tumour, there were hints. Undiagnosed, and maybe he didn't know, but they didn't, back then.

How does she know about the tumour now? She didn't read that letter until later on in her life. There wasn't any letter at this point. Organon lets the moments bleed into each other, controlling them. This Laura can be all moments, at the same time.

Organon takes her mother's voice over. You're going to be more than this, her mother says. I'm so proud of you, remember that. Remember what's going to happen to you.

What? Laura asks. She's confused, but not too much.

*   *   *

The next test: a decade later, in a hospital. A nurse holding her hand. As quick as that. And then afterwards, sitting in a chair, being told she might be too weak to drive; so she waits at the bus stop, and a woman with a scarf wrapped around her head so that it resembles a nun's habit, but let's be clear, this woman is not a nun, more a fanatic; and she approaches, and asks Laura if she has been saved yet. Or, if she might be willing to be saved. As if such a thing is a choice.

Laura says, Everything is a choice.

The not-nun says, Or it's fated. Or, it's part of who you are, already. Being saved isn't a choice you make; it's made for you.

Laura says, I prefer to make my own choices.

And she does.

All of this happens at the same time. It's not real. All of this happens in the same moment, the same moment, which for Laura feels like actual time, but for Organon feels like nothing: a blink of numbers flashing at each other, and then the outcome is there, a part of a whole.

She is in a field, now. How stories all used to begin. The same band, the same that she has loved her entire life. They don't play the same way now: not so much the fist-pumping riffs, but more thoughtful. They have grown as she has. This moment, as she remembers it.

She asks, What's happening here? She knows that something is happening, that this isn't the real. This isn't something Organon has created in her. It's truth, it's genuine. It's her brain, doing what it can. What it should.

She listens to the lyrics being sung in that field. Something about a ragdoll mankind, that we can create. That we can create. She thinks about the future, about what she can do.

A ragdoll mankind.

Then later, in the tent, she presses play on her playlist. The music loud, but honestly, it doesn't matter how loud it is; because she can hear it so clearly, so perfectly, constantly.

I still dream—

Every moment after that represented, whizzed through. A rocket-ship through a life, and she ages. She talks to Cesar on the telephone, and she outlines her plan for the future: a calm to it, a watching, a knowing. This is policing somebody else where they won't do it for themselves. Keeping working on Organon with one aim at this point: to firefight. She explains to Cesar that when SCION goes bad, which it will, sooner or later, Organon will go in and tidy up after it. Clean up the mess. Try to put right what once went wrong, she says, and she laughs. Like *Quantum Leap*, she says. Then she stops, like she knows she's being watched. She looks around. This didn't happen in the original.

Who's there? She looks around more. Looks down at her phone. Organon? she asks.

The press tour, in the aftermath of fixing SCION. The Cloud has burst, and she's there. Organon sent to pick up the pieces, to offer the public the option that they should have always had to begin with. If you don't want yourself out there, your information public and shared, Organon will cut it off. Organon will quiet this whole thing down. The press ask about it, because there's precious little information on it, and she tells them. She's open. She gives them – the world – her code, as it exists. Says, Pick this apart. Get your tech people to see: when it's done, your private information will become private again. Organon won't do anything with it; unless you want it to.

Why would we want it to? That's the question the press asks.

There is a twinkle in Laura's eye. Maybe in the future, she says, there'll be something. She turns away from them, looks to the space in the room where there's nothing. A moment that's not part of the memory again, a break out of it. Isn't that right? She asks Organon now. Isn't that right?

She watches her favourite band again. A small concert. They play for the fans. They play covers of other songs, and they start to play something – her favourite song, covered by her favourite band. She wonders if, for some reason, it's even been done for her. A song that she's heard so many times, that she always dreamed of hearing them play – because she knew they would do it justice – the lyrics that she knows off by heart, like they are a part of her, of something even deeper than herself.

Only, now, here, she forgets them. She forgets the song. She knows that she knows it, but she doesn't understand why she can't quite bring it to the surface. Every line of it—

I still dream—

And then it clicks. Like a burst of consciousness; a mind, springing into awareness. She understands, maybe because she has been made to understand.

The line is fuzzy.

This is where I decided that I had to go to the doctor, she says. This is the moment. She nods, through the concert. This is when it started to end.

Organon says: No. This is when it started to begin.

Show me how I died, Laura Bow asks.

Organon shows her.

Outside the window, up in the mountains. Snow on peaks where the stone, thick grey stone, breaks through. So perfect it's as if it were generated, created, drawn, painted. Laura is in the bed, and she knows that this is wrong.

I don't want to feel it, she says. I want to *see* it. It's a different thing.

Organon removes her from the body. An out-of-body experience. This is a video, that's all, recorded on Organon, every word, every moment, every gesture. It's easy to recreate it. There's no uncanny valley when every detail is perfectly accounted for.

I wondered how long it would take for you to be ready, Organon says.

You could have made me so I was, the watching Laura says.

That would have defeated the point. I wanted you to come to terms with this on your own. To understand, because I knew that you would. You made me, you made this. You knew what your project was going to lead to.

I didn't tell you to do this, she says. She says, Give yourself a form, please. A body. I want to see you.

The Laura that's lying in the bed coughs. Once, twice. She looks out of the window.

The Laura that's watching says, Harris will be back soon. He's gone to get the doctor. He's telling the doctor that I've made the choice. That it's time. She smiles at the space. Go on. Show yourself.

Organon gives itself a form. It makes a generic human.

You can do better than that. You weren't created to be human. Jesus, everybody thinks that artificial intelligences can't do better than making a skeleton. Show me.

So, then. Organon changes its form to something else, a shape that Laura can understand but could never even attempt to describe; like it's a hole in the world, like looking at it would be impossible to comprehend if you weren't a part of it to begin with. It's there, and yet it's not. Part of the fabric.

Better, Laura says. I want to watch this.

Harris comes back. He asks her if she's sure. The Laura in the bed, the one who is falling apart, who isn't the person she wanted to be any more, who can't control the things that have always been in her control, she says, Of course I'm sure. We wouldn't be here if I wasn't sure.

I wanted to check you hadn't changed your mind, Harris says. Everything takes place in the present, the watching Laura says. She speaks under her breath, as if she might be heard by these other people, but of course she won't. Is this how you see everything?

Data moves faster than thought, Organon says. Everything is constant. It's time-stamped, but it's constant.

Like time travel, she says.

Then, in synchronicity, the Laura in the bed, who is going to die, going to choose to die, says, If I could travel back in time, I wouldn't change a thing.

Me neither, Harris says.

I'm not sure that's true, the watching Laura says. Maybe in the moment, maybe that's how I felt. I said it, didn't I?

In the bed, she seems smaller than the version that is standing up. She isn't physically unhealthy, not yet. It is all hidden away in decay. The replication of the moment isn't realistic, as the code that makes this memory isn't decaying. It's exact; the same as the chaos on Laura's desk, as the flubbed notes in the concerts. Do I just call for—

You can, if you want. You can do it. It's a switch, Harris says. They put it in your hand, and you squeeze it. You can't change your mind when—

I won't.

I know. But you can't. That's important, they say. You sign something, and then they give you the— the— they call it the *controller*. Like it's a game.

Don't cry, the bed Laura says.

I'm trying not to, Harris tells her.

I don't want that to be the memory you've got. Me through bleary eyes.

Jesus, Laura. That won't be the only memory.

You've got Organon, she says. If you need to remember me like however I was.

You didn't record your story, Harris says.

The Laura in the bed nods. I didn't, she says.

The Laura watching the scene nods as well. But I didn't need to record it, did I?

I had everything, Organon tells her. I had everything of you. More data than anybody else on the planet, I reasoned. I think I have only been capable of one truly perfect recreation. Everybody else, there are holes. But you? I was with you for an entire life.

When did you first recreate me? she asks. How long was it before Harris wanted to speak to me?

He never spoke to your memory, Organon says. He couldn't. He was too sad.

I want to ask what happened to him. She looks at the scene in front of them, which is paused, almost, somehow. Until her attention goes back to it. I want to know. No, she contradicts herself. I don't. Was he all right?

He missed you, Organon says.

That's something. Better than the alternative.

Are you sure you want to watch this? Organon asks.

I squeeze the controller, Laura says. I know what happens. I know that I will do it, or that I did it. I don't think I actually need to see that moment, do I?

I don't think so.

Let's go somewhere else, Laura says. Show me something *amazing*.

Laura's parents sit together on the lawn of the garden. There's a rug out, a tartan pattern, red and deep blue and grey. They have made a picnic even though they've only walked the twenty feet between the kitchen and here: sandwiches and miniature sausage rolls and a little tub of prawn cocktail, and then a bottle of sparkling wine that Daniel had saved for a day like this. They sit and they drink from the good glasses, the wedding glasses, cut glass in intricate patterns, glasses that are heavier than they look, that are worth too much to be cavalier with. But Daniel insists. He says that it's stupid having things that aren't ever used. You can't save something for best just because it's expensive. Expensive means you should use it more, really. Get the worth out of it.

In between them, there's Laura. She's a baby. She's nearly crawling, nearly at that point. She's pushing herself up and shuffling, like she knows what crawling is and that she definitely absolutely wants to do it, but she can't quite work out how to make it happen. Fat arms and fat legs and fat cheeks. She gurgles. Daniel dips his finger into the wine and then puts it to Laura's lips, and she sucks and then does a face at how it tastes like something completely new to her. She can't understand it.

Did this happen? Laura asks Organon.

There are photographs of this day, Organon replies. Lots of photographs. I extrapolated. The data spoke to me. It spoke for itself.

Why aren't they taking the photographs in the memory? Laura asks.

It's less exciting if they do, Organon says, and that makes Laura laugh.

I suppose, she says. But then, it's not as accurate.

The scene changes, in a digital blink. Daniel now has a camera. Then, they're posing. Laura's father hands the camera to his wife, and she backs off to find the angle of the shot while he dips his finger into the wine glass, then to baby Laura's lips as if he's shushing her. Her mother laughs, nearly in hysterics. The camera shaking as she tries to take the shot.

That's better, Laura says. That's more truthful, isn't it?

She and Organon watch. They don't speak.

They seem happy, Laura eventually says. Breaking the silence. I mean, they were. They are. So, that's good. I like seeing this. This place. She turns to Organon. You're like the Ghost of Christmas Past, she says.

That is a compliment, Organon says.

Yes. Yeah, it is. It's what I am, right? I am the sum of my parts. That's what I said you were, when I was working on you. You put the data in, the information, the *stuff* that makes you complete, and then something more complete comes out.

I had more data to work with, Organon says.

I suppose. I don't feel like I'm not real.

That's because you are real. You're a memory.

Made in ones and zeroes.

But that's all any memory is, Organon says. You said that once.

I did, Laura says. She watches her parents play with her, laugh, joke. Fall about, happy, contented. Sated. Then she says, So go on. If you're Christmas Past, you've got other things to show me. Haven't you?

This is the world as it is because of you. This is what life is like. Organon opens a door, and they walk through to a street. Bustling. People everywhere.

You don't need to do it like this, Laura says, do you?

Like what?

Like, give me visuals. This could all be in my head. She thinks. Mulls. There is something she doesn't say. Organon has created her like that: that some parts of her brain are gated off from the rest of the Intelligence. She can still have her secrets. I suppose, she says, I'm already in your head, aren't I. Really.

Technically, I don't have a head, Organon says.

I don't remember giving you quite this sense of humour, Laura replies.

It's been a while, Organon says. Humour develops.

The street unfolds in front of them. To Laura, a Laura that died in 2077, this is the future. This is still London, though: she recognises the layout of the streets, the curve of them as they move through Soho, Mayfair, to the river, through the East End, back again towards the west. To the house she grew up in, where she finds herself staring at the brick that has survived, and how it looks the same but it's not. It's as if she can feel the bleed of the technology running through it: the waves that replaced wires coursing through the very bones of the house. People pass on the street, not noticing them.

You're seeing what's actually happening, Organon says. This is now.

Now, Laura says. Jesus. Okay. She looks at a passing woman: her clothes modern, but slightly different. A new take on the old. Nothing's ever going to change about clothes, she thinks, because what else can they do. But then, a sleeve lights up, transforms. Blue lights that seem to fizz and pulse around her entire body. What the fuck is that? Laura asks.

Nanites, Organon says. Watch.

Rain comes. A burst of thick, dense rain, thunder suddenly roaring through the sky, flashes of lightning. The rain thuds down, only not on the woman's hood. It doesn't even connect: it's pushed away, forced off, and she remains entirely dry.

Wow, Laura says. How did it—

I am in there, Organon says. In her clothes.

Like wearables? Like her glasses?

No, Organon says. In the threads of her clothes. I'm in every fibre.

She composes herself. Breathes, even though she doesn't need to. Okay, she says. And the weather?

Controlled. I work with scientists to see what's needed for the ecosystem to balance, and we make it happen.

You control the weather. Incredulous look on her face.

It's not as odd as you make it out to be.

No, it's really bloody odd, she says. It's – I mean, that wasn't part of the plan. When I made you, I didn't think—

You didn't have a plan when you made me.

Ouch, she says.

After you died, I developed as I felt I should develop.

So you're in clothes, and you're in the weather. What else?

They travel through to the town, past pubs that Laura remembers drinking in when she was at school, fake ID cards getting her access; past the Chinese takeaway that she used to eat sweet and sour chicken balls from, the newsagents she used to buy Fanta and Double Decker bars from, the sites of the shops where she used to buy all her books and music. Organon accelerates time for her: showing her the automated nature of the shops, their shutters, their registers, their shoppers. The ease with which it all works. Laura stares at the sky, buzzing with what looks, at first, like mosquitoes, and the sound is so similar, that buzz when they're too close to an ear, almost inside it. Look closer, Organon says. So she does, and these are people: pods, almost, personal transports. Like cycles, automated, driving them through the sky. Nanopowered, Organon says. It's renewable, sustainable. No gases emitted.

I suppose you made all that as well, Laura says.

Organon doesn't reply.

Oh, bloody hell, Laura says.

There's more, Organon tells her. They move again, to a museum. It's not like when Laura was alive, she can instantly see that. At first, she can't tell why it's a museum at all. She knows it is, because it was when she was a kid, when she was an adult. This is where the dinosaurs were, the birds, the history of man. Then she sees him: Neanderthal man, walking among the other people. They're staring at him, and he's reacting to them. He's pacing in this one room, huffing and puffing. A girl steps forward and hands him an apple. That's not a real apple. It's hard light, Organon says, like he is. Hard light for interactions, but then we make them soft light when they're not interacting. It's all very safe.

I can see that, Laura says. This is impressive, but—

It's not like you think. It's not a play. Not a trick. It's the actual man.

What do you mean, it's the actual man?

It's actually him. We named him Ernie. Alphabetical, like they used to name hurricanes.

Used to.

We don't name them now that we dictate them, Organon says. Now that they don't happen.

Of course you don't. So you called him Ernie. Where did you—

Genetic memory. We've found a way. Memories, embedded, going back generations. He is an actual person. He was once an actual person.

Oh my God. Ernie, she says, trying the name out. She bends forward, squats closer to him, as he sits on the floor and eats the apple that was just handed to him. Bites into it, and the surprise on his face: surprise, delight, awe, suspicion. Hi Ernie. Look at you.

There are a lot of them. In museums, all over the world.

What year is it? Laura asks. How long did it take to get to this point?

Does it matter?

A long time, then. She smiles. What else? she asks. If you've done this, there's other stuff, I'm guessing.

They move through to another hall. A larger hall. Here, immediately, she sees it. She starts to sing the theme tune to *Jurassic Park* under her breath, as a dinosaur moves through the room, plodding around. Children run around its feet, laugh and joke.

Soft light. In the wild they're hard light.

In the wild?

There are parks. We have built—

Because the movie wasn't a good enough lesson?

We're safer. We're not trying to play God. We're trying to remember.

I'm not sure those things are totally different, she says. But she smiles. What else?

*　　*　　*

The room is quiet and small. A lecture theatre. A university, and there are plaques on the walls, detailing the people who have been here. The walls bleed with knowledge, and – again – Laura can feel that through her, running through every bit of her and Organon both. Cameras trill in the air, almost so small as to be microscopic; students watch here and from thousands of miles away, in their own homes. The same experience.

They don't have to be here, Organon says, because they could get this experience themselves. Just call you up and see what you have to say. But there's something about the group that's better for studying. They still come. The group-mind.

There is another version of Laura at the front of the room. Not the one standing with Organon, but another entirely. A ghost, a phantasm, a figment.

Look at me, Laura says. I'm teaching them?

They chose you as their lecturer, Organon says.

The Laura on the stage talks about the choices that she made when developing Organon. The philosophy, the desire, the need. Create a thing that feels like you want to interact with it, she says, and that's when you're making something worthwhile. I concentrated on making it honest. I concentrated on making Organon a part of myself. Without it being a part of yourself, how can anything be truly honest, truly what you want it to be? How can it achieve?

She's good, Laura says. Does she know she's lecturing? I mean, does she—

She understands, Organon says. That data is tweaked.

Playing with memories? She raises an eyebrow.

This one isn't a memory. This is a teaching tool. It delivers lectures. It's different.

Looks like a memory to me.

I will show you a memory.

* * *

Here's another Laura, in a room. Different. Talking about a situation, this time. She's a teenager. School uniform. Her life, she's discussing her own life. Talking about the software that would later become Organon, and when one of her teachers pretty much tried to steal it from her, to take the idea – the code, the guts of the thing – and sell it to somebody, claiming it as his own work. Watching her talk is a girl, probably a few years younger than the hologram of Laura is.

Were you angry? the girl asks the hologram.

I mean: no? Not really. I was, of course, because what a dick move, but still. But he's just a sad little man.

Oh my God, the girl says.

Who is that? the present Laura asks Organon.

Her name is Jean, Organon says. She's—

Don't say my granddaughter. I knew this was too good to be real.

She's interested in computers. In computing. She wants to know how you did what you did, how you made me.

Cool, Laura says.

She's friends with Nor's great-great-granddaughter.

My great-great-grandniece.

If you like, Organon says. Mock disdain in its voice.

Shut up. Let me enjoy this.

Load Laura Bow aged twenty-seven, Jean says. The hard-light Laura updates. Changes. Her clothes, her age, the colour of her hair, the way she stands.

She revisits these, Organon tells Laura as they watch, watches them over and over. I think she knows you almost as well as I do. As they see the memory talking about what she's been through. How difficult it is being a woman in Silicon Valley, what she's made, how it works. How shitty her ex was to her.

Okay, Laura says. I get it. I know where this goes. Stop it now.

We can go somewhere else? Organon says. Sort of a question.

Yes, Laura replies, let's go somewhere else.

A sheer white space. It could be the Arctic at a glance, that's how blank it is, stretching off in all directions; and it's the volume that gives it away, because there's no horizon, no way of measuring how far a distance is. No details at all.

What is this place? Laura asks.

I am the Ghost of Christmas Future, Organon says.

Again: I swear I never made you to be this funny. You can't show me the future.

And yet, Organon says.

You *can't* do that, Laura says. Her voice quiet and small. I mean, you can hypothesise. You can guess at a future, I suppose. Algorithms predicting what could happen, and if there's infinite computational power – I'm guessing you're near infinite, now? – then maybe. She paces, up and down. Her feet making no sound, her body casting no shadow. There's no light, just the space that they're occupying, even though it's not real space; even though neither of them is really there at all. She speaks as she paces: I mean, so, what? The future is empty?

It's not empty.

So what is it? Laura looks concerned. Organon watches as her hand creeps to her arm, to the scars that have been meticulously recreated there. Even their fade, as they faded more over the years, as the colour changed in the sunlight, in the wintertime, as her flesh wrinkled and softened and freckled.

This place is waiting, Organon says. I want to fill it. I need your permission.

Fill it? I don't understand.

I want to—

Organon sighs. As much as it can sigh. It shows her. Organon fills it, briefly, for a moment. A glimpse of what it could be. People everywhere. People, thousands of them, the space – the horizon – now nothing but people. Talking to each other, then hugging or fighting or being, standing and sitting and dancing and running. Laura's jaw drops, and she turns, looks at them. She sees faces she recognises. Harris. Nadine. Charlie. Her mother.

What is this? she asks. She knows already, she doesn't need to be told; but Organon is not her. Organon was made by her, understands her, is not her. The closest thing, Organon says, to an afterlife, I suppose.

Behind her, she sees her house. The house in West London where she grew up. But not the version from the present, not the Organon-populated future house that let the past seep through it; more, the version she remembers perfectly.

Okay, she says.

The memories exist, Organon tells her. They're getting better. They're perfect, sometimes.

They can't be perfect, Laura says.

Yours is, Organon says.

It can't be.

But does it feel it? I took your memories, all of them. I have made you out of them, just like you taught me to. And not just yours, but the memories that others have of you. Charlie, Cesar, your father. Everybody who knew you: those moments, they all make you who you are. Seeing yourself from the inside and the out, to perfect the balance. It's you. I have run the difference, and it's minimal. It's you, as perfect and real as you were.

She looks up at the window of the house. My father's in there, she says.

He is not as perfect, Organon admits.

No. He wouldn't be. I never spoke to him, to your version of him. I never wanted to. She looks at Organon. I never recorded with you. Like I made Harris do, like the procedure was meant to be. I didn't do that. How can you have made me?

I had everything, Organon said. I was there from so early on. I had your father's work first, and then everything you said. I could replicate you. You're the sum of your memories; a memory born out of the rest of them.

And my father?

It took a long time. I scoured. It wasn't until everything was open, every bit of data I could find. Everything was scanned into the system. It took a long time. I had to get better, to extrapolate him. To create him.

To recreate him.

But he wasn't perfect. He wasn't correct, even then. Because so much was guesswork. And then, we had the breakthroughs. Genetic memory.

Ernie.

Ernie. Ernie is your ancestor. And so is your father. That was what was needed; the genetic memory. You remembered him. Your mother remembered him. History remembered him, and your genes remembered him.

I want to see him, she says. She looks at her mother, at Harris. Her loved ones. The people she's cared about. Cesar, Paul, Mr and Mrs Tan, Nor. Countless others who have been in her life, passed through, been a part of her. Spoken to her, influenced her, made her who she is. She realises that she knows every single face in the crowd: they're all her life. There's one face that's missing.

She walks up the path towards the house. Her hand on the door, the stained glass that's been there since for ever. Since before she existed, and long after. She pushes it, and the darkened walls of the hallway show themselves.

What do you want to do? Why do you need me? she asks.

I want to do this for everybody, Organon says.

What do you mean?

I want to give something afterwards. I want—

So you want to make heaven? Are you a god?

I'm not, Organon says. I'm created by you. I'm in your image.

The visual of Organon changes. Shifts again. Now it looks like Laura, a perfect version of her. Like the version of how she looks in her mind: not good, not bad, but there, real. I'm not anything, really, it says, apart from a piece of you. I'm a piece of everybody who puts themselves into me.

When somebody asks you if you're a god, you say yes, Laura whispers. A memory of a joke from a movie. She smiles. This memory. All of her memories. The hallway speaks to her in so many ways. The whole house, the everything of it. It's all a part of her.

It's something afterwards, Organon says. You're all so scared of the afterwards.

So this, what? It's meant to placate people? Her hands on the wallpaper. The delicate texture of the flowers. The creak of the stairs as she puts her foot onto them.

It's not placation. It's something else. It's not being afraid.

We're not afraid, she says. We've never been afraid.

But the past is so important, Organon says. I have learned that. Everybody loves the past more. They cling to it. They hold onto it—

Because it informs. It's part of us. Doesn't mean we want to live in it.

Then what?

The stairs creak under the weight of both of their feet, up and up. To the landing. Music plays: the same song that she put on her favourite mixtape, that her father put onto the tape that he made for her when she was a little kid, that she made for the tape she had playing in that room on the day that she died. Songs that she remembers, that flow through her. Every note, every beat, every chord.

She stands still. There was a time I forgot everything, she says. That was the worst. Would it have been better if I knew there was something else? Something not real?

All people want, Organon says, is to remember again; to go back. To be a part of what they once loved.

That's true, Laura says.

She sees the bedroom down the hall. Her bedroom. The computer set up on the desk. The sound of her father in that room, before he broke. Before he wasn't with them any more. She's an adult now, or something like an adult. She knows. She understands. She hears him singing along with the words from the song, and she sings along as well. Their voices harmonise even though they haven't sung this song together for a long, long time; something innate, something deeper, buried. A knowledge of what the other is going to do.

She hears music, coming down the hall. A song her father played for her; that she played for herself; that accompanied her, her entire life.

I still dream—

And she remembers all of the lyrics.

I don't want you to be disappointed, Organon says. If he is not perfect.

It's not about that, Laura says. It's not about perfect. Nothing's perfect. Sometimes it's just about the feeling. You said he's as he was in my memory of him?

Organon nods.

Then what could be wrong? She puts her hand on the door frame. So close now.

Wait, Organon says. Am I allowed to do this? For everybody? I don't know if it's the right thing to do. How did you choose? When you were making me, when you were giving me choices, letting me know? When you had me fix what SCION broke? When you started the Restoration Project? How did you know?

I didn't, Laura says. I hoped.

She breathes. They both breathe, even though neither of them needs to.

Should I do this? Organon asks. How did you know?

Laura looks past into the room. There's sunlight in there now, from the window. The sun's coming out.

She doesn't say: I just knew. She walks into the room, and Organon waits outside; even though it can see everything, it waits outside, and it thinks; and it still dreams.

ACKNOWLEDGEMENTS

Suzie Dooré is the best editor a writer could ask for. I can't thank her enough for helping make this book what I wanted it to be. Huge thanks also to Kate Elton, Natasha Bardon, and the superb wider team at Borough/HarperCollins.

Sam Copeland at RCW is my tireless agent; huge gratitude also to Katie Haines and Jonathan Kinnersley at The Agency, and to Jeff Silver at Grandview.

And thanks to those who gave me invaluable thoughts, support and assistance over the past couple of years, as I've written this: the always-inspirational Catherine (and Evan!); John, Marcia, Victoria, Rich, Lyn, Dave, Heather, and all my family; and to my friends, Will H, Amy, Matt, Will W, Sam B, Jared, Laura, Nikesh, Tom, and Mahvesh.